USA TODAY bestselling autho[...] London, England. She is m[...] sons—which gives her [...] insight into the ma[...] film journalist. Sh[...] getting swept up in [...] sensual excitement, funny and [...] and tortured men and glamo[...] where laundry doesn't exist. Once she tu[...] her computer she often does chores—usually [in]volving laundry!

Annie West has devoted her life to an intensive study of charismatic heroes who cause the best kind of trouble for their heroines. As a sideline she researches locations for romance whenever she can, from vibrant cities to desert encampments and fairytale castles. Annie lives in eastern Australia with her hero husband, between sandy beaches and gorgeous wine country. She finds writing the perfect excuse to postpone housework. To contact her, or join her newsletter, visit annie-west.com.

Also by Heidi Rice

Revenge in Paradise

Billion-Dollar Bet collection

After-Party Consequences

By Royal Arrangement miniseries

Queen's Winter Wedding Charade
Princess for the Headlines

Also by Annie West

His Last-Minute Desert Queen
A Pregnancy Bombshell to Bind Them
Signed, Sealed, Married
Unknown Royal Baby
Ring for an Heir

Discover more at millsandboon.co.uk.

FOR BETTER OR WORSE?

HEIDI RICE

ANNIE WEST

MILLS & BOON

All rights reserved including the right of reproduction in whole or in part in any form. This edition is published by arrangement with Harlequin Enterprises ULC.

This is a work of fiction. Names, characters, places, locations and incidents are purely fictional and bear no relationship to any real life individuals, living or dead, or to any actual places, business establishments, locations, events or incidents. Any resemblance is entirely coincidental.

Without limiting the author's and publisher's exclusive rights, any unauthorized use of this publication to train generative artificial intelligence (AI) technologies is expressly prohibited. HarperCollins also exercise their rights under Article 4(3) of the Digital Single Market Directive 2019/790 and expressly reserve this publication from the text and data mining exception.

® and TM are trademarks owned and used by the trademark owner and/or its licensee. Trademarks marked with ® are registered with the United Kingdom Patent Office and/or the Office for Harmonisation in the Internal Market and in other countries.

First published in Great Britain 2025
by Mills & Boon, an imprint of HarperCollins*Publishers* Ltd,
1 London Bridge Street, London, SE1 9GF

www.harpercollins.co.uk

HarperCollins*Publishers*, Macken House, 39/40 Mayor Street Upper, Dublin 1, D01 C9W8, Ireland

For Better or Worse? © 2025 Harlequin Enterprises ULC

Billionaire's Wedlocked Wife © 2025 Heidi Rice

Queen by Royal Command © 2025 Annie West

ISBN: 978-0-263-34468-4

06/25

MIX
Paper | Supporting
responsible forestry
FSC™ C007454

This book contains FSC™ certified paper and other controlled sources to ensure responsible forest management.

For more information visit www.harpercollins.co.uk/green.

Printed and Bound in the UK using 100% Renewable Electricity at CPI Group (UK) Ltd, Croydon, CR0 4YY

BILLIONAIRE'S WEDLOCKED WIFE

HEIDI RICE

MILLS & BOON

To my big, beautiful family—
both biological and found.

Your support means everything! xx

CHAPTER ONE

CERYS JONES SAT in the bustling pavement café in Barcelona's Gothic Quarter and tugged a tattered leather-bound journal out of her rucksack. She took a steadying breath as she opened the book, preparing to read the final entry for the first time. She'd read the other entries many times—ever since finding her mother's old diary buried in a drawer in her father's study the day of his funeral. It had taken her six months to get up the courage to read what her mother had written the night she ran away while on holiday less than two hours' drive away.

Cerys stared blankly at her mother's loopy, chaotic handwriting, so unlike the neat script in the rest of the book...

Blinking back tears, she read the last words the woman she could barely remember now had written, searching for any clue, any hidden explanation as to why Angharad Jones would choose Álvaro De Montoya Hernández, the Eighth Duke of Cantada, over her husband and child, and devastate all their lives...

I met a man today who made me feel totally alive for the first time in my life. I never believed in love at first sight. But Álvaro, the Spanish duke who owns the vineyard Bill and I were touring with Cerys this afternoon, was BREATHTAKING.

I'd lost Bill and Cerys somehow, and I smacked into him coming out of his office. He caught me, to stop me from falling... And something happened... something so exhilarating it hurt. It was as if a fireworks display was going off in my belly as this man looked at me, as he held me... It's something I've never felt for Bill, but I could see he felt it too.

We talked, but when I told him I had to go—that my husband and daughter were waiting for me—he caught my hand and told me to meet him, in the cove below our hotel, at midnight tonight.

I'm married with a child. He's married with three children and another on the way. But somehow the guilt I should be feeling—at even contemplating doing such a terrible thing—isn't there. Because as I write this on our hotel room balcony—while Bill is busy snoring in the bedroom, having had too many beers in the bar—all I can feel is that fierce, raw, unstoppable yearning for something more. More than my husband, more than our mundane life in Cambridge, more even than my darling Cerys...

Meeting Álvaro has awoken me from a coma, and beckoned me into a dream of what my life could *have been if I hadn't got pregnant too young, and then married a man who has* never *made me feel all those things you're supposed to feel when you're in love.*

Those things I always thought didn't exist... Until this afternoon. Until Álvaro.

Cerys closed the book and took a fortifying sip of the strong black coffee she'd ordered twenty minutes ago.

Then shoved the diary back into her rucksack. And let out a heavy sigh.

Well, that was a massive anti-climax.

Her mother's scribbles didn't make any sense. Not to Cerys.

Who jettisoned everyone who loved them for a chance to have epic sex with a complete stranger? Admittedly, Cerys hadn't quite gone all the way yet, so she had no idea what epic sex entailed—but she'd kissed her share of guys and she had *never* had the urge to run off with any of them.

After her dad's death, Cerys had been forced to sell her family home. But it hadn't been hard because the empty rooms were even lonelier now than when her father had been alive and locked in his study, busy ignoring his daughter. Jacking in her dead-end job at a coffee shop and deciding to use the small legacy to work her way across France to Spain for the past six months had been an even easier decision... Learning French and then Spanish, absorbing the culture, working in bars and restaurants and tavernas, having no responsibilities, no ties, no need to please anyone but herself, had helped to push her grief and confusion to one side.

But always in the back of her mind had been the quest to understand why her mum and Álvaro De Montoya had chosen to destroy two families fifteen years ago.

Her dad had never stopped blaming her mum for breaking up their family—and Cerys had felt his emotional distance like a wound, throughout her childhood and adolescence. The few memories she had of her mum were of a warm, vivacious woman who had loved her unconditionally—the way her father never had. But if Angharad had loved her only child, why had she left her? Cerys had barely even warranted a mention on that last page.

She was generally a positive person, but lurking in her subconscious had always been the sense that if she had been a better-behaved daughter, a more loving child, her mum wouldn't have chosen Álvaro over her, only to die tragically, not long after. And her dad wouldn't have found it so difficult to spend any time with her. But expecting the answers to all her questions from her mother's journal had clearly been overly optimistic, even for her.

She hefted the rucksack onto her shoulders and checked her phone for directions to the youth hostel she'd booked for tonight, when a headline from a local celebrity news site popped up on the screen.

Her heartbeat slowed as she stared at the blurred paparazzi shot of Álvaro's eldest son, the current Duke of Cantada, Santiago Álvaro Antonio De Montoya Lopez. Then she checked the timestamp. He'd been photographed attending an exclusive art gallery opening with a stunningly beautiful woman less than twenty minutes ago in the Plaça Reial, right here in Barcelona.

Was this the sign she'd been hoping for? It was certainly a weird coincidence, given that the famously ruthless billionaire businessman was based in Madrid.

On impulse, she keyed in directions to the splendid neo-classical square. It was only a ten-minute walk away.

Cerys headed through the back alleys, energised by the prospect of getting a glimpse of Álvaro's son in the flesh. According to the Spanish press, who seemed obsessed with 'the scandalous De Montoyas', Santiago was the image of his father. Maybe seeing him, even at a distance, would give her some clue as to what on earth had possessed her mother to run off with a hot stranger for a few weeks of sex, scandal and more sex and leave the child who had needed her so desperately behind for ever.

'I do not care what Alejandro told you, Gabriela, I am not going to propose to you,' Santiago said tightly, standing on the balcony of the Plaça Reial gallery. The square below was alive with the city's vibrant nightlife. But he wasn't aware of the majestic palm trees or the ornate Baroque fountain at its centre, or the people gathered in groups at the pavement cafés enjoying the balmy evening, because all he could see was Alejandro's face as he contemplated strangling his younger brother.

It had probably been Andro's idea of a joke—to inform Santiago's casual bed partner he was currently looking for a wife—but there was just enough truth in the joke to infuriate him. It had certainly made this evening's trip to Barcelona, to break up with Gabriela, even more excruciating.

But then he should have known Alejandro would laugh at Santiago's decision to find himself a suitable bride by the end of the summer. Alejandro had never been burdened by the scandal which had destroyed their family fifteen years ago and continued to linger like a bad smell over Santiago's reputation. Because, unlike Santiago, Alejandro did not bear an uncanny resemblance to their father. Nor did Alejandro have to corral their unruly seventeen-year-old sister Ana, because he was not the head of the De Montoya household.

Gabriela pouted. 'But Santiago, don't you still want me?' she asked plaintively as she ran a scarlet-tipped fingernail across his nape.

He grasped her wrist to pull her arm from around his neck. He didn't like to be fawned over in public, or in private for that matter.

The truth was, he should never have started his affair with the socialite two months ago. But that had been the day his business manager had informed him that Isla de la Luna, the exclusive resort Montoya Investments had bankrolled in the Balearics, which was due to open at the end of the summer, had received some unfortunate publicity from an article comparing his father's decision to run off with some British whore fifteen years ago and Santiago's inability to commit to one woman.

It was at that point he had decided he needed a wife.

Santiago had quickly discarded the idea that Gabriela might be a suitable bride, though. Sleeping with her had not been particularly memorable, plus she was even more petulant and entitled than his sister Ana. She would make a terrible role model for Ana, whose volatile emotions reminded him far too much of their mother, and who clearly needed the guidance Santiago would require his wife to provide. But when he made that ultimate commitment, he needed to choose a woman who would excite him enough in bed that he would not be tempted to stray... As his father had.

Ana's latest school expulsion had made Santiago determined to find a suitable bride before his sister returned to school—if he could find a school that would take her. Telling Alejandro of his intentions, though, had been an avoidable mistake.

'Our affair is over, Gabriela.' He'd tried to let her down gently, but she did not appear to appreciate subtlety.

'I see.' Gabriela blinked, her eyes sheened with hurt. He dismissed her reaction. He had not given her cause to expect more—they hadn't slept together in weeks.

'I must escort you home now. I have to return to the *castillo* tonight to deal with Ana—and it's a two-hour drive.' The De Montoya ancestral home was a place he hated to visit—the cruel memories of his childhood always there when he returned to the Castillo de las Vides—but he would need to find someone to watch over Ana for the summer now, before he returned to Madrid to locate a bride.

He cupped Gabriela's elbow and steered her through the crowd of people supping vintage cava and waxing lyrical about unimpressive art, determined to escort her out of the gallery before she made a scene. He did not need more headlines in the Spanish press about what a heartless bastard he was.

A crowd of onlookers was waiting in the plaza to greet them. Although held back by security guards, the crowd surged forward, holding their phones up to take intrusive shots. The limousine he'd had waiting pulled up.

But as the chauffeur opened the back door, Gabriela tugged her arm from his grasp.

'Would you mind if I took the car home alone?' she asked, her eyes misty with emotion. 'I doubt you want to witness me falling to pieces over something that meant nothing to you.'

'Of course,' he said, despite the inconvenience.

He kept a sports car at his penthouse apartment a few streets away. He would not be able to work on the drive to the *castillo* without the chauffeur-driven limo as he had intended, but having to deal with his ex-lover's tears would be a great deal more inconvenient.

After the car drove away, he was contemplating how the hell to get past all these damn people with their phones in the air when he heard a panicked cry—which diverted everyone's attention.

'Thief! *Ladrón!* Stop him—he's stolen my bag!' a female voice shouted in a mix of outraged English and Spanish.

A man, no doubt the thief, shot through the crowd carrying a pack, followed by a girl. She wore sneakers, a T-shirt and denim cut-offs, which showed off her toned legs as she headed towards Santiago. Her short chestnut curls bounced as she ran, surrounding a face which looked young despite her fierce frown.

He caught a whisper of her scent—like the wild summer flowers his mother had loved—over the aroma of heat and garbage from the square. But as the girl shot past him, he clocked how fast she was moving.

Is she mad?

If the girl caught the thief, he could become violent. Barcelona's pickpockets usually had no desire to tussle with their victims, but only a week ago a tourist had been stabbed on Las Ramblas during a street robbery.

A fierce protective instinct struck him in the solar plexus as the girl sprinted after the thief into the labyrinth of dark alleyways, away from the open plaza.

You little fool.

Santiago tugged off his suit jacket and slung it to one of the guards. 'Hold this!' he shouted in Catalan.

He sprinted after the foolhardy girl—leaving the square, the barrage of phone cameras and quite possibly his common sense behind him. He was no woman's knight in shining armour, just ask Gabriela, but even he wasn't cynical enough to do nothing while a girl Ana's age risked injury or worse over a lost bag.

CHAPTER TWO

CERYS PUMPED HER LEGS, her lungs working overtime as she entered the narrow side street.

She kept her gaze fixed on the man fifteen yards ahead of her, and her bright blue rucksack as it bobbed past the dwindling crowds of people. And tried not to think about Álvaro De Montoya's son—and the forbidding frown on his devastatingly handsome face—when she had sped past his nose.

The rucksack held everything she possessed, including her phone.

Why hadn't she paid more attention?

Her lungs heaved and her legs began to ache. She darted past a rubbish cart and swung round a corner, gaining ground. Her pack weighed a ton, and the thief was flagging. She could catch him, if she just kept running…

Her mind drifted as adrenaline and panic powered her through the pain.

She hadn't been thinking at all when he'd swiped her rucksack because she'd been transfixed by Santiago De Montoya—after spotting him on a balcony above the square.

She'd been glued to every aspect of his body language while he was deep in conversation with his girlfriend.

He had looked so tall and striking in the designer suit, his features so harsh and arresting in the light cast by wall sconces—the patrician nose, the stubbled jawline, the high cheekbones and the waves of carefully styled jet-black hair. But he had also been strangely detached, his stance radiating controlled irritation, while his date—a leggy, poised blonde—had seemed desperate. The woman had looked heartbroken when they'd appeared together at the building's exit moments later. But just as the arriving limo had obscured Cerys's view she had felt her bag detaching from her shoulders, the straps cut.

'Stop running! *Estùpida!*' The gruff shout coming from behind Cerys echoed off the walls of the alley.

Just as she was trying to make sense of it—*who was calling who stupid*—the thief stopped abruptly at the far end of the street and turned to face her.

He was only a few yards ahead now. Sweat dripped off his features. But this close she could see the scars on his face, and the anger in his eyes. And how enormous he was.

Oh, crap!

She skidded to a stop. The running footsteps behind her echoed in the silent alleyway, but were barely audible above her thundering heartbeat.

The thief shouted something in Catalan, then dumped the bag at his feet and tore it open.

'Stop, that's mine...' she shouted as he grabbed her travel wallet and her phone and stuffed them both into his back pocket.

She rushed forward without thinking, determined to stop him, as he began yanking out her clothes and throwing them onto the cobblestones, searching for more valuables.

'No, not that, please.' She grabbed his wrist as he lifted

out her mother's journal. This close, she could smell his sweat—acrid, bitter. Fury flashed across his face, before something which felt like a brick slammed into the side of her head.

She shot backwards and landed on her back, dazed—when several shapes appeared, large and blurry, to grab her attacker with a roar of rage.

Her vision cleared, enough to see four people become two, the other man throwing a series of sharp punches. She tried to sit up, her face numb, her bum in agony where she'd hit the paving stones.

Was she dreaming? She had to be, because the man grappling with the thief was the same man she'd watched avidly minutes before. But as the dull thumps and grunts echoed in the alley—the two men tearing at each other, struggling to land punches—she couldn't shake the sense of unreality. Of floating in a strange and painful dream.

What was Álvaro's son doing here? He didn't look detached any more, his jacket gone, his shirt torn, his face rigid with fury. He gained the upper hand, wrapping his forearm around the thief's throat from behind, but then the guy elbowed him hard in the ribs. He bent over, grunting in pain… The thief scrambled away, pausing to grab the dropped journal as he disappeared into the darkness, his face bleeding.

'No!' she cried, lurching onto unsteady feet.

Everything hurt, but she had to get the diary back. She could work for more money, get the travel documents reissued, but the journal was the only connection with her mother she had left.

She tried to run but strong arms banded around her waist from behind, dragging her back against a rock-solid chest.

A musty and compelling mix of laundry detergent and citrus soap and salty sweat filled her aching lungs.

'I have to get the book,' she cried in Spanish, struggling against the cast iron hold without success.

'Stop, it is gone.' A breathless whisper, low with determination and demand, rasped in her ear. 'Be still.' His voice rose with temper and incredulity as she continued to struggle. 'There is no purpose in being hurt for something you can replace.'

But I can't replace it.

The thought echoed in her head, even as her strength and panic deserted her until all that was left was dizziness and exhaustion.

Her heavy legs dissolved, her knees buckling, and suddenly she was floating. An impossibly handsome face hovered above her—reminding her of someone else she was sure she'd never seen in real life before. The strong, angular features were so striking and forbidding, but also so familiar, the chocolate-brown eyes shadowed with concern and judgement.

The pain surged, her heart contracting in her chest, but with it came the spurt of adrenaline as a word jumped out at her...

Breathtaking. He's breathtaking.

Her rescuer's shirt had been torn open, revealing the tanned column of his throat, and she could see the stubble on his jaw, along with the already darkening bruise on his brow. But as he stared at her, prickling excitement rippled over her skin. His laboured breathing matched her own. The sensation sank low in her abdomen and surged...

...as if a fireworks display was going off in my belly.

The description exploded in her consciousness, perfectly describing how she felt: disorientated, dismayed, confused and yet vividly, viciously alive.

'What is your name?' he demanded.

She shook her head, trying to dispel the phantoms, the rush of nausea and dizziness... And that desperate scalding heat...

It took every last ounce of effort to whisper the name lodged in her brain as she dropped into oblivion.

'*Álvaro...*'

'She is sleeping now, Your Excellency. Let her rest, but she should be woken every two to three hours for the first twenty-four to check for a concussion.'

Santiago raked his fingers through his hair, while the young medic stuffed the last of his equipment into his bag.

'Terrific,' he murmured. The bruise on his brow stung as he cursed his foolish decision to get involved in the first place.

How the hell had his night gone from annoying to catastrophic?

'Wait!' he demanded as the young man headed to the door of his apartment. 'Can you not admit her to hospital?'

He did not need this responsibility. He had to leave tonight, to handle Ana's latest misadventure. His staff in the city would all be in bed by now so he could hardly wake them to come over and check on his unwanted guest. And something about the girl had a diabolic effect on his usual caution.

Plus, why had she whispered his father's name before passing out?

The medic smiled. 'She's battered and bruised, but

there's no reason to treat this as an emergency, unless you wish to make a private referral.'

No way!

He recoiled at the suggestion. The press already had photographs of him haring off after her. He did not want to feed the story even more—which was why he did not intend to contact the police about the assault and robbery until tomorrow, once he was at the *castillo*.

'Is she okay to travel at least?' he asked, his frustration mounting. 'I have to drive to Girona tonight.'

The staff at the *castillo* would have to watch her.

The medic nodded. 'As long as you make sure to wake her up every two to three hours,' he repeated, as if Santiago were an imbecile. Then the young man's gaze shifted to the painful area on Santiago's forehead. 'Are you sure you're okay to drive?' he asked. 'You look a bit battered yourself, Your Excellency.'

Santiago frowned, making the skin around the bruise smart. 'I'll survive,' he said flatly.

The thief had landed a few lucky punches, but he'd been hit a lot harder as a boy, when he had made the mistake of questioning his father's judgement.

The medic nodded. 'Have a doctor check her over tomorrow. But bed rest is really the only treatment for concussion.'

Santiago saw the young man out. Then swore under his breath. He'd showered and changed, packed a bag and taken it to his car in the garage while the medic had been checking over the girl. But now he had no choice—he would have to bring her with him.

The thought of carrying her again did not appeal to him in the slightest. Although she was not heavy, the feel of her in his arms when he had brought her back here, while she moaned and dropped in and out of consciousness, had disturbed him. Almost as much as the whisper of his father's name on her lips.

The compelling scent of wild flowers had invaded his senses and he couldn't seem to stop staring at her face—as he toted her the short distance to the apartment building. She was pretty, nothing more—her full lips somehow a little too large for her gamine face, the bruise on her cheek only increasing the sense of fragile beauty. But it was the memory of her huge blue-green eyes, her gaze burning with intensity, which had disturbed him the most...

Because her forthright inspection had made him feel transparent, in a way he did not appreciate.

She looked impossibly young—maybe even still a teenager—and was stupidly naïve, too. Why else would she have run headlong into trouble? Requiring him to break the habit of a lifetime and rescue her.

He stood in the doorway to his bedroom and watched her, curled on the bed, fast asleep—the medic had given her painkillers at least for the bruising. Tugging his phone out, he texted the *castillo*'s housekeeper, María, asking her to prepare a room for the girl, while explaining he would need someone to stay up to watch her. Then he texted his EA in the Barcelona office. Mateo would get the message tomorrow. Someone would have to see if her belongings could be retrieved from that back alley. He'd had to leave the bag and clothes behind—with his arms full of her. But, given Barcelona's reputation as the Catalan capital of petty crime, he expected her belongings to be gone by morning.

Tough.

The thief had already taken the items of value. Surely

she would have travel insurance to cover the losses. And if she were foolish enough not to, that was not his problem.

Steeling himself, he entered the room and scooped her up from the bed. She stirred in his arms, her luminous eyes opened and seemed to stare into his soul, sending a rush of unwanted reaction through him.

Dammit.

'*Hola,*' she said softly.

'*Hola,*' he replied.

'*Gracias. Lo aprecio mucho.*'

He wondered what she was thanking him for, but then her cheek pressed into his T-shirt and her eyelids drooped. The trusting, strangely intimate gesture had his heart hammering his ribs.

'*Ve a dormir,*' he said, deciding her ability to speak Spanish coherently meant she could not be that concussed.

She sighed, then obeyed his command, dropping back into sleep.

After carting her down to the garage, he buckled her sleeping form into the passenger seat of his convertible. He congratulated himself on a clean getaway as he drove out of the garage and began the night drive to the ancestral estate.

Not so successful was his battle to control the wave of unwanted awareness as the girl's captivating floral scent filled his car...

CHAPTER THREE

CERYS EDGED OPEN her eyelids, then slammed them shut again, the blast of sunshine threatening to laser off her retinas.

Why did her face feel as if it were on fire, too?

She touched her cheekbone.

'Ow.' She groaned. *That hurt!*

Then she moved and all the other sore spots on her body wept in unison. Her bum most of all. What had happened to her? Because she felt as if she'd been slam-dunked from a great height, into a soft lavender-scented cloud.

'*Hola, señorita. Estas despierta?*' The bright, excited female voice came from beside her cloud.

Who the...?

She risked opening her eyes again. And turning her head, which amplified the throbbing in her face, and the headache blooming behind her eyes. *Fabulous!*

A girl—or rather, a beautiful young woman—sat in an ornate chair, staring back at her with wide chocolate-brown eyes, which reminded her of someone, but she had no idea who.

'*Hola! Como estas?*' the girl said, her stunning face breaking into a grin, which only made the combination of thick black hair falling in carelessly perfect waves, striking bone structure, smooth olive-toned skin and those captivating eyes more spellbinding.

'Hi,' Cerys replied, hopelessly disorientated. Where was she? How had she got here? And why was the girl speaking Spanish?

Although the girl wore modern clothing—a flattering and expensive summer dress covered in sunflowers—Cerys had the weird thought she had travelled back in time as she took in the huge bedroom. The ornate furniture looked like something from a bygone era, all carved wood and velvet upholstery. While the lavender cloud was actually a magnificent four-poster bed, draped with white linen embroidered with gold. The scent of lavender detergent and fresh earth added to the strange feeling of being cast adrift in someone else's life.

'Where am I?' she managed at last, because the girl seemed to be waiting for her to speak.

'*Castillo de las Vides*. The Castle of the Vines, where my family—the De Montoyas—have lived for many generations...' the girl said in accented English. 'My brother Santiago is *el Duque* now. And the wine we produce here is the very best in Spain.'

'Sorry, where?' Cerys asked when the babble of information finally ceased. She'd never heard of this place. Or this family. Had she? What was she doing here?

The girl's grin widened.

'We can speak *Inglés*, if you prefer,' the girl offered, her heavy accent doing nothing to detract from the excitement in her voice. 'But Santiago told our housekeeper, María, you speak Spanish. I heard him say it yesterday.'

Maria? Why did she have a vague recollection of being woken in the darkness and asked questions by an older woman in a language she didn't understand?

The girl pulled her chair closer, the mischievous sparkle in her eyes becoming astute.

'Santiago drove you here in the middle of the night, and carried you to this bedroom himself. And you were asleep all day yesterday. But he hasn't told anyone your name. It's so romantic. He never brings any of his *chicas* here.'

Chicas?

Cerys frowned, her head screaming. She didn't know what that meant, but from the girl's expression she could guess.

'I'm not your brother's *chica*,' she said, because that was one thing she was certain of. She'd never heard of this guy. And she wasn't sure she had ever been anyone's *chica*.

The girl's brow furrowed. 'Are you sure?'

'Yes, because I've never met him,' she said. Although... Something was pushing at the edges of her memory—dark eyes like the girl's, but so serious and intense they made her stomach muscles quiver.

The girl's eyebrows rose, but as she opened her mouth to question Cerys further, an older woman Cerys vaguely recognised appeared, carrying a silver tray. Stern but polite, she spoke in rapid Spanish to the girl, while placing the tray over Cerys's lap and lifting a silver dome to reveal a lavish cooked breakfast which had Cerys's stomach realising how empty it was. All the time the older woman continued to argue calmly with the girl, who protested, then begged, then pouted, all in Spanish, but was finally ushered out of the room. The girl swung round at the door to wink at Cerys.

'My name's Ana, I am *el Duque*'s sister. Do not fear, I will be back to investigate later,' she said, then was shooed through the closing door by the woman who Cerys had guessed must be María.

Investigate what, exactly?

The housekeeper smiled at Cerys, while speaking in a soothing voice, but all in Spanish. Then tucked a napkin in the neck of the cotton nightdress Cerys was wearing—which she didn't recognise either.

A lump caught in Cerys's throat, the motherly gesture calling to a vague memory from long ago which made sadness squeeze her ribs. She swallowed down the inexplicable swell of tears.

As she struggled to eat the fluffy tortilla accompanied by toasted bread and a delicately spiced tomato salad, the housekeeper continued to question her gently in Spanish.

After a few mouthfuls, Cerys had to put the fork down. She was exhausted and it hurt her jaw to chew, plus her stomach was rebelling against the thoughts racing around her sore head.

'I'm sorry, I don't speak Spanish,' she said to the housekeeper, who seemed surprised. 'And the breakfast is delicious, but I can't eat any more.'

The woman nodded, unoffended, and lifted the tray. She said something which included the name Montoya.

'Thank you so much for looking after me,' Cerys said as the housekeeper left the room. The woman only smiled.

Cerys was still staring out of the large bay window ten minutes later, studying the acres of vines interspersed with woodland which covered the surrounding hills, trying to make sense of all the questions in her head...

Why was she here? Who were these people? And why was her mind so blank? She didn't even know how she had acquired the bruises on her face and her backside.

Or where the simple oversized nightdress she was wearing came from.

She jumped when a sharp knock sounded on the door. 'Come in...' she said.

Heat scorched her sore face when a tall man walked into the room—making the palatial bedroom suddenly feel poky. She didn't recognise him, but he seemed to have a physical effect on her—making her belly jiggle and heat spread across her collarbone and down into her...

She crossed her arms over her chest, far too aware of the loose-fitting nightie, and her nipples pebbling into stiff peaks beneath the thin cotton.

He stepped closer and the light from the window illuminated his face. The square jaw, the patrician nose, the serious expression and those eyes... A deep, dark brown, with flecks of gold in the irises. Why did she recognise his eyes? They were like the girl's but also not—because they had none of her amusement or excitement... Or transparent emotion.

In a fitted shirt and expertly creased suit trousers, he was magnetic. In fact, she couldn't stop staring at him as he crossed the room and sat in the chair the girl had vacated.

'*Buen dia.*' His clipped Spanish accent did nothing to reduce the scalding heat rising up Cerys's neck like a mushroom cloud. 'I am Santiago Álvaro De Montoya Lopez. *El Duque de Cantada.* Do you remember me?'

So, this was the brother Ana had mentioned.

Cerys wanted to say yes, because she *definitely* remembered his eyes—so disturbing and compelling—but nothing else about him was familiar. Not even the discolouration on his brow beneath the tanned skin. How had he become bruised, too?

While he studied her intently, waiting for her answer, she decided she couldn't possibly have met him before, because she would not have forgotten anyone this overwhelming—and frankly, hot. She managed to shake her head, his presence so intimidating it had robbed her of the power of speech.

His eyes narrowed, his gaze becoming even more piercing, if that were possible—the sceptical expression made Cerys feel guilty, but she had no idea what for.

'We met in Barcelona, two nights ago,' he said in perfect English. 'You were injured, during a street robbery. Do you remember this?'

She shook her head again, then cleared her throat.

'No, I... I don't think I have ever been to Barcelona.'

Her voice came out on a perilous quiver, which would have been embarrassing if she weren't so confused right now, about everything—her bizarre reaction to this man most of all.

He raked his hand through the thick waves of dark hair. 'You most certainly have been to Barcelona,' he corrected her.

Before she could respond, he stood and paced to the window to stare out at the vines, his shoulders rigid with tension. Or was that irritation?

'I'm sorry,' she said, the confusion clearing a little. However she had ended up here, it was obvious she was a nuisance. 'You've been very kind.' She lifted the sheet and placed her bare feet on an antique silk carpet. 'But I can leave now...'

He swung round from his contemplation of the landscape.

'*Madre de Dios*,' he hissed, impatience flashing in his eyes. 'And how do you plan to do this?' he demanded.

'When you have no money, no travel documents, and very few clothes?'

She stared at him. 'I… I don't have any clothes? Seriously?' She folded her arms around her waist, feeling naked under that searing judgement. At which point she realised she didn't even have a bra.

'You do not remember this either?' he said, frustration making his stern expression even more forbidding. That said, she knew how he felt—because she was getting quite exasperated herself.

How could she have got herself into this much of a fix? Or was this some weird anxiety dream?

Gee thanks, subconscious.

Hopefully, she would wake up any minute, because Señor Hot was fast turning into Señor Super Pissed-Off.

'The thief who stole your bag? The chase across Plaça Reial?' He fired questions at her as he strode back across the room. 'Your immature decision to tackle a man twice your size? The fight we had? The drive here from the city? You said my father's name, Álvaro, before you passed out. You remember none of this? *Nada?*'

'No…' she said, feeling less accommodating by the second. Why was he so furious? She was the one with no clothes and no money. 'And shouting at me isn't going to make me remember. In fact, it's making my head feel like it's about to explode. So maybe stop doing that.'

He swore again—but at least he did it under his breath—then he sat back down in the chair beside the bed and dropped his head into his hands.

But as he rubbed his face he flinched, and she realised he had touched the raw spot above his eye. She knew how that felt. Then one of the questions he had fired at her rushed back.

The fight we had?

'I didn't... I didn't hit you, did I?' she asked, horrified. While she couldn't remember much of anything, she hoped she hadn't intentionally hurt another human being, however annoying they were.

He peered at her through his fingers, the frustration replaced by confusion.

Yup, so know how that feels, too.

'The bruise above your eye?' she asked again, scared to hear the answer. 'I didn't give you that, did I? When we had our fight?'

He dropped his hands and straightened in his chair, his broad shoulders making the ornate piece of antique furniture creak—and seem nowhere near as imposing as he was. But his expression was still giving her serious what-on-earth-is-she-talking-about-now? vibes.

'You asked if I remembered our fight,' she tried to explain again. Could this conversation get any more awkward? 'I really don't remember fighting with you...' Although she already had the sense that he would not be a difficult man to start an argument with. He seemed quite inflexible and a lot impatient. 'But if I hurt you, I'm very sorry.'

The fierce frown suddenly disappeared. He dropped his head back against the seat and the minutes ticked by as he stared at the ceiling. Cursing. Softly. In Spanish.

Okay, what had she said *now*? He was making this conversation unnecessarily difficult. Maybe it was the language barrier. Although his English seemed perfect. Perhaps something had been lost in translation.

But when his gaze met hers again, what she saw in his expression astonished her. And made the jumping beans in her belly go into overdrive.

'What's so funny?' she asked.

A sensual smile curved his lips, adding to the wry amusement in his eyes, and making him look even more... Well, hot. Frankly.

How was that fair? she thought, annoyed with herself now as well as him. How could she possibly think he was attractive when he was being such a jerk?

'*We* did not have a fight, *chica*...' He let out a gruff chuckle.

Although she should be relieved that she hadn't punched him, his amusement at her expense was starting to make her wish she had. And the use of the word *chica* in that intimate tone was not good for the jumping beans in her still mostly empty belly.

'*I* fought with the thief who robbed you,' he stressed. 'After he slapped you.' His gaze roamed over her face, making her brutally aware of her sore cheek—and the prickle of sensation everywhere else. 'I am not a violent man,' he added, which almost sounded like an apology. 'But the abuse of women is something I will not tolerate. *Ever*.'

The smile had died, the sparkle of amusement gone from his eyes. Cold fury crossed his expression. The moment felt so compelling she shivered, even though she was the opposite of cold. However overbearing he was, it seemed he had a strong—and unbreakable—moral code...

'Thank you, then. For helping me,' she said, feeling guilty now for having snapped at him.

He'd obviously rescued her from the man who had robbed her and hurt her—and brought her to his home, and she had been ungrateful.

'*De nada*,' he said, approval highlighting the golden shards in his irises.

'If someone could lend me some clothes, I'll get out of your hair...' It was obvious he didn't want her here. So, getting the heck out of his home was the least she could do to return the favour.

But when she went to get up, her legs shaky, his frown returned. 'Get back into bed,' he demanded. 'You can barely walk.' The edge of authority was so sharp she obeyed him without thinking.

'But I...' she tried to protest.

'What is your name?' he interrupted.

'Cerys.' The answer popped out instinctively.

He nodded. '*Y tu apellido?* Your family name? What is this?'

She opened her mouth, expecting it to appear in her head the same way her first name had... But nothing, absolutely nothing, was there. The panic she had been contending with when he arrived snaked around her ribs and squeezed. She blinked furiously as idiotic tears stung her eyes.

'I... I'm not sure,' she stuttered, both frantic and suddenly bereft.

How could she not know her own surname? This was horrendous. She felt as if she had been robbed of something far more precious than her clothes, or her money or her passport...

She pressed her fingers to her lips, realising the full import of the huge empty space in her head...

'Do you know my name?' she managed, feeling utterly pathetic now, but also scared. Because why would he have asked her name if he already knew the answer?

After studying her intently for what felt like several hours, but could only have been a few seconds, he shook his head. The intent expression became shadowed—with pity or concern or disapproval, she wasn't sure, because he masked his emotions so well.

Either way, she felt humiliated. How could she go anywhere, *do* anything, *be* anyone, if she didn't know who she was?

She trembled and sniffed. 'Oh, God,' she whispered, staring at her hands, which were clasped so tightly in her lap the knuckles had gone white.

He pressed a large palm to her shoulder. 'Do not cry,' he said softly.

She shifted against his touch, and he lifted his hand immediately, but the feel of it still buzzed over her skin—which wasn't comforting at all really.

'I won't,' she said, determined not to let the tears queuing up in her throat fall in front of him. Because that would somehow be so much worse.

She hated to be dependent on anyone, but what she hated more was to know she needed his support, because deserving his help felt like a test she was bound to fail. She did not know why she knew she had to be self-sufficient, but she clung to the insight because it was a clue—however small—to that blank space inside her.

'We will let the doctor examine you. And then we will work out who you are.'

His offer wasn't exactly welcoming, but his tone was so pragmatic and commanding it still felt reassuring. If anyone could find out who she was, she was sure it would be this man. But when he stood up, she grasped his wrist.

'But what if you can't…?' she said. 'Find out my surname?'

He frowned. 'You will stay here until I do,' he said, as if it was obvious.

'But... Y-you don't want me here,' she replied. 'And if you don't want me here, I don't want to be here.'

She couldn't stay. She had no money. How would she pay him back? And she refused to rely on his charity and largesse, especially as he'd made it clear he found her presence in his home inconvenient at best.

He glanced at her fingers on his wrist, making her realise she was clinging to him. She released him instantly, even as the riot of sensation where her fingers had touched his skin made her breathing accelerate alarmingly.

'You will stay here because you must,' he said in that forthright manner he had that made absolutely no effort to spare her feelings. 'Until we discover who you are.'

It was true, of course, but, even so, she felt utterly miserable—small and insignificant and lonely—emotions which also brought back hazy recollections, but, like all her other memories, they were a jagged blur of sound and colour and shadows.

Without another word, he strolled from the room and shut the door decisively behind him.

Cerys went back to staring at the view, even more anxious now than she had been before Santiago Álvaro De Montoya Lopez had walked into her life and witnessed it going into freefall... *Again*. Apparently.

'I believe she has a form of amnesia, Your Excellency. It is not uncommon after a trauma such as you have described to me. The mind will sometimes seek to protect the psyche from an event or emotions that are difficult to cope with.'

Santiago turned from his contemplation of the vineyards on the south-facing terraces above the *castillo*'s

East Wing, the knot in his stomach tightening as his head began to throb.

Dr Mendoza's calm observation was not what he had wanted to hear—which had to explain why he felt the opposite of calm right now himself.

He should not have touched the girl this morning, that much was obvious. He had stayed away from her ever since he had deposited her in one of the guest bedrooms in the West Tower at three a.m. two nights ago, following the drive from Barcelona. That would be the guest bedroom which was as far away from his own private quarters as it was possible to get her. Then he had left María Hermosa and her staff to deal with her.

Why had he given in to the unfamiliar urge to comfort her? Because the memory of her subtle shudder when he'd briefly placed his hand on her shoulder was still echoing uncomfortably in his groin an hour later... Not to mention the sight of her nipples, drawing into tight peaks under the almost transparent garment his housekeeper must have loaned her. And then there had been that subtle scent—flowery and fresh—which had an even more devastating effect on him today than it had in the car, during the endless drive to get here.

He did not usually enjoy physical contact, was not a naturally tactile man, unless erotic pleasure was involved. Nor was he a man who had any gift for comforting distraught women—just ask Ana, or his mother for that matter, whose distress he had failed to alleviate when he was a boy.

He shook his head, determined to dispel the wave of old guilt. And grief.

But how could he have controlled the urge to comfort her? The girl had looked so forlorn and lost in that moment. He had not lied when he told her he hated to see any woman abused. That was surely why he had lost his cool so spectacularly with the thief in Barcelona. The sight of the brute swatting the girl off him like a fly had stirred a deep-seated rage he remembered also from his childhood, which had exploded like a storm.

But this morning the instinct to protect her had felt more personal—and all the more disturbing for it.

'You do not think she is faking this memory loss then?' he asked, his usual cynicism kicking in. She had no money and no possessions, how easy would it be to throw herself on the mercy of a wealthy man, by pretending to have no recollection of who she was? 'This very convenient confusion about her identity,' he finished, in the hope that maybe the girl was not as vulnerable as she appeared.

'I do not believe so. She was distressed about her lack of memory, Your Excellency. As anyone would be in such circumstances,' the doctor replied, the faint rebuke in his tone making it clear he thought such an assessment of the girl's symptoms was beneath Santiago.

Santiago ignored Mendoza's gentle reprimand. His cynicism had served him well over the years. But, unfortunately, his common sense—and his ability to read people—was telling him the girl was not lying. Despite her vulnerability, she had been determined not to appear defenceless, had even taken him to task for his hectoring questions.

'She informed me she wishes to pay for her stay if she remains here,' the doctor added, clearly having been charmed by Santiago's new house guest. 'Although I have advised another couple of days of bedrest before she contemplates finding employment. I would also suggest having her referred for a scan at the Girona hospital, just to ensure there are no underlying issues.'

'Okay,' Santiago replied.

Her insistence she pay her way was of course ludicrous, especially when she was still suffering from the effects of that brute's blow. Perhaps the sight of the yellowing bruise on her cheek was another reason why he had taken pity on her and made a foolish attempt to prevent her crying.

Although again, pressing his hand to her shoulder had not felt entirely like pity when she had responded to his touch, her gaze darkening with…

He cursed inwardly.

Forget that look. It meant nothing. And you certainly do not wish it to mean anything.

It seemed he would be stuck at the *castillo* at least until the end of the summer now—before he could find a new school that would enrol his troublesome sister for the autumn semester. He'd already exhausted all the best private institutions in Spain, which meant looking further afield.

Although at seventeen she was nearly a woman, Ana remained as stubborn and disobedient as ever. Leaving her in the care of the staff here for the summer would be a recipe for disaster. She had the ability to charm them all into becoming her partners in crime—even María was not always immune to her exuberant determination to be a thorn in everyone's side, most of all her oldest brother's. And the many governesses he had hired over the years had never been able to control her either.

All of which meant he had already had to make the infuriating decision to relocate his business interests here for the next two months to watch over her himself. The good news was, after a few months of having him punishing her bad behaviour, by the end of the harvest she would be begging him to attend whichever new school he picked—and it would also give him time to prepare her for his impending marriage, once he found a bride.

The bad news was, he would be spending a whole summer in this mausoleum, which held far too many unpleasant memories. And now, added to that, there would be this girl here indefinitely too—whose presence provoked him in a way he had never experienced before. Not even while dealing with Ana.

'How long do you think it will take for her to regain her memory?' he asked.

And leave, he wanted to add, but didn't. Because he suspected Mendoza would be less than impressed with the callous sentiment. Not that he cared what people thought of him, but Mendoza had been here the night his mother had died… And he did not want the man suggesting grief counselling again to cure Santiago's 'detachment issues', when Santiago had never considered his ability to contain his emotions a problem.

'That is impossible to say with any certainty, Your Excellency. Although usually these episodes do not last very long, amnesia is not something you can cure. The brain adjusts to trauma at its own pace and in its own way. But you could perhaps consult a psychiatrist for a more thorough assessment.'

'Let's see how it goes,' he said noncommittally, already discarding that idea.

If they couldn't cure the problem, what was the point of letting a psychiatrist poke around in the girl's head? In his experience, such an intrusion would only make the whole episode more traumatic. She certainly had not lost her ability to stand up for herself, which was the main thing.

'She is well otherwise?' he asked.

'She is tired and still bruised, and distressed obviously about the amnesia, but otherwise she is fit and well, yes. There are no signs of any more concerning injuries. The scan would just be a precaution.'

'Okay, arrange the scan and send me the bill for her treatment,' he said. It was the least he could do to ensure she was healthy and could leave as soon as was humanly possible.

But when the doctor nodded and headed out of his study, he called after him.

'Do you know how old she is, Mendoza?' he asked, because it was another aspect of his unexplained reaction towards her that he found deeply unsettling. She seemed so young, innocent even—what if she were even younger than Ana? Wouldn't that make Santiago's awareness of her—that jolt of arousal when her breath had guttered out and she had trembled under his touch—nothing short of depraved? The memory of his father—and his unscrupulous dealings with women—loomed large.

'She says she has just turned twenty.'

Not younger than Ana, then. Thank God.

Santiago frowned, his suspicions aroused again, even as relief flooded him. 'How does she know her age, if she has no memory of her own name?'

'Random pieces of information are not unusual in these circumstances.'

What a shame she does not have any more useful pieces of random information then.

After the doctor left, he called María and gave his housekeeper the news that Cerys would be staying until she regained her memory. Or they could find out more about her.

He had already contacted the Barcelona police about the assault and given them a description of the thief. Maybe he would get lucky, and her documents would be found. Her accent suggested she was English. Mateo had contacted the British consulate in Barcelona, so they could alert them if anyone enquired about a missing girl.

The housekeeper took the news with her usual competence, but then reiterated what Mendoza had said about the girl insisting on paying for her room and board.

'Once she is fully recovered, find her something to do then. And pay her accordingly,' Santiago replied. If she were faking her amnesia to play on his sympathies this would disabuse her of the idea that he was in any way a soft touch. 'I have no objection to her working here once she is well enough.' And there was always work to do during the summer—he had frequently had to lend a hand himself in the fields during the harvest. Then an idea struck him. 'Ana needs someone to watch her. I simply do not have the time to be my sister's keeper twenty-four-seven. Give the girl the task and tell her to report back to you if Ana gets up to her usual mischief.' He huffed out a breath. 'Especially with any of the local boys or my male employees.'

His sister was vivacious, beautiful, completely uncontrolled and also dangerously naïve—but because she was also extremely intelligent, she had realised her ability to enslave the opposite sex as soon as she had reached puberty, and had become even more of a handful as a result—which was precisely why she needed a woman's guidance. But until he found a wife to provide that, this girl could keep her company. She wasn't much older than his sister, but maybe she could distract Ana from her usual tricks. Plus, they both spoke English. Keeping his sister entertained and out of trouble would certainly be a way for Cerys to more than earn her keep. And it would relieve him of the onerous task of dealing with Ana while he was also juggling vineyard business, the upcoming harvest, all his other businesses and investments... And rebooting his quest to find a suitable bride, which had been put on hold for the past forty-eight hours.

He had to host the annual Cantada Summer Fiesta in three weeks, so he would endeavour to find a date for the event who he could add to his shortlist—a shortlist which had precisely zero names on it at present.

As he tucked his phone into his back pocket, he congratulated himself on finding an excellent solution to the problem presented by his unwanted houseguest.

Now all he had to do was get on with his life and ignore her existence—which would be easy. The seventeenth-century *castillo* had over six hundred rooms in four separate wings, the vineyards stretched for over two thousand hectares, the winery and bodega was a huge operation which would be full of people working—and tourists doing tours—as they prepared for the harvest during the coming weeks. He was going to be extremely busy. And if the girl was going to ride herd on Ana she would have her hands full, too. So there was no reason he would ever even need to see her or speak to her again. Let alone touch her.

Excelente! The problem of his unwanted houseguest was solved.

Now all he had to do was find a wife.

CHAPTER FOUR

Three weeks later...

'IT'S SO IDYLLIC HERE, it must be tough having to leave for school at the end of each summer,' Cerys said as she rubbed the towel over her wet hair and grinned at Ana.

Her new friend—well, her only friend really, as Cerys still couldn't remember her other friends *yet*—laughed and levered herself out of the river pool to sit on one of the rocks shaded from the morning sun by gnarled tamarind trees.

The laugh wasn't like Ana's usual laughs though—infectious and full of mischief—it had a cynical edge which Cerys recognised from her first encounter with Ana's brother. Or rather, the first encounter she could remember.

She had bumped into him—literally—only once since that first day in *Castillo de las Vides*. That had been three days ago, while she had been running across the *castillo*'s courtyard to meet Ana for the day's planned excursion. She hadn't been able to see his eyes behind the aviator shades he wore, but the memory still made her shiver. Because she had felt his gaze sear her skin as he gave her a perfunctory greeting before walking away.

He really did not like her, and she had no idea why.

There were so many things she'd wanted to say to him in that moment—all of them about Ana—but she'd been completely tongue-tied. And more than a little spellbound by the sight of him in work-battered boots, a sweat-stained T-shirt and faded muddy jeans. The stubble on his chin, the messy disarray of his hair and the funky smell of sweat and earth had made her realise he must have been in the fields before dawn.

The truth was, she found the Duke of Cantada fascinating, and not just because Ana never stopped talking about him.

It hadn't taken her long to realise Ana was still somehow convinced they were secretly a *thing*—which was beyond ridiculous, the man could barely stand the sight of her. But she had also figured out that Ana's exuberant determination not to follow any of her brother's rules stemmed from a desperate desire to attract his attention. Attention which the austere man seemed determined to withhold. He only made time for his little sister once a day, when he would summon her to his study after breakfast for a ten-minute lecture to which Cerys was cordially not invited. He never ate any meals with Ana, or spent any quality time with her, not since Cerys had been given the job of 'watching her' anyway.

She'd wanted to ask him why, when she'd rounded the corner and nearly run him down. But when he'd grasped her arms to stop her from falling on her face—the hot spurt of sensation had stopped her from saying anything at all. And by the time she had untied her tongue he'd been gone. She hadn't told Ana about the encounter, though, because it would only feed her friend's obsession about their non-existent affair.

'This is the first summer Santiago has let me stay at

the *castillo* for years—and only because you are doing a good job keeping me out of his way,' the girl announced, the defeat in her voice making Cerys feel bad for her. And angry with her brother.

Why couldn't he ever spend any time with her? Ana was so generous and witty and smart. Cerys had warmed to her instantly—even though her livewire personality still exhausted her.

'I don't consider it much of a job. I still can't believe he's paying me just to have fun with you,' Cerys said.

She wasn't about to look that gift horse in the mouth though, especially as her memory was still so patchy. At least she'd been able to let go of the crippling fear and confusion of those first few days after she'd found herself at the *castillo* with no idea who she was. It was good to have a purpose, and she was convinced now her memory would return. She had acquired a working knowledge of Spanish so swiftly she must have been able to speak it before, and she was also getting weird insights into her past and her personality. Nothing concrete, nothing useful yet—like her surname! But those flashes of recognition made her optimistic that Dr Mendoza's assessment was correct. That if she just relaxed and tried not to stress about it, her missing memory would repair itself. And what could be more relaxing, and invigorating, than accompanying Ana on a series of excursions in this incredibly beautiful place?

They'd become inseparable in the last three weeks. Ana knew the area well and had made suggestions for excursions each day which Cerys had been happy to follow, doing everything from cycling to the nearest village for ice creams, going on a tour of the winery with the young bodega manager Joaquín—who Ana had flirted with mercilessly—or having regular picnics at this glorious swimming hole about an hour's trek from the *castillo* through the estate's woodlands.

'Santiago does not consider spending time with me fun at all,' Ana said, the dejection in her voice making Cerys want to shout at the man.

'Well, he's an idiot then, isn't he?' she said. She reached for the fruity sangria they had packed for their picnic. 'If he took the time to get to know you better, he'd see what an incredible person you are,' she added, determined to defend her friend and take the sadness out of her eyes.

Ana smiled, but the sadness remained. 'He does not want to know me better. It is because of our mother, I think. María once said I was like her. And now I think that is why Santiago hates to be with me—because it brings back the memories of when she died.'

Cerys straightened. She'd heard whispers about the terrible tragedy which had engulfed the Montoya siblings fifteen years ago and left both their parents dead. But that was all, because it seemed the household was sworn to silence on the issue. Even Ana had never mentioned her parents' death before now. Cerys had also discovered that Santiago had an aversion to the use of mobile phones other than for business purposes, because he had a pathological hatred of social media, but she'd never really got to the bottom of why that was either. Now she wondered if the two things were linked. She hadn't wanted to probe and as she still didn't have a phone of her own she couldn't search the internet for clues. But she also wanted to respect the family's privacy, convinced any hang-ups Santiago had were none of her business.

But as she reached forward to place a comforting hand on Ana's arm, and saw the abject misery on the girl's face, she couldn't help thinking all this secrecy about the past might not be a good thing. Wasn't it always better to talk about your feelings, your emotions? However painful they were. Why couldn't Ana's brother see that isolating and ignoring his sister for something she had no part of—because she'd only been two when her mother died—was only perpetuating the trauma of those events? And making the behaviour he wanted to correct all but inevitable.

How exactly was Ana supposed to get his attention, without causing trouble?

'If that's true, he should address it,' she said softly. 'He's the adult here, Ana. He ought to be able to see whatever happened to your mother is not your fault.' A wave of emotion—strong and visceral—rose up her chest, making her sure her assessment was correct. 'He certainly shouldn't punish you for it, just because you take after her.'

Ana raised her head, her eyes misty with emotion. 'I think he does not mean to be cruel. But it was a very difficult time for him. Alejandro told me once that the scandal was awful. Santiago was only sixteen, trying to be the *Duque*. I think he is still very angry with our father.' Ana swallowed, swiping her eyes, and showing a maturity Cerys had never seen in her before. The word *scandal* though, seemed to echo in her subconscious, triggering a selection of shadowy images she couldn't seem to suppress or interpret.

'Do you... Do you know how your parents died, Ana? Or what the scandal was that Santiago's so angry about?' she found herself asking, suddenly desperate to know more, even though she wasn't entirely sure why.

Ana shrugged. 'I don't know all the details. I tried to look it up once on the internet and Santiago had my phone confiscated for a whole month! It was horrible. He told me it would be very upsetting for me—and that it was all lies anyway. At school, the other girls would whisper, but they were scared of being punished too if they said more.' But then her face lit up as she shifted onto her knees on their picnic blanket, the energy Cerys was used to returning in a rush. 'But what I do know— and Santiago doesn't know I know, so you must never ever tell him—' she added, her voice dropping to a conspiratorial whisper '—is that our father, who was very, very handsome, fell deeply in love with a very beautiful woman, who was also married, and he ran off with her that summer. Then they were burned alive in a terrible car accident! My *madre* was pregnant and she was so upset she lost the baby and died too, from a broken heart, only days later... It was so dramatic!' Ana gave a hefty sigh, but the feverish excitement on her face was that of a teenage girl who couldn't empathise with her family's terrible losses because she had been far too young to know any of the people involved. To Ana, this was just a romantic story that had happened to strangers.

But as Cerys's stomach clenched, her insides churning, her heart throbbing painfully in her throat, the story felt personal somehow, the trauma hideously real to her— which made no sense at all because she didn't know these people either...

She clasped her arms around her waist, trying to ride the vicious wave of emotion sweeping through her body, and contain the visceral pain in the pit of her abdomen.

'Cerys, what's wrong? You have gone very pale...' Ana's panicked whisper seemed to come from far away. But it managed to pierce through the churning agony in Cerys's stomach, the cramping pain.

She dragged in a jagged breath. And then another. And clasped her stomach tighter to brace against the shadows as they transformed into faces, sights and sounds which seemed to punch her in the gut as each one appeared—a young woman, her smile warm and sweet, a forbidding man, his face devoid of emotion, an angry voice telling her that her mummy was never coming home again, cold rain on her skin making her shiver and shake.

'She's dead now, and she deserves to be—for what she did to me.'

She shook her head, struggling to break free of the images. Were they memories? They had to be, memories lodged deep in her psyche, which had nothing to do with Ana's family or their long-ago tragedy. But something in Ana's story must have dragged them out of her subconscious.

At last, she managed to breathe deeply enough to stop shaking, to feel the warm afternoon sun on her skin. Whatever those images were, wherever they came from, all she knew was that she wasn't ready to deal with them, not yet.

'I am so sorry, Cerys.' Ana's concerned voice drew her the rest of the way out of the nightmare, and back to the sun dappled riverbank. She listened to the calming sound of water trickling over rocks, inhaled the bittersweet scent of the tamarind trees, the heady fragrance of the wildflowers, waiting for her friend's face to come back into focus and the last of the vicious tremors to subside.

She nodded, determined to make it so, but suddenly wary now of letting those nightmares back in. Whatever had happened to her in her past, she didn't want to go back there again until she was ready. Certainly not yet. Was that why her mind had sealed off her past?

'It's okay, Ana. I'm okay really,' she said.

'What happened?' Ana asked, her dark eyes filled with curiosity now as well as concern.

'I... I really don't know. One minute you were talking about your family's past. And the next...' She sucked in another shaky breath as it occurred to her, whatever had once happened to her, Santiago must have suffered what sounded like a terrible trauma. One that, unlike her, he had never managed to escape.

Guilt and sympathy washed over her. And he'd only been sixteen, thrust into what sounded like a media storm—because his was an aristocratic family in the public eye—after the violent death of both his parents in a matter of a few days.

She'd dismissed him as an autocratic, unsympathetic, exceptionally rigid and judgemental man. Ana had said he was still angry. But how could she judge him now, for struggling to face whatever trauma he'd suffered then, for dealing with it the best way he knew how—by refusing to spend time with his sister, by closing down discussions about that long-ago scandal—when she herself didn't have the courage to face her past either?

'It felt like the memories locked in my head were trying to come out, but I really didn't want them to, because they weren't happy ones...' she managed because Ana was still searching her face, the avid curiosity in her gaze making the gold flecks in her irises shine.

'Perhaps you should not let them out,' Ana offered. 'If they are so sad they will make you ill.'

Cerys let a weak smile lift her lips. Trust Ana to get right to the heart of the problem.

'It feels a bit cowardly not to, though,' she said. 'And I may have to, if I'm going to figure out who I am. I can't expect your brother to keep me on a salary indefinitely.' Especially as she was already so sure he didn't really want her here.

In fact, she already had a deadline. Ana was due to start a new school at the end of the summer—even if she had rejected all her brother's choices so far. Either that or the rumour among the staff was that Santiago was planning to get married, so his wife could 'handle' Ana, something Ana was even less on board with from her running commentary on all the awful women her brother had chosen to date in the past.

Cerys had made a point of not engaging with Ana's opinions of Santiago's dating history, because it would only fuel Ana's obsession with pretending that Santiago and her could be an item. But she had secretly agreed with Ana that the *Duque*'s marriage plans seemed remarkably unromantic and pragmatic to the point of being deeply cynical—assuming they were true.

But whatever happened with the *Duque*'s search for a *Duquesa*, or a suitable boarding school for his sister, Cerys knew she would be surplus to requirements in six weeks' time. She certainly couldn't stay in the *castillo*, taking a salary from Santiago, once he didn't need her here anymore.

'I have a brilliant idea,' Ana said, an excited smile spreading over her face. It was an expression Cerys knew she needed to be wary of, because it usually meant she was going to have to dissuade Ana from some wild scheme.

'Hmm, let's hear it then,' she said, humouring her friend as she sipped the sangria and tried not to contemplate how hard it would be to leave Ana, and María and all the friends she had made on the staff, at the end of the summer. If her memory didn't return in time, she would have to throw herself on the mercy of the British consulate, because she was sure she had to be English. But she would miss everyone so much. And the *castillo,* which had become a home—despite its owner wanting her gone.

'If my brother is in search of a bride, why doesn't he marry you?'

Cerys sprayed the sangria she had been drinking across the picnic blanket. 'Ana, are you mad?' she finally managed through the coughing and spluttering.

'Why is this *loco*?' Ana asked, looking genuinely puzzled by Cerys's reaction. 'He wants someone to look after me, so he does not have to do it himself. This is what María told me. Why should it not be you, when you are so good at it?'

Cerys wiped her mouth, aware of the hot blood charging into her cheeks. 'You're seventeen, Ana, you know why,' she said, even as the visceral hum from three days ago, when Santiago had grasped her arms, began to thunder in her ears and ripple through her abdomen.

'No, I do not.' Ana pouted. 'If his reason for finding a wife is to give me a mother, then why should I not have a say?'

'Because that can't possibly be his only reason, Ana. And anyway, I hardly know him...' she murmured, trying to keep her exasperation front and centre so she could avoid thinking about the hum, which was starting to take on a life of its own.

Instead of being deterred from her mad scheme by logic though, Ana let out a triumphant laugh. 'But if you marry him you will get to know him very quickly. Do you not think he is handsome? And he is a very good lover. It is what his *chicas* say when they think I am not listening.'

'Ana!' she shrieked. 'Oh. My. God. Don't *say* stuff like that, he's your brother.' Cerys slapped her hands over her ears, horrified now by the girl's shocking candour, and the throbbing sensation which had dropped like a brick into her abdomen. A very hot brick.

She *definitely* did not need to be thinking about her boss's prowess in bed, because being the focus of his attention for precisely ten seconds three days ago—not to mention a whole ten minutes three weeks ago—still had the ability to make her wake up at night hot and sweaty and on edge... Not that she would ever mention that to Ana. It was bad enough that she already knew she was less worldly-wise than her charge who was three years younger, but she had spent weeks now trying very hard not to acknowledge what felt like a small crush on Ana's brother. She'd been keeping a lid on it so well up to now, despite Ana's provocation, and now her friend had blown her cover to hell. Something Ana was far too astute not to notice.

'*Sí*, but he is not *your* brother? No?' Ana grasped Cerys's wrists to pull her hands down from her ears, which were doing precisely nothing to halt the conversation.

'Ana, please, I told you already, I don't think he likes me much. At best, he sees me as staff, at worst an inconvenience,' she murmured, humiliation adding to the vivid blush. They could probably see her cheeks on Mars right now they were so hot.

'Then we must make him see you,' Ana said, still completely undeterred. 'Tomorrow is the Fiesta,' she added. 'It is the perfect opportunity.'

'The perfect opportunity for what?' Cerys asked warily, the determined set of Ana's jaw starting to concern her. Surely she couldn't *actually* be serious about this.

'For Santiago to see you as a woman—and a bride. No?'

'Absolutely not, Ana.' It was official, Santiago's sister had lost her mind. 'And anyway, I can't go. I'm not invited.'

Thank God.

Preparations for the exclusive Cantada Summer Fiesta to mark the beginning of the harvesting season—and Catalan's national feast day celebrating St John the Baptist's birth—had been consuming the staff for weeks at the *castillo*. It was pretty much all anyone talked about. One of the main reasons she and Ana had been roaming the woodlands and forests each day had been to keep out of everyone's way. Of course, Ana had dropped several hints already about Cerys attending the lavish party. And Cerys had to admit she'd been tempted—because the event sounded so enchanting and super exclusive and something she knew she had never attended before. She had also been touched by how keen Ana was to have her there, but now she was beginning to realise her friend might have had an ulterior motive.

'This is not a problem,' Ana replied. 'Alejandro is arriving tomorrow, and he will not have a date, as he never commits to one woman,' Ana continued. 'I will ask him to escort you.'

'No way! I've never even met your other brother,' she replied. In fact, all she knew about the famous, or rather infamous, Alejandro was that María had referred to him as a *chico muy malo*, and that whenever his name was mentioned all the housemaids blushed.

'And I don't have anything to wear either,' she added, hoping to put an end to the discussion once and for all, because she could feel it slipping away from her in the face of Ana's enthusiasm.

'I have many beautiful dresses that will fit you,' Ana countered. 'And I need you there, because both my brothers will ignore me, and without you there I will die of boredom. *And...*' She paused to take a breath and grab a spicy pastry from the picnic hamper, brandishing it as she continued. 'Very soon all your memory will be returned...' She took a hefty bite, but then her face fell as she swallowed. 'Will you leave? When you know who you are again?'

'I don't want to—I'd love to stay the rest of the summer if I can. Assuming, of course, there isn't anyone waiting for me back home.' But even as she voiced the thought, the shimmer of loneliness told her that, wherever her home was, there was nothing for her there. The fact that no one had contacted the Barcelona police or the British consulate looking for her in the past three weeks surely confirmed that.

Ana's eyes darkened with concern. 'I wish you to stay too, which is why—even if you do not wish to marry Santiago—you *must* show him how valuable you are.' She dumped the half-eaten pastry in the basket and jumped off her rock to grasp Cerys's hands in hers. 'Come to the Fiesta with me. If I don't cause any trouble, he will want to keep you here, I know it. And you will enjoy the party. Especially once the dancing starts.'

'I'm sorry, Ana,' Cerys said, calmer now that at least Ana had stopped talking about marriage. 'I really don't think that would be appropriate.'

Especially as being anywhere near Santiago makes all my brain cells melt. And a few other things beside.

But Ana clung on, the wide-eyed expression becoming desperate.

'*Please*, Cerys, without you there I will be so bored

I will be forced to flirt with all the boy waiters—which will make Santiago super mad with us both. Then neither of us will be able to stay for the rest of the summer.'

'That's blackmail, Ana,' Cerys said, trying to remain immune to the girl's pleading, and not smile at her outrageous antics.

'You know I can't help myself when I'm bored. Or lonely,' she replied. And Cerys felt her heart break for the girl. '*Por favor*, Cerys, *please*. The Fiesta is the best event of the season. The courtyard will be full of lights, there will be flamenco and then dancing in the orchard, the food is always superb and Santiago will serve Cantada's finest wines and cava. And we will be invisible if you want. No one will even know we're there.'

'Ana, stop…!' She dragged her hands free but knew she had lost the battle. The girl was just too persuasive. And a part of her was so tempted at the prospect of attending the event.

Would it really be so wrong to give in to the urge to accompany Ana? Santiago would be unlikely to notice her after all, he'd be far too busy hosting the event. And stopping Ana from flirting with the waiters was totally part of her job description.

'*Por favor*, Cerys. It will be such fun.'

Cerys sighed. 'Okay, I'll go. But I'm not talking to Santiago…' Especially as he would surely be there with a date and he wouldn't want her there, if he noticed her at all, which she was sure he wouldn't, especially if she kept a low profile.

Ana jumped up and whooped with glee. 'We will find you an amazing gown this afternoon. And I will tell Alejandro to escort you as soon as he arrives tomorrow.'

'No, you mustn't! I'm not going with Alejandro,' Cerys said, panic making her pulse race again.

'But everyone wants to date Alejandro, he is very handsome and charming. Even if he is also *uno chico muy malo*,' Ana said, undeterred.

'No,' Cerys said forcefully. 'I'm not confident with bad boys.' In fact, she was fairly sure she had never had a proper boyfriend—which explained why she found Santiago so overwhelming. He was, after all, incredibly handsome, and commanding and forceful and, from what Ana had said, also very experienced with women. 'We're going to blend into the background, okay? I don't want Santiago to notice me.'

Ana plopped back down, her brow furrowing. 'But this is silly. How will we make Santiago jealous if you have no date?'

Precisely.

'Promise me, Ana. I'm only going if you agree to my terms. No Alejandro, no tricks, no jokes, no wild schemes, no flirting with the waiters and no daft attempts to attract Santiago's attention.'

Ana threw up her arms. '*Bueno*, but you won't have as much fun,' she said, disappointment weighing down every word.

Cerys smiled, relieved. 'Of course I will, I'm going to my first ever Catalan fiesta,' she said, pleased she had managed to corral Ana—while also prising another nugget of information about her past out of her brain. Not only had she never been to a Catalan fiesta, she was sure she had never been to a party as exclusive as this one promised to be—because she had a vague recollection of serving people, rather than being served.

As they packed up the picnic and Ana began to rattle

off the selection of dresses they could choose from for Cerys's debut, anticipation began to build in her chest.

After everything that had happened in the past three weeks, maybe she deserved this moment. Santiago wouldn't even notice her, so it would be a chance to observe him again, without putting herself in the spotlight. Or risking her employment. After the deeply distressing things Ana had told her about his past, she couldn't stop the deep well of sympathy for him taking hold too. And watching him with the woman he might be planning to marry—because he would surely have a date at the Fiesta—would also stop Ana getting any more ridiculous ideas, and cure Cerys too of the silly schoolgirl crush she seemed to have developed after two fleeting encounters.

Not to mention the inappropriate hum.

By nine o'clock the following evening though, Cerys realised she had totally underestimated her new best friend's ability to cause absolute chaos…

CHAPTER FIVE

'I MAY HAVE to murder your little sister,' Cerys muttered under her breath, so embarrassed she wanted to die.

The stupidly handsome man beside her chuckled, his green eyes a different shade to his siblings, but filled with the same mischievous twinkle as his younger sister.

'Trusting my sister was your first mistake, Cerys,' he said easily. 'The only thing you can rely on is that Ana never *ever* does what she is told.'

'Good point,' Cerys said and smiled back at him, trying to relax as he led her through the dark hallways of the *castillo* towards the sound of exuberant music, the buzz of conversation and the clink of champagne flutes.

Night had fallen a few minutes ago, signalling the beginning of the Fiesta, the cooler evening air a necessity for any social event in Catalonia during the summer months.

Cerys released the breath clogged in her lungs as she and her 'date' entered the stone gallery above the *castillo*'s magnificent central courtyard. Festooned in fairy lights and decorated with lavish floral arrangements, the space below was already filled with guests—men in lightweight designer suits and women in summer gowns in vibrant colours which made them look like colourful butterflies or extravagant peacocks. The red glow on the horizon was iridescent as the sun finished its descent over the rolling patchwork of vines as far as the eye could see. Bougainvillea climbed in flamboyant splendour up the castle's stone walls—and the scent of the flowering vines filled the air with redolent perfume. Delicate, perfectly spiced tapas were being served on silver trays—along with glasses of the *castillo*'s famed cava—by liveried wait staff. Cerys knew the kitchen had been working on the feast for days. A Latin band added the rich vibrant rhythms of the Catalonia rumba. The dancefloor set up under the trees at the edge of the courtyard had several couples on it already, dancing to the infectious beat.

The tension making Cerys's stomach jump and jive with the music relaxed.

'Wow,' she murmured, captivated by the laughter floating in the air, despite the formal setting. It was all so romantic and exciting, something to tell her grandkids about one day. She hoped.

'You approve?' Alejandro asked.

'It's...' She sighed. 'It's stunning. Your home is so beautiful.'

'Not *my* home—the *castillo* and the vines belong to Santiago,' he said, surveying the scene. The hollow tone made Cerys wonder what the story was with the De Montoya brothers? Why weren't they close? Perhaps it was their very different personalities. Santiago was so serious and responsible and forbidding. While Alejandro, on the other hand, was so debonair and charming and defiantly shallow.

'*El Duque* is welcome to this cursed place,' he murmured. 'But anyway,' he said, a practised smile curving his lips as the dark expression lifted. His gaze roamed over her. 'The *castillo* is not as beautiful as you are.'

Cerys smiled, flattered by Alejandro's easy charm—which was so unlike his brother's rigid judgement. 'Why, thank you. I bet you say that to all the girls,' she quipped.

He chuckled. 'I see my reputation precedes me,' he replied, the devil-may-care twinkle back in his eyes.

Even on their ten-minute acquaintance, Alejandro De Montoya Lopez was everything Cerys had expected him to be—tall, dark, dangerously handsome, impossibly charming and even more of a handful than his sister.

But for some reason he did not stir her senses the way his older brother did. His amusement, though, at Ana's machinations was helping to calm the explosion of nerves when he had appeared in the doorway to Cerys's sitting room instead of Ana, and announced he had been blackmailed into escorting her to the Fiesta.

She had already felt way too exposed in the dress which Ana had insisted she wear. A stunning sky-blue chiffon creation which flattered her figure—but was too tight in the bust—and silver heels which clicked on the stone steps as Alejandro led her down into the courtyard.

'By the way, just to be clear, this is totally not a date,' Cerys said, scanning the crowd to find Ana—who had probably gone into hiding after her latest stunt. 'I don't expect you to stay by my side tonight. I really don't want to cramp your style.' Although, from the industrial strength flirtatiousness she had already witnessed, she suspected not even a new ice age would be able to do that. 'I'm not even supposed to be here.'

'And miss the chance to annoy my brother? No chance,' her non-date replied, his gaze fixed on something across the courtyard.

Her stomach started doing the rumba again when Alejandro escorted her into the courtyard and the other guests began to notice their arrival. While the women and even some of the men only had eyes for Alejandro, she felt hideously exposed—and out of place.

'I just hope he doesn't spot me gatecrashing his party,' she said, crossing her fingers behind her back.

'Too late,' Alejandro murmured. 'It seems Ana was right about Santiago wanting you all to himself. Either that or he has just swallowed a bee,' he said, then wrapped his arm around Cerys's hips to draw her to his side. 'Let's make this convincing,' he whispered, nuzzling her ear.

She shuddered when he kissed her neck, so shocked by the unexpected contact, and the sudden shift from amused to seductive, she couldn't process what was happening before the crowd parted and Santiago appeared from nowhere.

'I thought we agreed, Andro,' the Duke announced, his voice tight with anger. 'The staff are off-limits.'

Her boss looked magnificent, because of course he did, in a tailored designer suit. Clean-shaven and with his hair trimmed, his patrician appearance—that air of dominance and demand—was even more controlled than usual, but for the stark expression and the muscle twitching in his jaw. Disturbing arousal rushed over Cerys's skin as his scalding gaze raked over her, but then his statement registered. The brick in her abdomen plummeted towards her toes as she became painfully aware of the guests nearby—who belonged at his fiesta, unlike her—watching and listening and whispering behind their hands.

The nerves in her stomach tangled into a tight knot and the last of her confidence dropped off a cliff. She was staff, he'd just made that abundantly clear. She should never have agreed to come.

Alejandro raised his hands, palms up, in a defensive gesture, but the mocking tone was anything but when he replied. 'Don't be such a bore, *hermano*.' He chuckled, but his laugh had a brittle edge. 'Cerys isn't staff tonight, she's with me.'

'I should leave,' she whispered, wishing the flagstones could open up and swallow her whole, but no one seemed to hear her, even though Santiago's furious gaze remained locked on her face.

'What's the problem, Santiago?' Alejandro piped up, the charming smile becoming caustic. 'Couldn't get your own date, so now you want mine?'

The shocked gasps from the crowd echoed round the event, feral and excited, while mobile phones appeared from nowhere to document the scene unfolding.

Cerys stepped away from Alejandro's side, still far too aware of Santiago's fierce gaze riveted to her face. He didn't even seem to be listening to his brother. Because all his attention—all his fury—was focused on her.

Why was he looking at her as if she were the only person here? It was unnerving, and disturbing... And weirdly exhilarating, but not in a good way.

'I'm sorry,' she murmured. But as she turned to flee, Santiago stepped forward and grasped her elbow.

'We must talk, in private,' he said, his low voice edged with demand.

'It's okay, I'll leave. I know I wasn't invited.' She tried to tug her elbow loose, scared of what he wanted to say. Was he going to fire her? In front of all these people? 'Please accept my apology,' she added, desperate to repair the damage. 'This was a massive mistake.'

'It's too late for that,' he said. But as his grip tightened and he began to steer her away from their audience, Alejandro's voice sliced through the whispers of the crowd.

'Hey, who said you could steal my date?' he asked, but he sounded more amused than affronted.

Santiago glanced at his brother, his gaze flat and remote and so chilling Cerys shivered.

'Find some other unfortunate woman to warm your bed for tonight,' he said, the tone so scathing that Cerys felt brutally ashamed. Whatever was between the De Montoya brothers, she had made it worse by coming here tonight.

The crowd gasped. But instead of being offended, Santiago's brother only laughed at the insult, a cynical smile on his lips. 'Unfortunate? I don't think so.' He shrugged but then sent Cerys a cavalier salute. 'Sorry, Cerys, you're on your own, but good luck with my boring brother,' he said, then strolled off into the crowd as if he didn't have a care in the world.

Even so, Cerys knew she owed him an apology too. Why had she chosen to make a spectacle of them both? But before she could say anything, she was being marched across the courtyard, Santiago's hand still firm on her arm.

Instead of returning to the *castillo* though, he headed past the kitchen staff, busy plating up more canapés, and towards the orchard on the far side of the dancefloor. Cerys's stomach sank like a stone. She had intended to keep a low profile, and arriving on Alejandro's arm had been an idiotic decision, but never in a million years had she anticipated the *Duque*'s response to seeing her at the event being this negative.

She spotted Ana, standing by the band, her face a picture of remorse. Cerys shook her head, blinking back tears. She didn't want her friend to feel bad. Ana was young and foolish but her heart was in the right place—even if she had totally underestimated her brother's reaction to her latest stunt.

They continued past the dancefloor and into the orchard which surrounded the *castillo*. Was he going to march her right off the property and kick her onto the street in her borrowed ball gown?

Could this actually get any worse?

But as she stumbled and he tugged her back to her feet without breaking stride while they headed through the lemon trees, the prickle of temper pierced through the fog of mortification and panic.

What had she done that was so terrible? Why did he think it was okay to treat anyone with this level of contempt? He'd not only insulted his brother, he'd also insulted her, and for what?

Okay, so she was being paid by him... And she had been forced to throw herself on his mercy in the past month, because she had nowhere else to go. But did she really deserve to be hauled out of his party like a piece of trash? In front of all these people? To be made to feel she was so far beneath him, she didn't even deserve to be seen in public?

'You need to let me go. Whatever I've done, I apologise,' she said tightly, finally gaining some backbone. 'But FYI, you're totally overreacting.'

He grunted but remained silent, his grip tightening on her arm. To her surprise, a house appeared through the orchard on the edge of the vineyards, nestled among a grove of trees.

A house she had never even realised was here.

Covered in wisteria, it looked old but also well kept.

The stone veranda which surrounded the structure was sturdy and strong. The lights on the porch illuminated a selection of luxury outdoor furniture—a couch and armchairs—making it clear the house was in regular use.

As Santiago hauled her up the steps to the porch, she found the strength to yank her elbow from his grasp.

'Stop dragging me about. I don't care if you're my boss.'

If she was going to lose her job because of his temper tantrum, so be it. She couldn't spend the rest of the summer scared of his reaction. Scared to put a foot wrong. Nor could she be invisible. If he despised her this much, she would have to leave. And while it terrified her to think of where she would go, she had to hope she would be okay. Her Spanish was much better now, her memory would return once she got up the guts to confront those scary shadows in her head, and she was healthy. She could work, in the fields if she had to. It wouldn't be easy without ID, but if she contacted the British consulate and informed them of her situation, surely they could help her…

'I know you didn't invite me to the party,' she tried to explain while he loomed over her, saying nothing. 'But Ana wanted me there. And even though I work for you, I'd like to know what you think gives you the right to treat me like a disobedient child. To humiliate me like that in front of everyone. And throw insults at your brother.'

She congratulated herself on getting the words out past the massive lump of panic and confusion in her throat. But as soon as she'd got them out, she had to fold her arms around her stomach to stop herself from shaking.

He stood there, staring down at her, silent and forbidding, his expression fraught with… What exactly *was* that expression? Because she had no idea what he was even thinking at this point. He didn't look angry any more, he looked wild.

'Just tell me one thing,' he said through gritted teeth, the muscle in his jaw clenched tight. 'Have you slept with my brother?'

'I... *Wh-what?*' The girl's eyebrows shot so far up her forehead Santiago was surprised they didn't launch off her face. 'Are you nuts? I met your brother for the first time ten minutes ago,' she said, clearly so shocked by his accusation the denial came out on a barely audible hiss.

The grinding fury which had been driving him ever since he had spotted Alejandro pawing Cerys five minutes ago finally downgraded enough to allow him to breathe. He loosened his tie, ripped open the top buttons of his shirt, the formal wear strangling him. Not unlike the vicious spurt of raw, feral emotion which had blindsided him when he had seen them together. An emotion he had never encountered before.

Jealousy.

As he took several careful breaths, he was finally able to identify the reaction which had swept through him like wildfire as soon as he had caught sight of Cerys across the courtyard on Alejandro's arm.

Jealousy... And vicious, uncontrolled desire.

The dress was one he vaguely recognised. Was it one of Ana's? But on Cerys it looked different—seductive, erotic. The floating layers flowed over her curves, cupping her spectacular breasts, while the glittery heels made her legs look about a mile long. The lights on the villa porch, which he left burning always to dispel the ghosts when he came here to escape the *castillo*, illuminated the sprinkle of freckles across her nose, not quite hidden by the dusting of powder. Her short cap of chestnut curls caressed her neck as her ragged breathing seemed to cut through the noise—of his throbbing pulse, and the distant snap of castanets from the flamenco performance which had just started. The smudge of make-up on her lids sparkled in the twilight and deepened the unique colour of her irises to a translucent mix of mermaid green and sky blue.

'*Bueno.*' He ground the word out, his insides in an uproar of need. His hunger for her was so intense he felt unhinged, untethered from his own sense of self.

He skimmed a finger down her cheek, her vicious shiver of response vibrating in his groin.

'Because you already belong to me,' he managed, around the thick ball of desperation in his throat.

He grasped her wrist and tugged her towards him, aware of her eyes widening with shock—but also flooding with awareness.

She must feel it too, this physical force which linked them, and had tormented him for weeks. This erotic compulsion which had become a living, breathing monster in the past few days—with her in his home, but always out of reach.

She shuddered. 'I... I do?' she said on a whisper of breath as she searched his face, the rise and fall of her breathing making her breasts press seductively against the too-tight bodice, threatening to spill out—and snap the last thin thread on his control.

How had he been reduced to this? Every time he spied her from his study, running across the courtyard each morning to rendezvous with his sister, every time he had found himself walking through the forest on the opposite bank of the river where Ana had told him they swam regularly, the clamouring need had increased...

Until a week ago, when he had finally earned the reward he had never acknowledged he had been seeking... Spotting her through the trees, her high full breasts displayed to perfection in a bikini she must have borrowed from Ana too, because it had barely contained the luscious flesh. And the need had exploded through his veins like wildfire.

He had vowed that night while he stroked his turgid flesh and imagined those full breasts swaying into his palms, that he would not ask Ana about her again, would remain locked in his study working for the siesta hours to avoid another glimpse of her wearing only a few scraps of spandex, her luminous skin glistening with moisture.

But his latest vow had been shot to hell three days ago. He had been crossing the courtyard after a difficult four hours in the fields, checking the yield, organising the schedule for harvesting with the winery manager, when she had run around a corner and straight into him. Suddenly his arms had been full of her fragrant flesh, his lungs filling with her scent—summer flowers and female musk. And those eyes—so bold, so inviting, so conflicted—had stared at him out of the heart-shaped face he had become obsessed with.

It had taken all his control to release her.

But tonight...*tonight* was too much. He couldn't let her go again.

His hands moved up her arms, edged her forward until he could lower his mouth to hers, the desperation to taste her intoxicating, tormenting.

'I want to kiss you, Cerys,' he whispered across her

lips. 'I have wanted to for weeks,' he finally admitted to himself as much as her.

Why had he tried to deny this hunger for so long? When his attempts to control his reaction had only made the need more acute? What, exactly, was he trying to prove?

She let out a sob, arousal darkening her eyes to black. 'Okay...'

Her husky agreement was like a gunshot, threatening to destroy what was left of his control. As the fault lines snaked out, his hands trembled, but he forced himself not to shatter. Not to take what he craved so desperately. Not. *Yet*.

He desired much more than a taste of her, but the sheen of innocence still clung to her—despite the crushing jealousy which had consumed him when he had seen his brother touch her.

He must tread carefully.

He had never taken a mistress, had prided himself on always being able to control his libido, unlike his father. But it was clear he had been kidding himself all along. Because all it had taken was the right woman to unleash that feral, elemental part of himself, to awaken those same needs and desires which had torn apart his family—and destroyed his childhood.

He should be ashamed, disgusted, but somehow all he could feel was the searing desire to claim her as his. But before he gave in to the hunger, he must ensure he did not exploit her, the way his father had exploited so many women.

'Do you desire me, too?' he asked.

It was a crude request, one that was beneath a man like him—he was usually so sophisticated with women, his sexual needs easy to contain and compartmentalise. But not with her... *Never* with her.

She blinked, but then she bit into her lip, tugging the pouting flesh with her teeth, and his hunger surged.

'Yes,' she whispered. 'I think so.'

Think?

He pressed his forehead to hers, tried to calm his ragged breathing and get a grip on the vicious need, his hands shaking as he caressed her hips through the thin material of the dress.

He had to make her understand what this would mean, so she could make a clear choice.

'I do not sleep with my employees, Cerys.' The words were torturous to say, because they had the potential to deny him—deny them both—what they so desperately needed. But he couldn't respect himself if he allowed the animal desires his father had given free rein destroy what was left of his own ethics.

'If we do this, I can no longer pay you to watch over Ana. Do you understand?'

She stared, the confused expression like a bullet to his heart. The heart he had believed could never be harmed, never be touched by any woman.

'Are you saying I'd have to leave?' she asked. 'If we kissed.'

'No... *Dios*, no,' he said. He clasped her bottom, no longer able to keep his hands from caressing the firm flesh he had yearned to touch again, day and night, for weeks. He cradled the thickening erection against the shimmering blue fabric which he was already desperate to rip from her body, so he could see all of her at last.

Calm down, Santiago. Do not scare her. Do not make her run.

'I would wish very much for you to stay here, for the rest of the summer... Or until you want to go.' He knew from his conversations with Ana that her memory was returning, although she did not know enough yet to find her way home.

Maybe this also explained the increased urgency which had consumed him over the past week. If he did not take her now, she might be gone. And he would never know what it was to feast on her. And unleash this part of himself, at least once.

This yearning would surely burn itself out, as all passions did eventually. She was not of his class, was not even Spanish, did not even know her own name, and was far too young for him, not just in years but, he suspected, also in experience. However many boyfriends she had in her past, she could never be as jaded as he was—a man who had lost his innocence long before he had lost his virginity.

But he wanted her too much now to concern himself with the future. With what would happen when he returned to Madrid. Or her memory finally unlocked all its secrets. Even his hunt for a suitable wife had been sidelined as his obsession with her grew. He hadn't even considered inviting a date to the Fiesta, because he had no desire to touch another woman but her.

'I want you to stay for the summer.' *In my bed*, he almost added, but stopped himself. Because it would be crass, and surely she must know what he was offering— a summer by his side, until this incessant hunger ceased. 'Ana likes you—enough to do as she is told for once. But if we do this, I cannot have you on my staff. You would have to stay as her friend, her companion. As my guest.' *And my lover.*

Her face brightened, the confusion clearing as the arousal flared. The need in his pants throbbed.

'That would be amazing. I love Ana, we've become friends. I always felt a bit weird taking your money when we have such fun together. And I love being here—it feels like home, the first real home I've ever had. I don't know how I know that, but I do,' she said, with an openness that disturbed him on some level.

The *castillo* had not felt like home to him, not for a very long time, but something about her enthusiasm for the place reminded him of the boy he'd once been, before he had witnessed the ugly reality behind the elegance and charm of his family's life.

He swallowed, pushing the unhappy memories down. This relationship was about physical desire, nothing more... Or less. It had not one thing to do with that naïve child, who had once believed in something that had never been real. That boy was long gone. And good riddance. He never wished to be that trusting, that naïve, ever again.

'If you're really sure it's okay for me to stay here as a guest?' Her eyes searched his face, her hand touching his cheek. Her palm felt cool against his skin, and so soft. 'I'd be happy to accept. Thank you.'

He nodded, no longer able to find words, spellbound by the enthusiasm in her face. How could she be so trusting, and yet also so vulnerable?

'And if you really *want* me,' she said, still sounding a little astonished, 'I really want you, too.'

'*Bueno!*' he rasped, his control snapping. Grasping her in greedy handfuls, he boosted her into his arms, knowing he had to get her inside the house before he took her mouth, because he did not believe for a second they would stop there. And while the villa was secluded and away from the *castillo*, he did not want to risk being interrupted.

She let out a startled gasp but wrapped her legs around his waist and clasped his head between her hands. He marched into the villa, slamming the door shut behind him—the giddy excitement he sensed in her reaction a powerful aphrodisiac to his already rampant desires... He framed her face in his hands, captured her mouth and thrust his tongue deep to taste her at last.

He devoured her heady sobs, the sweet shallow darts of her tongue, and let the control he had clung to for weeks burn away in a firestorm of need...

CHAPTER SIX

CERYS GRASPED HANDFULS of Santiago's hair and kissed him for all she was worth. Giddy shock turned to desperate pleasure as he explored her mouth—conquering her with a purpose which made her yearn.

She wasn't sure how everything had changed on a single heartbeat, from panic and temper to vicious need and validation. But it felt so life-affirming, she was not going to question it.

He wanted her to stay at the *castillo* as a guest, to be Ana's friend rather than her paid companion. But so much more than that, Santiago wanted *her*—the way she now understood she had always wanted him.

She feasted on his lips as his arms wrapped around her. The ridge of his erection pressed against her. She squirmed, wanting, needing more—although she wasn't entirely sure what.

He jerked his head away suddenly. His dark gaze scoured her face before he deposited her on the kitchen table.

Her breathing was so rapid her head was spinning. Was he done? Was that it?

She was ready to beg when he rasped, 'I want to see all of you.'

She bounced her head in a rapid nod.

He clasped her neck, his thumb stroking the pulse hammering against her collarbone.

'Say the words,' he demanded. His callused palm rode up her thigh, under the chiffon, to drag her to the edge of the table.

'Yes, yes,' she gasped.

His lips found the pulse under her ear as he wrenched down the gown's thin strap. The sound of rending fabric filled the room.

'Wait, Ana's dress...' she managed, her head angling instinctively to give his mouth more access.

'I will buy her another,' he murmured, his voice hoarse, as he tore the bodice to free her breasts from the inbuilt bra.

He swore in Spanish, his eyes becoming glassy as his gaze raked over her swollen flesh. He cupped her heavy breasts, then bent to suck one hardening nipple into his mouth. She sobbed, the sharp drawing sensation so exquisite she could feel it deep in her abdomen as he tormented one breast, then the other.

She thrust her fingers into his dark silky hair, to hold him to her, to demand more. Her breathing became laboured, the need more so as arrows of sensation shot from her breasts to her core. He hooked her legs over his hips to rub the ridge in his pants at the melting, aching place between her thighs.

Her breath heaved as she clung onto his shoulders, the sensations too much and yet not enough. She felt trapped, devoured, tormented, the pleasure persuasive, provocative, painful, the aching empty space at her core hungry to be filled.

As if he had read her mind, he lifted her into his arms

to carry her to the open staircase, murmuring something in a language she didn't understand.

'I don't... I don't speak Catalan,' she whispered, kissing his cheek, his jaw.

'*Vamos arriba...*' he murmured, caressing her bottom, the erection still pressed intimately against the place now yearning for relief. 'Upstairs,' he repeated in English. 'We must find a bed.'

He took the stairs two at a time to reach a mezzanine level. A huge bed took up most of the sparsely furnished space. A large open window looked out across the orchard, the lights from the *castillo* and the party they had left what felt like a lifetime ago sparkled through the trees. The scent of a citronella candle burning on the window ledge provided the only light in the shadowy room.

He dropped her on the bed to kick off his shoes, drag off his jacket. He ripped off his shirt and tie, then went to work on his trousers.

She propped herself on her elbows to watch, her breath catching.

Her excitement surged. She'd thought he looked good in clothes, but without them... *Oh, wow!*

She devoured the sight of taut roped muscles, defined pecs, the ridged abs divided by a happy trail of dark hair. His sleek tanned skin gleamed in the candlelight. The vicious hunger flared, along with the ripple of trepidation, when he fished a foil packet out of his pocket, then shoved off his trousers.

The erection, so long and thick, thrust towards his belly button from the nest of dark hair at his groin while he rolled on the condom.

Had she ever seen anything so magnificent...? Or so

intimidating? She swallowed, her throat thickening with anticipation, and panic. She didn't think so.

He climbed on the bed, caging her in, pressing her back. His lips nuzzled her neck as he dragged off the torn dress and her panties.

She clasped her arm over her breasts, suddenly shy, instinctively aware no man had ever seen her *this* naked before.

'No, Cerys, do not cover yourself,' he murmured.

She shivered as he lifted her arm free, her breasts heavy under that scalding gaze. He skimmed his thumb under a thrusting nipple, still wet from his mouth.

'I must kiss you,' he said.

She nodded, expecting him to kiss her mouth again, but instead he trailed his lips along her collarbone, then licked and sucked his way down her body—worshipping each yearning spot, each throbbing pulse point—until the ragged moans were queuing up in her throat.

After feasting on her tender nipples, he drew lower to skim kisses over her ribs and circle her belly button before sinking between her thighs. Grasping her buttocks, he lifted her to his mouth.

She sobbed, struggling to catch her breath, to control her fraying emotions, and the shocking pleasure as the explosion of heat and endorphins consumed her.

Fireworks in my belly...

The thought whispered across her consciousness as his tongue swept over the very heart of her, the rasping lick making her hips buck. A groan broke free.

'Shh...' he murmured.

But then he captured the tight bundle of nerves—already so needy, already so swollen—and sucked hard.

She cried out, soaring up, the fireworks exploding from her core to cascade through her entire body.

He held her hips, worked her with his lips, demanding more. The waves of pleasure built again, too fast. Another brutal climax crashed over her, layering on top of the last, intensifying the explosion, forcing her to ride the inferno.

At last, he allowed her to collapse onto the bed, exhausted, spent.

He rose above her, his gaze fierce. Bracketing her hips, he angled her pelvis and pressed the huge erection against her core, before thrusting hard and deep to claim her completely.

The brutally stretched feeling overwhelmed her, before the sharp pinch of pain made her flinch. And gasp.

He stopped, lodged so deep inside her she couldn't tell where she ended and he began.

He buried his face in her hair, swore in Catalan, then lifted his head to bracket her face with unsteady hands.

'Am I your first lover, Cerys?' he said, his voice husky with shock.

'I... Yes,' she whispered, positive she had never felt so exposed, so vulnerable, so taken before.

He swore again.

'I'm sorry,' she said, sure she had done something wrong. Why else would he look so horrified? 'I should have said something...' Although of course, until this moment, she hadn't been sure...

'Do not apologise,' he whispered, his thumb stroking her lips, his expression devastated. 'Does it hurt?'

'No, not at all,' she lied. Whatever she'd done, she didn't want to make this even worse.

He shifted slightly and she winced before she could stop herself.

A wary smile curved his lips, the devastation gone from his eyes, to be replaced by something strained, and guarded, and a lot less revealing.

'Did you lie to me, Cerys?' he asked.

She tried to smile back, but emotion tightened her throat—because the moment of connection felt lost. For a second, he had looked at her as if she mattered to him, and it had felt so good to really matter to someone.

'No... I... It's just not super comfortable,' she managed.

'Then I must be gentler,' he said, the strain in his face making her heart thump her ribs.

Stroking her hips, he drew his hand down until his thumb delved to locate the place where their bodies joined.

She moaned as he circled and caressed the tender bud, making her buck against his touch.

'Does this help?' he asked.

She nodded. 'Yes... Please, do it again.'

He let out a strained chuckle. But then he caressed the perfect spot until she was panting, moving against him, forced to impale herself more on the rigid erection to find relief.

He groaned and stopped stroking her, to hold her hips. 'I must move, Cerys, but you must tell me if I hurt you.'

'Okay.' She sighed, so close to the edge now, she didn't care what he did, as long as he did *something*.

He drew out. So slowly, so carefully. Then sank back, to fill her impossibly again. She moaned, the pleasure immense, the discomfort fading, to be replaced by a delicious coil of tension deep in her sex.

'Is it okay?' he asked.

'Yes, please, but move faster... I need more.'

'Yes, Cerys.' His low chuckle at her demands made her smile, even as he began to move faster, thrust harder.

Her sobs joined his grunts as he rolled his hips to drive deeper. Until she was clinging to his shoulders, meeting those steady, punishing thrusts to take even more.

She groaned, yearning for more, even though it felt impossible to take more. The pressure on her chest became almost as immense as the pressure between her thighs.

He clasped her buttocks to thrust into her to the hilt, to brand her as his completely. Her body gathered, tightened—reaching, rising—and soared again.

The raw pleasure—which had felt so far out of reach only minutes before—crashed over her as he shouted out his own release, and they flew over together at last.

Cerys lay in the shadowy room, floating in a cloud of bliss, only vaguely aware of the shocking emotions stirring inside her. Scary, *enormous* emotions. Until Santiago shifted. He was still *there*, still so large and firm inside her, the weight of his muscular body pressing her into the mattress, making her aware of every part of her which felt tender, sore—and utterly, totally alive for the first time in her life.

He eased out of her so carefully the ragged emotions consumed her. She blinked rapidly to control the tears which threatened.

How could what they had done feel so epic? When their chemistry had always been there, ever since that first morning, when he had marched into her room at the *castillo* and demanded to know if she remembered him.

She frowned. How could she still not remember their first meeting, in Barcelona? When so much about him had always felt familiar. Almost as if she'd known him in another life... She strained to illuminate the hazy memories which had scared her so much yesterday, but the information remained rooted in the shadows.

Santiago rolled onto his back beside her. The deep rasps of his breathing were barely audible above the thunder of her own heartbeat.

But then the music from the *castillo* drifted in on the night air, through the open window.

The Fiesta!

Panic rose like a wave at the thought of Ana, of Alejandro, of all the staff and guests who had seen them leave. *Together.*

What would everyone think, if they figured out what had happened?

Their lovemaking, which had been so wonderful and life-affirming and exciting in the moment, suddenly seemed shocking. She'd just had epic sex with the boss!

She shot upright, tugging the sheet with her to cover her nakedness, then spotted the torn remnants of Ana's designer gown lying in a heap by the bed.

Shame engulfed her.

She went to scramble off the bed when a hand reached out and grasped her wrist, preventing her escape.

'Cerys, what is wrong?'

She glanced over her shoulder. Santiago lay on his back, still gloriously naked and unashamed—and the renewed pulse of arousal blindsided her all over again.

He lifted up on an elbow, his grip remaining firm on her wrist while he searched her features with that all-consuming intensity which gave none of his feelings away, but made her sure he could see right into her soul.

Why did that feel far too revealing now?

Maybe because she didn't really know or understand

this commanding and enigmatic man at all. Any more than she understood her livewire reaction to him.

'I've torn Ana's dress,' she blurted out, grasping for something coherent to say.

He stared at her for the longest time, then said simply, '*I* tore Ana's dress. And I will buy her a new one.'

'But you can't, or she'll know what we've just done...' Cerys replied, certain that would be bad. Perhaps, if they could just pretend this hadn't happened, everything would be okay. She wasn't sure how she was going to control the vicious hunger still buzzing over her skin, even now, after he'd given her not one but several spectacular orgasms, but she'd have to figure it out. *Later.* She pulled her wrist free. And shunted to the edge of the bed to scoop up the remnants of the dress, the torn chiffon like a symbol of her fraying emotions.

'I should get back to the *castillo* before anyone notices how long we've been gone,' she began to babble. 'If I go in through the kitchens and then just head to my room, no one will see me.' She sat back on the bed. Where were her panties? Her shoes? 'I can ask María in the morning for the name of a good seamstress. I'll say I tore the dress by accident and that...'

'Stop, Cerys.'

Arms, roped with muscle, banded around her waist. Suddenly she was surrounded by him, cocooned with her back against his chest, his thighs bracketing her hips, his feet on the floor on either side of hers, his cheek resting on her hair. She could feel his breathing, harsh and heavy, on her neck.

The shattering emotions rose up to consume her, restricting her breathing as tears scalded her eyes.

'*Breathe*, Cerys,' he demanded in that cool, controlled voice.

She dragged in an unsteady breath, releasing it slowly as he held her.

'I'm sorry. I don't know what to do. This just feels so wrong...' How could she have given in to this hunger, this need, without a thought to the consequences, or her circumstances?

'Do not apologise,' he said as he captured her chin and turned her head so he could peer into her eyes.

'I will purchase a new dress for my sister. Not you.' His gaze raked over her, assessing, searching. But the detachment, the control she had always sensed before, was gone. He seemed different somehow—less rigid, almost tender, despite the guarded look in those dark eyes.

She let out a shattered breath and swallowed down the new surge of panic. And need.

He brushed his thumb across her cheek, to hook her hair behind her ear. The gentle touch, and the concern in his eyes, had the emotions welling all over again.

The yearning to belong to him, to belong here though, was the scariest thing of all...

'And I will buy you a new wardrobe, so you have no need to borrow Ana's clothing again,' he added, the certainty in his voice almost as disturbing as the strange sense of connection, of intimacy, which felt too needy...

She shook her head. 'You can't do that, Santiago. I can't accept it. How on earth would I explain your generosity to Ana? She already thinks we're...'

'Forget about Ana. This is not about my sister. This is about us.'

Us.

The word struck at the heart of all her insecurities. All

the things she worried about late at night. The crushing loneliness—the intermittent surges of anxiety—which she had no trouble dismissing during the day, when she made herself concentrate on living in the moment and tried not to panic about her lost past. But they tormented her before she fell asleep, or in dreams, when the images which had disturbed her yesterday sneaked into her head without warning.

'But...there is no us,' she said.

She couldn't let his approval or his generosity—or the hot look in his eyes, which he was making no attempt to hide—mean too much. She was lonely, yes, and anxious too now, about why her memory hadn't fully restored itself yet. What if she was the one holding it back, subconsciously? Because she wanted to stay here, always...

'Cerys, we have become lovers.' His unruly thumb skimmed down, to press against the skittering pulse in her collarbone. His gaze darkened, making her heart lurch in her chest. 'Of course there is an us.'

Lovers.

Her pulse skipped and bobbled, her breathing accelerating again.

Was he saying what she thought he was saying? That he wanted to make love to her *again*? That this wasn't a mistake? A disaster? One night of madness they both needed to forget.

How would that even work, when he was a duke—and she was, quite literally, a nobody?

'I am your first lover.' The possessiveness in his voice was reflected in his fierce expression. 'Your *only* lover. If wrong has been done, it is by me, not you, Cerys.'

'No, Santiago, don't say that...' She leapt off the bed and out of his arms, dragging the torn dress up to cover her nakedness from that searing gaze that still made her feel so needy. 'I wanted you to make love to me, very much...' She swallowed. 'And I enjoyed it, a lot.'

He draped the sheet across his lap with a relaxed grace which suggested he was covering himself to protect her modesty rather than his own. Then his lips curved in a sensual smile.

'I am glad,' he murmured.

Her whole body flushed with heat and embarrassment when he let out a low chuckle, so husky it scraped over her skin. And provoked a reaction in the parts of her he had already awakened so thoroughly.

'I'm going to shut up now. I keep making it worse,' she said, knowing she had never felt more gauche and out of her depth in her life. 'I just... I don't want you to feel bad about me being a virgin. Because you absolutely shouldn't. You didn't know. Because I didn't tell you... And I should have.'

'Except you didn't know either...' he murmured softly, still with that devastatingly sensual smile on his lips, although his expression looked serious rather than amused.

But as she struggled to figure out how to explain herself, so he would see that if anyone was at fault here it was her, he snagged her wrist and drew her towards him.

'I do not think what we did was wrong,' he said, the confidence in his voice belied by the intense expression. 'We have a rare and exceptional chemistry, Cerys. Something I have never felt before.' He took her hand, threaded his fingers through hers to tug her closer, until she was positioned between his thighs. Even though he had to look up, seated on the bed, he still seemed dominant somehow. His thumb stroked her wrist. Her heartbeat became even more erratic, the approval in his gaze overwhelming. 'I have never wanted a woman as I have wanted you. Ever since our first meeting.'

That would be the meeting she couldn't remember and so desperately wished she could.

'It is a hunger which has only become more desperate, more compelling every day since...'

'I... I know,' she managed even though her throat was so dry it felt as if each word was scratching her throat like sandpaper. She hadn't been able to read the signs before tonight, because she'd never experienced this desire before now, she couldn't have and still have been a virgin. But she understood it now—the dreams she'd had about him, the fear whenever Ana talked about their 'secret affair' because she wanted it to be true, when she knew she shouldn't... Her endless curiosity about him, which she had tried unsuccessfully to ignore.

He tilted his head to one side, the quizzical expression only making him more handsome. He was so much less rigid and forbidding, excitement rippled through her.

'So, you felt it too?' he asked, but it didn't sound like a question.

She cleared her throat, trying to clear the sandpaper. 'Yes, I did,' she said. 'Very much.'

It all made sense now, why she had been so fascinated with him. Why she had agreed to Ana's foolish scheme to come to the party, to wear the dress. It had always been for him... Because, in some secret corner of her heart, she had wanted him to see her as a woman instead of an employee, a nuisance, a burden, a responsibility he didn't want.

Did that also explain why she could still feel his touch too, on all the places on her body he had already pleasured, already possessed? Her breasts pressed against the sheer fabric she clung to, her nipples already rigid with need again. How was that even possible?

He gave her hand a gentle yank until she found herself perched on his knee, her bare bottom resting on one muscular thigh. The intimacy felt so powerful and compelling it hurt.

Slowly, gently, he lifted her arm until the torn dress fell into her lap, exposing her breasts. The dark possessive gleam in his eyes was as exciting as it was disturbing, especially when he circled the taut nipple with his thumb. She let out a soft sob, the ripple of reaction immense as the stiff peak swelled under his touch.

'Your body does not lie, Cerys.'

He leant down to press a kiss to the pouting tip but drew back when she shuddered.

'Can you feel how much I want you again?' he asked provocatively. The wicked seduction in his tone was playful, and impossibly beguiling from this serious, sober man.

Her heart hammered her ribs—the rare insight he was giving her into the man behind the mask of the *Duque* even more erotic than the insistent press of his erection against her thigh.

'I'm not sure I can do it again yet,' she said, unable to hide her regret. 'I'm still a bit sore.'

He chuckled, the sound husky and raw. Then pressed his forehead to hers. 'I love that you are so forthright, Cerys. And so honest.'

Love... The word rebounded in her heart—calling to something inside her which felt even more exposed than her bare breasts.

Had she ever felt like enough, ever been loved unconditionally? Was the yearning to be seen, to matter, another glimpse into her past? And how did Santiago know how to locate those forgotten needs so easily? How did he make her feel so cherished, so important, when they hardly knew each other?

But even as she asked the question, she tried to suppress the sudden yearning, the desperate longing to have him mean it. To have him want her to be his. *Always*.

He wasn't talking about love in the emotional sense. They'd had sex only once and, as they'd both discovered, it had been a first for her. So obviously she wasn't super experienced when it came to sexual intimacy. But in some ways, he was more of an enigma now than he had been before tonight. Was the feeling of validation just the afterglow talking? Perhaps it was also relief, that the disapproval she had sensed before had always been a result of the sexual sparks he had been trying to suppress… Because she was his employee.

'These are both very attractive traits,' he continued. 'Almost as attractive as your spectacular breasts,' he murmured, his eyes gleaming as he raised his eyebrows lasciviously.

She laughed, relaxing despite the ball of emotion jammed in her throat.

Who knew Santiago Álvaro Antonio De Montoya Lopez, the ninth Duke of Cantada, could be so charming? So relaxed? So seductive?

She recalled what Ana had told her the day before, about the scandal which had all but destroyed his family. Was that why Santiago had seemed so responsible and rigid? Because he'd had to be for so long? Seeing him like this, relaxed, playful, made her heart lift. He was probably like this with all the women he slept with, but still she was glad she could make him forget about his responsibilities—so many responsibilities—if only for one night, because he'd given her so much too.

'Do not fear, I will not ravish you again tonight.' He slung his arms around her waist, to draw her more securely into his lap. And to press his lips into her hair. 'But I do not intend to let you go either,' he added. The possessive tone was still there, but lighter and even more seductive now.

The easy hug—and the growing sense of intimacy—had her heartbeat going haywire. But she forced herself not to freak out again. Or let herself get too carried away.

This might be how all men behaved after sex. After all, if she had been blown away by those orgasms, why couldn't he be blown away too? Enough to say tender, affectionate things he didn't really mean. She just needed to make sure she didn't take it too much to heart. And let it all mean too much to her. He'd offered to let her stay at the *castillo* as a guest for the duration of the summer, and that would be more than wonderful enough.

'Are you already wet for me again…?' he murmured against her hair, his lips nuzzling the pulse point in her neck. The provocative question made the heat pulse and pound at her core.

'Hmm…' she moaned as he caressed her breast and toyed with the swollen peak. Sensation arrowed down, making the tender spot between her thighs clench and release.

'Would you like me to make you come again, Cerys?'

'Oh, yes, please,' she said, and he laughed. She squirmed in his lap, her brain too sluggish, too distracted, to process anything but the feel of his palm sliding over her belly. The calluses on his fingers made her shiver as he eased his hand under the chiffon bunched in her lap to locate the throbbing bundle of nerves between her legs aching for his touch.

He captured one thrusting nipple between his lips, sucking strongly, while his fingers explored the slick swollen folds.

She gasped, panted, moving her hips instinctively against his hand to encourage him to touch the place where she needed him the most.

He circled and caressed but couldn't quite find the perfect spot he had located so easily before. She gripped his wrist to direct him lower... A fraction of an inch was all she needed.

'No, Cerys,' he said, resisting her entreaties. 'First you must promise.'

'Promise what?' she said, frantic now.

'That you will share my bed until the hunger stops. And there will be no more talk of mistakes.'

Her needy flesh clamoured, yearned, the longing so intense she couldn't breathe, couldn't think.

'Say yes,' he demanded, his thumb so close to the aching, tender, desperate spot which would take her to heaven again. 'And I will give you the relief you seek.'

It seemed like such a small request, to make the yearning stop, so she could reach that sweet pinnacle. Again.

She nodded.

'Say yes,' he demanded. 'You must say the word.'

'*Sí*, yes, yes,' she choked out on a desperate sob, and he stroked across the very heart of her. *Finally*.

The pleasure exploded along her nerve endings, the glittering shards cascading through her body as he worked the desperate flesh. Ruthlessly, efficiently.

She was still quivering, still steeped in the heady rush of afterglow, as he scooped her up and placed her in the centre of the bed. He gathered her into his arms, the thick erection pressing against her bottom. She writhed against it, wanting him inside her again, needing that connection. But he shifted back.

'Be still, Cerys. I must give you time to heal before I take you again,' he murmured against her hair, his voice strained but his arms cradling her so securely.

Again?. Yes, I want you again. So much.

And not just because of the incessant need. But also because his patience, his thoughtfulness, had made her feel more cared for than she had for so long. Too long.

Had she ever felt as safe, as sheltered, as she did right now? Somehow, she didn't think so. A part of her knew she should be wary… That this desire to be wanted, to be needed, to be held, might be about much more than just sex—for her. But she didn't want to be cautious any more as the exhaustion swept over her and she snuggled into his arms and let herself drop into a sweet, secure oblivion.

CHAPTER SEVEN

CERYS AWOKE GRADUALLY to stare at dappled sunlight hitting the wall opposite in a room she didn't recognise.

Oh, no, not again. Where am I?

Before the panic—that she'd lost another chunk of her past—could set in though, the citrus scent of the lemon orchard and the musky scent of sex invaded her senses. And sharp, vivid memories from the previous evening overwhelmed her senses.

Alejandro's teasing smile, the sultry fragrance of bougainvillea and expensive perfume on the night air, Santiago's angry glare, the humiliating march through the orchard... And then.

She breathed through the adrenaline rush, powered by a string of evocative images, each one more erotic and exhilarating than the last...

She levered herself into a sitting position, aware of all the places where she was pleasantly achy. The bed was empty beside her, but the indent on the pillow confirmed the memories were real.

She and Santiago had slept together last night. They'd had passionate, exciting, intoxicating and scarily intense sex—and discovered he was her first lover.

And he hadn't regretted it. And neither had she. Even though they'd ripped Ana's dress in the process.

'I tore Ana's dress. And I will buy her a new one.'

She scrubbed her hands down her face, a silly grin forming.

Wow. Just wow.

And, best of all, the dreams hadn't come last night... The shadowy memories which had scared her before. Because he'd held her as she fell asleep. And promised to keep her.

Until the hunger stops...

She sighed and flopped back onto the bed, to stare at the ceiling and try to take stock of what it all meant—feeling overwhelmed, but also secretly thrilled.

Last night had been nothing short of incredible. For so many reasons.

The discovery that sex could be amazing if you were with someone who knew what they were doing—and Santiago *definitely* knew what he was doing—was just one of those reasons. He'd been so focused, his usual intensity and control all centred on her. And, as a result, her first time had been nothing short of mind-blowing.

Of course, she had to be careful not to make too much of what was basically a physical attraction. Fleeting and exciting but not necessarily unique. Or at least not for him. And just because it had been her first time, she needed to make sure she didn't fall into the trap of confusing sex with emotional intimacy. Because her life was already confusing enough.

She was glad he had insisted she no longer be paid to watch Ana, that he wanted her to remain at the *castillo* as the family's guest.

She frowned. Although how was that going to work? How would Ana react once she discovered she'd been correct about their attraction to one another? Maybe it didn't have to be too big a deal? Cerys could simply spend her days hanging out with Ana and her nights hanging out with Ana's brother...

All the tender achy places throbbed in enthusiastic agreement.

Yeah, maybe don't think about the nights or you'll be unable to focus on anything else, and Ana will notice and be impossible.

Easing off the bed, she spotted a pile of her clothes neatly folded on the chair opposite her—with a note attached that had her name scribbled across it. But there was no sign of Ana's torn dress or the heeled sandals she'd borrowed.

She dragged the sheet with her to shield her nakedness, feeling shy despite the fact the house was quiet and it had to be close to noon. Santiago was probably at work already—because he was *always* working, even on a Sunday.

She opened the note. Heat climbed up her chest as she spotted the scrawled S at the bottom. Then the hot blood exploded in her cheeks as she read the rest of it.

María has supplied the clothes and will arrange a replacement for Ana's dress. Enjoy your beauty sleep, but when you are ready come directly to my study. I have a proposition for you.
S

Embarrassment came first—because now María would know all about last night. It probably hadn't even occurred to Santiago how their affair was going to affect the *castillo*'s staff. She would have to tell Santiago she wanted to keep their arrangement on the down-low. She'd formed a strong bond with the staff and considered María a friend. She didn't want the housekeeper, or anyone else, to feel uncomfortable around her because she was basically sleeping with their boss.

But surely that wouldn't be a problem for him. She doubted Santiago wanted to make too big deal of this liaison either, given his aversion to gossip and his pathological need for privacy. So they were all good.

Warmth swelled though as she read the list of typically curt instructions—or rather orders—again. Santiago might be an exceptional lover, but he was also far too used to having his every command obeyed without question.

She'd found him so daunting before now, that aura of command more than a little intimidating. But she could still remember his charming smile, the playful note in his voice and the way he'd held her as she slept. She'd seen a completely different side of him last night—not so much commanding as protective, possessive even. It only made him more attractive. But now she had agreed to a wild summer fling with the guy—the logistics of which had to be the proposition he was talking about— she would have to set a few boundaries. Or she'd end up getting steamrollered by that iron will.

Boundary number one: impress upon Santiago she didn't take orders from him any more… Well, not outside of the bedroom anyway—where taking orders from him was super hot.

After reviving in the villa's surprisingly modern power shower and soaping her hair and body with toiletries that carried Santiago's woodsy scent, she tugged on the T-shirt and shorts combo María had chosen for her. Perhaps she and Santiago could confine their fling to this villa on the edge of the vines. They could make a secret pact to meet here at nightfall, after the *castillo* was asleep—because it was obvious he already used the place as some kind of getaway. It was so secluded and private it would be perfect. Sensation rippled over her skin at the thought of her midnight trysts with *el Duque*...

Something tugged at her memory... An odd feeling of *déjà vu*. Almost as if she'd done this before...

Her breath caught, the sharp twist in her abdomen reminding her of her raw reaction to Ana's story two days ago... But then her mind engaged, and the tension in her stomach eased.

She couldn't possibly have had an affair with anyone before now, not if she had been a virgin. Good to know being a total novice had some upsides.

She huffed out a strained laugh, recalling the hopelessly awkward conversation she'd had with Santiago the night before, when she'd made a complete twit of herself reassuring him about taking her virginity. Why had she assumed he even cared about that?

As she headed back through the orchard, she could hear the staff clearing up after the party.

A blush mottled her chest. Had anyone noticed they hadn't returned to the event?

She paused in the trees and watched the *castillo*'s maintenance guys—all of whom she knew by name—busy dismantling the dancefloor.

She decided midnight trysts were all well and good, but if she was going to spend the summer here, as Santiago's guest, she would need to establish a few ground rules—to preserve her pride, as well as not complicating her friendships with the staff. She was more than happy not to be paid a salary any more, especially as she and Santiago would be sleeping together, but she wanted to make herself useful, so she didn't feel like she was taking advantage of his generosity. And while he'd been very sweet to offer to buy her a whole new wardrobe, no way could she let him do that. He'd been paying her a very generous salary—while also providing room and board—so she already had some money saved.

She switched directions before the crew could spot her and headed towards the *castillo*'s kitchen entrance where María's office was situated. Even though Santiago had told her to come directly to the study, she wanted to thank the housekeeper for bringing the clothes—and track down Ana. Her friend was probably still fast asleep, but she needed to let her know she hadn't been kicked out after all, and apologise about the torn dress… Her blush intensified at the thought of how the heck she was going to explain *that* without getting the third degree on where she'd been all evening from Santiago's sister. Because Ana would definitely have noticed the two of them hadn't returned to the party.

She slipped through the back door. María stood in the doorway to the kitchens, busy directing a group of housemaids who were taking breakfast trays up to the party guests who had stayed the night.

Everyone stopped to stare at her. And the trickle of embarrassment became a flood.

Cerys cleared her throat.

Just play it cool, Cerys. They don't necessarily know about your midnight tryst with the boss.

'*Hola, cómo estás?*' she said, trying not to feel as if she had a huge red X sewn onto her T-shirt.

Talk about awkward.

She should probably be grateful Santiago had had the foresight to ask for some fresh clothes, because getting caught trying to sneak back into the *castillo* wearing the torn dress would have been a lot worse.

Instead of her usual smile, though, María hurried towards her wearing a concerned frown, while the maids, most of whom Cerys considered friends, all began to curtsy.

When María reached her, though, the friendly housekeeper curtseyed too.

And awkward became mortifying.

What the hell?

'María, stop,' she managed in Spanish, tugging on the housekeeper's elbow to lift her out of the curtsy. 'What's going on?'

The housekeeper straightened, but her eyes were still filled with a deference which made Cerys even more uncomfortable. Had Santiago said something to them? Surely this couldn't be a reaction to their disappearance from last night's fiesta.

María spoke to her in Spanish in hushed tones, something about *el Duque* waiting for her and how she had no need to enter the house through the kitchens any more.

Why not?

Before she could ask the question though, María was directing her past the genuflecting housemaids, who wouldn't meet her eye, and up the stairs to the *castillo*'s entrance hall.

She was still trying to figure out what was going on when María knocked firmly on Santiago's study door and ushered her inside, before disappearing again.

Cerys stood dumbly in the entrance to the elegantly furnished room. She'd never been invited to Santiago's office before, but it wasn't the ornate antique furniture—or the shelves filled with textbooks and legal tomes—or even the huge mullioned window which offered a spectacular view of the *castillo*'s vineyards that intimidated her the most. That would be the six other people—who were seated around the main desk—staring back at her, all dressed in business attire, especially when they all stood up abruptly.

Cerys's discomfort sky-rocketed, but it was nothing compared to the giddy rush when Santiago stood up from behind his desk and crossed the silk carpeting to greet her. Could he look any more dashing in the tailored pants and shirt, the sleeves rolled up to reveal the tanned forearms which had held her so securely last night?

'Cerys, you are awake, finally,' he announced in English, the slight reprimand in his tone more amused than censorious.

But the telltale blush still surged into her face when he tucked a knuckle under her chin and tilted her head up. His lips captured hers in a firm, demanding kiss, intensifying the adrenaline rush, and the weird feeling of unreality. She sucked in a shocked breath—because he was basically announcing their relationship to all these people.

Why would he do that? She tried to make sense of his behaviour, while also controlling the foolish feeling of validation.

He placed a proprietary hand on her hip to lean down and whisper confidentially in her ear, 'We will take that kiss to its logical conclusion later, but first we have something important to discuss.'

We do?

Hot arousal tangled with the confusion in her belly—which had kicked off ever since she'd walked into the kitchens and the staff had stared at her as if she had just flown in from Pluto. The people in the study—who were making her feel woefully underdressed—had the exact same look on their faces: part fascination, part awe.

Santiago ordered them all to be seated again. Taking her trembling fingers in a firm grip, he led her back across the office—introducing her to each person in turn. She instantly forgot most of the names, but did gather—from her not entirely fluent Spanish—they consisted of his legal team from Madrid, a private detective from Barcelona and representatives from both the British consulate and the Barcelona police. An elegant Spanish man, who had been introduced as the British ambassador's representative, jumped up to offer her his seat beside Santiago's desk, then bowed and retreated to stand at the back of the room.

'Santiago...' she whispered, trying not to feel intimidated as he let go of her hand to retake his seat beside her.

Why was everyone staring at her? And why had Santiago asked her to come to his study during what was some kind of business meeting, when she knew nothing whatsoever about any of his businesses?

'I... I really don't think I should be here,' she added when he simply sent her the charming smile she remembered from the previous evening. It had enchanted her then, and made her feel cherished and seen, so she clung to it now. Whatever was going on, he seemed pleased to see her—and he didn't seem to regret last night—which was good, right?

'I have a proposition for you, Cerys, which I believe will suit us both very well, but there is work to do first. We must discover your identity as a matter of urgency—which is why I have hired Señor Pérez, who has an exceptional reputation for investigating missing person cases,' he continued, indicating the detective, who was busy tapping out something on his phone. The older man looked up and sent her a friendly smile, which had her anxiety downgrading a notch. 'He will need to question you and take photos before he returns to Barcelona today to begin an in-depth investigation and track down your stolen ID documents.'

'That... That would be amazing,' she said, moved that he was so keen to help her. Recovering her memory was something she had struggled with, because she now suspected that, on a subconscious level, there were things in her past she didn't want to discover. But with his support, surely it would be easier to face those truths? And to rebuild her life once their fling was over. 'And so helpful... But...' She hesitated, forced to state the obvious. 'But I'm not sure how I'll pay for that.'

Would they have to rethink their arrangement? He'd been adamant last night she couldn't work here any more if they were sleeping together. But she would need a salary to cover the cost of Señor Pérez's services, because she doubted they would be cheap.

His brows rose, and then he chuckled. 'I will pay Señor Pérez, of course,' he said.

'But I can't let you do that, Santiago,' she said, her cheeks on fire again. 'It's really kind, but you're not responsible for...'

'Let me explain, Cerys,' he interrupted. Then he pressed his hand to her shoulder, the way he had done all those weeks ago. The gesture had the same effect now as it had then, the warm weight making her insides clench and her pulse thunder in her ears.

'I am not a kind man, Cerys. But I have always strived

to be an honourable one...' he added. 'Which is why it is very important to me that you do not feel exploited.'

Exploited? *What?* Her heart smacked against her chest wall.

She'd always known Santiago had a strong moral code, ever since he had come to her rescue in Barcelona—even if she still couldn't recall the details of that encounter. And now she knew why he felt that way. Because, from what Ana had told her, his father's dishonourable behaviour had done so much damage to his family and their reputation. But she didn't want him to feel he'd taken advantage of her last night. Because he hadn't.

This had to be to do with her virginity. She had convinced herself it hadn't bothered him after all, but now she recalled the stricken look on his face when he'd realised.

She was still trying to figure out a way to explain to him she had been more than willing, without embarrassing them both in front of their audience, when he continued.

'That said, I also have an ulterior motive because, without proper ID documents, it will not be possible for us to be legally wed...'

'For us to be...? *Wh-what?*' she croaked, her throat constricting with shock.

She leapt out of her chair, not caring about their audience any more, as her anxiety went from a confused ten to a nerve-jangling ninety in a single heartbeat.

'Wh-what did you just say?' she asked, her voice raw.

He let out a low chuckle, apparently completely unfazed by the fact she was freaking out. Turning to their audience, he asked that the two of them be given some time alone, adding that María had prepared lunch in the main dining *salón* next door for everyone.

The men and women all filed dutifully out of the room. But as soon as the door closed behind them, Cerys's stomach pitched and rolled over.

'Did... D-Did you just say *wed*?' she managed, sure now she must have been hallucinating.

He stepped towards her and grasped her hand. 'Cerys, breathe,' he said, the same way he had the night before.

She sucked in several precious lungfuls of air, trying to put a stranglehold on the panic. But it wasn't as easy this time, especially with those chocolate-brown eyes searching her face, the approval in his expression only freaking her out more.

It had meant so much to her. His tenderness, his care with her... But this couldn't actually be happening... Could it? Why would a man like Santiago want to marry her, and after only one night?

'I should thank you,' she began, her whole body racked by tremors she couldn't control. 'You were amazing last night. You made me feel so s-special. And I loved every minute of it, even the uncomfortable bits...' She started to babble. God, was she actually making any sense at this point? She dragged in a few more breaths, trying to calm her rampaging heart before it could burst right out of her chest. 'But you don't have to marry me. I don't expect it. You didn't exploit me. Not at all. I'm not vulnerable or anything.'

His brows drew together.

'Of course you are,' he said, but then he took her other wrist to draw her back into the circle of his arms. His forehead rested on hers and her breathing hitched, the painful yearning in her abdomen becoming unbearable.

She wanted his proposal to be real, but why? When it felt like too much, on so many levels.

'You have no memory of who you are,' he said gently. 'And yet I made love to you anyway. Can you not see this makes you very vulnerable?'

'But it doesn't...' She gulped in air, still struggling to breathe, the desire to belong to him so overwhelming it felt wrong too. Hadn't she always been independent? Why would she want this? Need this to be true? 'I don't want you to feel like you have to marry me—that's mad.'

'Shh, Cerys. I do not feel I *have* to marry you. I *wish* to marry you.'

She jerked in his arms, the words like a shot to the heart. But even as they spread through her body on a wave of desperate yearning, she scrambled back.

'You...you can't be serious.'

Surely this had to be about her virginity. But that would be *nuts*... They were living in the twenty-first century, not the nineteenth.

'I am very serious,' he said, his pragmatism finally starting to calm the tremors racking her body. 'I require a wife, Cerys. Someone who can manage my home, bring some much-needed stability to my family and, most of all, someone who can be a good role model for Ana...' An affectionate smile edged his lips. 'Handling Ana is not an easy task, and yet you have proved remarkably adept at it in the last three weeks.'

'Ana's my friend,' she said. 'It wasn't hard.'

'And if we marry, she will be your sister-in-law. And this will be your home. Are these not things you want?'

She blinked. A family, a sister, a home?

The longing reverberated in her chest because somehow, she knew these *were* things she had wanted, wished for, for a very long time. Maybe forever.

The wave of gratitude, that he would even offer her something so precious, overwhelmed her.

She swallowed heavily, trying to stop the wave from washing away what was left of her common sense. How could she accept him, when she suspected he was offering her everything she had ever wanted for all the wrong reasons?

'Yes…but… Why would you want *me*?'

'This is easy to explain, Cerys…' he murmured. 'Or better yet, let me show you…'

He pressed his hands to her cheeks. The rough calluses felt cool against her hot skin, but did nothing to chill the heat throbbing in her sex now, as well as her face. He was looking at her as if she mattered to him, the fierce approval in his gaze more potent than any aphrodisiac.

Lifting her chin, he pressed his lips to the pulse point in her neck. She shuddered, her response instant and forceful.

Her breathing accelerated and the heat swelled—her sex already softening, clenching, desperate to receive him again, when his lips found hers.

She was panting too heavily to find the words—or the will—to object when he unbuttoned the front of her shorts and slid his hand into her panties.

She sobbed as his thumb brushed the swollen nub. Already so needy.

'You respond to me with such passion, Cerys. I find it irresistible.'

The words floated through her, as forceful and demanding as his touch on her yearning flesh. But when he circled her clitoris again, bringing her so close to another shattering orgasm, shame washed over her.

She lurched back, yanking herself out of his arms. Her gaze took in the prominent ridge in his suit trousers. Then shot back to his face. He didn't look quite so pragmatic now, his expression fierce, the playfulness gone.

She fumbled, frantic to rebutton her shorts even as her clitoris still yearned for his expert touch. She'd almost gone completely to pieces again, the desire for him so intense it hurt...

She wanted the security he represented, the safety. Was impossibly moved he would offer her something so wonderful, something so huge. And she loved the thought of being a part of his family, of having a home. But she had an awful feeling she was already halfway in love with him. While he was talking about responsibilities, and practicalities, and chemistry.

The disparity was so stark—it scared her.

'It's... The sex, it's not enough. Not for a marriage,' she managed.

'Why not?' he replied, as if he really didn't get it.

'Because...' She cleared her throat, annoyed her voice had come out on a high-pitched squeak. 'We're not even in a relationship.'

He thrust his fingers through his hair, looking frustrated.

'I was your first lover, Cerys. You have spent nearly a month in my home. And you have no one. We spent the night together. I gave you your first orgasm. In fact, I gave you several. You are already wet for me again. And yet you think this is not a relationship.' He swore in Catalan.

'Okay, but...'

Bright flags of colour slashed across his features. And his eyes narrowed.

'But what? What is the problem, and I will fix it,' he said, as if her accepting his offer of marriage was a business deal he could negotiate.

It probably was to him… But how could it be to her, when he had already captivated her so completely?

'I just… I realise that you want to be married, for lots of practical reasons. But even so…it seems… I don't understand why you would choose me…' she tried again, feeling cornered now, and far too aware of the spurt of adrenaline, that foolish bubble of hope and exhilaration—that he would *want* to marry her—which left her feeling even more needy than the promise of another spectacular orgasm '…when we barely know each other…'

He stepped closer, close enough that she could see the shadow of beard growth already appearing on his jaw, and the flecks of gold in the rich chocolate of his irises. He cupped her cheek, making her shudder, and ran his thumb across her lips.

'I know you well enough.'

But you don't love me.

The pathetic thought echoed across her consciousness. But she stopped herself from voicing it—scared he would laugh at her, because she would sound so naïve and sentimental, compared with his pragmatism…

She dragged his hand away from her face, because she really couldn't think when he was touching her with that possessive gleam in his eye. She took a breath, trying to calm her confusing reaction, and got a lungful of the woody scent which clung to him. The rush of awareness became even more disconcerting. How had she become addicted to that scent in a single night?

'But I don't understand why you would want to marry *me*,' she managed, already hideously exposed.

'As I told you, I am in need of a bride. I have business interests which have been unfavourably impacted by…' He paused, frowned. Clearly, Santiago was not a man used to explaining himself. 'I have always believed in marriage,' he continued. 'It is a steadying influence for any family. And my family has needed stability for a long time.' It was a wholly unromantic statement, but also revealing.

A burst of sympathy made her ribs feel tight.

She already knew he had been responsible for his younger siblings for many years. And Ana had told her two days ago what a burden that had been for him—becoming the head of the household and a Duke when he was little more than a child himself. Was that why he was such a workaholic? So focused and intense and emotionally detached most of the time. Of course, it had to be.

But as much as she might sympathise with his desire to bring stability to his family, it didn't really answer her question. Surely, there had to be so many more suitable candidates than her to be his wife.

'But what if we never discover my identity?' she asked.

'This will not happen.' The deep grooves on his brow lifted. 'Señor Pérez is one of the best. But if it takes longer than expected, we will go through with the religious ceremony on the wedding date, and then arrange to legalise our union as soon as we have the necessary documentation.'

The wedding date?

'You've already chosen a *date*?' she asked, stunned all over again.

He nodded. 'Three weeks from now. I do not wish to

wait, Cerys. Once we are a couple before God, we can travel to Isla de la Luna, a resort I own in the Balearics, for a honeymoon. Our marriage will be excellent publicity for the launch. But quite apart from that, you fulfil all my requirements in a wife.' He touched her cheek again, apparently unable to keep his hands off her. 'And I wish for everyone to know that you are mine.'

'*What* requirements?' she asked, exasperated now as well as confused and so wary her stomach felt as if it had tied itself into a knot. But what scared her most was the balloon of hope parked under her breastbone, which was expanding no matter how hard she tried to suppress it. And was already big enough to have her questioning what exactly she was objecting to.

Santiago wanted to marry her. A man who fascinated and excited her beyond measure. Who had so many qualities she adored too. His determination to protect the innocent, his dedication to his family, to his duty, and his unbreakable code of honour, not to mention his insane work ethic. Above all, though, he had always made her feel safe, even when she'd thought he disliked her... And last night, he had made her feel cherished, feel important in a way she knew she never had.

If she married him, she could live at *Castillo de las Vides* for ever—a place she had come to adore. She would be Ana's sister for real. And while she knew she would want to work—because she had her pride—would it really be so terrible to have a home, to share in a heritage, a legacy? Something she knew she had always yearned for too.

'Cerys, I have wanted you since the moment I set eyes on you. There is something between us. Something that I cannot explain. A hunger which has turned me into a man ruled by his desires. A hunger which has only become more intense since last night. But I refuse to be a man like my father, who allowed his libido to consume and destroy everything he touched. I believed I was immune to such a weakness. But apparently, where you are concerned, I am not. I wish you to become my wife, so I do not risk destroying something I have sworn all my life to protect. As he did.'

His father?

She could hear the pain in his voice, and the anger. And see the conviction in his eyes. And for the first time since she had met him, she realised he had vulnerabilities too.

Suddenly she saw so clearly what she had not seen before.

Santiago was a passionate man who hid his passions behind a wall of duty and control. And somehow, without ever intending to, she had destroyed that control. And he was determined to get it back...

She pressed a hand to her chest, to control the spike in her heartrate.

Why was she so scared of saying yes? Who could say the marriage he wanted couldn't work for both of them?

Yes, it would be nuts on so many levels. But what if there *could* be a commitment? And how could she not believe in the intense physical connection he was talking about when she felt it too? What if their passion could lead to genuine intimacy, genuine affection—genuine caring and respect?

She suspected he would never be an easy man to live with, to love—but she couldn't imagine a greater gift than the opportunity to try and build something with a man like him.

There were so many things about him, so many elements to his character, she respected. And frankly, what did she really have to lose? What if she *never* discovered who she was? Who she had been? And why her brain had blocked out her past. What if, subconsciously, she didn't *want* to be that person any more? What better way to start a new life than to take this leap of faith he was offering and see where it took her? Where it took them both.

She understood, of course, he saw this marriage in practical terms—that it wasn't an emotional commitment for him. But who said she had to play by his rules?

Of course, marriage was still an extreme solution, but then she suspected that Santiago—for all his outward calm and control—was a man of extreme passions, if last night was anything to go by.

The balloon in her chest threatened to cut off her air supply.

'Okay,' she said.

His eyebrows rose and his face flushed. She had surprised him. No, she had astonished him. Why did that feel so exhilarating?

'You will agree to a marriage ceremony?' he asked. 'In three weeks' time?'

The whisper of uncertainty in the question felt strangely empowering. While Santiago's reasons for wanting this marriage were prosaic, her answer still mattered to him. It felt like a start... A start to something more. Maybe.

'Yes, but I have some conditions,' she said hastily.

It would be a mistake to let Santiago have everything his own way. He was a guy used to giving everyone orders and having them obeyed, so she had to make it clear from the start, if she was going to be his wife she wanted to be his equal.

That said, she'd never bargained with a duke before, and she suspected Santiago wasn't used to giving an inch when his brow lowered ominously.

'What conditions?' he demanded.

Good question!

She racked her brain. What did she want out of this marriage? 'I want to spend quality time with you,' she blurted out, knowing that would be key.

They were still virtual strangers, mostly because he'd been avoiding her until last night. But indulging their physical bond wasn't necessarily going to build intimacy, especially as she suspected Santiago was a master at keeping his emotional needs under lock and key.

He let out a gruff chuckle, then cradled her neck to drag her closer. 'I promise we will have much quality time together,' he said, his hand sliding over her hip to cup her buttock and make her vividly aware of his need, as well as her own. Her clitoris throbbed, already begging for his touch again.

It took every ounce of her strength to flatten her palms against his chest and ease him away. 'I don't *just* want to spend quality time in your bed. I also want to be able to talk to you.'

'About what?' he asked.

She sighed. This negotiation was going to be tougher than she had anticipated. The man was nothing if not obtuse. 'Just *everything*...the *castillo*, your work, my work...'

'You will not work, we agreed,' he interrupted.

'Yes, but that was before...' She swallowed, the enormity of what she was discussing starting to intimidate her again. 'I'll want to work if we're married. I'm not comfortable with you paying for everything. I'd want to contribute.'

She could see he wasn't happy with that suggestion.

'I am a rich man, there is no need for you to work,' he declared. Then he grasped her wrist to tug her back into his embrace. 'And do not worry, you will be contributing a lot… And I will ensure you won't be bored, as I intend to keep you very busy.'

The playful, seductive tone had a predictable effect, but she eased him back again, more firmly this time.

'It would make me feel like a burden,' she managed. And she sensed she had felt like a burden too many times before in her past.

'Okay. What is it that you wish to work at?' he countered, stumping her.

She had no idea what her skills were—other than those vague memories of working an espresso machine and pulling pints—but surely, she had to be able to do *something*.

'Well, I'm not entirely sure. *Yet.*'

'Then perhaps we can delay this discussion until after we are married,' he offered reasonably. Far too reasonably really.

She huffed. 'Okay, but in principle, I want to work. Once I've figured out what I can work at.'

'Noted,' he said, the confident smile somehow managing to be both patronising and indulgent.

'I also want to be able to talk to you about Ana, and Alejandro.' Because they would be her family too now. 'I want to know more about you, and your past and your family dynamics,' she probed gently, knowing she'd have to understand all those things if she were going to be a real member of his family.

'What does this mean? Family dynamics?' he said, the tone aloof and dismissive.

She forced herself not to be hurt by the flippant response. She knew his father's affair had hurt him, but it was far too soon to get him to confide in her about the tragedy that had befallen his family. She suspected, though, that was the key to why he was so determined to lock all his feelings away and pretend they didn't exist. But she couldn't break down all those barriers at once. What she had to establish, though, was that this was a marriage not just in name—and in the bedroom—which was what she suspected he wanted. That this marriage could eventually be a partnership too.

She sucked in a careful breath. Maybe even a loving one.

'Well, for example, I'd like to know what the issue is with you and Alejandro,' she offered. Surely understanding his sibling relationships would give her some clue to his thoughts, his feelings.

'There is no issue with Alejandro,' he said, the fierce frown returning—but she could see she had hit a nerve, because the muscle in his cheek was twitching. 'He is my brother and I love him, even though he goes out of his way to provoke me,' he added, apparently unaware he was contradicting himself.

'And Ana?' she soldiered on. 'I know you want me to be a good role model for her. But it's your attention she really wants. Maybe if you spent more time with her...?'

His gaze flattened. 'I have spent time with Ana every day this summer.'

For ten minutes, during which time, according to Ana, he'd mostly lectured his sister.

She could also recall the way he'd spoken to Alejandro at the party. Had he even realised he had insulted his brother? That he might even have hurt his feelings?

She sighed. There were so many things she wanted to be able to discuss with him about his siblings, about why he had such a fractious relationship with both of them. Was what Ana told her true? That her resemblance to their mother was the reason Santiago avoided her?

But she didn't want to press the point. *Now*. All she really needed at the moment was a commitment that nothing would be out of bounds. Because she knew she would never be able to live life the way he did—denying her emotions and keeping them under strict control. Or keeping secrets. It just wasn't who she was, or rather who she wanted to be. Because one of the most compelling emotions she had dragged up from her past was the yearning for closeness and connection, which she had become more and more sure in the past weeks she must once have been denied.

'But you don't mind talking about you and your family, about your feelings…' She struggled to find the right words, so he wouldn't slam down those barriers again.

All she needed was a chance. Something to work with, so that their marriage had the potential to be more than just sex, and convenience, and an astute business arrangement for him, and security and safety for her. *Eventually*. 'Stuff other than, you know…' the blush exploded in her cheeks '…orgasms.'

He let out a husky laugh. 'I suppose this is okay.' He sighed. 'If you really wish to talk about boring things.'

'It's not boring to me,' she said, knowing how much she longed to know everything about this enigmatic and endlessly fascinating man.

'I will agree to this,' he said as he curled his fingers

around her neck and tugged her towards him. 'Although I must warn you, Cerys. Where you are concerned, I find orgasms the most interesting topic of conversation.'

She laughed, feeling euphoric because she had received the concession she wanted—and she doubted Santiago gave many concessions. 'I like that topic of conversation too,' she agreed, her breathing accelerating again.

He was looking at her as if he wanted to devour her in one quick bite—which was so…intoxicating.

'So, we will be married?' he demanded.

'*Sí*,' she whispered.

Marriage to Santiago De Montoya Lopez was going to be a rollercoaster ride—and, she suspected, a battle of wills for the ages. But what was life if not a rollercoaster ride? One that you either chose to climb aboard or were thrown off by fate. Her certainty that life could be short, and that you had to grab what you could with both hands rather than risk having nothing at all, was so vivid her heart jumped into her throat.

'*Bueno*,' he said, then grasped her waist to lift her onto his desk. Dipping his head, he went to work unbuttoning her shorts and dragging them off with her panties.

'Santiago!' she gasped, naked from the waist down in seconds, her heartbeat now pumping furiously between her thighs too. 'We can't do it *here*,' she said, aiming for shocked but getting exhilarated instead as he freed the huge erection from his trousers and produced a condom.

His gaze met hers, the erotic intention unmistakable as he rolled on the protection with ruthless efficiency. 'We can do it anywhere we wish, Cerys. We are engaged.'

He drew his finger through her slick folds, stroked the yearning bundle of nerves with his thumb, making her buck against his hold.

She cried out, the dart of pleasure so strong it nearly undid her.

'I can feel how much you need me, Cerys,' he said, the awe in his voice making the hope swell.

When had she ever felt so wanted, by anyone? Perhaps it was just sex, but still it felt immense, important.

He cupped her bottom, dragged her to the edge of the desk to position the huge erection at her entrance. She shuddered and flinched, gripping his shoulders as she braced herself for the heavy thrust which she wanted and needed so desperately.

Instead of impaling her again, though, he gathered her chin and lifted her gaze to his.

'Can you take me like this, Cerys? You are not too sore?'

That he was determined not to hurt her, when she could see the hunger in his face, made hope swell into her throat.

She nodded, blindsided by an emotion which felt like more than excitement, more than just fascination. More than just that desperate, undefinable urge to live in the moment and enjoy whatever life threw at you... An emotion that was terrifying.

'I want to feel you inside me again,' she said, her heart thundering when approval darkened his expression.

'You must tell me if it is too much,' he said.

He hooked her legs around his waist and eased inside her with infinite patience, infinite care, but he didn't stop until he was seated to the hilt.

She pushed the terrifying emotions back, to concentrate on the rising tension, the brutal bliss just out of reach. He rolled his hips, slowly, carefully, out, then back. Then faster, harder—until all she could feel was the animal hunger, the deep strokes of him inside her, the desperate need. All she could hear was his grunts, her sobs, the slick slap of flesh against flesh. The basic elemental need became so huge, so unstoppable, it was like a runaway train, speeding her towards that desperate oblivion once more.

But as she crashed over, into his arms, and he shouted out his own release, the painful pressure in her chest— the frantic fear that there was much more at stake here already than she understood, or could control—exploded too.

CHAPTER EIGHT

Three weeks later

'So, you're really going through with it, then?'

Santiago swung round from the mirror in the small vestry—where he had been checking his cravat—to find his brother standing with his shoulder propped against the doorframe. The casual pose and the relaxed tone, though, was contradicted by the incredulous expression on Alejandro's face.

About damn time.

Santiago put a stranglehold on the surge of anger and frustration.

His brother's hair was a mess and his cravat hung around the open collar of his shirt untied. But at least he was here—*finally*—and wearing the suit which had been designed for him so he could be Cerys's *padrino*. It was traditional for a girl's father to represent her at a Spanish wedding ceremony, but Cerys had been certain her father was not living, from the nightmares she had already dredged up from her past, so Alejandro had agreed to walk her down the aisle. But, as usual, his brother had clearly not understood the gravity of that commitment.

'You were supposed to be here an hour ago, Andro,' he replied, attempting to relax his jaw and not sound furious. He did not have time to start an argument. His wedding was due to commence in less than twenty minutes.

His brother shrugged. 'I got hung up in Girona this afternoon.'

No doubt in some woman's bed.

Santiago's jaw tightened, his own sexual frustration adding to his irritation at his brother's late arrival.

He had chosen not to make love to Cerys for the past few days, to prove to himself that he could control the insatiable desire. But now he was concerned he would be unable to control his physical reaction during the ceremony. Which would not only be humiliating—but had the potential to reignite the salacious speculation about his insatiable sex drive, which this marriage was supposed to curtail.

In the past three weeks it had become a struggle to leave Cerys sleeping in the secluded villa on the edge of the vines each morning at dawn to go to work in the *castillo*. And even more of a struggle not to tear her clothes off her as soon as she arrived to join him there each evening. He had even taken to waking her during the night, to have her again. And using sex to placate her whenever the nightmares woke her from dreams.

At least the sex had diverted her from attempting any more conversations about his past whenever they were alone together. Cerys must have heard of the De Montoya Scandal by now—but he had no wish to discuss it. This marriage would finally repair the rest of the damage his father had caused. They could not make their union official in the eyes of the state until Pérez came through with her ID documents. But the detective believed he had found something which might help uncover her identity, which he was bringing to the *castillo* tomorrow.

With the Isla de la Luna resort due to open in a couple

of weeks, his business manager had been overjoyed at the prospect of them honeymooning on the island and Santiago would prefer to have the civil marriage conducted beforehand. The publicity department had a press release ready to go too, which would hopefully put an end to the comparisons with his father once and for all.

It had been important to him to have their marriage blessed in the family chapel, if for no other reason than to prove to himself that he had finally shaken off the shackles of his past. And his father's crimes.

But the more he hungered for Cerys, the more he wondered if that were true.

Three days ago, he had noticed the bruised shadows under Cerys's eyes. And he knew they were caused not just by the endless wedding planning and the demands he made on her at night, but also by the nightmares which woke her frequently.

She was emotionally fragile, her memory clearly returning, and yet every time he took her, the need only become more acute—to the point where he had taken to making excuses to snatch stolen moments with her during the day. The soft sobs of her arousal, the feel of her tightening around him, was something he had begun to crave like a drug. Three days ago, he had even demanded she come to his study so he could hand over his mother's mantilla—the black veil traditionally worn by Spanish brides. Of course, he had no real interest in whether she wore the mantilla or not. But contriving that particular reason to see her had been a misstep, leading to questions about his mother. Which had then led to him ravishing her on the desk to divert her attention again. In the end he had been so ashamed of himself he'd ended up insisting on a three-day separation until the wedding…

But, of course, the three nights without her in his bed had only made his appetite more insatiable.

He sighed. At least this self-inflicted celibacy was due to end in a few hours.

Night had fallen ten minutes ago, and the centuries-old chapel on the vineyard's grounds—where the exclusive ceremony would be performed—had been full of the invited guests for over an hour.

He had decided against a big society event—partly because the wedding planner had nearly had a breakdown when he had insisted on arranging this blessing ceremony before the Isla de la Luna launch at the end of the month. But mostly because he had always had an aversion to any kind of press attention. They would have exclusive photographs taken on Isla de la Luna, but the press release would only be issued for this event once Cerys's true identity had been discovered and they could legalise the union.

But he'd also had no desire to wait.

It was unlike him to rush anything, but getting Cerys in his bed permanently as soon as possible had seemed like the best way to control this obsession. Now, though, he wasn't so sure about that either. Because the more he had Cerys, the more he seemed to want her.

'I'm really not interested in hearing about your latest conquest, Andro,' he replied tightly. 'I'm just glad you finally showed up.'

His brother arched a sceptical brow, but as usual appeared unbothered by Santiago's criticisms.

'You look tense. Wedding nerves, *hermano*?' he goaded.

'Why would I be nervous?' Santiago replied, annoyed

by the suggestion. 'Marriage to Cerys fulfils my requirements.'

However swift his decision to offer Cerys marriage had been, he did not regret it. She wasn't just diverting in bed, she called to some elemental part of him which he could no longer deny—not yet anyway. Her innocence, of course, had also been a decisive factor—the realisation when he had thrust so heavily inside her the first time that she had never given herself to another man had been both disturbing, and deeply unsettling, on one level—but also strangely cathartic on another. Because as soon as he had realised the truth, he had been consumed with the possessive urge to ensure he remained the only man ever to touch her.

He had wondered, late at night, if it was this urge which had driven his father to finally choose one of his many mistresses over his mother. Was it this same elemental obsession which had made his father choose to run off with that British tourist? Because, if it was, surely it made Santiago's marriage to Cerys even more imperative. And while Cerys's lack of a past might have been an issue, if she were a virgin at twenty, surely her life must have been sheltered. Plus, he found her personality—that impulsive optimism, her willingness to see the best in him, while also challenging and exciting him—surprisingly enchanting. And surely her desire to be a part of his family could only be beneficial if it meant he could concern himself less with Ana's constant disobedience and Alejandro's determination never to take any damn thing seriously. To have Cerys act as a go-between with his siblings suddenly seemed like a perfect solution. She was so sunny and bright. Ana already adored her and he knew Alejandro had been charmed by her, too.

'Uh-huh? Really?' Alejandro said, not sounding convinced. 'You're marrying a girl you've known for less than a couple of months. A girl you don't know anything about—and neither does she. I know she's hot,' he murmured. 'And according to the staff you can't keep your hands off her, but why the hell are you marrying her when you could just keep her in your bed until she remembers who she is and goes home?'

Fury consumed him. Lunging forward, he grabbed his brother by his lapels and thrust him back against the doorframe.

'Don't speak of her like that, as if she is no better than one of our father's whores,' he growled.

Instead of fighting back, though, Alejandro stared at him, his gaze direct.

'Calm down, Tiago,' he said. The nickname which Andro hadn't used since they were boys cut through the surging fury, to the familiar shame. 'That's not what I meant.'

Santiago unlocked his fists and released his brother.

The fury had come from nowhere. He had revealed too much. What was wrong with him? Why had he reacted so strongly to Alejandro's familiar attempts to goad him?

'Have you got feelings for her, Tiago, is that it?' his brother asked.

The thought struck fear into his heart.

'Don't call me by that name,' he said, struggling to control his panic. They weren't those boys any more. They had once been close, but that was before Santiago had betrayed them all by keeping his father's sordid secrets from the rest of his family.

'I told you months ago I was in search of a wife,' he continued, knowing he was reasoning with himself now as much as his brother, but determined to make his motivations clear. No one had said anything about love. Nor would they. 'And we are well matched.'

Sexually. Which was the only connection which mattered to a man like him.

But why did he sound so defensive? He had nothing to explain, nothing to apologise for. This had always been his intention. Yes, the marriage was sudden, but it still served his purpose.

'Obviously, her lack of memory is an issue, but Pérez believes he may have located some of her belongings. It is only a matter of time before we will know her identity.'

'And you don't want to wait until then?'

'We are saying our vows in…' he glanced at his watch '…precisely ten minutes. So, no. I do not wish to wait.' He glared at his brother. Why did he care so much about this marriage? 'She was innocent, Andro, so I also have a responsibility here that you would not understand.'

His brother stiffened and hurt flickered in his eyes. But Santiago dismissed it.

Given Alejandro's reputation as a womaniser, he had probably deflowered a thousand virgins in his time.

But then his brother swore under his breath. 'I knew it, this is because of what happened to our *madre*. It's all part of your dumb white knight complex, isn't it?'

Santiago tensed, resentment burning under his breastbone.

His brother did not understand. Would *never* understand. Because he had not been there when their mother had… He swallowed, forcing the raw memories back, and thrust his fingers through his hair. Alejandro did not need to understand.

'If you don't wish to stand as Cerys's *padrino*,' he said,

forcing the bleak memories back under control, 'I will find someone else.'

He should never have asked Alejandro to fulfil the role when his brother was so unreliable.

'Cerys isn't the problem, you are,' his brother remarked, his voice heavy, and not at all like the devil-may-care playboy he presented to the world. 'Does she even know what she's getting into with you?'

Santiago felt the question like a blow. What the hell was that supposed to mean?

The delicate melody from a single guitar floated into the vestry, the opening bars of the musical arrangement which had been chosen to accompany his bride's arrival.

'Make yourself presentable to represent Cerys, or leave,' Santiago said. 'It is your choice.'

Alejandro was still staring at him, tension snapping in the air between them, when Ana dashed into the vestry in the *padrina's* gown she was wearing to represent Santiago in place of their mother. He felt a surge of pride at how grown-up she looked. And how excited.

Even though Cerys's ability to corral his younger sister had been one of the reasons he had chosen her as his bride, he had been quietly astonished by how enthusiastic Ana had been about the match. And how well behaved she had been in the past three weeks.

'Cerys is here, and she looks stunning,' Ana announced, then her head swung between the two of them. 'What are you two arguing about, because everyone can hear you shouting at each other and it's embarrassing.'

Shame washed over Santiago, alongside the rush of anticipation. And desire. He just needed to get through this damn ceremony so he could have Cerys to himself again. Thank God, the festivities after the blessing had been performed were only due to last for a few hours.

'*Madre de Dios*, Andro, you are a mess.' Ana rushed over to Alejandro to tie her brother's cravat. 'You must go to Cerys and calm her down. She is nervous. As any new bride would be.'

She grinned at Santiago, but the innocent excitement in her eyes made him feel oddly guilty. His sister had insisted on viewing this marriage as a love match—and it had suited his purposes to let her. But now he wondered if his decision not to tell her the real reasons for this union would hurt her when she discovered the truth.

Alejandro batted her hands away. 'Leave it, I can tie the damn thing myself.' He sent Santiago a warning look, then flashed the dangerously cynical smile which said he cared about nothing and nobody. It was a smile Santiago had always hated, until this moment. 'Let's get this done then.'

Ana sent Santiago a curious look as Alejandro marched out.

'What *were* you two shouting about?' she asked, her concern making Santiago tense even more. 'Because it sounded like more than your usual fights about Alejandro's wicked ways.'

'*Nada*,' he said, determined to forget it.

He had not one thing to feel guilty about. Cerys knew what this marriage offered—and what it did not. She wanted security and he needed stability. And they both enjoyed the sex. Maybe he enjoyed it a bit too much at present, but they would eventually tire of each other, they had to.

The music swelled from the chapel, the guitar joined by a string quartet.

'Come...' He folded Ana's hand over his arm, to lead her into the chapel. 'We are late.'

'Yes, Your Excellency,' Ana said cheekily, but for once he had no desire to reprimand her. Because all his thoughts were on the woman who was about to walk down the aisle towards him.

And finally bring this infernal yearning to an end.

Is this really happening? Why does it feel so wonderful...? And yet also so terrifying.

Cerys's hand trembled as she held onto the abundant bouquet of roses and orange blossoms the florist had pressed into her hands on her arrival at the old chapel in the *castillo*'s grounds.

The romantic music reached a crescendo, lifting the hairs on her neck, as Alejandro appeared by her side and held out his elbow.

'Are you ready, Cerys?' he asked gently in Spanish, his usually easy-going smile a little strained.

She nodded, despite the gathering storm of emotions at the prospect of becoming Santiago De Montoya's wife *for real*.

How was it possible she already cared for Santiago so much? A man who, even after three weeks of virtually non-stop intimacy, still seemed like such an enigma.

Maybe it was just the endorphin rush of incredible sex.

Or the way he always managed to make her feel safe.

Late at night, though, as she drifted into an exhausted sleep, his arms holding her so protectively, the dreams had come. Vivid, confusing, terrifying dreams, which always made her feel powerless. And empty and alone.

And then there were the memories which swirled

through those dreams, just out of reach—memories which were becoming more vivid every time they appeared.

A woman's face, the same shape as her own, her voice rich with love but her eyes filled with regret and sadness. A man's face, his blue-green eyes, so like hers, flat and emotionless and chillingly disapproving. Words on a page in large looping letters which she couldn't seem to read. And the sense of dread—the feeling that she and Santiago had always been linked. But not in a happy way.

'Are you sure?' Alejandro murmured, his usually relaxed expression surprisingly intense.

'I…' She hesitated. But then the confusing guilt was overwhelmed by a burst of urgency. Santiago was waiting for her. He needed this commitment and so did she. She pushed past the wave of anxiety—the sense of being adrift and untethered. 'Yes. Yes, I am.'

Alejandro searched her face, but then he nodded. Tucking her against his side, he led her into the chapel. Everyone sitting in the pews stood and turned towards her as the music swelled. She dismissed the pulse of sadness that she didn't know most of these people. But then she spotted Ana and Santiago, standing at the end of the aisle by the altar. Ana turned to flash a quick grin over her shoulder.

Cerys smiled back. But then her gaze found Santiago—his tall frame strong and indomitable—and her wayward emotions surged with the music.

He turned his head as if he could sense her need to see his face. Their gazes locked and passion flared—sharp and true and endlessly exciting—but with it came a fierce sense of connection.

His gaze raked over her, his appreciation so vivid her steps faltered. The ceremony, the congregation, even Ana and Alejandro became a blur—and all she could see was him. And that hard, handsome face which had become so precious.

Breathtaking.

Her lungs squeezed, as they had so many times—every time he touched her with such hunger, as if she were the only person he would allow to see his need. Every time he held her with such care.

She knew there was still so much of himself he kept hidden from her. But surely if she could be patient, and unlock her own secrets, she could coax his secrets out into the open too.

Alejandro placed her hand in Santiago's and stepped back.

Santiago's gaze intensified, the hot look—full of purpose and demand—rushed over her skin. She smiled, forcing the misgivings back.

Nothing could stop this marriage being wonderful. Because, whatever the truth was about her past, her future would soon be bound to this man now, for better or for worse. And she trusted him to take care of her.

Because she intended to take care of him, too.

CHAPTER NINE

'*Ay Dios mío!* I thought that would never end!' Santiago gripped his new bride's hand, rushing through the lemon orchard towards the house on the edge of the vines.

The local priest had blessed their marriage three interminable hours ago. Then the wedding feast had dragged on for several eternities—every single one of the small congregation toasting their health with the *castillo*'s finest vintages and indulging in the lavish spread of Catalan and Spanish delicacies prepared by an army of chefs. If the long wait to be alone wasn't frustrating enough, he had been forced to dance under the stars with his new wife. To have Cerys in his arms, the simple but stunning white silk dress only enhancing his need, had been nothing short of torture. But finally, *finally*, he had her all to himself... And he intended to consummate this marriage now, without further delay.

'Santiago, slow down before I break a leg or, worse, ruin this beautiful dress.' Cerys's breathless laugh did nothing to ease the sense of urgency and desperation in his gut.

Dios, she had looked so stunning, and so hopeful, walking towards him on his brother's arm. The need—dark and dangerous and unstoppable—had blindsided him again, but right beneath it was a sense of desperation.

The fear that if he did not claim her as his as soon as was humanly possible, if he did not possess her, she might slip through his fingers like moon dust. Which was, of course, ludicrous. She was his now, before God and his family, which meant they had the universe's blessing to feed this infernal hunger until it finally burned itself out.

Stopping, he bent to scoop her up and over his shoulder.

She let out a very un-*duquesa*-like shriek.

'Santiago! Put me down!' she yelped, her muffled voice filled with exasperated laughter.

He found himself chuckling too, despite the incessant craving making his palms sweat. And his groin tighten.

'You are too slow,' he said as he gave her bottom a playful swat and was rewarded with another indignant shriek. 'And I am tired of waiting.'

She wriggled furiously, inflaming his desires even more, if that were possible.

'Don't you dare drop me!' she demanded as he bounded up the steps to the veranda with her bouncing on his shoulder.

'Do not panic,' he replied, the foolish grin spreading into his heart. When was the last time he had enjoyed himself this much, anticipation warring with a sense of fun which had been absent from his life until Cerys? 'You are far too precious for me to risk dropping you.'

She stilled as he carted her over the threshold.

The villa had been decorated with bouquets of wild flowers from the meadows by the river at his request, for their first night together as man and wife. Her scent had always captivated him and he knew how much she had enjoyed the excursions she made to swim there with Ana.

He was not a romantic man. He did not believe in love

and had never been given to romantic gestures, nor was this marriage supposed to be anything more than a means to an end, for both of them. But when he deposited her on her feet and her gaze connected with his—the translucent blue-green of her eyes sheened with surprise and happiness—his heartbeat slowed.

Her cheeks flushed, her eyes widening as her gaze swept over the hundreds of candles in glass jars illuminating the profusion of summer blooms. The romantic setting was only enhanced by the heady fragrance of the flowers—and the subtle scent of Cerys, sharpening his hunger for her... Always for her.

'Santiago, it's...wonderful.' Her breath hitched and her eyes twinkled with tears in the candlelight. 'Thank you. No one has ever done anything so thoughtful for me.'

'How do you know this?' he asked, her candour, her emotion, suddenly making him feel exposed.

She bit into the full bottom lip he had been yearning to taste all evening, her expression so open and vulnerable and unafraid it scared him a little.

'I just... I know.' She pressed a fist to her chest. 'In here. Does that make sense?'

While it really should not make sense, if he were being entirely rational, somehow it did to him. He had forced himself not to look too closely at why she might have accepted his proposal. But he had always known that her motives were nowhere near as cynical or calculating or selfish as his.

But why would she give herself to him with such passion, and hold nothing back? Was it bravery? Or naivety? Or both.

How could she allow herself to be so trusting when

she knew nothing at all of the darkness that lurked inside him?

She blinked, a single tear falling over her lid.

He pressed an unsteady palm to her cheek, her soft skin flushed with heat.

'Cerys, do not cry,' he murmured, disturbed now by the way his own heart was punching his ribs. Why had he given in to the impulse to hire a florist and have the villa decorated for their wedding night, when this marriage could never be a love match?

'I c-can't help it...' she sniffed.

He brushed away the single drop with his thumb, then cradled her cheek.

But as he dragged her into his arms, determined not to overthink the impulsive gesture, or her response to it, she pressed shaking palms against his chest, to prevent him from taking what he needed now more than breath.

Her gaze was full of longing and hope—her expression both vulnerable and defenceless—and yet also so fierce.

'Did you mean it, Santiago?' she whispered, the tender expression touching the cold, empty corners of his heart which he had relied on for so long to keep him detached, protected, safe. 'Am I precious to you?'

'Of course,' he said instinctively.

But as he drove his hands into her hair, the perfect chignon collapsing under his urgent caresses, the gruff acknowledgement had his heart slamming into his throat.

'You are mine, Cerys,' he added, desperate to believe he cherished her for one reason, and one reason only. 'And I want you more than I have ever wanted any woman.'

He covered her lips, swallowed her soft sob of startled surrender, and proceeded to feast on what was finally his—determined to control the panic and those wayward emotions as ruthlessly as he had controlled so much else in his life.

But as she clung to him and kissed him back, her hunger more than a match for his own, the emotion punched his throat with the force and fury of a sledgehammer.

This isn't love, it can't be... Not yet.

Cerys repeated the words to herself as Santiago devoured her, his furious kiss conquering every sigh, every sob.

He boosted her into his arms again, his large hands caressing her backside, the heavy erection in his trousers rubbing against the hot spot in her panties. She wrapped her legs around his waist and clung to him, kissing him back with every fibre of her being. Until the cautious words were swept away on a heady wave of desire. The swell of need gathered pace as she remembered how he had dragged her away from the wedding banquet and then whispered words she had never expected, never even hoped for.

'You are far too precious for me to risk dropping you.'

The marriage blessing had been terrifying and magical all at once. The only thing tethering her to reality had been Santiago's solid presence by her side, his gaze filled with passion and purpose as she'd whispered her assent to their union in English then Spanish.

How could this be a mistake, when everything had been so perfect?

She'd tried so hard to keep a firm grip on her expectations throughout the past three weeks, ever since she had agreed to his practical, pragmatic proposal. She mustn't hope for too much, too soon. If there could be more in their union, it would take time to grow—especially when

Santiago guarded his emotions so zealously. She didn't want to be too reckless, too needy, too vulnerable.

But it had been so hard to keep everything in perspective, as Santiago had said his vows with a firm command which had left no room for doubt. As he'd kissed her with furious need in front of all the people who mattered to him. As he'd watched her with appreciation darkening his eyes to a rich chocolate brown during the feasting and spun her around on the dancefloor as if they were the only people there. As he had grasped her hand and marched through the crowd, ignoring the back-slapping and laughter, his singular purpose had made her insides melt all over again.

The truth was her defences had already been in tatters before he had said the words which had made her heart melt. Because he had already shown her in so many ways today that she was precious to him.

But as he swung her high in his arms to march up the staircase to the bed where they had made love for the first time—and so many times since—the flicker of candlelight and the flowery perfume of the summer meadow bunched on every surface had her hopes lifting even higher.

When they reached the bedroom there were more candles, more flowers, and her heart became so huge she could barely breathe.

How could such an austere, forbidding man have done something so sweet and sentimental, just for her?

He dropped her on the bed, his expression focused and determined. She watched, transfixed by how magnificent he looked as he towered over her. Desire charged through her system like a drug. He tore off his jacket and tie and wrenched the tailored shirt out of his suit trousers. Buttons popped, his magnificent chest bared at last—the hard muscles bunched and tensed, the tanned skin, the sprinkle of hair trailing through his abs, softened by the glow of the candlelight. She shivered as he shoved off his trousers and stood gloriously naked before her—to roll a condom on the huge erection.

'Take off the dress, Cerys,' he growled, his voice rough with demand.

Her gaze snapped to his, to see the fierce frown.

'Now,' he added. 'Or I will destroy it. I cannot wait any longer.'

She nodded, snapped out of the erotic fog. Lifting onto her knees, she fumbled, trying to find the tab under her arm, but before she could drag it down, he had brushed her hands away.

She could feel his urgency, the fight to be gentle, as he hooked a finger under the straps and shoved them down. He found the zip at last, releasing her from the shimmering fabric, which had felt like a straitjacket for hours. She moaned as his lips found the pulse in her neck and suckled hungrily while he dragged the dress down and freed her tender breasts from the constricting lace.

His hands were everywhere, caressing, stroking, divesting her of the gown, the lingerie she had worn especially for him, until she could feel the night breeze against her skin.

He captured one stiff peak between hungry lips as his fingers found the slick folds of her sex and circled the swollen nub. She lurched off the bed, already so close.

He pressed one finger, then two inside her, finding the spot he knew would take her over and caressed it with ruthless efficiency. The first orgasm slammed into her, driving her up—too far, too fast—even as he grasped her hips and drove into the tight clasp of her body.

Impaled, possessed, she struggled to breathe, couldn't think, the adrenaline, the need lost in the burst of furious emotion. And desperation.

She needed this, needed him. *Always.*

She gripped his shoulders, the rocking thrusts taking him deeper still. So deep she could feel him touch her soul. The second orgasm layered onto the first, building harder and faster, terrifying in its intensity. She tried to hold back, to hold on, as the powerful erection stroked in and out, filling every part of her to bursting, and taking her to a place she had only ever been with him.

'Again, Cerys, you must come for me again. Now you are mine.'

As if by his command, her body responded, the pleasure cascading through her in a thousand glittering shards of sensation. She cried out, feeling terrified and exhilarated, scared and yet cherished.

The shout of his release was like a validation, a promise, sending her soaring over that final ledge and plunging her into the beautiful abyss.

CHAPTER TEN

Santiago strode across the courtyard, aware of the morning sun already beating down on the remnants of last night's festivities, which were still being cleared away by the crew employed by the event planner.

When was the last time he had indulged himself like this? And stayed in bed until noon.

Cerys had woken him just after dawn, writhing in the throes of a nightmare, calling out for her mother. But when he'd roused her the rest of the way, she had been unable to recall the details of the dream. Luckily, he had known the perfect way to distract her. To distract them both.

He frowned, recalling how they had both drifted back to sleep, sated and content in each other's arms.

Uneasiness settled in his gut. For the first time in—well, for ever, really—he would happily have stayed in bed all day, because his work did not excite him as much as Cerys. He pushed the unsettling thought to one side, the memory of her face the night before—full of hope and possibilities—when she had seen the flowers, though, only disturbed him more.

He tugged his phone from his pocket to check the time. Pérez had arrived at the *castillo* twenty minutes ago, with an item which the detective believed could be one of the possessions Santiago had described being pocketed by the thief in Barcelona.

He hoped to hell the item held the key to Cerys's identity. And helped unlock her memory the rest of the way. He had hated seeing her confusion and panic this morning, the sadness on her face when she had struggled to recall the details of her dream. But more, he knew he was becoming too invested in this relationship. Once the legalities could be settled, and the prenuptial agreement signed, he could surely begin to get this union in perspective. Perhaps the decision to have the marriage blessed in the family chapel according to the De Montoya tradition had also been a mistake—bringing emotions into play which had no place in this arrangement—but how would he have been able to persuade anyone the marriage was real if he did not make vows before God? And why did he still feel as if the impulse to do so had been a lot less pragmatic than he might wish, that deep-seated urge to claim Cerys in all the ways that mattered something he could no longer ignore.

He jogged up the back stairs and headed to his study. When he arrived, Pérez was waiting for him.

'Your Excellency, I apologise for waking you on the morning after your wedding,' the man began.

'It was a church blessing for the union, to recognise it in the eyes of God. The marriage, however, will not be legal until we have Cerys's ID documents,' he replied gruffly, trying to convince himself as much as the detective that yesterday's service had been a necessity demanded by religion and tradition. Nothing more. 'So, I'm hoping you have news for us that will tie up the loose ends.'

'I'm afraid I do not have any of your betrothed's ID documents,' the man said, dashing Santiago's hopes.

But then the detective reached into his briefcase to produce a tattered leather-bound book. 'But my contacts in Barcelona discovered this for sale on the black market, which I believed might be the item you described.'

Adrenaline shot through him, swiftly followed by relief. It looked exactly like the book the thief had taken from Cerys's bag that night. The one item she had been so determined to retrieve.

'Well done, Pérez,' he said.

'This is the book you described to me?' the man asked.

'Yes.' He had only seen it fleetingly, but he was sure of it.

But as Pérez passed him the book, the detective frowned. 'I'm afraid to say the man who sold it to me had already shown it to a journalist.'

'I see… Why would a journalist be interested in it?' he asked, annoyed. They had not released any details about Cerys, her amnesia—or their wedding—to the press yet, so that yesterday's ceremony could remain private. Why had those damn vultures been snooping about?

'Perhaps you should read it first,' Pérez replied, which was hardly an answer. But then the man's gaze became shadowed with something that looked uncomfortably like sympathy. Who the hell was that aimed at? 'It appears to be her mother's journal,' he added. 'It also explains why she may have been in the Plaça Reial that night… Because you were.'

What?

'Okay. You are sure?' he said.

The man nodded, still looking grave.

But then Santiago's heart lifted, along with a large portion of the guilt which had been bothering him for weeks now, ever since he had taken her virginity.

Why did it matter why Cerys had been in the plaza? Perhaps she had heard of the family scandal which had made him a figure of public scrutiny for years. So what? If the journal belonged to her mother, it would surely hold the clues they sought to reveal her identity.

'Regardless, this is good news,' he said, taking the book from the detective.

This wasn't just good news—it was excellent news. Finally, Cerys would have a way to unlock the rest of her memories. The doctors had all said her recovery had been delayed because she had been in an unfamiliar place ever since the assault. That if they could discover her real name, the details of her past, it would jog her memory loose, and speed the process up considerably. She had remembered so many fragments already, but verifiable details would help to create a much fuller picture.

But while he hated to see her struggle, he knew his motives were also selfish.

He wanted her to know everything. Wanted her to be fully herself again, so there would be no more nightmares.

After last night, and the impulsive decision to have the villa decorated, he suspected she was already developing deeper feelings for him. And while in some ways that served his purpose, he hated the thought that until she was fully healed she could not know her own mind completely. Nor did he want her to be so vulnerable. Because surely this was why he felt so driven to protect her.

Of course, he was also curious to discover more about her. Where she came from, who she was, why she seemed to expect so little of people, while at the same time giving so much of herself. Because her open and generous heart had begun to captivate him—which also could not be good.

Sitting down, Santiago opened the cover of the book. But then the name of the owner scribbled across the facing page leapt out at him and seemed to grab him around the throat. The anticipation curdled in his stomach, becoming sharp with shock… And then dread.

Angharad Jones.

The name which had been etched on Santiago's consciousness for fifteen years. The name of the woman who had helped to plunge his family into scandal and grief and extinguished hundreds of years of honour. And for what? To satisfy his father's indiscriminate libido and her own.

The dread spread, its tentacles wrapping around his ribs. Nausea rose up like venom, poisoning everything in its path—everything that had happened in the last three weeks, the last two months even. The way Cerys had captivated and excited him, the longing and hope in her eyes last night curdled, until all that was left was the bitter taste of irony. And all those cruel memories which he thought he had conquered a lifetime ago.

He swallowed to stop himself from gagging. Then flipped through the book blindly, until he reached the final entry.

Pérez murmured something that sounded like an apology, but Santiago could barely hear it over the discordant throbbing in his ears as he read what Cerys's mother had written fifteen years ago—on the night she had run away with his father.

Fury and fear and hopelessness tangled in his gut like venomous snakes. It was a feeling he remembered far too vividly. From when he had looked into his own mother's sightless eyes, registered the empty bottle of pills on her bedside table and known he had not done enough to save her. Or his baby brother or sister.

His hands shook, his breath sawing out, the control he had worked so hard to maintain threatening to shatter again and leave him even more alone.

The writing scribbled in bold black ink danced in front of his eyes. Sickening, disgusting, selfish words. This woman had destroyed his family. To satisfy her lust. To alleviate her boredom.

The horrifying truth dawned on him. Guilt solidified the brick in the pit of his stomach, freezing it into a block of ice-cold contempt.

The journal fell from his numb fingers onto the carpet.

He stood, shaking with anger and disbelief, even as his stomach twisted with shame.

I have defiled our family chapel by blessing a marriage to the daughter of my father's whore there.

Yesterday's marriage would not be recognised in law until the legal documents had been signed. But how could he annul the vows he had made before God, when they had consummated them not once but many times last night, and again this morning? No priest would condone it. And anyway, a journalist already knew Cerys's identity.

He stared blankly at Pérez. 'This journalist, what do they know?'

'They knew of your interest in the book. And the connection to the incident in Barcelona. It is already common knowledge that the woman you rescued that night has been living in your household ever since. Although I do not think it is known that she has lost her memory. Your household are extremely discreet.'

Except how do we even know she has really lost her memory?

The familiar cynicism went some way to fill the hole in his gut.

What if it was always a lie, to trick me into a commitment?

Santiago swore, the poison rising in his throat. No wonder Pérez had looked so concerned when Santiago had confirmed the journal belonged to the woman he had chosen to make his wife.

The story would break very soon, that they had been married in his family's chapel. Even though they had not released the information to the press yet, they had made no attempt to hide it either. And while his staff in the *castillo* knew of his hatred of gossip, last night's guests would not necessarily be as discreet.

And when Cerys's identity was revealed, the whole world would know his shame—that, like his father, he had thrown all caution and control away simply to satisfy his own lust.

'I am sorry, Your Excellency,' the man said again. 'I know this news is a surprise.'

'A surprise?' He barked out a bitter laugh as he picked up the book from the carpet, the fury so cold inside him that his heart felt frozen. 'I need you to find out when the story will break.' At least then he could prepare, do some kind of damage limitation, although at this point he had no idea what that even looked like. He could refuse to go ahead with the civil ceremony, but the blessing had already been performed. It would only be a matter of time before the press discovered that too. Even though the congregation had been asked not to post anything on social media, he had not thought it necessary to swear them to secrecy indefinitely.

'I must speak to my wife,' he said.

The word tasted sour on his tongue, but instead of the fury he wanted to feel, heat surged up his torso as he imagined the sight of her—her naked curves, soft and supple and dappled by sunlight—when he had torn himself away from her less than twenty minutes ago.

His wife...

The woman he had been so desperate to marry that he had not even delayed until their marriage could be conducted legally. Because of an obsession he *still* could not control.

He forced himself to take a breath.

Cerys Jones had captivated him, much as her mother had once captivated his father. That much was obvious. And it seemed that a part of him still yearned to feed that obsession. But he was in the driving seat now.

When the gossip sites and the scandal sheets got hold of this story, the main purpose of this marriage would be destroyed. But he would not let Cerys, or the foolhardy emotions she had begun to stir in him, get the better of him again. And from now on he would control the narrative. Ruthlessly and without compromise.

He allowed the cold, controlled fury to build as he walked back through the orchard and the poison seeped into his soul. The incriminating journal felt like a brick in his pocket. But the sun which had felt so warm less than an hour ago could do nothing to thaw the block of ice building around his heart—or repair the gaping hole in his gut.

Cerys scrubbed the steam off the bathroom mirror, then pressed her fingers to her jaw, aware of the rough patch where Santiago's stubble had abraded her skin.

She stared at her reflection in the mirror—and let the

sensual memories of their early-morning lovemaking crowd out the shadowy images from her nightmare.

She'd woken again in a daze of heat and longing ten minutes ago, to find Santiago gone and the sun high in the sky. Somehow, not having him there beside her had spooked her. But the residual hum of arousal, and the long hot shower, had helped quell the anxiety from the nightmares—which had been so vivid and so disturbing when Santiago had woken her earlier. Before he had helped to drive away her fear on a wave of heat.

A loud rap on the bathroom door made her jump.

'Cerys, get dressed and come downstairs.' The sharp command in Santiago's voice sent a chill through her.

Why did he sound like the man she had met that first morning in the *castillo* nearly two months ago now? And nothing like the man who had made wild, passionate love to her last night, and slow, sensuous love to her less than an hour ago.

She rushed to open the door, the prickle of unease frightening her.

'Santiago, wait!' she said, surprised to see him heading back down the stairs.

She clutched the towel to her breasts, far too aware of her nakedness when his hot gaze raked over her skin.

'Is something wrong?' she asked.

When his gaze met hers, the tight muscle twitching in his jaw contradicted the heat burning in his eyes. 'Get dressed.'

'What's wrong?' she asked again, his harsh judgemental expression making her shiver despite the sunshine pouring through the bedroom's open window. And reminding her of the man from her dreams who always seemed to look through her as if she wasn't there.

'Do as I ask...' The command was unmistakable, as if she were one of his employees again and not the woman he had wanted to become his wife. 'And you can drop the innocent act now. I know who you are.'

Drop the innocent act?

She stood frozen, shocked by the searing tone and the bite of contempt as he disappeared.

She rushed to dress herself, trying to calm the panic in her gut, the sudden feeling of being nothing. Of being nobody.

Who was this man? And what had happened to the man who'd vowed to cherish her the night before? The man who had gone to so much trouble to make her feel safe and protected.

She walked down the stairs ten minutes later, the creased wedding dress making her feel hopelessly self-conscious. Santiago sat in the far corner of the room, the casual combo of jeans and a T-shirt and his forbidding expression reminding her of the morning she had bumped into him fresh from the fields. The burnt-out candles which had looked so magical last night, and the cloying fragrance of the flowers, which were starting to droop in their vases, seemed to mock her too, drying up all the hope and excitement of the previous evening.

'Wh-what...? What did you mean, you know who I am?' she asked.

'Do you recognise this?' he asked, lifting a red leather book from the coffee table beside his chair.

A wave of sadness and confusion washed over her, swiftly followed by a shocking flash of recognition. Her stomach twisted, the cramping pain like a knife to her gut.

'That's... That's my mother's journal,' she gasped.

She gulped in air, her lungs so tight she could hardly breathe. Her mother's face—bold, beautiful, wreathed in smiles and laughter—swirled in front of her eyes, but then it dissolved, the image becoming shadowed and so sad... Dark earth piled on a freshly dug grave, her father's unforgiving expression, the cruel words he'd spoken to her on that terrible day so long ago.

'Don't cry for her. She's dead now, and she deserves to be—for what she did to me.'

'She's... She's gone...' She pressed trembling fingers to her lips to contain the brutal sob, the sudden tidal wave of grief... Her brain was battered by a parade of vivid memories from her nightmares, which now made a sickening sense—as the jagged shards slotted into place. And became real.

Her mother sitting on a hotel balcony scribbling, her face fading into nothingness. Her father, young and angry, then older, always uncaring and indifferent, his eyes flat and cold and remote.

Tears scalded her eyes, her breathing so painful she couldn't draw enough air into her lungs. But when her gaze rose to meet Santiago's, and she saw the suspicion in his eyes, she recognised him too. Not as the man she'd first met in the *castillo*, the man she had weaved so many dreams about in the last few weeks, but as the man she'd watched so furtively from the shadows of the Plaça Reial—detached, indifferent, and with another woman. His was the same face of the man who had carried her back to an apartment in Barcelona as she drifted in and out of consciousness.

Theirs had never been a chance encounter. She had come to Spain to discover more about the mother she'd lost as a little girl... And the family of the man who had compelled Angharad Jones to make that fateful decision...

The scandal which had disturbed her so much when Ana had recounted the barest of details came back to her now in its entirety, in a grim parade of newspaper headlines and gossip column editorials.

'So now you remember who you are, Cerys Jones,' he said, the brittle cynicism bewildering. Why was he looking at her like that, as if he despised her?

He stood, holding the book, and walked towards her. His movements were stiff with outrage and lacked his usual grace.

Hooking a knuckle under her chin, he lifted her face, the angry heat in his eyes scalding her skin.

'Ironic, is it not? That we share the same destructive passion as our parents,' he said, the matter-of-fact, almost careless tone only adding to her panic and confusion. 'Amusing too, that I believed you were unique, when you simply stirred in me the same weakness my father succumbed to. Tell me, when did you recover your memory? Before or after I proposed to you? Or was it ever really lost at all?'

Pain lanced through her. But his ruthless contempt was not as awful as the terrible loneliness which engulfed her. And the yearning for his touch, his approval, which she still couldn't seem to quell, despite his cruel accusations.

Her mind and body had played a hideous trick on her, eliminating her memory just long enough for her to fall headfirst into the delusion that he cared for her. But worse than that...

She drew back and locked her knees, determined not to collapse, not yet, even as the brutal memories still bombarded her. And her battered brain wrestled with the full impact of how her reality had become so twisted, like a cruel joke, now the truth was staring her in the face.

'Do you have nothing to say?' he asked, the tone cutting.

She shook her head, unable to find the words. She hadn't made up the amnesia. Why would she? To what purpose? But she didn't have the strength to defend herself.

She'd always believed she had a connection to Santiago, but she realised now the connection had been the scandal that no one talked about. The scandal that had haunted so much of Santiago's childhood. To realise it had haunted so much of hers too, though, was no comfort. Because what should have brought them closer was ripping them apart.

'Why do you not answer?' he asked, the derisive tone matched by the brittle judgement in his eyes.

She swallowed down the yearning. He thought she'd lied to him for months, thought she'd pretended not to know who he really was? She didn't even want to guess why he would think such a thing… Because all it would do was confirm how little she really knew and understood him. She'd known his reasons for this marriage had been pragmatic, but she'd never believed he was a cold man, far from it.

'I… I can leave,' she offered, even though it hurt to even contemplate such a thing. But she had to cauterise the hope. Because all her naïve dreams about this marriage had been exposed now to the harsh glare of reality.

One dark eyebrow lifted, the sceptical arch matched by the tight smile.

'How very noble of you,' he said. 'But I'm afraid we are due to honeymoon shortly on Isla de la Luna. Have you forgotten that one of the purposes of this marriage was to garner some good publicity for that venture?'

She recoiled at the chilling tone. 'But how can we go on honeymoon now?'

'Of course we can. Now we have your identity, we can make this marriage official.'

'But... But you don't want to be married to me any more?' she whispered, as shock layered over the sick feeling of inadequacy.

'Unfortunately, what I want and what I need are not the same thing,' he said, as the last of her hope died inside her. 'The press is already aware of your identity,' he continued. 'When the story of our betrothal breaks, the vows we have already made will get out too,' he said, the flat, emotionless tone only scaring her more. 'It is too late to undo the marriage now. It would only bring more scandal on this family, which has already suffered enough at your hands.'

She flinched at the furious contempt in his face and the clipped tone, which suggested he was holding onto his temper with an effort.

'None of it was deliberate,' she managed, forced to defend herself.

Even as she said the words, though, the hideous irony struck her.

She'd come to Spain to find out why her mother had run off with Santiago's father that night. And now she understood her mother's decision, because she had done the same thing with Álvaro's son. She had loved his attention, become intoxicated by their livewire sexual chemistry, enough to believe she could build a future with a man she barely knew...

That her mind had tricked her into throwing all caution

away, the way her mother had, was beyond ironic. But so much worse was the yearning that would not stop—for Santiago to still want her, for him to believe she had not meant to hurt him…

'What our parents did was wrong,' she said. 'But my mother was young and in love for the first time,' she continued, not even sure any more if she was trying to defend her mother's choices now, or her own…

Santiago barked out a harsh laugh. 'Don't be foolish. There is no such thing as love. They were two selfish people who decided that screwing each other was more important than facing up to their responsibilities. The only difference is that with your mother, my father chose not to cover it up.'

'How… How do you know that?' she asked, shocked anew by how bitter he sounded.

'Because their affair was not the first time he screwed a woman who was not his wife,' he countered, spitting out the ugly words as if they tasted sour on his tongue. 'Your mother was just one of many women my father took to his bed during his marriage. The first time I saw him humping one of his mistresses was in the bodega when I was eight years old.' The golden shards in his irises glittered with contempt, but under it she could see the pain that child had endured too. And the disillusionment. 'I kept his secrets, out of some childish sense of loyalty, but after that day I knew exactly who he was.'

Despite the hideous things he had said to her, the terrible things he had accused her of, sympathy welled up in her chest because she could hear the shame in his voice.

She'd always known that the tragedy which had befallen his family had had a marked effect on him, that the twin burdens of grief and responsibility thrust upon him as a teenager had made him a man who was determined never to feel too much. But now she understood—his whole childhood had been marred by his father's actions, the one tragic betrayal involving her mother simply a culmination of so many other lies. Did this explain his refusal to trust her now?

'I'm sorry, Santiago. Your father sounds like a selfish man, unworthy of your loyalty and respect. But this is not the same…'

And we don't have to be the same, she thought frantically.

Last night, this morning, every time he had taken her with such need, such passion… It hadn't been just about the sex, and chemistry, it had been so much more than that. She'd seen a man who wanted to make an emotional connection, even if he couldn't admit it to himself or her.

Why was he making them both pay for something they had had no part of?

She reached out to touch his arm—desperate to comfort that boy, desperate to connect again with the man she had seen in the rare moments when he had let his guard down. Moments which seemed even more precious now.

But instead of accepting her compassion, the muscles of his forearm tensed and he drew away from her touch. His expression remained cold and unmoved.

'You're wrong,' he said, the cutting tone thick with sarcasm. 'My decision to have you, no matter the cost to my family and my reputation, proves that I am my father's son after all,' he added, but beneath the brittle anger she could also hear the regret. 'I kept his secrets because I was too scared not to. And because of my cowardice, my mother never understood what a bastard he really was. She had no way to protect herself against his lies—when the truth was exposed for the whole world to see—and so she took her own life.'

His jaw hardened as Cerys's stomach churned. 'What... what are you saying, Santiago? I thought your mother died in childbirth?'

Wasn't that what Ana had said? What the press reports had implied? That the shock of her husband's death had caused his mother to go into premature labour and the subsequent loss of blood had led to her death and her baby's.

'She killed herself, and as a result the child inside her,' he hissed, and her stomach turned to lead as she realised what he was saying. His mother hadn't died from a miscarriage, she'd committed suicide. Which meant what Santiago had endured that summer had been even more horrendous.

'I didn't know she had the pills. I should have realised how much pain she was in...' he continued. He heaved a tortured breath, his gaze becoming haunted. 'She still believed he was a good man, that he was worthy of her love, because of my silence.'

She pressed her palm to his cheek, the muscle in his jaw so rigid her instinct was to soothe. 'That's not true, Santiago. It wasn't your fault. You were just a child.'

His gaze flashed to hers and he jerked his head away from her touch. 'I was man enough to keep his secrets from her for eight years. I knew who he was, and I said nothing. If she had known who he really was—that he had *never* been faithful—she would not have been so shocked by the affair, so devastated when he died. That's on me and I will bear the responsibility for it for the rest of my life.'

'Santiago!' she gasped. 'How can you believe a child of eight could be more culpable than a man of thirty?'

It explained so much, she thought. Why he was so determined to protect his siblings, why he had been determined to protect her—because he believed he had failed to protect his mother... But also why he found it so hard to share his feelings, to be vulnerable, to admit he needed support too. Because he had always been the one to take on the responsibility, to pay the price for his father's crimes...

But where did all these terrible truths leave them?

'We can't legalise this marriage. Not now. Surely you can see that, Santiago,' she said carefully, even as her heart shattered.

She understood now exactly how much he had lost. How badly he had been hurt. But how could she ever hope for more from him now, when she would always be linked in his eyes to the events which had destroyed his childhood?

'We do not have a choice,' he replied, the flat tone only hurting her more.

'But why not?' she asked, desperate now. Leaving the *castillo*, leaving Ana and María and all the other friends she had made here—even Alejandro—would hurt immeasurably.

The friendships she'd made in Spain over the course of a few months had been more intense, much deeper and more real than any others she had made in her life before now, because she'd always been held back by the fear of abandonment which had dogged her until she'd woken in Santiago De Montoya's home.

But how could she stay, when being with Santiago, seeing how much he despised her, would hurt so much more?

The full impact of what she had done dawned on her.

She'd let herself fall in love with this hard, cynical man. Even though he'd never really given her any reason to hope for more from this marriage, she'd felt cherished and important. But what they'd had was a lie. Even if one day he could believe she hadn't faked the amnesia, how could she ever atone for sins that weren't even hers?

She'd spent her whole life being judged for her mother's desertion by her father. She couldn't go through that again—it would destroy what was left of the woman she had discovered in his arms. The woman she might always have been meant to be—reckless, yes, impulsive, and so much like her mother, but also full of passion and hope and love.

'This marriage can still end the scandal which has destroyed my family's honour and reputation—and held my business back for fifteen years...'

'But won't my true identity only reignite the scandal?' she said, trying to make some sense of what he was saying, while her mind was still reeling, her heart still in turmoil.

'Not if we simply state that I knew who you were all along. A marriage between us can then create a new narrative—a love match between us will right the wrongs of our parents' affair... And add a positive spin to the story before we part.'

'B-but you don't love me,' she murmured, sickened by the brutal yearning in her heart. 'You never did... You don't even believe in love...'

'That is easy enough to fake,' he said. 'Especially now we know what a good actress you are.'

She shuddered at the bitter tone.

'I... I won't do it,' she said. 'I can't...'

But when she stepped away from him he clasped her upper arm, dragging her back until his mouth was so close to hers she could feel his breath on her lips.

'Yes, you will. If you care about Ana, about Alejandro, about the future of this family.'

'You... You know I do, but how can telling another lie make this okay?'

God, why had she ever agreed to go through with his marriage bargain? When she'd known she was falling in love with him weeks ago. Maybe even from the first moment he'd held her.

She sucked in a breath, struggled to free herself from his hold. But he held her too firmly.

'Love is always a lie,' he said, shattering any hope that might remain. 'But whatever I have discovered today, I still want you, Cerys,' he murmured, the heat in his eyes part promise, part threat. 'That is one thing that has not changed.' His gaze dropped to her breasts, which had peaked painfully beneath the thin silk, still yearning for his touch. 'And it seems your body still wants me, too.'

She tugged free, scrambled back, stunned by the vicious spike of arousal, the melting sensation at her core.

'I... I don't care what my body wants,' she said, because there was no point in lying, he knew her body too well. He was the only man who did. But where once his touch had given her such joy, all it did now was make her feel more ashamed.

'I don't want to hurt Ana, or your family's reputation,' she added, because she could see that he wasn't wrong about the impact her real identity would make when the press broke the story—especially if they ever discovered that nobody had known her connection to Angharad Jones until today. It wouldn't just reignite the old scandal, it would affect Santiago's reputation personally. He would be viewed as a fool or, worse, a man like his father, too blinded by his own lust to be patient, to think coherently.

Her frantic mind tried to come up with a solution... But she couldn't get past the reality that it wasn't his fault she had lost her memory, any more than it was hers. And that he would never have proposed to her in the first place if he had known who she was.

'We will make the marriage official and then honeymoon at the Isla de la Luna resort,' he murmured, his voice so flat and his eyes so shuttered she could see nothing of the man she thought she knew. 'Once we return in two weeks' time, you can live at the *castillo*, I will live in Madrid, but we will continue to be seen in public, on occasion, until a divorce will not cause too many questions.'

Two weeks? Could she survive for two weeks without letting him know the true depths of her feelings for him, and exposing herself even more?

She thought of all the years she had spent, hiding the hurt from her father, making herself believe it didn't matter if he couldn't see her. That she didn't need his approval, or his love. And it occurred to her that by the time he had died, over six months ago now, none of that hopeful child had been left.

Perhaps going through with this charade for the sake of appearances, would cure the feelings she had developed for Santiago. Feelings which she knew now would never be returned. Even though going through that brutal rejection again would be so much worse, because Santiago had always been a better man than her father. The next two weeks would force her to face the truth, and finally teach that naïve, impulsive, reckless girl not to throw away her heart so easily, or trust too quickly.

Hopelessness engulfed her as she nodded.

'I... I can give you two weeks to repair the damage my identity will cause to your family's reputation,' she said. 'But I won't sleep with you,' she added hastily.

How could she, when she still yearned for his touch?

Something flickered in his eyes, something fierce and possessive, but it was gone so quickly she was sure she must have imagined it. He touched his thumb to her cheek, slid it down to press against the pulse in her collarbone. She pulled away, but the vicious jolt of reaction was impossible to disguise.

'If this is what you wish, Cerys,' he said, but she could see the cynical glitter in his eyes. 'We will leave for Isla de la Luna as soon as your documents can be issued,' he announced. 'And I will have the legal team alter the prenuptial agreement—so the terms of our divorce are already agreed—which you will need to sign.'

The stabbing pain sharpened when suspicion flickered in his eyes.

She nodded. 'Of course.'

Did he really believe she would refuse to sign it? That she would want to prolong this agony? Or profit from a marriage which was devoid of hope now?

As he strode away, her heart sank to her toes. Because pretending not to want him—not to love him—when they were alone together was going to be the hardest lie to pull off of all... But maybe if she could fake *not* loving him, *not* caring for him, or that little boy who had lost his trust in love so long ago—it might become true.

CHAPTER ELEVEN

'WHEN DID YOU *discover your wife was the daughter of your father's mistress, Your Excellency? The child of the woman who destroyed your family.'*

'*Cerys? It is said you did not even remember your own name when you met His Excellency the Duque, is this true?*'

'*Es esta una pasión por los siglos de los siglos, Excelencias?*'

Santiago pressed his hand to the small of his wife's back to direct her past the press piranhas who had been lying in wait at the Ibiza heliport for their arrival.

They'd been legally wed that morning in a short civil ceremony at the *castillo*, witnessed by his legal team. The press release had been issued to announce their marriage and the honeymoon on Isla de la Luna, but it seemed to have done nothing to quell the furore which had been raging for forty-eight hours—starting only a few hours after he had first been handed Angharad Jones's diary.

'No comment. *Sin comentarios!*' He ground the words out as he attempted to shield Cerys from the throng of reporters and photographers all vying for her attention.

His security guards pushed the crowd back from the entrance to the private dock. But even so, he felt Cerys flinch as ever more intrusive and provocative questions were hurled at them in both Spanish and English while they walked the short distance to the launch which would transport them to the island.

He ushered her on board, squeezing her hand as they headed down to the cabin, while the crew cast off. But she dragged her hand free as soon as they were out of view. Much as she had done that morning after they had pledged to honour their marriage vows before the officiant. As if she could not tolerate his touch a moment longer than was necessary.

He took the seat opposite her as they sped away from the private dock. He gripped the leather as the boat lifted into the surf. But he couldn't take his eyes off her profile as she stared out onto the horizon.

She looked pale and tense, her eyes shielded by dark glasses. But he'd seen the shadows under them that morning, when she had arrived in his study to sign the paperwork which would confirm their union and the terms of their divorce. The designer dress the stylist had picked out for the occasion hugged her full breasts and sent a familiar shot of heat through his system.

They would have the resort to themselves—it wasn't due to open for another two weeks. And while he was loath to spend time alone with his wife—when his emotions were still far too volatile—he had also been pathetically pleased to have her within reach all day.

He had given a statement to the press two days ago, stating that he and Cerys were very much in love and that their parents' past had not one thing to do with their future. But the old story—scandalous runaway couple, deadly car accident two weeks later, his mother's subsequent miscarriage and death—had been dredged back up anyway. And the scandalous new twist—that the *Duque*, who looked just like his father, was now wed to Angharad Jones's daughter—had been titillating a nation ever since. Hell, it had spread across several continents. His company's press office had even been contacted for comment by media outlets as far afield as New York and Sydney.

He'd thought he could control the narrative. He'd been wrong. But it wasn't the press furore which had disturbed him the most in the last three days...ever since he had read her mother's diary—and had his emotions thrown into a blender—the demons only intensifying all his fears about how much he had allowed himself to feel for this woman.

He'd wanted to punish Cerys, and he'd done an excellent job, but he'd also ended up punishing himself. He'd been working every hour he could during the day to stay away from her... But at night, as they'd slept in their separate bedrooms in the villa, away from prying eyes, he tossed and turned, desperate to touch her, to hold her, to have her need him as much as he still needed her.

As he studied her, her head downcast, her arms folded around her midriff, something twisted inside him.

Her skin was so pale, her gaze hollow. They had barely exchanged a word since the morning after the church blessing... But even so, their furious argument that day continued to haunt him. Her attempts to comfort him when he'd blurted out the truth about his mother's death... Why the hell had he told her about his mother's suicide, when he'd spent years maintaining the lie she had died in childbirth? And why had Cerys been so devastated by the revelation?

A part of him hadn't wanted her sympathy. But another part of him, the part that had always been determined to keep that truth hidden, had been stunned by her reaction.

She had played her role well in public, had been dignified and aloof as befitted his Duchess... When they were alone, though, she had retreated into herself. But why did he miss the eager, energetic, enthusiastic woman who had once captivated him so much, if the identity of that woman had always been an act?

Having to touch her, to hold her in public, had been its own special kind of torment—especially when they found themselves alone each night and she had rushed off to the villa's second bedroom. Because the yearning for her, always for her, was still there, no matter how many times he tried to suppress it. Why could he not get over the hunger, now he knew who she really was?

Swallowing heavily, he blurted out the demand he had not wanted to voice for days now—every time she closed herself off from him. 'Why are you afraid to look at me when we are alone, Cerys?'

Her head rose, but the tension in her expression made the twisting pain in his gut sharpen.

'I'm not afraid to look at you,' she said above the churn of the water, but he could hear the tremor in her voice and knew she was lying.

'Take off the glasses,' he asked, not convinced by her denial.

She hesitated, but only for a moment, before she lifted them and placed them in her lap. As well as the shadows, he saw wariness. And suddenly he knew she must feel it too, this hunger. This need.

'I'm looking forward to seeing the resort,' she said, the carefully polite tone making the agony in his gut swell, followed swiftly by anger. 'Ana says it's supposed to be beautiful.'

He nodded, recalling his sister's eager send-off before

they had climbed into the helicopter that morning, en route to Ibiza. The fierce hug the two women had shared.

Cerys had kept that part of their bargain. Her strength and poise had been nothing short of heroic when they had informed his siblings of her true identity. With his typical nonchalance, Alejandro had thought it amusing, while Ana had been excited with the romance of it all. That they had both accepted the news—and Cerys's relationship to the woman who had destroyed their family—without question had given him pause, and made him question his own fury when he had discovered the news. How could both his siblings accept her mother's crimes were not her responsibility so easily?

'Perhaps you and Ana could visit the island together when she comes home for Christmas?' she offered. 'She'd love to spend more time with you... I'm sure that's why she's so difficult at times. She just wants more of your attention. And I think our divorce will be tough on her.'

He tensed, the mention of the divorce he had insisted on making the twisting agony become a hollow ache in his chest.

'There is no need to concern yourself with Ana's welfare,' he snapped.

She flinched as if he'd slapped her.

But she said nothing, did not react, did not defend herself. She simply turned back towards the horizon while slipping the sunglasses back on, shutting him out again.

But as he watched her retreat into her shell again, the hollow ache grew.

Perhaps he should apologise for the remark. Cerys's friendship with Ana was something he had always known was real. But *how* could he apologise to her without confronting the fear which had begun to build...? That he might have made a mistake. That the amnesia had always been real. That his reaction to her identity had been about much more than the past.

They remained locked in a fraught silence until the boat powered down, to glide into the bay below the main resort buildings at Isla de la Luna. They were greeted by the resort manager and an army of bellhops as they stepped onto the wooden dock.

The rocky cove was one of several on the two-hundred-square-kilometre land mass which he had purchased uninhabited five years ago. The island was now home to a luxury private villa with an infinity pool, a guest house and eight en suite bedrooms above a horseshoe beach. Smaller luxury cottages were situated next to the resort hub, where a fully equipped gym, a bar and restaurant, a pool complex, a cinema and a Michelin-starred chef were also available to serve the guests.

The heliport was still under construction, which was why they had been forced to fly into Ibiza. But this was the first chance Santiago had had to view the facilities.

A company photographer appeared to snap pictures of them disembarking for the press release which he had agreed with his marketing team. Articles about their honeymoon had already been sold to all the top travel magazines, providing the perfect advertisement for the venue as an exclusive private island rental. At a cost of half a million euro a week to hire as an entertainment or vacation retreat, the resort would be able to recoup its construction costs in less than five years, as long as he did not use it too much himself.

He pressed his palm to his wife's back to guide her to the waiting buggy, and was rocked by the shiver of response she could not hide.

Why would I ever want to come here again without her?

The bitter realisation forced him to face the truth he had been avoiding, that his business interests might never have been the primary reason he had insisted on legalising this marriage and embarking on a two-week vacation—when he never took vacations.

He could smell her, that intoxicating perfume of wild flowers and female musk, as her hip pressed against his on the buggy's narrow bench seat. The hollow ache he didn't understand and did not want to acknowledge tangled with the heat swelling in his groin as the buggy bounced up the road to the resort hub. His gaze became fixed on the rigid line of her spine and the glow of sweat on her cleavage. That damn dress displayed too many of his wife's charms in his humble opinion. The cap of carefully styled curls which framed her high cheekbones and translucent skin only tormented him more, because he couldn't plunge his fingers into the silky mass, or see her luminous blue-green eyes—now hidden by her sunglasses—go dark with need.

'Your Excellency, would you like to tour the facilities at the resort hub?' the manager asked from his seat at the front of the buggy.

'No, take us directly to the villa,' he replied, his gaze still riveted to his wife's profile. 'And tell the staff we would prefer as much privacy as possible during our stay.'

Cerys's head spun round at that request, her cheeks turning a becoming shade of pink.

Finally, he had got his wife's attention without having to demand it.

It took another twenty interminable minutes for them to make the journey on the narrow island track. And ten more for the luggage to be unloaded and the manager to give them a brief tour of the villa before he finally left them alone.

As Santiago stood on the open terrace, contemplating the pool and the beach in the cove below, the need to cut through the oppressive silence increased.

Cerys had remained by his side throughout the endless tour, complimenting the manager on the beauty of the surroundings and the impressive professionalism of his staff. But as soon as the manager said his goodbyes and the buggy had sped off down the road, she had stepped away from him, reestablishing the distance he had come to hate.

As the buggy disappeared over the hillside, she turned, probably intending to retreat to one of the villa's eight bedrooms. Panic sprinted up his spine, but he forced his anger to the fore to disguise it. He reached out to grab her wrist, knowing he could not let her escape from him again.

'Santiago?' Her gaze snapped to his, her shuttered expression making the anger twist and churn in his stomach. But as he captured her other wrist and tugged her around to face him, suddenly he could no longer be sure if his anger was directed at her... Or at himself.

'Don't walk away from me again, Cerys,' he said, the hollow ache becoming a chasm he no longer understood but knew he had to fill. Somehow.

She felt it too, she had to. This incessant need that still controlled them both. Why the hell were they denying it, when they were both being punished for it anyway?

Cerys blinked and stiffened. This was the first time Santiago had touched her in private since that fateful morning after their wedding when he had accused her of so many things.

She forced herself not to struggle against his hold, even as she could feel her pulse beating double time in her collarbone and her nipples tightening into taut peaks to press against the linen of her dress.

He had hurt her. Humiliated her. Judged her. And made her feel like nothing, as her father had for so many years. How could she still want him, still love him so much? It wasn't fair.

'Santiago, what are you doing?' she managed, her voice breaking, even as her spine stiffened.

'Renegotiating our agreement,' he said gruffly, then he grasped her waist to bring her flush against his hardening body.

He lowered his head, his lips so close to hers she could taste his hunger. And her own.

She jolted in his arms, shocked by the soft sob which burst out of her mouth. The pounding heat sank into her sex. He licked across the seam of her mouth, coaxing, careful, requesting entry, and her lips opened before she could stop them.

He explored her mouth, revelling in her surrender, claiming her as he had so many times before. And she was powerless to resist him, her need feral and elemental.

But when he cupped her bottom, tugging her against him until she could feel the full weight of his need, she let out a sound of protest and braced her hands against his chest to wrench herself out of his arms.

'Don't... I can't...' she began, panic rippling through her, the yearning so intense, but the ball of anger and humiliation he had caused anchoring her to reality again. 'I don't want to...'

'Why not?' he asked, his frustration yanking her the rest of the way out of the erotic fog. 'The last few days have been hell. Why should we not make this bargain more bearable?'

'I won't sleep with you. Not when you believe I lied to you about the amnesia.' She tugged her hands free of his grasp, determined to stand her ground, no matter what it cost her. She loved him, but she refused to be a doormat. Refused to let him use her, when he had created the distance between them. Demanded it.

He swore softly and thrust his fingers through his hair.

'I stopped believing that days ago, Cerys. I'm not sure I ever really believed it,' he said, the confession surprising her. But something about the way he said it, grudgingly and without an apology, only made the anguish inside her—which had been building for days—so much worse.

He'd shut her out. And blamed her for something that had never been her fault.

'But you wanted to believe it?' she asked, not ashamed any more to demand answers. '*Why?*'

His gaze met hers, the shame unmistakable before he could mask it. 'Why does it matter now?' he said, the weariness in his tone giving her pause. But she steeled herself against the desire to let him off the hook again. To allow the pain he had suffered as a child take precedence over the pain he had caused her. They had both suffered. Both lost so much. But she wasn't the one who had allowed that pain to destroy what they might have built together.

'It matters to me, Santiago.'

Admiration flared in his eyes and echoed in her heart, but then a harsh laugh broke from his lips.

'You drive a hard bargain, Señora De Montoya. And I mean that literally,' he said.

Her cheeks heated. But she forced her gaze to remain

fixed on his face. She knew a distraction technique when she saw one now… Hadn't he always used sex to stop her getting too close? And like a fool she'd let him. But she wasn't going to fall for that again. No matter how much it cost her.

'I've kept my end of this bargain, Santiago,' she said flatly. 'You can't change the terms of our agreement just because you're horny.'

But as she turned to leave him *again*, he snagged her wrist and held on.

'I want my wife, Cerys. Not just a woman to warm my bed. There is a difference.'

'But I'm not your wife, not really,' she replied, her pulse thundering under his thumb, but her gaze bold and direct. 'This is a temporary marriage in name only, until the scandal has died down again. And then we'll go our separate ways. That's what you wanted.'

'And if I have changed my mind?' he countered.

'You don't get to change your mind, Santiago,' she said, her voice breaking.

The ache in her belly became sharp and jagged, ripping through her defences all over again. But she pushed against the desperate yearning, the longing to have him see her, to have him cherish her again. Because she knew now that he never had, not really. Or he would never have turned on her the way he had.

'If you think I'm going to sleep with a man who hates me you're wrong,' she murmured.

'It is not you I hate…' The words burst out. 'It is *them* I hate…'

He tugged her closer until he could rest his forehead on hers.

'I'm sorry I ever made you believe that, Cerys,' he murmured, his voice raw.

She could feel the tremors racking his body and knew that finally some of the barriers he had erected around his heart were breaking down. But while she couldn't seem to step away from him again, nor could she bring herself to accept his apology.

'Telling me you're sorry is not enough, Santiago,' she whispered.

'Tell me what I must do to fix this and I will,' he said.

She dragged herself back, to stare into his eyes. Seeing the torment, seeing the regret he couldn't hide any more was a start. But she still needed answers. So many answers.

'Then tell me why...' she murmured. 'Why you pushed me away?'

Santiago let out a deep sigh, finally forced to admit to himself what had kept him awake these last three nights...

Not the loss of her body, but the loss of her.

'Reading your mother's journal... It brought back so many demons from that night, when I found my mother. Demons I thought I had conquered, but then I realised I never had. Because wanting you made me feel defenceless, like that boy again. It was easier to pretend what we had was a lie than to accept that I needed you so much.'

Cerys had come into his life and made it richer, sweeter, lighter. And he wanted that back more than anything. It had never been a mistake to ask her to marry him. He could see that now so clearly.

'I am sorry I made this marriage about the past. I don't *want* to live there any more. We can make this what it was always meant to be. It doesn't matter to me that you are her daughter.' He'd always believed she was vulnerable, that she needed his protection, especially when she had struggled to remember her own identity. Why had he not realised until this moment that she needed his protection now more than ever? She had no one. If they divorced, she would be alone, left to handle the press without his support.

'What matters now is that you are my wife.' The guilt dropped into his gut like a stone. Why hadn't he acknowledged too that she had been damaged as well by that cursed affair? She'd lost her mother, just as he had. Why could their shared loss not bond them tighter together? Make them stronger.

All he wanted was to get back what they'd had before he'd read that damn journal.

'You still need a family...' he said. 'A home. And I can still give you that.'

She drew away to stare into his eyes and the shimmer of tears made his insides clench. Why didn't she look pleased with his offer? Hadn't he bared his soul enough?

She blinked slowly but, as she stared back at him, all he could see was the regret in her eyes which made him feel defenceless again.

'And what would I be giving you, Santiago?' she asked softly.

Panic joined the grinding pain in his gut. Was this a trick question? What did she expect him to say?

'I still require a wife,' he said, even though he wasn't sure any more that his hunt for a suitable bride had ever been the real reason he had proposed marriage to Cerys—after only one night. Had he ever been able to think clearly, to think pragmatically, where she was concerned? 'And you are still the only woman I want.'

At least he knew that was still the truth.

'That's not enough for me any more, Santiago. I want more. And I always did. So much more.'

He cursed under his breath. His panic and confusion increased tenfold until the grinding pain in his stomach felt like a monster, ready to rip him apart.

Was she punishing him for being a hot-headed bastard three days ago? For accusing her of things he had always known in his heart she was innocent of? He knew he deserved to be punished for hurting her like that, but why could she not forgive him, when she had forgiven so much else? So they could go back to where they'd been.

'What more is there?' he asked at last.

'*Love.*'

The single word struck his chest. And seemed to ricochet in his heart—the heart he had guarded so carefully, protected so zealously, for so long. The heart he had never been able to protect from her.

'*Dios!*' he swore, suddenly terrified. 'What nonsense is this?'

She flinched, much as she had done when he'd spoken to her so harshly on the launch, but instead of looking weary or hurt, he saw the spark in her eyes he had missed so much.

'It's not nonsense to me, Santiago, because I love you.'

Cerys's heart broke at Santiago's stricken reaction before he could mask it.

It had been so hard in the last three days and nights to contain her feelings for him, and deal with the death of all the hopes she'd harboured for their marriage. Containing the incessant yearning every time he looked at her with desire in his eyes, every time his palm settled on the small of her back—so protective, so possessive—to shield her from the press, to declare her as his. Or his fingers gripped her elbow, her hand, her wrist to keep the pretence alive that he was madly in love. All of it had been torture for her.

But knowing she still loved him, and knowing he couldn't return her love, had been so much worse.

This morning, when she'd signed the marriage documents, while he stood beside her, so close and yet so closed off, it had hurt the most. Because instead of being a beginning, it had been the end. And the irony of that had seemed exceptionally cruel.

It had hurt too, hugging Ana goodbye and knowing she was unlikely to ever see Santiago's sister again—because by the time she returned from her new boarding school at Christmas, their divorce would surely have gone ahead.

The pain had been even more brutal as she had watched the *castillo* disappear from view that morning as the helicopter had lifted into the sky. Scanning the patchwork of vines, the woods she had roamed with Ana, the villa on the edge of the orchard Santiago had filled with wildflowers just for her, and knowing the place she'd wanted to make her home could never be one now, even though she had agreed to remain there until the divorce.

But when he'd told her on the boat ride here that she need not concern herself with Ana's welfare any more, the thick fog she had used to anaesthetise her from the pain for days had been ripped away...

And his crude attempts at seduction had finally forced her to confront her own culpability.

How could she have been such a coward? So what if she loved him! Why had she let him set the agenda?

Again.

She wanted to leave the past behind. Their parents' crimes had never been their crimes, and she was glad he understood that now. Glad he had finally admitted that he had accused her to protect himself.

But she had wanted to make a life with him... So why had she *ever* been ready to settle for a marriage without love? To let him hide behind the shield he put around his emotions and never let her in, not all the way.

Was there still a tiny portion of that little girl lurking inside her who had always blamed herself for her mother's desertion? The girl who had internalised her father's rejection without even realising it.

Before meeting Santiago, she'd always been so wary of sex, so scared of allowing herself to be vulnerable, to commit to anyone. She'd yearned for a family but had always felt responsible for being alone. Because her father had never seen her when he looked at her, never loved her after her mum's desertion, never made her feel valued or cherished. So, when Santiago had looked at her the morning after their wedding wearing the same expression her father had worn so often—with judgement and indifference—she'd internalised that too.

Surely that had to be why she had been so scared of fighting for what she needed.

From what Santiago had told her about his father's affairs, she knew her mother had been wrong to think Álvaro De Montoya was a man who could love her. Their brief, selfish affair had been an illusion built on desire and desperation—and it had *always* been bound to fail.

But why had she given up on her feelings for Santiago so easily? When she knew in her heart Santiago was a much better man than his father had ever been.

She'd seen those precious glimpses of the boy his father had tried so hard to destroy. The playful, kind, protective man. The man who loved and respected his family so much he had blamed himself for his mother's suicide. The fierce, possessive lover who had always put her pleasure above his own—and had been distraught at the thought that he had taken advantage of her. Even the obsessive workaholic who had fought so hard to provide a stable home for his family ever since he was sixteen.

But inside that man was also the boy who was terrified of taking a chance on love. Terrified of exposing himself again to the rejection he'd suffered as a child from the man who should have protected him.

'If you love me,' he said, his voice breaking, 'why will you not agree to stay in this marriage?'

She placed her hand on his cheek, the five o'clock stubble abrading her palm.

'Because I need you to love me back, Santiago,' she said, finally demanding what she should have demanded weeks ago, when he had first proposed to her.

His jaw tensed. 'But I'm not sure I am capable of that...' he murmured, but behind the doubt she could hear the terror.

Tears prickled at the back of her eyes, because she could see the broken boy so clearly now, behind the man.

'Oh, Santiago. Of course you are.'

He lifted his head, his gaze tortured, and so vulnerable... He let out a ragged breath. 'How can you know that?'

She nodded, tears falling down her cheeks, suddenly realising it had always been so simple. That by loving him, being open and honest about her feelings—and forcing him to be open and honest about his own feelings too—she could make him see that he deserved love, just as she did.

'You're just scared,' she said. 'Because your father made you feel responsible for his failings. Just like my dad made me think that somehow, I was responsible for my mum running out on him. But the truth is neither of us deserved to be judged for what they did.'

He shuddered, as if the last of the barriers he had put around his heart were crashing down before her very eyes. She knew it hurt. Because it hurt her too, to see him so scared and so unsure.

'But you have to open your heart to me, Santiago,' she said, letting the last of the fear go. 'You have to make yourself vulnerable to love again. You have to be honest with me about your feelings. *All* your feelings. Or we'll never really have any more than they did.' She sent him a watery smile, her desperate need for him to let her in the rest of the way all that mattered now. 'And look how that turned out.'

He brushed a tear away with his thumb.

'I do have feelings for you, Cerys. So many feelings I do not recognise. Feelings I have been terrified of admitting, even to myself,' he said.

She pressed her hand to his cheek, letting her heart lead when his eyes flared with emotions he had never let her see before.

'Ditto,' she whispered. 'Do they still scare you?' she asked, her breath trapped in her lungs, the anticipation more than she could bear.

He pressed his forehead to hers, let out a long sigh. '*Sí*, but losing you scares me more…'

She clasped his head, drew him back so he could see everything she felt, everything she needed. 'They terrify me too, Santiago, but the good news is, being scared together is so much better than being scared apart.'

He let out a harsh laugh, his eyes darkening not just with desire now, but also with longing. And love.

'You are so brave, Cerys,' he said, making her heart swell against her chest. 'You make me feel brave too.'

She grinned back at him. 'Brave enough to give those feelings a chance?' she asked, but she could already see the answer in his eyes.

'I am not sure I ever had a choice,' he said ruefully. But then he dragged her into his arms and placed a gentle kiss on her lips, full of emotion and desire. 'But yes, brave enough to try…'

Tears of gratitude spilled over her lids and she sniffed, the emotion so immense she could feel her heart shattering all over again. But in a good way this time. 'Then I guess we're still married,' she whispered.

He laughed, the sound deep and husky with relief. But then he yanked her the rest of the way into his embrace, urgency surging between them. 'Will you let me have you now, Cerys? My wife. My love.'

She nodded—because her hunger was vicious and desperate too.

'*Gracias a Dios.*' He grasped her waist and lifted her into his arms. But as he carried her into the bedroom, it wasn't just her sex which was throbbing so hard she felt giddy with need and longing, it was her heart, too.

They had barely got through the bedroom door before he was stripping her dress from her, palming her bottom, sucking her turgid nipples through the thin lace of her bra, his hand sinking into her panties to find her wet and needy.

They tore off each other's clothing and he positioned her on the bed on all fours. She choked out a sob, the need a rush of pheromones and emotions.

'I cannot wait... Can you take me?' he asked, his voice gruff with desperation.

'Yes...' The word was dragged from the depths of her soul. Even though a part of her knew she was giving up an essential part of herself, she knew now it would be safe in his keeping.

But then she couldn't think any more as he drove deep into her yearning flesh. She gasped, the thick intrusion as immense as always as he impaled her in one all-consuming thrust.

She sobbed, taken, possessed, the orgasm already building—so fast, so furious, so devastating. He pumped his hips, forcing her to take more, to take all of him, until he hit the spot only he had ever found.

She cried out as the first orgasm crested. His hands captured her swinging breasts to anchor them both, so he could pump harder and faster—another orgasm built, fusing with the first, turning torturous pleasure to exquisite pain.

The delirious climax shattered in endless waves, leaving her raw, spent, exhausted, as he shouted out his own release and collapsed on top of her.

But then he whispered into her hair, his arms wrapping tight around her, 'You are my wife, my *duquesa*, my love, Cerys.'

Her heart crested at the astonished wonder in his tone, the sure steady feel of his heart beating against her back.

'I never want to let you go again,' he said, his voice thick with emotion.

'Ditto, *el Duque*,' she murmured, her heart soaring as his rich chuckle of appreciation reverberated in her soul.

EPILOGUE

Ten months later

'Feliz cumpleaños, Ana!'

A cheer went up around the courtyard, which was decked out in a cascade of fairy lights. The birthday girl beamed at Cerys as she accepted the congratulations of the friends she had made at the local high school in the past six months. Ever since Cerys had insisted her sister-in-law come home for good from her latest boarding school to live permanently with her and Santiago at the *castillo*.

Santiago's arms wrapped around Cerys's midriff and he pulled her back against his chest to nuzzle her ear. 'You spoil my sister, Cerys,' he whispered, but she could hear the amusement in his voice and knew he was joking.

It had been a little awkward at first, having Ana home—especially as Santiago seemed incapable of keeping his hands off her for more than a few hours at a time. But it had been the right thing to do, she decided as she watched Ana blow out the candles on the huge cake María and her team had been working on for days.

Ana deserved a home too, and it had been nothing short of wonderful watching Santiago finally start to bond with his sister. And watching Ana grow into a much more mature and sensible young woman—give or take the odd outrageous attempt to provoke him.

Plus they still had enough privacy—the *castillo* had six hundred rooms, and they lived in the villa on the edge of the vineyards. Not only that, but they also had to do a lot of travelling, to Madrid and Barcelona, for her new job as the *castillo*'s hospitality manager, as well as for Santiago's work.

She knew her husband had created the position to appease her—when she'd started making noises again, a few weeks after their honeymoon was over, about working for a living. But she also knew she'd pleased him with how much she'd loved doing it. And how much she had managed to achieve, which had actually surprised her a lot more than it had ended up surprising Santiago, who had turned out to be her biggest cheerleader.

She'd been nervous as hell that first day, not sure her extensive skills as a barista, a barmaid and a waitress really qualified her to manage anything. The good news was, at first it had only been her running the new programme which she had developed herself. She'd been able to reassure herself that if her ideas were dumb and she failed, at least no one would be made to pay for her mistakes but her.

She now had a staff of six people, and the new luxury wine-tasting banquets, which finished off the tours the vineyard had been doing for years, had not only boosted that area of the business but had also garnered some fabulous reviews and were now a thriving success. The fact that she adored her job didn't hurt either, and the chance to contribute something to the family and the man who had given her so much.

'She deserves to be spoilt, she's been invaluable as a hostess this month,' she shot back.

She'd hired Ana to host some of the new summer banquets they had added to the schedule as soon as she'd finished her final exams at the local high school. And while Santiago had frowned a little at the thought of his sister working for him, Ana had loved it—and quickly proved herself to be reliable and hard-working. And her confidence had soared every time Santiago showed her he trusted her and praised her work, which Cerys had encouraged him to do at every available opportunity.

She had adored arranging the surprise party, knowing that Ana would love the chance to celebrate her eighteenth birthday with her schoolfriends and the colleagues she'd made at the bodega. But as she watched the girl rush through the crowd to hand the first slice of cake to the bodega manager Joaquín—who was brooding silently from his place on the sidelines—she was glad Santiago was too busy nuzzling her neck to notice the bright light of infatuation in his sister's eyes. She supposed she'd have to have a sisterly chat with Ana about that.

But she didn't want to come on too strong.

Because, *wow*, she knew exactly what that giddy rush of first love felt like when Santiago's hands settled over her belly, and her heart did a backflip.

After all, she was still totally infatuated with Ana's brother.

She sighed and covered Santiago's hands with hers, stupidly happy, but also nervous.

The DJ she'd hired began to play a recent pop track Cerys knew Ana loved, while the disco lights on the temporary dancefloor set up under the trees began to throb in time with the heady tune. The teenagers began to cheer again, pairing off to dance.

'Is this our chance to slip away?' Santiago murmured against her ear, his hands still caressing her belly in that slow, seductive way he had that made all her pheromones throb in time with the music's bass beat.

Cerys grinned, even as the anxious little knots in her belly tweaked.

Once they were alone tonight she would have to tell him about the test she had taken that morning. The test no one but María knew anything about—and only because she'd had to ask the housekeeper to procure it for her while she'd been busy in the last week organising Ana's party, as well as developing a new banqueting roster for the autumn.

The test she had been sure, before she took it, she wanted to be negative.

It was too soon, they hadn't discussed children, she wasn't even sure how the heck it had happened, given that she had been on the pill. But there had been that one incident two months ago when she had forgotten to renew her prescription. She'd only missed a couple of days though, and Dr Mendoza had reassured her she would be very unlikely to conceive, so she hadn't even mentioned the lapse to Santiago…

But when she'd taken the test that morning—just as a precaution, because she'd been feeling so tired lately and had even been sick one evening, after work—and the extra red cross had appeared, her somersaulting heart had told a very different story.

Apparently, she was overjoyed. But when she glanced over her shoulder now, to press a hand to her husband's cheek and whisper, 'Absolutely, María said she'd keep an eye on things...' all her nerves about her news reappeared...

Santiago grunted. '*Gracias a Dios.*'

Holding her hand, he headed through the crowd of gyrating teenagers until they reached Ana.

'*Feliz cumpleaños*, Ana. I'm so proud of you,' he said, pressing a fatherly kiss to his sister's forehead.

Ana grinned, flushing with pleasure at his praise. Then she threw her arms around them both to thank them for the party.

'We will leave you now to enjoy yourself. Be good, okay?' Santiago added.

Cerys had to blink back a sudden rush of emotion. He would make such a wonderful father. He was so protective, so sure and steady, but also so kind and so affectionate in his own gruff way.

Ever since he had begun to let his guard down, he had begun to understand how much he had to give and to gain by letting people in. And she had seen him grow into the man he had always been meant to be. And it made her so happy.

But even as the joy burst in her chest, the knots in her stomach remained...

She was worried about how he was *really* going to feel about this new responsibility, when he'd already had so many other responsibilities thrust upon him in his life. She knew he would accept it instinctively, and if he knew how excited she was about the pregnancy he would keep any misgivings he had about the baby to himself.

But ever since that scary, beautiful day on Isla de la Luna, when they had made a commitment to each other to let go of the past so they could build on their future together, trust had been the key. And admitting what you needed, as well as what you wanted, however terrifying it was.

But if she was going to discover what he really thought about becoming a dad, she would have to bend that promise a little and keep her own reaction to the news neutral, so he wouldn't feel the need to hide his true feelings again.

'Don't worry, Santiago. I won't do anything you two wouldn't,' Ana replied cheekily, breaking Cerys out of her thoughts, and making Santiago curse softly under his breath.

'*Dios*,' Santiago said as Ana skipped off to join her friends. The mix of concern and compassion and pride in his eyes as he watched his sister disappear into the crowd made Cerys's heart melt even more. 'That does not reassure me in the least,' he grumbled.

Cerys laughed.

But as he grasped hold of her hand to lead her through the orchard to their private villa, away from the raucous party, the throbbing pop music and teenage exuberance was soon drowned out by her erratic pulse… And she had to swallow to contain the prickle of anxiety once more.

'I love you so much, Señora De Montoya,' Santiago murmured as he pressed his wife back against the closed door of the villa, unable to keep his hands off her. 'I hope you know that…' he added, cupping her face as he kissed her lips.

She kissed him back, with hunger, with love, but when he eased back and she smiled at him, he could see the flicker of uncertainty, even panic, in her eyes, too.

And his heart got trapped in his throat, right behind the words which he had been so desperate to say to her all day long… Ever since he had returned home from the fields to take a shower before Ana's party and spotted the corner of the box half buried in the bathroom trash.

And of course, once he'd realised what it was, he'd had to dig out the test itself, then avidly read the instructions...

The burst of joy in his heart and the rush of pure masculine pride and pleasure had been so immense, once he'd realised exactly what he was seeing, he'd been lightheaded. In fact, he'd had to sit down on the bed and spend several moments forcing himself to breathe... He'd never fainted before in his life, but he'd been so giddy it had been touch and go there for a while.

All he'd wanted to do in that moment was find Cerys, throw his arms around her, lift her up, spin her round and then probably never let her go again in this lifetime.

But that had been three hours ago now. Three hours as he had watched her preparing the last of the arrangements for Ana's party. Dealing with the guests, coordinating the surprise, greeting everyone... And he'd waited for her to drag him to one side to tell him the news. And she hadn't.

Not only that, but once he'd calmed down enough to think straight, he'd realised that she must have known about the pregnancy when she'd come to the bodega to meet him for lunch eight hours ago now... And again, she'd said nothing.

He'd been watching her so closely in the past hour, unable to stop himself from touching her, running his hands over the space where their child was already growing, while willing all his fears to subside. But now as he watched her glance down and tug her bottom lip beneath her teeth, the panic which had been building like a summer storm threatened to consume him. And forced him to ask himself the question he had been trying not to ask for three hours.

What if she wasn't as overjoyed about this news as he was?

Their life had been wonderful, exciting, so full of fun and love in the past ten months. But it had also been chaotic, insanely busy and overwhelming. She had built a career for herself at the bodega, built a home for his family in the *castillo*, become his wife and his *duquesa*, forced into the public eye, while deftly handling the media attention which he had always hated with charm and grace.

He knew she loved him. He would never doubt that. But maybe she was not ready for this development. Maybe she was exhausted by all the changes. And what right did he have to push this on her, when she had already taken on so much for him?

But what the hell would he do if she didn't want to keep his child? When he wanted so much to see her body grow round with his baby, to see her nurture it, to see her become an amazing mother…

They had changed the narrative of their family's history, from tragedy to triumph, with their love. But it had been exhausting as well as exhilarating at times. He understood that.

But as he watched her struggle, he felt the rush of love consume him all over again.

They had built this marriage on honesty. On trust as well as love. And they would get through this moment like so many others. He had to believe that.

Tucking a knuckle under her chin, he lifted her face until that translucent blue-green gaze connected with his.

'Cerys…' he said, skimming his thumb over her bottom lip, chewed raw now. 'Is there something you wish to tell me?'

She blinked slowly, the pink flush galloping up her

neck, but the naked hope in her eyes had every one of his fears dissolving as the giddy rush of joy forced him to lock his knees again.

'You... You know?' she whispered. 'How do you know?'

He grinned. *Dios*, this woman... How could he adore her any more?

'Five minutes spent digging through the bathroom trash...' He huffed, trying to sound indignant but getting overjoyed instead. 'Why exactly do you use so many tissues, by the way?'

Her gaze lit up with the innocent joy he loved.

'You're not upset?' she asked, even though she had to be able to see his answer, because it felt as if his whole body was lit up too.

'About the fact that you are having my baby?' His gaze dipped and he pressed his hand to her belly, to caress the spot where their son or daughter was probably already the size of a pea. 'No... I am ecstatic.'

He dipped his head to capture her sob of relief on his lips in a reverent kiss. But then he reached around her waist to pull her tightly against him, the heat surging as it always did, alongside the joy, and whispered in her ear, 'Your tissue addiction, though, is a problem we may need to remedy.'

She was still laughing as he carried her up to their bedroom to show her exactly how much he worshipped and adored her... And how much he would love all the children he hoped to give her one day.

* * * * *

QUEEN BY ROYAL COMMAND

ANNIE WEST

MILLS & BOON

For dear Abby Green

Who organises the best surprises!

CHAPTER ONE

ANNALENA PAUSED IN the palace's opulent vestibule. All around were the trappings of old wealth and power. The floor of multicoloured marble. Gilded lanterns, huge tapestries and statues by ancient masters.

The triple-height space was topped by a frescoed ceiling that art lovers travelled the world to see. It showed the continents, their people portrayed with improbable romanticism. Grand princes, warriors and scholars. The only women were naked or nearly so, subservient or simpering admiringly. Naked women because that was what the men who'd commissioned it liked to look at, and subservient because that was their place in the world.

Some things apparently hadn't changed in three hundred years.

If Annalena and her grandmother had been male, the powers that be wouldn't have spurned them so insultingly.

'Can I help? Are you here for a tour of the public rooms?'

She turned to see a guide, gesturing to the tourists gathering on one side of the vast space. 'No, thank you. I'm here on business.'

His eyes widened as he tried and failed not to stare at her clothing. As if he couldn't believe she could have business in the royal palace.

Despite her nerves, Annalena felt her lips twitch as he walked away.

She'd thought hard about what to wear to today's meeting. Formal, of course. Initially she'd reached for the suit she'd worn last week to meet the international consortium looking to invest in a joint research project.

But she'd changed her mind and opted for tradition.

Once upon a time she'd hoped the man she'd come to meet was nothing like his father, with his complete disregard for anything except making quick money, no matter the cost to the country. But Benedikt had shown himself to be just as imperious and greedy. Uncaring of tradition and the fact some things were too precious to be destroyed. Her grandmother had raised an eyebrow when she'd seen Annalena ready to travel to the capital. But there'd been laughter in her eyes and approval in her tone when she'd said, 'I see you plan to make a statement, my dear. Good for you. It's a perfect time to remind him we're all custodians of our country. It's not all about his bank balance.'

Annalena made her way across the vestibule towards the royal offices. Her low-heeled shoes tapped purposefully across the expensive marble.

As she neared the closed door, security intervened. 'I'm sorry. This is closed to the public.'

She surveyed the dark-suited man and smiled, belying her thumping heart. For she *was* an interloper, worried at the possibility of failing. Because of her family she'd never had the luxury of being just average, but nor did she belong here. 'I know. I have an appointment.'

She didn't know whether it was a curse or a blessing that so few people in the capital knew her by sight. In the Grand Duchy of Edelforst she was well known. But in Prinzenberg's capital it was different. Her fault for avoiding the place so long.

Who could blame her, given her family history?

Dread pooled in her stomach and a shudder rippled down her spine. She'd grown up viewing this as the sinister centre of the disaster that had engulfed her family.

She'd never set foot in this building and had hoped never

to do so. But some things were more important than personal inclination. Besides, she wasn't a child, to be frightened by long ago events.

Yet she couldn't help wondering if Benedikt was as dangerous as his father had been.

The guard looked at her closely. Annalena told herself it was because she didn't look like the usual sort of visitor. She couldn't have betrayed her disquiet. She'd been too well trained to conceal emotions behind a serene mask.

'I wasn't told about a visitor. Who are you seeing?'

Annalena pushed her shoulders back, projecting some of her grandmother's hauteur. 'His Majesty. A ten a.m. meeting.'

'Just a moment, please.'

The guard frowned, half turning away as he spoke into a mouthpiece. Heads turned in their direction.

Good. Let them stare. The more people to witness her arrival, the less chance anyone would dare throw her out.

For the hard-won appointment she'd finally managed to schedule had been cancelled very late last night.

Cancelled without explanation, let alone apology or an offer to reschedule. Given the difficulty she'd had trying to make contact with the man, she shouldn't have been surprised. It was clear she, and her concerns, weren't important enough for royal attention.

That made fury fizz in her veins. She welcomed it as an improvement on nerves.

The people she represented had been patient. They'd followed the proper channels. Yet every attempt to get a hearing had been stymied, every submission met with offensively vague responses.

His Majesty wasn't interested.

He'd soon learn his mistake.

Yet she had to force herself not to press her hand to her stomach where butterflies the size of Alpine eagles swooped and swirled.

The guard turned back. 'I'm sorry, His Majesty's staff have no appointment scheduled.'

'One was made and I've travelled some distance to be here.' She withdrew her phone and showed him the original email.

The man's eyebrows rose as he read her name. He looked decidedly uncomfortable when he met her eyes again. 'I'm very sorry, ma'am, but I was told…' He stood straighter. 'I can't admit you.'

Which was what she'd expected. 'Very well, I'll wait.'

She walked around him to a gilded, antique chair a few metres from the door.

He hurried after her, but not in time to prevent her sitting. 'I really have to ask you to—'

'This is a public area.' She smiled at him. 'Perhaps you'd inform His Majesty's office that I'll wait until it's convenient to see him.'

She knew the King would consider any time inconvenient but she'd given up waiting for him to act decently. If she had to shame him into meeting, so be it.

Faces turned in her direction, the sightseeing group and staff too. The harried guard whispered urgently into his mouthpiece.

Annalena settled in her seat and tapped her phone. She might as well answer work emails while she waited.

She was absorbed in a report when she heard voices. Without looking up she knew the door to the offices had opened and someone was conferring with the guard.

She checked the time. Half an hour had elapsed. Maybe they'd hoped she'd grow bored and leave. Fat chance!

High heels clacked then stopped before her. Annalena kept reading.

'Excuse me, ma'am.'

It was the guard. She looked up to see he was accompanied by a woman in a sleek charcoal suit, silk shirt and air of sophistication. Her perfect make-up didn't conceal the way her mouth clamped tight.

'Hello,' Annalena said, taking the initiative. 'Are you from his Majesty's office? I—'

'I'm afraid you're wasting your time. The King isn't available.'

Annalena blinked slowly, letting her eyes widen as if no one had ever spoken across her before. Clearly she wasn't going to be offered the courtesy of an introduction either.

The woman lifted her chin. 'You were sent an email. The meeting was cancelled yesterday.'

Annalena let the silence stretch. 'It took well over a month to arrange this meeting and I've come from Edelforst solely to see the King on an urgent matter. I know he's here today so I'll wait and hope space opens up in his schedule.'

The nameless woman frowned, eyes narrowing as she opened her pinched mouth. Annalena forestalled her. 'If you'll excuse me, I'll get back to my work while I wait. His Majesty isn't the only one with a busy schedule.'

She turned to her phone, but not before she saw the woman's jaw clench while the guard beside her veiled a smile.

Annalena's last comment was unnecessary. She'd been raised to be polite, especially given her position. But the woman was rude and Annalena didn't take kindly to bullying. That was what the King of Prinzenberg and his minions tried to do.

So much for her grandmother's insistence the new monarch would be an improvement on the old. Her 'informed sources' had got it wrong.

Heels clicked away and a door closed. Yet it took Annalena a good five minutes to pick up the thread of the report.

She was halfway through it when someone cleared their throat.

It was the burly security guard. Behind him followed a man who deposited a tray on a small table that had appeared beside her. The scent of coffee hit her nostrils and she inhaled appreciatively. Coffee, cream, sugar and cinnamon biscuits.

She beamed at the newcomer, reading his name badge. 'Thank you, Reiner. I didn't have time for morning coffee.' And she'd been too nervous to eat.

He smiled and shook his head, nodding towards the guard before he left. 'It was Udo's idea.'

She turned. 'Udo. That's very kind. I appreciate it.'

Faint colour crept across the big man's cheeks and he murmured something non-committal before returning to his post.

It seemed the King's personal staff were happy to ignore her but other palace employees weren't.

What did that say about the new King of Prinzenberg? That common courtesy didn't matter to him?

Now she found it difficult to concentrate on work. She stared at the screen but it wasn't words she saw. It was Edelforst's wide valleys, the meadows and vast forests, farmland surrounded by towering mountains. The villages and compact towns. The people who loved their land and had struggled hard for generations to support themselves.

Her vision blurred, eyes glazing.

Everything rode on this. She couldn't afford to lose.

'Your Majesty…'

Benedikt shook his head. 'I told you to ditch the title, Matthias, at least when we're alone.' He'd never liked royal pomp. That had been his father's thing.

Thinking about the old man soured his mood. Even now King Karl cast a long shadow.

'Of course.' His private secretary and closest confidant grinned. 'But I worry one day I'll forget in public and call you Benno.' He paused. 'We need to find a gap in your diary.'

Benedikt laughed and leaned back from his desk. 'Good luck. I've seen the timetable for the next month.'

'I'm not talking about later in the month. I mean today. There's a…problem with the schedule.'

Matthias had handled his schedule for years, juggling commitments in Prinzenberg along with Benedikt's business interests across three continents. He couldn't remember problems before. Not in that tone of voice. Not with that frown of disapproval.

'Tell me what happened.'

'Nothing I can't handle, but—'

'Tell me anyway.'

His old friend sighed. 'The same thing. Staff here take it upon themselves to vet who and what you see. They think they're doing right but forget to consult me first.'

'They're still loyal to my father. Or at least his ways.'

Benedikt's mouth tightened. He'd been young when he discovered how little he liked his father's ways. Which was why, from the time he'd had any say in it, he'd spent so much time outside Prinzenberg even though he loved it. He'd only returned full-time following his father's recent death.

'They'll learn. I'll make sure of it. But it takes time.' Matthias sighed. 'Meanwhile, you have a visitor.'

'If he's not on the schedule I haven't got time.'

'She *was* on the schedule. I put her there. But someone decided she didn't need to see you.' He let that sink in. 'She turned up anyway. She's been in the palace vestibule for almost three hours. I've only just found out.'

'Three hours! In the vestibule?' He paused, watching Matthias's expression turn ever more sombre. It seemed worse was to come. 'Who is she?'

'The Grand Duchess of Edelforst's granddaughter. Princess Annalena.'

What was a member of Edelforst's most senior family doing here? What administrator in their right mind thought it okay to put her off and not tell him?

As if Benedikt didn't have enough to deal with. His coronation was fast approaching and he was still fighting spot fires left by his father, made more difficult by the fact his father had been secretive about so much. Karl had jealously guarded his business dealings as well as his power and prestige, even from his heir.

Relations between the Grand Duchess and Benedikt's father had been frosty, if not downright inimical. As the Grand Duchy was a semi-autonomous province of Prinzenberg, in the end his father had left the place to run itself.

The Grand Duchess had a lot of power in the province, which had traditionally been ruled along matriarchal lines. Outside her province she technically had no political authority but she was respected, even revered nationally, though she hadn't been seen outside Edelforst for years.

Insulting her granddaughter was *not* how Benedikt wanted to begin their relationship. He'd planned to visit but kept being delayed as he uncovered yet more urgent problems left by his father.

There was a knock on the door before it opened. He sighed and rose, an apology forming for her wait. But surprise caught his tongue as Matthias ushered her in.

The young woman's dark blonde hair was plaited, arching over her head in an old-fashioned coronet that added to her height. Instead of modern dress she wore a dirndl of forest green, figured with silver. A decorative apron of pale green covered her skirt, the fabric betraying its cost with a shimmer of silk.

Her tightly fitted, laced-up bodice moulded a narrow waist and round breasts, the low décolletage revealing the edge of an embroidered white blouse beneath it.

There was no cleavage on show and her skirt fell just below her knees but Benedikt's skin prickled in instant male awareness.

His skimming glance rose to the dark green velvet ribbon around her throat with its silver pendant. Worn like a choker, it emphasised her slender neck and the soft-looking skin sloping down to her breasts.

Benedikt swallowed, shocked by his instant response. His fingers twitched and his lower body hardened, his breath stalling.

The dirndl was the national dress of Prinzenberg, rarely worn in the capital except at festivals. Even in her province of Edelforst, it wasn't worn daily. His parents had regarded it as terminally old-fashioned and he'd thought of it as appealing but country cute.

This woman wore it like a weapon.

She looked magnificent. And incredibly sexy.

His first appraisal took in her traditional clothes and slender body. His second lingered on her face. Taking in eyes the green of a mountain tarn and lips that curved like the proverbial Cupid's bow.

Dimly Benedikt was aware of his heartbeat quickening and her eyes widening as she stared too, looking almost as taken aback as he was.

His vision flickered as something hard and fierce pulsed between them. Something he felt low in his belly and high in his tightening chest.

Imagination, he told himself. The result of too little sleep and too many hours unravelling the murky web of his father's business dealings.

Matthias broke the silence, murmuring introductions before bowing his way out. Leaving them alone.

Benedikt moved from behind his desk. 'It's a pleasure to meet you, Princess.'

He held out his hand just as she lowered her gaze and bobbed in a brief curtsey that was graceful but not at all subservient.

His hand fell. She mustn't have seen him reach to shake her hand.

When she lifted her head her steady stare set off warning bells. She didn't look like a supplicant. Nor a well-wisher. Her even features were composed, almost expressionless. Too expressionless.

'My sincere apologies that you had to wait to see me. That was most unfortunate.'

'As you say. But I managed to get some work done while waiting.'

Her words were even yet held a note of provocation. A reminder that her time was valuable too?

He gestured for her to precede him to a pair of leather lounges facing each other. 'Please, take a seat.'

There was a refined rustle of silk as she passed him and he found himself watching her graceful walk. Not the hip-swinging sway of a woman in high heels to which he'd grown accustomed. Her movements were more fluid and she sank onto the chesterfield with a grace that made him imagine her swirling around the palace's grand ballroom in a long gown.

'I only learned a few minutes ago that you were here.'

Her eyes widened before her forehead crinkled in a frown. 'Yet I spoke to one of your staff soon after I arrived.'

She doesn't believe a word you said.

It was there in her carefully bland expression and too tight jaw. And the angle of her chin, not precisely aggressive but not compliant either.

Benedikt wondered what it would be like to have this woman compliant, or, better yet, pleased and eager to see him. His palms prickled with a phantom sensation as he imagined holding her. Her chin would lift, not in pride or wariness, but to bring her lips closer to his.

Adrenaline shot through his bloodstream, making his pulse pound.

He took a seat opposite and banished the fantasy. Later, when there was time, he'd unpick how she'd planted such thoughts in his hitherto pragmatic brain.

Unlike his father, he *never* let sex interfere with his obligations.

'My private secretary will get to the bottom of the miscommunication. In the meantime, again, my apologies. Can I offer you refreshments?'

'Thank you, no. I had some recently.'

No breaking bread with the enemy, then.

She certainly wasn't here as a friend, come to congratulate him on his accession to the throne.

His father had complained about her feisty grandmother, getting in the way of his modernisation plans.

When he was younger Benedikt hadn't paid much attention other than to silently applaud anyone courageous enough to get in his father's way. It seemed the old lady's granddaughter had the same strength of character.

'If you don't mind,' she said, sitting straighter, 'I'll get straight to business.'

'By all means. Which business, specifically?'

Which business?

Annalena sucked in an indignant breath. As if he didn't know full well! There could only be one reason.

How dared he pretend not to know?

He even softened his question with a slight smile as if he really cared.

As if she could be swayed from her purpose by that!

Annalena chose not to think about that moment of shocked reaction when she'd entered the room and seen him in person for the first time. Tall, well-built and suave in his expensive suit, he'd made her pause as an unfamiliar sensation triggered inside her.

His features were arresting, bold and attractive, enhanced by an intriguing groove down one cheek when he smiled. That, and the laughter lines at his eyes, gave an impression of warmth. As did those golden-brown eyes that contrasted so appealingly with his dark hair. But she wasn't fooled. He was as hard and autocratic as his father. They even had the same stubborn, angular jaw.

'The dam, of course.'

'Ah.' He paused, his expression impassive. 'What aspect did you want to discuss?'

Annalena resisted the urge to grind her teeth. He might have been asking what cake she'd like with her coffee.

Did he really think so lightly of their concerns?

You know the answer to that. He doesn't care any more than his father did. That's why you're here. Just because he looks... appealing doesn't mean he's even halfway decent.

She pinned on a cool smile, thankful that his arrogance temporarily banished her worry and her ingrained fear at being in the palace where King Karl, the bogeyman of her childhood, had lived. 'All of it. You know the whole idea is disastrous. I've come to make sure it's stopped.'

Now she got a reaction. His eyes no longer looked complacent. They widened in shock. His dark, angular eyebrows jerked down above his nose and his mouth lost its easy half-smile.

Obviously he didn't like head-on confrontation.

In which case he should have done something about this much earlier. For a moment satisfaction flared, but she stifled it. This wasn't about her but about keeping Edelforst safe.

He smoothed out his frown and spread his hands in an apparently open gesture. 'I'm happy to take you through whatever aspect of the project concerns you. But as for stopping it... That's impossible. It's a tremendous opportunity for the country and will bring huge benefits long term.'

Annalena curled her hands over the arms of her chair. 'Of course it's possible to stop it. Work hasn't begun.'

He shook his head, his lips curving in a half-smile, as if humouring her. But there was no smile in his eyes. 'It's not that simple. You may not be familiar with the ins and outs of commercial projects but commitments have been made. Contracts are in the final stages of negotiation.'

Patronising man! She might not have managed a hydroelectric project, but she knew about commercial negotiations, both on her grandmother's behalf and in her own work. Botanical research that identified compounds with potential medical and other uses was highly prized.

'If contracts are being negotiated they haven't been signed.'

'But statements of intent have, with penalty clauses if the project doesn't proceed.'

'You were so sure you could force this through, despite the opposition?'

'Opposition? You've been misled. A thorough feasibility study was undertaken and no negative issues were found that outweighed the benefits of the scheme.' He smiled, a charming smile that Annalena guessed would make a lot of women melt. Even she felt a tickle of appreciation low in her body. 'I'm happy to explain the scheme and put your mind to rest.'

Put her mind to rest!

How dared he? He made her sound as if she were too ignorant to understand what the scheme involved. As if she'd come here on a whim. She'd guarantee she knew more about it than he did.

Now she knew how he worked. He used charm to cloak his ruthlessness instead of the aggressive bluster his father had employed. One had threatened people into compliance and this one showed friendly concern that was barely skin deep.

Contempt fired in her blood.

He intended to brush their concerns aside. To downplay them and carry on regardless. Because, like his father, he had the power.

Her heart thudded so hard and fast she almost put a hand to her breast to calm it. Instead she kept her hands where they were, a lifetime's lessons in control and decorum coming to her aid.

She drew a slow breath. She'd come hoping they'd discuss this sensibly and he'd see reason. She'd hoped he wasn't like his father.

Above all, she'd hoped he wouldn't force her hand. Instead he was fobbing her off.

'There's nothing I could say to dissuade you?'

His smile was sympathetic. Or was that pitying? 'I'm afraid not. But—'

'Please! No more weasel words about tremendous opportunities and the public good. We both know they're false.'

She'd shocked him. He looked almost comically stunned, as if no one ever called him on his lies. If the situation weren't so dire she might find it amusing.

But this wasn't funny. They'd done everything they could. Submitted detailed reports and evidence. Experts had talked at length with royal administrators. From the moment the massive dam was mooted under his father's reign, everyone from her grandmother to scientists, sociologists and farmers in Edelforst had pleaded to save a huge proportion of their land from being flooded.

No one had listened.

There was only one way to stop this disaster, but it meant doing something so drastic Annalena had desperately hoped to avoid it. The thought of inserting herself further into this awful place filled her with dread. But this wasn't about her.

Shoring up her resolve, she drew some papers from her pocket and held them out, pleased her fingers didn't tremble. Though from this moment, her life would never be the same.

Benedikt of Prinzenberg rose and took the papers. 'What are these?'

'The documents that will ensure the dam isn't built.' Annalena sucked air into constricting lungs. 'Proof you're not the legitimate ruler of Prinzenberg. I am.'

CHAPTER TWO

SHOCK RAN THROUGH Benedikt like an electric current through copper wire. His fingers twitched and he had to firm his hold on the papers.

She was serious! Or the best actor he'd ever seen. He read hints of unease despite her raised chin and imperious stare. But she didn't back down.

For a stunning moment he felt a searing lightness, a dazzle of relief.

Because he hadn't wanted to be King. Monarchy meant King Karl and he'd never wanted to be like his father.

He'd seen hints of his father's darkness in his own soul long ago and feared following in his footsteps. The impatient, remorseless part of him that triumphed in getting his own way. In winning no matter the odds stacked against him. The pride. The thrill he got from risk-taking that in the past had verged on recklessness.

But he loved his country. He'd reconciled himself to his duty, knowing Prinzenberg needed him, now more than ever. With his father's death, he'd shouldered his inherited burdens, despite his old fear that royal power might exacerbate those ruthless tendencies he'd tried to conquer.

'You're accusing me of being a usurper?'

She drew a deep breath. Benedikt fought not to notice her breasts rise against her constraining bodice. A tactic to distract him?

'You're not entitled to be King. The coronation you're planning in a couple of weeks is a farce.'

Her words were as good as a slap to the face. Benedikt felt a muscle spasm in his jaw.

Did she really think she could get away with such a ridiculous lie?

He looked at the documents in his hand. The first was a copy of a marriage certificate, the writing old-fashioned but clear. It recorded the wedding thirty years ago between Alexandra Cecile Adelgunde Luise Von Edelforst to Christian Maximilian Eitel Luitpold Von Prinzenberg.

Benedikt's breath escaped silently, leaving his lungs empty.

Christian of Prinzenberg.

Once the Crown Prince. So much loved by the people that his name still was spoken with reverence, something that had always annoyed Benedikt's father.

All the country knew Christian had died tragically young and unmarried.

Benedikt sank onto the lounge, head spinning.

He read the certificate again, frowning. It had to be a forgery. He flipped the page over and found a copy of another certificate, this time a record of birth. For Annalena Alexandra Christiane Luise Von Prinzenberg, dated eight months after the wedding.

Von Prinzenberg.

It was the royal name, held only by the country's ruler and their direct family.

Despite knowing this had to be fraudulent, Benedikt felt a tickle of unease track down his spine.

After Christian then his father the King died in quick succession, Benedikt's father, Karl, had inherited the title. He was a distant cousin of Christian's. It had taken almost a year of careful checking and deliberation before he was officially named heir to the throne, his name changing to Von Prinzenberg. The name Benedikt now carried.

He lifted his gaze to the woman opposite. She sat straight-backed, knees bent and ankles crossed neatly. Hands clasped in her lap. Only the rapid and rise and fall of her breasts and the pulse thrumming at the base of her neck betrayed she was anything other than completely composed.

'You expect me to fall for this fraud?'

She flinched minutely but held his stare with those deep green eyes. 'It's not a fraud. It's the truth.'

Benedikt shook his head. 'These papers don't prove anything.'

'On the contrary.' She leaned forward. 'They prove I'm the rightful ruler. I'm the only child of Prince Christian, who should have been King after his father. I'm his rightful heir, born before your father took the crown.'

'If you believe this fabrication.' Benedikt's hand fisted, crumpling the papers.

'You think by destroying those, you can hide the truth? You believe *me* so naive as to bring the originals?' She sat back, eyebrows lifting. 'Those are copies. The originals are held safe. Don't think you can bury the truth.'

'I'm not in the habit of burying anything.'

Her huff of disbelief was loud in the thick silence. 'Like father, like son,' she murmured.

Benedikt opened his mouth to challenge her but stopped. He more than most knew his father had kept secrets, some shameful. But he couldn't let himself be distracted.

'How do I even know you're Annalena, granddaughter of the Grand Duchess of Edelforst?'

She looked the right age and he knew the real Annalena was blonde. He'd seen her once as a child on a rare visit to the province.

That had to be it. She was some crazy impostor. But why pursue a lie that would be easily found out?

'You can call my grandmother, and there are people here in the capital who can vouch for me. Meanwhile…'

She dug out a small card and passed it to him. It was a driver's licence, worn around the edges. It looked real. The only anomaly was that the woman in the photo wore a plain white T-shirt and her hair in a high ponytail.

He stared. It was the same woman but the difference from the one sitting here was enormous. The picture showed someone relaxed and half smiling, with none of the buttoned-up tension emanating from the figure before him.

He put the licence and papers on the seat beside him. They'd be investigated fully.

'It's still not true. You can't be Queen.'

One eyebrow rose mockingly. 'You should know Prinzenberg was one of the first European countries to acknowledge the rights of female heirs. Males don't take precedence when it comes to inheriting the throne.'

He stopped her with a slicing gesture. 'I'm fully aware of our constitutional history. It was an essential part of my education *as son of the King*.'

Her lips curled in a grimace, the first evidence of unfettered emotion he'd seen in her. Her tone was heavy with repugnance. 'He might have ruled but that doesn't mean he had the right to.'

Deep inside, Benedikt felt the truth of that. Not because he had doubts about his father's right to inherit the throne, but because the country had deserved someone far better. Someone who cared more for it than themselves.

He breathed out slowly. That was his mission, and his obligation, to redress his father's wrongs and be the head of state his country needed. He hoped he was up to it, that his father's taint didn't undermine him.

'Of course he had the right. He was the previous King's closest surviving relative.'

She merely shook her head as if the nonsense on the papers she'd brought were true.

He'd never been gullible, even as a child. Growing up with

a father like his had ensured that. Karl had been cold, emotionally abusive and regularly twisted the truth to suit himself.

Benedikt rubbed the back of his neck where tension clamped. The six weeks since his father's death had been taxing. His schedule was diabolical and he couldn't waste more time on this.

'I'm not interested in fairy tales. I *know* this can't be true.'

In the afternoon sunlight her braid gleamed like gold as she tilted her head. Far from looking put out, she appeared curious. As if he were an intriguing specimen to be examined. 'How can you be certain?'

'Because if your story were true, your mother would have told the old King she was pregnant with his grandchild and secured your place on the throne.'

His guest didn't look flustered. 'He didn't outlive my father for long. The King was already dying when my father was killed in that accident.'

Impatience made Benedikt grit his teeth. 'That doesn't explain why she didn't come forward. Why hide you? Why keep the supposed wedding secret?' He rose. He'd had enough. 'Your story doesn't hold water. I don't know what your game is but you didn't think it through.'

He grabbed the papers, about to turn away.

'They kept the wedding secret because the old King was pressuring my father into an arranged marriage. He was gravely ill and wanted his son married before he died. He'd chosen someone but Christian, my father, couldn't marry her because he was in love with my mother.'

'Fairy tales,' Benedikt repeated. 'That's all you offer me.'
'It's true!'

She shot to her feet, eyes ablaze, and Benedikt found himself snared by the emotion he read there. It punctured his estimate of her as coolly conniving. She looked full of passion.

His pulse kicked.

'The King was worried about the country's finances and

wanted him to marry the daughter of an American billionaire. Someone with plenty of money to invest in Prinzenberg.'

A sliver of ice punctured Benedikt's chest.

Someone like his mother.

Karl had been charming when he chose and Benedikt's mother had fallen for his wooing, then lived to regret her choice, finally realising he cared more for her money than her. Karl's pretence of affection had ended after several miscarriages and the stillbirth of a second son. With the news she'd never be able to give him a spare heir.

Benedikt's most vivid childhood memories were of her distress at her husband's casual cruelty. If he had a choice he'd never marry. For him the very idea was weighted with pain and negativity, with trauma. Fury rose that this stranger should involve his mother, a woman who'd endured so much, in this scam. Benedikt still felt her loss deeply, and his grandfather's.

He stalked across, straight into Annalena's space. If that was who she really was. 'I've had enough of your games.'

He'd long ago learned to curb the volatile anger that could provoke reactions he'd later regret. But he had his limits.

Serious eyes met his with no trace of fear. 'My parents were in love but my father didn't want to disappoint *his* father so he stalled for time. Then they discovered I was on the way. They married in Edelforst with my grandmother's blessing. My father left, intending to choose the right time to announce their marriage, but he made my mother promise *not* to come to the capital. He insisted she keep their marriage and her pregnancy secret until he took her there.'

Despite himself, Benedikt was intrigued. It had the elements of a good yarn if nothing else.

'That doesn't explain why she didn't come forward later. Why no one else heard about this supposed marriage.'

Annalena crossed her arms, not pugnaciously but, he realised, defensively. Her shoulders curved in. Suddenly she looked vulnerable, making him notice for the first time how much smaller she was than he. Her feisty attitude had eclipsed so much.

'She was protecting me. She died soon after I was born and my grandmother stayed quiet for the same reason.'

'And you needed protection from...?'

'I was only a few weeks old when your father was proclaimed heir to the throne.'

'Still time to assert your claim. Why didn't they?'

She straightened, arms unfolding and shoulders pushing back. She tilted her jaw and, despite the fact she only came up to his shoulder, managed to look down her nose at him. As if she really were Queen and he some ragtag imposter.

'Because of what my father said before he left that last time. He wasn't looking forward to telling his father he'd married for love not duty. He didn't want to disappoint his sick father. But he had something else on his mind. A series of accidents had dogged him in the capital. Potentially fatal accidents.'

'You're saying he thought someone was trying to kill him?'

'Someone else was vying for power. Someone who saw the old King's illness as an opportunity. My father didn't want to reveal he was married until he had concrete proof and had neutralised the danger.'

She went on before he could interject. 'My father left Edelforst on a Sunday night and by Wednesday morning he was dead. In a car accident on a road he knew like the back of his hand. The first report mentioned an oil spill on the road at the only spot where the side plunged into a ravine. But the official, final report made no mention of it. There were other anomalies—'

'You forget there was no one else in line to inherit the throne. No one *vying* for power.'

Her expression changed, defiance and sadness replaced with something like regret. 'No one except the orphan who'd been raised at the palace beside the Crown Prince as an act of charity. Someone ambitious and older than Christian, who chafed at the fact he could never rise to the same heights of power. Someone who, within weeks of the Crown Prince's death, quietly married the American heiress whom the old King had favoured.'

Benedikt's blood froze, his skin turning clammy with horror.

'Your father. Who later became King Karl.' Her voice was implacable, her words missiles. 'That's why my family kept the marriage and my parentage secret. They didn't want him to kill me too.'

CHAPTER THREE

'WE HAVEN'T BEEN able to disprove it, but we've only had a couple of hours.' Matthias was grim as he met Benedikt's gaze across the desk. 'The priest who supposedly officiated at the wedding *was* the priest at that church on that date. He's retired but still lives nearby. The other witnesses, including the Grand Duchess, still live in Edelforst.'

'And?' There had to be more.

'I spoke to the priest. A trusted staff member is heading there in person to conduct an interview, but I knew you'd want an initial report.'

Benedikt nodded, appreciating his assistant's thoroughness but wishing he'd get to the point.

'You're not going to like this. The old man said he remembered the ceremony perfectly. He said it was the honour of a lifetime to marry the Crown Prince to the Princess he'd baptised in the very same church.'

Benedikt fell back in his seat, the air expelling forcibly from his lungs.

Was there no end to this nightmare?

He'd known Annalena of Edelforst was trouble from the moment she marched into this room and the floor shifted beneath his feet.

He'd put that visceral response down to tiredness from overwork. Taking over the labyrinthine mechanics of his father's commercial empire and trying to separate it from royal responsibilities and assets was even harder than he'd anticipated. His father had melded the two, running private business interests and the country to benefit himself and his cronies. Even his staff ran the country like a private fiefdom.

Then in strides Princess Annalena, who it seemed really was who she claimed, accusing him of being a usurper.

And his father of murder.

Benedikt had detested his father. The man had all but destroyed Benedikt's mother and set an example to his son of the sort of man he *didn't* want to become.

But murder? Even Karl wouldn't stoop to that.

Yet Benedikt felt a niggle of unease.

King Karl had been inflexible, selfish and devious despite his outward charm. Every stone Benedikt turned over, stepping into his shoes, revealed something questionable if not downright corrupt.

Grabbing the arms of his chair, he scooted forward, leaning across the desk. 'Did the priest give a reason for keeping the wedding secret?'

'The Prince and the bride's mother, the Grand Duchess, swore him to secrecy. He only talked now because the Grand Duchess said that after all this time, if he were asked he should tell the truth.'

'The truth!' Benedikt shot to his feet, shoving his chair back and stalking away. 'It's all a lie.'

'I did manage to track down the other witnesses.'

Benedikt spun around, but from Matthias's expression he knew that wasn't good news.

'Apart from the Grand Duchess, there were two. One was and still is her lady-in-waiting. I haven't spoken to either of them. I thought that was better done in person.'

Benedikt nodded. If the old lady was part of this scheme they'd have to tread carefully. As for her lady-in-waiting, she'd do whatever her mistress ordered. Who even had ladies-in-waiting any more?

'And the other witness? His name seemed familiar.'

'I spoke to him by phone. He had the same story as the priest. Brought in to witness a wedding but asked not to reveal the details until now.'

'How did he sound? Plausible?'

Matthias pinched the bridge of his nose before meeting Benedikt's gaze. 'Very. He was a lawyer then. He's now a judge with a reputation for probity and fairness. His name was familiar because he's on our list to help manage your programme of law reform.'

A harsh laugh escaped Benedikt. 'The old lady really pulled out all the stops with this plot, didn't she?'

'If it's a lie, it's a very good one. But we've only just started investigating. Face-to-face interviews might yield different results. Plus we have to examine the original documents.'

'I want someone to dig out all available information on Prince Christian's car smash.' Benedikt paused, hating the hollow feeling in the pit of his stomach. 'Do we have my father's diaries for the period?'

Like his predecessors, King Karl had kept a daily diary of royal business.

'No. Apparently your father only began the practice after he was crowned. And, instead of writing it himself, he had his secretary note down key business.'

So there'd be no confessions about crimes he might have committed. Benedikt didn't know whether to be pleased or disappointed.

'Thanks, Matthias.' Benedikt leaned one hip against the desk. 'Keep me informed of progress.'

This couldn't have come at a worse time, in the lead up to his coronation. Maybe that was why they'd chosen it.

'Have you decided what you're going to do?'

Benedikt met his sympathetic stare. 'What can I do except find out what really happened?'

Unlike his father, he didn't brush aside inconvenient truths. If her story were true...

It didn't bear thinking about.

Prinzenberg was in a worse state than he'd thought, public monies siphoned off to private individuals and a whiff of corruption where there was big money to be made. Benedikt had worked hard to prepare himself to become King one day but it would take all his skills, knowledge and time to set his country on the right track again.

The idea that a woman who'd never been near the royal court, much less the machinery of government, could take his place…it made his blood run cold.

Prinzenberg couldn't afford an amateur. It needed strong, strategic government. Benedikt was far from perfect but he was a highly successful businessman, thanks to his grandfather's mentoring, and he'd been raised to understand politics, public service and foreign diplomacy.

Matthias inclined his head in the direction of the room where Annalena awaited his return. 'And the Princess?'

Benedikt rolled tight shoulders. 'Let me worry about her.' He opened a desk drawer, reaching for headache tablets. 'Believe me, you've got the easier job.'

'Frankly, my dear, I'd never realised the practical implications of your career. It's fascinating, the work you're doing.'

Colonel Ditmar smiled warmly before taking a bite of cherry pastry. As a child she'd known him well, the kindly man with an engaging twinkle who always had time for a rather lonely little girl.

She hadn't seen him for years, though he still visited her grandmother. Seeing him reminded her how time marched on. He had the same upright bearing, bushy moustache and gravelly voice, but his moustache and hair were white now, and his face, like her grandmother's, was lined by age.

Annalena had been raised by a generation older than the parents she'd never known. It struck her how precious her time with those dear people was.

She shoved aside the thought of a world without her amazing Oma, instead recounting for the colonel an amusing story about a field trip fraught with complications.

His laughter eased the tension knotting her shoulder blades. It almost made her forget they shared coffee and cake not in her grandmother's elegant sitting room, but in an ostentatious salon full of ornate gilding and uncomfortable chairs.

Was there *any* room in the sprawling palace designed for comfort rather than show? She felt the constraining shadow of King Karl and his son in the very walls.

As if on cue, a door in the white and gilt panelling swung open and a tall figure appeared. Wide shoulders filled the space, then in stepped the man who called himself King.

Easier to think of him in those terms than as Benedikt. That was too dangerously informal. Annalena didn't have his measure. She didn't believe he'd resort to violence like his father but she didn't trust him. She couldn't let down her guard. Not when in one short interview he'd completely upset her equilibrium.

Upset it? The first time their eyes met it felt like an earthquake resonating from the pit of her stomach, overwhelming her body in waves of... What? Yearning? Recognition?

She roped in dismay. It would take a remarkable man to make Annalena yearn at first sight.

Her parents had fallen for each other at first sight. Far from finding that sweet or inspirational, for Annalena that had been a cautionary tale. Their love had been doomed, leaving her mother a widow while still a bride. Then she'd died of a broken heart as much as from illness, leaving her daughter orphaned. No wonder Annalena had never dreamt of romance. As for being swept off her feet...!

No, Benedikt might be remarkable but, she told herself, for all the wrong reasons.

Yet as he crossed the room, a warm smile easing his features as he greeted the colonel, Annalena felt *something*. A fluttering in her chest. The suspicion of an ache that for a moment left her breathless.

She watched him shake the old man's hand, refusing to let him rise from his seat, though protocol demanded it. Or would if he really were King.

Annalena swallowed convulsively as unease raised goosebumps across her skin. She'd done the right thing, revealing the secret of her birth. Every other avenue they'd tried had failed. But had she unleashed something larger than she'd imagined?

He turned, eyes appraising, and suspicion solidified into an atavistic fear that she'd set in motion something she couldn't control.

'Princess Annalena, I hope you've enjoyed your afternoon tea.'

She inclined her head, refusing to use the title he claimed. 'Thank you, yes. The colonel and I are old friends. It's been wonderful to catch up. Such a coincidence we should be visiting the palace at the same time.'

And such a convenient way for you to check I really am who I say. The colonel wouldn't be fooled by an imposter.

One dark eyebrow rose and she had the unnerving sense her opponent read her mind.

She almost wished he could. He had such a confident air it would do him good to realise it took more than good looks to impress a thinking woman.

His eyes narrowed on her then flared wide, more gold than brown. Heat bloomed inside her and she hurriedly turned to her companion. She was *not* discomfited. She was simply remembering her manners.

'Colonel—'

'It's been so good to see you, dear Annalena. But I must get on. Business to see to, you know.'

He rose and she stood too. 'Of course. It's been lovely. I'll pass on your regards to my grandmother.'

He leaned in and kissed her cheeks, the brush of his moustache and the scent of butterscotch taking her straight back to childhood.

Then he was gone, leaving her with the brooding man who ruled this place.

Suddenly she felt very alone.

Annalena straightened her spine after picking an imaginary piece of fluff off her skirt. 'Are you at least convinced now that I am who I say?'

'There seems little doubt.' He moved nearer, not as close as the colonel had been, yet she *felt* his presence as a physical weight pushing against her. She couldn't quite get her breath, her breasts straining against fabric that suddenly felt too tight. He extended his arm and it took all her self-control not to flinch. 'Your driver's licence.'

'Thank you.' She took it, careful not to brush his fingers. 'I assume you had it checked.'

'Naturally. Proving your identity is the first necessary step.' He gestured to her seat. 'Won't you sit?'

Annalena subsided onto the chair and watched him take the colonel's seat. He looked completely composed and in control. She didn't know what she'd anticipated but was annoyed at his equanimity. Especially since she felt anything but calm. 'And the next step?'

He reached for a poppy-seed pastry, taking a large bite and chewing before answering. 'Sorry, I didn't have time for lunch.'

She folded her arms. 'I know the feeling.'

His huff of laughter surprised her, sending a skittering sensation through her middle. His sombre eyes crinkled at the corners making him look…

Deliberately she turned towards the generous spread she'd been too keyed up to enjoy. A slice of chocolate gateau caught her eye. If ever there was a day for chocolate this was it. She helped herself, a welcome distraction from this man who so confused her.

She didn't trust him, yet being with him made her feel energised and self-aware. The sharpness of her breathing. The cinch of fabric at her waist. The weight of her mother's locket at her throat. The scrape of her nipples against her bra.

'The next step?' she asked as she slid a fork through dense chocolate and fluffy cake.

'Proving your claim to the throne is false, of course.'

His absolute certainty surprised a laugh out of her. All the proof she'd given him and she hadn't even created doubt in his mind. 'Good luck with that.'

'You find this amusing? You're enjoying yourself?'

Now she heard it, not uncertainty but steely threat. He wasn't as sanguine as he appeared.

Her grandmother had spoken in scathing terms about his father. Was the man before her just as callous? As ruthless? It was a chilling possibility. But nothing would happen to her under his roof. Too many people knew she was here.

Seeking distraction, Annalena popped a piece of cake into her mouth, focusing on the rich flavour and texture, rather than the scorching glare turned her way. She swallowed and licked her bottom lip.

'If you think this is how I get my kicks you really are out of touch. No person in their right mind would do what I've done today for fun. I didn't *want* to come. I didn't *want* to reveal the truth about my parents. I'm happy with my life, thank you very much, and I'd rather get on with it.' She put down the delicious but barely touched cake, the fork rattling on the plate. 'If you'd done the right thing in the first place, none of this would be necessary.'

'This? Your attempt at blackmail? You're blaming me?'

Impossible man! 'Blackmail implies I'm doing something wrong. But right and the law are on my side. The crown is mine by right. Building a dam that will destroy so much of Edelforst is wrong.'

'Don't be so simplistic.' He shook his head and, in the first gesture she'd seen that revealed weakness or perhaps tiredness, he raked his fingers through his dark hair. Infuriatingly it fell perfectly back into place. 'You can't see the bigger picture. Some land will be inundated but the owners will be compensated handsomely. We're seeking sustainable ways to create power. This hydroelectric project will bring huge benefits.'

'You sound just like your father.'

His head jerked back, making her wonder what the relationship had been between the two men.

A muscle in his jaw worked. 'You spoke to him about this?'

She snorted. 'Chance would be a fine thing. We tried, my grandmother and I. Along with numerous delegations. But he refused to meet anyone. All the projections we sent him, all the scientific studies, the petitions and detailed analysis... All we got was a vague assurance that all input would be considered. Then the announcement that the dam would go ahead exactly as planned, *for the public good*.'

'It can be hard to accept change but when there's a clear public benefit—'

'*Public* benefit? Are you serious?'

Her skin felt too tight to hold in her outrage. It felt as though ants crawled across her flesh. She wanted to leap up and stride around the room, waving her arms and releasing some of her pent-up emotions.

Instead she took a deep breath and looked out at the manicured formal gardens, seeking calm.

'You *have* read the documentation, haven't you? You know most of the power generated and the profits will go to private companies beyond our borders?'

'Only a percentage and only for a limited number of years. You can't expect them to help fund such a big project without getting some return.'

Annalena turned and met his steady gaze. Even now, in the privacy of the palace, he refused to admit the truth. The disparity between the press release he quoted and the true plans was vast.

She dragged in a shuddering breath. He was as brazen as his father, not even a hint of concern that he was selling out his people so others could profit. So *he* could profit.

Her shoulders slumped and she sagged in her seat. He was persisting in the lie his father had created.

She'd hoped a frank discussion would make him see the dam was a monumental error that would do environmental, social and economic damage. But there was no reasoning with a man who didn't see beyond the lining of his own pockets, for surely he'd get a cut of the profits.

Which meant her only hope was following through on her threat to wrest away the crown. She felt sick with dismay.

Annalena didn't want to swap her career for a life hemmed in by pomp and ceremony, especially since King Karl had tainted that world. She wasn't cut out for a royal life and feared she'd be overwhelmed as well as unprepared. Growing up with a title and a famous grandmother, she'd always been different to her peers. It had taken longer to make friends and be accepted. Some people still treated her differently. How much more isolating would it be as Queen?

Despite her fighting words earlier, she'd hoped this could be resolved simply. He'd tell her he'd changed his mind about the dam and she'd return home.

She couldn't give up without one last try.

'If you agreed not to proceed with the dam, and put it in writing, I'd consider signing away my rights to the crown.'

What was under that ground there that she so wanted to protect? Gold? Rare elements?

According to the summary Benedikt had read, the land was barely productive agriculturally and of little real value.

But to offer such a bargain…

She must have powerful reasons. To concoct a lie about being the true queen wasn't something to undertake lightly.

And if by some million-to-one chance there was something in her claim, why agree to give it up for a dam?

He was missing something. Benedikt hated that feeling. He had a flair for business but most of his success came from hard work and attention to detail. He never allowed himself to be caught unprepared.

But Annalena of Edelforst had done just that. He felt as if she'd ripped the antique carpet out from beneath his feet and he'd suffered concussion from smashing his head on the floor.

In the hours since she'd flounced into the palace, he and Matthias had followed up her claim of royal lineage. He made a mental note to review the files for the dam project as soon as possible.

He'd only had time to read the summary report, because he was trying to get across so many things in a short time. His father had been selective about which royal matters he took on, keeping real power to himself, jealous even of his son who'd one day inherit. Now Benedikt paid the price for that.

'Do we have a deal?'

She had to be kidding. There'd be no deal of any kind until he knew exactly what was going on and why.

'I don't do deals with people who try to blackmail me.'

He had the satisfaction of seeing her eyes widen in dismay. A softer man might almost feel sorry for her.

Except she was trying to manipulate him, something he abhorred. His father had revelled in making people dance to his tune, playing on their vulnerabilities.

Was that what Annalena had attempted with her big, doe eyes? Making a production of eating that gateau as if it were a prelude to sex? The way she'd taken her time biting into it then chewing, eyes flickering half closed as if in sensual delight, then licking away crumbs from her sweetly curved mouth.

Heat eddied in his belly, drawing tight and low, provoking anger at how easily she affected him.

'My answer is no.'

She sat higher, fingers curling around the arms of her chair. Her mouth flattened, jaw tightening. And her eyes…they were slits of green fire, hot enough to scorch.

A childhood memory stirred. An old legend about the dragon that had haunted the high Alpine reaches of Prinzenberg. Not only could it breathe fire, but also turn to stone anyone foolish enough to meet its stare.

Benedikt breathed deeply, meeting that incendiary look. His pulse quickened as adrenaline pumped hard and he welcomed it, welcomed the surge of response. He told himself it was because, after months grappling with his father's convoluted backroom deals and half-truths, he found honest dislike refreshing.

Bizarrely, her searing look *was* turning him to stone.

His lower body was weighted and hard. That sizzling gaze was like a hand stroking his skin, reminding him how long it had been since…

There was a rustle of silk as she rose. 'In that case we're finished here. I have an appointment with a constitutional lawyer tomorrow.'

Benedikt stood too, closer than he'd intended. Close enough to feel her heat and inhale her light floral scent. 'Because you're giving up your claim?'

Her fiery stare turned cool. 'I didn't come here to walk away empty-handed.'

Unfortunate but predictable.

'Then you won't walk away.'

Her gaze searched his and he had an uncanny sense of familiarity. But they'd never met before. He'd only seen her at a distance once in his youth.

'Why are you looking at me like that?'

'You don't think you can drop that bombshell then stroll away?' Benedikt shook his head. 'Until the succession is clarified, you'll stay here.' His lips curved in a feral smile. 'As my guest.'

CHAPTER FOUR

'ARE YOU *THREATENING* ME?' Annalena hoped the quiver in her voice was anger.

He looked different, as if beneath his control lurked something untamed. His sharp smile contrasted with that heavy-lidded, almost lazy stare that she knew was anything but indolent. His tall frame almost hummed with energy.

'Of course not. Threat implies something unreasonable.' He folded his arms, making her even more aware of his height and the impressive breadth of his chest. 'I'm sure you'll agree I've been remarkably fair-minded in the circumstances.'

She considered reminding him it was *his* fault they'd got to this stage, by refusing to heed the information sent to him about the hydroelectric project. But a glance at that rigid jaw told her recriminations were pointless.

'Once the confusion about your arrival was cleared up, you've been treated courteously. I listened to your story. I set in motion enquiries to verify or disprove it.'

So he *had* taken action to confirm it. Annalena didn't know whether to be relieved or worried. Would his agents try to steal the original documents? Would they harass her grandmother?

'Meanwhile you've enjoyed my hospitality and the company of an old friend.'

'Only because you wanted to verify my identity.'

'That too.' He paused, his lowered eyebrows giving him a brooding look. Yet to her dismay even that didn't mar his dark charisma, a charisma she didn't want to notice. 'Given your allegations about my father, my behaviour has been remarkably restrained.'

A micro expression flitted across his features. Repudiation? Who would want to believe their father was a murderer? For a moment she felt a surge of sympathy.

Automatically she opened her mouth to apologise for any distress caused, then realised how absurd that was. The truth wasn't her fault and she wasn't broadcasting it publicly. She was giving him the opportunity to deal with this behind closed doors.

'Thank you for the meeting,' she said through gritted teeth. 'And the refreshments. But it's time I left. We can speak when you've completed your enquiries.'

She was turning away when he spoke. He didn't raise his voice. It was smooth, almost soft. 'You really think *that's* reasonable behaviour, Annalena?'

Something tickled her spine as he said her name. It felt like the caress of a feather, drawing her flesh tight and making her insides quiver.

Her hands fisted. 'You're accusing *me* of being unreasonable?'

That brooding stare locked on hers and she had the strangest sensation that she couldn't step away. Those intense eyes pinioned her. His gaze flicked to her mouth then her eyes and tension notched higher, a sense of *anticipation* unlike anything she'd experienced.

'You've spent a long time angry with my family, fixated on our apparent crimes. But consider this from my perspective. I was unaware of the issues you raised until today.' A muscle jerked in his jaw, making the harsh set of his features suddenly more human. 'The allegations are serious and I'll get to the bottom of them.'

'But—'

'If true, they have the potential to cause alarm, if not panic in a country already reeling from the unexpected death of its king. If true, they'd cause a constitutional crisis. In the circumstances, it's *sensible* for you to stay while we sort it out.'

She shook her head. 'I've already provided the documentation you need. But I don't need to stay here.'

She'd hated the palace, or what it represented, all her life. It had been home to the scheming criminal who'd killed her father and, she was convinced, her mother too. Oma had insisted her daughter had died from grief for her husband.

Annalena's nemesis went on, his voice implacable. 'If you're really the Queen, you'll need to get used to living and working here.'

The idea shot a bolt of cold steel through her ribs.

No, that wouldn't happen.

She'd sign over her rights to the crown once the dam was stopped. She had no desire to be Queen. Her life was fulfilling. She had no aptitude for court politics and no desire to learn.

'Meanwhile, having you here will be more efficient. I want this sorted quickly, don't you?'

'Naturally. But I can stay elsewhere in the city while you do that.'

That had been her plan, to visit the university and spend a few days catching up with colleagues.

'What are you afraid of, Princess?'

She wanted to tell him she didn't use her title and preferred he didn't, since he made it sound like a challenge. As if he thought her unworthy of it.

More, she wanted to scoff at the suggestion she was afraid. She was a competent professional, respected by her peers and the people of Edelforst.

Yet coming here into the lion's den was more daunting than she wanted to admit.

This was a world she'd avoided. Where his poisonous father had ruled, backed up by cronies who either couldn't see or didn't care how flawed he was. She'd rather be safely back home, surrounded by her work and her friends.

Annalena sucked in a shocked breath. Maybe she and her beloved Oma had more in common than she'd suspected. The old lady was as sharp and indefatigable as ever, but her physical world had gradually narrowed so she found it hard to leave home. That was why Annalena had come alone today. The Grand Duchess rarely left her castle and then only to visit familiar, nearby places.

'Princess?'

How she detested that casually raised eyebrow and mocking tone. As if this stranger sensed the trepidation she'd barely been aware of herself.

He didn't know the first thing about her. He was prodding, pushing her into agreeing.

It was infuriating that it worked. If she stayed she could negotiate the deal Edelforst needed and it would be finished all the sooner.

Besides, reading the glint in his eyes, she suspected if she didn't accept his hospitality he'd lock her in. He could make her his prisoner rather than a guest. Would he dare?

Despite his courtesy, she sensed his deep-seated implacability. Did she want to test it when, in the end, they'd have to negotiate?

She exhaled, forcing out the tension behind her ribs. Slowly she lifted her chin to meet his stare.

'Very well. I'll accept your *gracious* invitation.'

Her voice dripped disdain. They both knew there'd been nothing gracious about his words nor had there been an invitation, merely an ultimatum.

For a second she thought she saw the hint of a flush across his cheekbones but of course it was imagination.

Benedikt strode down the corridors towards his office. He knew he was scowling, jaw clenched, yet couldn't yet mask his discontent. The few staff members he met scurried out of his way.

Great. They probably thought the honeymoon period with their new monarch was over and he was reverting to type. His father's type. King Karl had been renowned for his bad temper when things didn't go his way.

That was enough for Benedikt to rein in his anger. In his darker moments he'd recognised his father's influence, his early years learning about the world and relationships from a ruthless narcissist.

He was lucky the old man had grown bored with parenthood so increasingly Benedikt had been raised by his mother. Karl had mainly intervened to interrogate his son on his learning, set impossible goals, and chastise his failures. Or use him as a hostage to the Queen's compliance, ensuring she acted the devoted consort even when their marriage broke down.

Eventually Benedikt had been allowed to summer each year in the US when his mother vacationed there, visiting her father. Without that Benedikt might have grown as monstrous as Karl.

Away from the palace he'd learned right from wrong and how to control his impulses rather than reach out and take. But it hadn't been easy and even now he sometimes had to step back and consider his decisions.

Benedikt slowed, doing his best at least to look unperturbed.

Technically he'd got what he needed. Annalena was here where he could keep an eye on her. Where she couldn't get up to more mischief before this crisis was resolved.

But the woman had an uncanny ability to make him lose his cool. He'd had a lifetime to learn to mask his thoughts and feelings because his father had always played on emotions and weakness to his advantage.

With this one woman Benedikt felt too much.

He couldn't pin her down, alternately thinking her a liar or deluded. *Surely* her allegation about his father was untrue.

As for the secret marriage, that must be a romantic fable concocted by her grandmother.

Yet something about the Princess Annalena had an authentic ring. A reluctant laugh huffed out. Even dressed like a milkmaid, she had more imperiousness in her little finger than some monarchs he'd met.

And charm too, when she chose to use it. He'd seen her with Colonel Ditmar and felt jealous of the old man. That smile…

Despite her wince when he called her Princess, she had the hauteur that came from a blue-blooded pedigree. She'd made him feel like an oaf though he'd been raised as Crown Prince.

She'd reminded him that he hadn't invited her to stay, but ordered it. As if he were his father's son in the worst possible way.

She was right. In that moment you'd happily have ordered security to stop her leaving.

Because they needed secrecy until this was sorted.

Or did the need to make her stay say something about his disturbing reaction to her?

Benedikt raked his hand across his scalp. He didn't have time for *reactions* to any woman.

Having her here was necessary. He needed to control the spread of her preposterous story until he could disprove it.

Yet you didn't confiscate her phone. It would only take one call from her to the press.

No matter how tempting that had been, he was determined to prove himself different to his father. He was a fair-minded man, not a tyrant, even if he was determined to take control of this situation. Besides, if she'd planned to wreak immediate chaos, she'd have done that already.

He couldn't work her out. She demanded he take her claims seriously, yet in the next breath talked about giving up the crown if he'd stop the dam.

Surely that proved this was a scam. How many people would give up the chance for wealth and royal privilege?

Despite his difficulties untangling his father's more dubious arrangements, and reminding palace staff that they worked for the people as much as the King, there was no denying there were benefits to being ruler.

He entered his office, walked through to Matthias's desk in the next room and propped his hip against the desk. 'Any news?'

'Nothing conclusive. Sorry.' Matthias leaned back in his seat. 'The Grand Duchess and her lady-in-waiting will be interviewed tomorrow and I've arranged for an expert to view the original documents.'

'An expert?'

'Someone who knows about fraudulent documents. The police and courts have used him.'

'And the Grand Duchess is happy about that?'

'Very happy. Which makes me wonder. If it were all a hoax…' His troubled gaze met Benedikt's. 'Her only condition is that the documents be examined in her presence. And that if there's still any doubt about them, they be transported by someone of her choosing, who will remain with them throughout the whole process.'

Benedikt stiffened. 'She's implying *we* might do something nefarious with the papers!'

Matthias's expression was solemn. 'As if she doesn't trust you.'

'Which would make sense if her claims were true. Maybe she thinks I'm like my father.' A nasty premonition stirred in Benedikt's gut. 'Any news on the car accident?'

'Only the summary is digitised and it doesn't say much. Accident due to reckless driving. I've requested the physical files. But I did track down someone who was there soon after the crash. They were nervous about speaking but eventually confirmed a significant oil spill right across the road.'

'Which doesn't tally with the official report.'

'No, but there could be an explanation. We can't jump to conclusions.'

Yet Benedikt's thoughts turned irresistibly to the implications if this were all true. If the well-being of the nation rested on the narrow shoulders of a woman with no experience of government. Who, he'd discovered from Matthias's digging, made a living researching plants.

How useful would botany be in the complex work of managing a government? In dragging Prinzenberg out of the shadows cast by his father and into a more equitable, prosperous future?

A shiver ran down his backbone. It wouldn't come to that. It couldn't.

The country needed someone with experience of government, international affairs, social issues and economics for a start. Someone to bring the nation together. Who understood the royal court and politics. Whose education and personal experience had been tailored to make them a suitable monarch.

It needed *him*.

Annalena paced the gravelled path through the topiary gardens, heading for the parklike grounds she'd seen from her suite.

It had been over twenty-four hours since she'd arrived at the palace and, apart from her restless hours trying to sleep, she'd only been able to relax during a couple of walks through the gardens.

Being in the open air, preferably in wilderness, had always been her go to in times of stress. At home she headed for mountains and forests when she needed to clear her head.

No chance of doing that here. The palace was an opulent prison.

Her spacious suite, stuffed to the gills with ornate antiques, was nevertheless extremely comfortable. Nothing was too much trouble, including sumptuous meals worthy of a fine restaurant, which she'd eaten in stately solitude in her private sitting room. Benedikt had excused himself, saying he had to work, presumably frantically trying to disprove her story.

But she was aware of eyes on her whenever she ventured from her suite. Whenever she opened her door there was an usher at the end of the hall, ready to assist. Though those ushers looked more like security staff.

To stop her leaving?

Her case had been collected from her car and brought to her suite. She'd have preferred to get it herself, to enjoy the freedom of being beyond the palace perimeter for a few minutes, but Benedikt had insisted.

Annalena wasn't fooled. He wanted her where he could keep an eye on her. He'd even suggested that instead of visiting the university today she stay close, to be available for any clarifications he required.

She could have insisted but hadn't wanted to press him into a corner. It was easier to accede to a reasonable request than force him to reveal his true colours. That could mean armed guards barring her from leaving.

At least now you can pretend you're a welcome guest.

Despite the tension cramping her neck and shoulders, she snickered. He probably feared she'd tell her story to a reporter. As if she wanted the world to know!

Nothing could be further from the truth. Annalena had a fascinating, satisfying career, friends, and a home she loved in Edelforst.

Coming to the capital, bearding the beast in his palatial lair, had been a desperate last resort. Not an attempt to wrest the crown from him.

Maybe if she'd been raised expecting to be Queen things would be different. If she'd learnt about politics, government and economics, she'd have considered it. But while her grandmother was a proud woman who hated that Annalena's birthright had been stolen, she was a pragmatist and fiercely protective. She'd seen what King Karl was capable of and preferred to let her granddaughter build a life for herself, safe from the threat of harm.

The bonds of love between granddaughter and grandmother were strong. That was why, when Annalena had rung last night, she'd let the old lady believe she was staying in a hotel as planned. No need to worry her with the news she'd sleep under the enemy's roof.

Benedikt of Prinzenberg was used to command, having people obey. He was a quick thinker, powerful, and hated being crossed. Yet he wasn't completely like his father. His dismay when she'd spoken of murder had been genuine. She didn't fear for her life.

Yet he disturbed her in ways she couldn't name.

Being around him was like standing before an approaching thunderstorm. Everything felt charged and weighted with anticipation.

Annalena rubbed her hands up her arms as she left the formal gardens and stepped onto the springy turf of the private royal park. Ahead, a sweep of grass curved between stands of large trees to where afternoon sunlight glittered on a small lake.

She paused, inhaling the scent of growing things, then exhaling some of her tension.

Soon he'd have to acknowledge the truth and they'd come to an agreement. Then she could leave.

She didn't want to spend another night in his palace.

Down near the lake, they'd said.

What was she doing there, far from the palace buildings? Was this a tactic to make him come to her? To show she had the upper hand?

That would be petty and, despite the earthquake of disruption Annalena of Edelforst had caused, he didn't think her that.

Troublesome, yes.

Worrying.

An absolute disaster, for his country and everything Benedikt was trying to do here.

Yet despite the shockwaves still reverberating through him, not all his thoughts about Annalena were negative.

Because those thoughts don't come from your brain, but a more primitive part of your body.

Her combination of touch-me-not condescension and earnestness, not to mention a mouth created for kissing, kept distracting him. Her eyes flashed and her cheeks flushed when she spoke about the hydroelectric project and he'd wondered what else would excite her passion. *Who* else.

If she knew, would she use his distraction to her advantage?

She was here to negotiate, or said she was. A savvy negotiator turned any weakness to their advantage. He needed to do the same.

Benedikt paused by the water. She was nowhere in sight but must be close. Somewhere nearby security staff were keeping a discreet eye on her. They hadn't reported her trying to leave.

That was one positive at least. One positive out of a minefield of negatives.

He ploughed a hand through his hair. He couldn't believe how the day had unfolded. One after another, facts had been assembled and the truth he'd believed all his life distorted into something completely different.

But he didn't have the luxury of personal feelings. He had a nation to consider. That had to be his focus.

A sound caught his attention and he headed towards it, pine needles muffling his footsteps. He heard muttering then an off-key voice softly singing the refrain from a hard-rock anthem of a decade ago.

Benedikt paused. It couldn't be...

But he knew that voice. That husky, unmusical, but strangely beguiling voice belonged to the buttoned-up woman who threatened his country's peace and prosperity.

It made her seem approachable. Vulnerable. Not the keen-eyed competitor ready to rip the kingdom from his hands. Nor the foe whose femininity sidetracked him.

He stepped into the forest and there she was, squatting before a large tree, phone in hand, photographing something on the ground. The singing became a periodic hum as she shifted her weight, leaning in for a better picture.

Benedikt rocked back on his feet, taking in the view. She wore a T-shirt of dark khaki and jeans that clung taut against the curves of her backside, hips and thighs.

He swallowed and shifted his weight.

He must've made a noise because she swung round, twisting on the balls of her feet, her long ponytail flying across her shoulder.

There she was, the woman he'd seen on her driver's licence. Surprised but not uneasy, features alight. The set of her shoulders, the glow in her eyes and the curve of her lips told him she was happy.

Or had been until he'd appeared. He watched two tiny vertical lines appear above the bridge of her nose and her expression turn blank.

She rose in a fluid movement that spoke of fitness and agility. An instant later her phone had disappeared into a pocket and she stood, straight as a soldier on parade, facing him.

He found it unsettling.

Not that she should mask her emotions for this confrontation. But that he should mind.

Perversely, he wanted to know more about the woman who enjoyed grubbing on the forest floor and sang heavy-metal songs as they should only ever be sung in the shower. The woman who'd looked so joyful.

He'd like to know that woman.

'You were looking for me?'

'I didn't think I'd see you foraging in the leaf litter.'

It wasn't a criticism but she took it as one.

'I was told I had the freedom of the grounds.' She saw him taking in her appearance and pushed her shoulders back. Unfortunately that pushed her breasts against the fitted T-shirt and Benedikt had to work to keep his attention on her face. 'If I'd known we were meeting I'd have changed my clothes. I didn't pack for a stay in a palace.'

Benedikt smiled but his muscles felt stiff. Not just his facial muscles. 'That doesn't matter. I prefer casual.'

Her eyebrows rose as she surveyed his dark suit, white shirt and silk tie.

'I've come from the office. I've been working all day.'

Again he'd said the wrong thing, reminding her that she was filling in time instead of meeting colleagues at the university as she'd planned.

He looked past her to the red fungi she'd been photographing. Or perhaps it was the tuft of tiny white flowers beside them.

For a bizarre moment he wished he could question her about that, hear her talk about her work. He wanted to meet the lighthearted woman who found wild vegetation more fascinating than a grand baroque palace full of priceless art and heirlooms. Or, apparently, the chance to be Queen.

He wanted to engage with her without royal responsibility weighing him down.

He stifled the selfish urge. His country needed him to focus on resolving this problem, quickly!

Her gaze turned laser sharp as if she read his thoughts. Yet when she spoke she sounded wary, not eager. As if she didn't want to hear his news. 'You have news?'

'I do.' He watched her intently, trying to read any microexpression. 'It seems you *do* have grounds to claim the crown of Prinzenberg.'

CHAPTER FIVE

ANNALENA FELT HER features freeze, like ice spreading across a mountain tarn in winter. She even heard the warning crackle of shifting ice beneath her feet, as if she'd stepped beyond the bounds of safety.

It took a second to realise the sound wasn't ice, but twigs cracking beneath her shoes as she instinctively backed up.

That made her stop and draw in much-needed oxygen.

There could be no retreat. No sign of vulnerability. Not while negotiating with Karl's son. He'd use weakness to his advantage.

This was what she needed. His admission was the first step to stopping the dam. To saving homes, jobs, habitats and people's way of life.

Yet being next in line for the throne was *so* not what she wanted, fate's joke at her expense.

Deep breaths. Now the negotiations begin. Now he knows the power in your hands he'll agree to your terms. It will be over soon.

She breathed out, willing her taut frame to relax. 'You admit I'm the rightful heir?'

His expression gave nothing away. What had she expected? A bitter rant? Threats?

Before she'd left home, she'd anticipated all that and more. But once she'd met him, her expectations had altered. Despite his earlier antipathy, she'd never felt in physical danger as she would have with his father.

Benedikt was annoyed and authoritative but she couldn't believe he'd harm her. If she did, she'd never have stayed overnight. She'd have persuaded Colonel Ditmar to escort her out, or found another way to leave.

Or are you naive? You're in a secluded grove with a man you barely know and no witnesses.

Old nightmares brushed hoary fingers across her nape. Nightmares of the father she'd never known in a car that tumbled into an inferno at the bottom of a mountain.

A shudder racked her from the base of her skull to her heels, now planted wide on the ground.

'I admit that...' he paused as if reluctant to continue '...it appears possible. There are facts to be confirmed before we know for sure.'

Of course he wouldn't give in immediately. He'd hang onto power as long as possible. He mightn't be his father but he was a powerful man who didn't want to relinquish authority.

Annalena wanted to say she wasn't interested in taking it off him, but that was her bargaining chip. She had to stay firm until they reached agreement.

'How many people know?' she asked.

'Only those who need to.'

He shoved his hands in his trouser pockets, in the process pulling his jacket open to reveal a broad, hard-looking chest.

She blinked. He hadn't moved but that change of stance reminded her of their biological differences. He was taller and, by the look of it, fit. No doubt he was physically stronger.

She was sure he wouldn't harm her.

Yet you didn't tell Oma you were staying in the palace. You let her think you were in a hotel.

Because her grandmother had lived through the trauma of losing a beloved daughter and a son-in-law. Despite her fierce intelligence and iron will, that had changed her. Annalena hadn't wanted to worry her.

He asked, 'How many have *you* told?'

'None.' Before she could prevent them, more words spilled free. 'But my grandmother knows I'm here, and a lawyer has extra copies of the documents. If I don't return—'

Benedikt's oath was loud in the quiet grove. 'You think I'd harm you? You really believe…?'

She saw his disbelief, then his features settled in an outraged scowl before he turned and strode away. He reached the far side of the glade then spun back, his long paces eating up the distance, bringing him to a halt an arm's length away.

It felt closer. He all but crackled with energy. She felt it lift the fine hairs on her arms and nape, drawing her skin tight with goosebumps.

Eyes like molten metal held hers. It was like looking into a furnace, so bright it hurt.

'Whatever you believe about my father, whatever he may have done… I. Am. Not. Him.'

His chest rose mightily and she saw the frenetic beat of his pulse at his temple.

When he spoke again his voice was softer yet heavy with repressed emotion. 'I don't deliberately hurt people, Annalena. I won't harm you.'

She believed him. His horror at her words was real. She still felt the shock of it reverberating around them.

Annalena nodded. 'I know.'

'Do you? You take my word for it? Isn't that too trusting?'

An outsider might think so. She'd have thought so earlier. She didn't pretend to understand everything about him, but the man she was just beginning to know didn't fill her with dread.

On the contrary, he filled her with an uncomfortable feminine yearning stronger than she'd ever experienced.

Instead of wanting to shrink from him, she wanted to get close. It was one of the reasons she had to ground herself firmly whenever he was around. So as not to give in to temptation and get closer.

'I'm not saying we're on the same side. I'm not naive. But I believe you.'

He didn't look convinced. 'Yet you took precautions in case you disappeared.'

So she'd had a moment of uncertainty and fear. But her fear had more to do with her turbulent reaction to him than any true belief he'd harm her.

She lifted one stiff shoulder. 'I was going into battle. I couldn't take risks.'

Was that understanding in his gaze? 'Especially given what happened to your father.'

Her heart jolted. 'You believe now that it wasn't an accident?'

'I don't know. I doubt we'll ever know, given how much time has elapsed. But there are discrepancies in the reports.'

For the first time Annalena noticed lines of tiredness around his eyes, worry imprinted on his forehead and bracketing his mouth. She'd sensed yesterday that he wasn't close to his father. But to confront the possibility Karl had been a killer...

'Where do we go from here?'

His mouth kicked up at one corner, like a tick of approval. 'Charming as this place is, I vote we move to somewhere we can be more comfortable.' He gestured for her to walk with him. 'Shall we?'

Annalena cast a glance around the clearing. Personally, she'd rather have their discussion here. She found the palace oppressive. But admitting that would hand him an advantage. He mightn't want to harm her but she needed her wits for this negotiation.

A quarter of an hour later they entered a large walled garden. Unlike the topiary garden, this wasn't regimented. Paths meandered and there was a riot of colour from flowering trees, shrubs and annuals.

'Let's talk here,' she said impulsively. He paused mid-step, and she hurried on. 'Surely you've had enough indoor meetings?'

'Why not? I know just the place.'

He led her around a circular path to a summerhouse surrounded by scented, climbing roses in shades of cream, yellow and bronze. Opening the door, he invited her to precede him.

A few paces in Annalena stopped, breath catching. The octagonal room was filled with light from the many full-length windows, despite them being half obscured by roses.

White-painted furniture looked comfortable with an abundance of cushions in pastel gelato colours. The ceiling was wallpapered with a vivid print of a lavish garden from which peeped exotic birds and animals. Suspended from the ceiling was a chandelier, not antique crystal, but of glass in a multitude of colours, creating rainbows across the room.

The place was whimsical and welcoming and lifted her spirits. She'd never thought to see anything so delightful in the palace.

Between two windows was a tall cabinet crammed with books, drawing Annalena. The titles weren't organised alphabetically or by size but by some arcane logic, presumably known only to the owner. They seemed well read and most were about plants and gardening.

She swung around, taking in the lovingly tended pot plants. The small tables strategically placed beside the seats. She could imagine afternoons here with friends. Or curling up on that long sofa with books from the cabinet and a piece of cherry torte. It would be a cosy place to work on her laptop.

'This is marvellous! Just...perfect.'

In the doorway, Benedikt's expression was inscrutable. Finally he stepped inside, looking around as if he hadn't seen the place in a while. 'I'm glad there's one part of the palace you approve of.'

Apparently she hadn't hidden her dislike for the place well. 'I'm not really into gilding and formality.'

'You grew up in a castle. Your grandmother still lives there.'

She lifted one shoulder. 'Some of the rooms there are very grand but not all the spaces are formal. It's old and quirky and...comfortable.'

'And this palace isn't?' Before she could answer he continued. 'You don't have to be polite. No one in their right mind would call Prinzenberg's palace cosy.'

'But you have this. Whoever designed it knew how to create a welcoming, relaxing space.'

'My mother's talent. You should have seen our New York penthouse.'

'Your mother designed this?' Annalena looked around with new eyes. It couldn't be any more different to the parts of the palace she'd seen. 'She could have been a professional designer.'

'I agree. But it wasn't seen as compatible with her royal obligations.'

Annalena's gaze sharpened. Was he telling her a queen wouldn't have time for another career? That if she took the throne, she'd have to give up her profession?

But his expression as he surveyed the room suggested he wasn't thinking of her.

She racked her brain for everything she could remember about the now dead Queen. An American who'd increasingly spent more time overseas than in Prinzenberg. She'd borne the King one live son and one stillborn. In the last few years before her death she'd appeared at the King's side only at a few key royal events.

Had she been unhappy? Was that why Benedikt looked pensive? Annalena had barely had time to adjust to the possibility when he turned that bright stare on her, sending heat arrowing through her body.

'We need to discuss the future.'

She nodded, subsiding gratefully into a chair. Time to finalise this.

* * *

Wary eyes met his. 'Have you looked at the material about the dam? It proves—'

'We'll talk about the dam soon. Our first priority is the crown.'

Benedikt watched her stiffen, the corners of her mouth crimping down.

'The issues are linked. I told you, if you kill the dam project, I won't press my case to be Queen.'

'Saving that valley means more to you than ruling the country? With all the wealth and influence that brings?'

If so, she was remarkable. Through the ages, all around the globe, people had struggled and connived, even killed to win a crown.

A vast chasm carved open his belly. Was that what his father had done? Killed for a crown?

He'd probably carry that suspicion for the rest of his life. Another weight to add to his already heavy burdens.

'Yes, it does mean more to me. There's no benefit to Edelforst from the project, only destruction. The power generated will be diverted elsewhere and so will the profits. There are better, more cost-effective ways of generating power than flooding the valley. We'd lose our heartland. We can't allow that.'

Was that a royal 'we'? With that spark in her eye and tone of condemnation, she was every inch the displeased monarch.

'What about the next project you don't like?'

Her brow knitted in confusion. 'I don't understand.'

'If the government decides on a future policy that affects your province, a policy you disagree with. What will you do?'

'Bring forward our concerns, of course.'

'If that doesn't work and you lose the argument, what will you do then? Reassert your claim to the throne? Threaten a constitutional crisis to get your own way?'

'This isn't about *me*.'

Benedikt shook his head. 'It's absolutely about you. No matter what you say about altruistic motives, if it's proven you have a right to the throne, what's to stop you wielding that against me, or my heirs?'

'I'm not interested in being Queen.'

'But you *are* interested in what happens to Edelforst. Look how far you've gone to protect it.'

She opened her mouth then snapped it shut. 'I'll sign a document written by your lawyers, giving up my right to the throne, on condition—'

'Yes, I know. On condition the dam doesn't proceed.'

He'd heard more than enough about that. What he *needed* to sort out was whether he could legitimately rule Prinzenberg or be forced to hand it over to a woman who wasn't interested in it, and who had few if any of the skills to run it.

Not because she wasn't intelligent, but because she'd never learned. How long would it take a novice to come to grips with what he'd spent a lifetime learning? Especially with so many so-called advisers ready to lead her into decisions that would serve them rather than the country. Cronies who'd benefited from his father's rule and administrators with a vested interest in stifling public scrutiny.

Could Prinzenberg afford to wait years for her to catch up?

Benedikt thought of the problems he'd uncovered in just six weeks and knew they didn't have that much time.

He dragged in a sustaining breath. 'You could sign such a document. And I'm sure that at this moment you're convinced you'll abide by it. But if later you change your mind, *I'd* be the one facing the fallout.'

Her brow knotted. At least she hadn't jumped to contradict him.

'Look at it from my point of view. If it came to light later that you'd signed away your right to the throne to save your precious valley, it would seem like coercion. Maybe, technically, you'd be barred from taking the crown. But all hell would break loose. The people and the parliament could take sides. There'd be division and argument. Prinzenberg would be brought to its knees. It could take years to sort out.'

She sat stiffly, her eyes flashing pure green in her flushed face.

No wonder he'd thought her familiar yesterday. He'd believed he'd looked into that clear gaze before, and he had. But it wasn't Annalena's. The eyes he remembered belonged to Crown Prince Christian, the man whose death had ushered in his own father's rule. Those vibrant eyes looked down at Benedikt every time he passed the royal portraits on the way to his office.

She had her father's eyes.

If he'd still believed that right always won out, he'd be tempted to step away now. Let her have the crown while he pursued his own interests in America and elsewhere.

But Benedikt wasn't that unworldly. Living with his father, not to mention years in business and working for his country, had ensured that.

His country needed a strong monarch who'd protect and serve it well.

'You doubt my word?'

'I doubt that you fully understand the bomb you've primed to explode. Whether it's now or in the future, it *will* explode, unless we deal with it.'

'We can keep this secret. My grandmother kept the circumstances of my birth secret all these years.'

'Which is an extraordinary feat. But only a few, very loyal people knew.' He leaned forward, tempering his voice to hide his urgency. 'Think about what's happened since you came here. The people who have seen you and know you stayed here overnight. Administrative staff who are wondering why certain files have been requested. Only a hand-picked few have conducted interviews in Edelforst, but gossip will be circulating already.'

She slumped in her seat, eyes round. He had to make her understand.

'This is no longer about a very few, trusted people with your well-being at heart. It's gone beyond that. People will be curious and start digging. People who aren't necessarily loyal to me or you. People who learned under my father to use knowledge as a currency to win power for themselves.'

'Why do you keep them on?'

'I won't. But change takes time. I can't sack all his staff and advisers on the spot. I owe them the chance to prove themselves, or not. But my point is, we can't assume everything will be solved with your signature on a piece of paper. We have to prepare for a future when this secret may become public.'

He didn't mention the other possibility. That Annalena might change her mind down the track. What if she had a baby? Maternal instinct might prompt her to claim the throne for the sake of her child.

She stared into the distance, biting her bottom lip, and heat shafted to his groin.

His mouth firmed. He didn't need the distraction of sexual awareness on top of everything else. But it had been there from the moment she'd marched into his office and it wasn't fading. Seeing her in casual clothes, in something like her own environment, only heightened his response. As did her ignorance of or apparent lack of interest in her sexual allure.

How long since he'd met a woman like that? Even in college the women he'd met had been supremely conscious of their appearance and his reaction to them.

And that you were heir to a throne and a fortune.

Excitement tickled his backbone as he surveyed Annalena.

The sexual awareness wasn't one-sided. He'd seen the way her pupils dilated, her gaze on his mouth when he spoke. The way she leaned closer until she realised what she was doing and abruptly pulled back.

Yet she didn't care about his money or status. If anything, those counted against him.

That mutual attraction was the only positive he could see in this whole tangled mess. It would be useful when—

She shook her head, pink lips forming a moue of concentration that made him harden. How could he be susceptible to such an innocent expression?

'I can't see we have any other alternative but an agreement like I proposed.'

Benedikt took his time replying, tamping down his unsettling physical reaction.

He'd come up with an alternative and spent the night and all today testing its weaknesses. It would be difficult but not impossible. Unconventional, but so were the circumstances.

That fact that it was something he'd rather avoid was immaterial. It would be manipulative and ruthlessly efficient, but then wasn't he Karl's son? He swallowed bitterness that perhaps he'd inherited his father's conniving mindset after all.

'I have a solution. You'll get what you want for your province, no dam. I'll get security of tenure as King. And the country gets the stability and leadership it needs.' He paused. 'That's vital. It's not public knowledge and I don't want it to be, but Prinzenberg is facing serious problems. My father and his supporters stripped public assets for their own gain. There are other issues too that will take time to sort out.'

His heart thudded against his ribs. He hated sharing that but needed to make her understand the gravity of the situation.

This wasn't just about Annalena and Benedikt and their personal preferences. It was about the well-being of their homeland. He couldn't renege on that responsibility.

'And I thought it would be straightforward.' Her mouth twisted. 'What's your win-win solution?'

'Now you've opened this can of worms, we can't pretend it didn't happen. We have to move forward. We'll make the best of the situation, for everyone's sake.'

Her frowning stare met his. 'I get a bad feeling when you don't give me a straight answer. What's so bad you have to cajole me into accepting it?'

Benedikt spread his hands, palms up in a gesture of openness to show he had no hidden agenda.

'My coronation goes ahead in a couple of weeks and you'll be at my side.' He watched her eyes widen. 'As my bride. We'll be crowned together.'

CHAPTER SIX

ANNALENA SHOT TO her feet and across the room. When she reached the window and spun around it was to find him on his feet, watching her.

Did he think she was going to make a run for it?

He had the determined look of a man ready to stop her.

She stifled a snort of despairing amusement. How could she run? She was as mired in this situation as he. All through their discussion she'd told herself there would be a way out. Surely they could control things so everything went back to the way it had been.

But she'd found herself agreeing with every point he made. *Except the last one.*

A huff of gasping laughter escaped. She'd been right to worry. His solution wasn't merely bad. It was *catastrophic*.

She folded her arms across her heaving chest, holding in the rackety thud of her heart pounding against her ribs.

'That's preposterous.'

'It's logical.'

'Maybe to a robot that doesn't understand the nuances of people's lives. Not to a *person*.' She hefted another breath. 'It's inhuman.'

She stared at the man watching her so steadily. How could he even *think* it possible? He looked totally unruffled. Had he no sensibility? No feelings?

Yet there it was again, the throb of awareness that made it

seem as though they stood a mere breath apart instead of metres away. She experienced it each time they met. As if there were a link between them. Even his far-fetched suggestion hadn't dimmed it.

His eyes glowed as they locked on hers and suddenly the tight feeling in her chest and her rapid heartbeat weren't just about his outrageous idea.

No, he wasn't a robot. He wasn't unfeeling.

He was human and very, very male.

A twisting sensation started up in the vicinity of her womb.

A moment ago she'd been shocked. Now she was swamped by the certainty she was completely out of her depth with him.

Her head spun and she planted her feet wider.

'Actually, it's a very human solution.' His voice was low, almost intimate. 'We both have issues that need resolution. By combining our resources we solve both problems and do it amicably. Then we can move forward and so can our country. You love Edelforst but it's part of Prinzenberg and I assume you care what happens to the nation.'

'Marrying is a little more than combining our *resources*.' To her chagrin, heat climbed her throat and into her cheeks. 'You're talking about joining our lives.'

And your bodies. Don't forget that. He's not the sort of man to be satisfied with a paper marriage. And he'll want an heir to the throne.

That twisting ache low in her body intensified.

From the first she'd been aware of Benedikt's intense masculine charisma. It wasn't the aggressive, boisterous masculinity some men exuded. But he was a powerful, virile man, an intelligent man who challenged and intrigued her. She was always intensely aware of him, mind and body.

She wasn't gullible enough to think he was proposing a temporary arrangement. Royal marriages didn't work like that, especially when both husband and wife had claims to the throne.

His eyes narrowed. 'You have plans to spend your life with someone else? You have a fiancé? A partner?'

Her chin lifted. She'd bet he knew there was no such person in her life. As well as researching her birth and her right to the throne, his staff would have compiled a report on her.

'Not at the moment.' Not ever. Because there'd never seemed time with her family obligations and her career. The circumstances of her birth and her parents' deaths had impacted her ability to throw herself carelessly into romantic love. Deep in her psyche, love and tragedy were inextricably entwined. Was it any wonder she hadn't taken that risk yet? Wariness, even fear, had kept her from the possibility of an intimate relationship. 'That doesn't mean I won't meet someone right for me in the future.'

He lifted his shoulders, the lazy action emphasising the leashed power in his rangy form.

'Perhaps with time we could be the right person for each other. Successful matches don't always begin with romance.'

He was talking about a match for dynastic reasons. What about the personal? Finding someone to share your hopes and dreams, your fears and delights?

She'd never been hung up on dreams of white bridal dresses and confetti. But through her rather isolated childhood and adolescence she'd hankered for someone with whom she could share her life. Now, approaching thirty, that had solidified into a desire for family, a partner and maybe children. But above all someone who loved her for herself, not for what she could do for her country.

'What about you? Do you have a partner? A fiancée?'

She waited for his instant denial. And waited. Her eyes rounded.

For the first time since the conversation began, his gaze strayed away from her. 'I—'

'You have a long-term lover and you'd throw her over without a second thought? Just to shore up your position?' Annalena backed a step and found herself pressed against the French door, hands splayed against glass. 'How could you—?'

'It's not like that.' He dragged his fingers through his hair, then, as if realising the gesture betrayed emotion, pushed his hands into his trouser pockets.

She stalked across the room to stand before him. She wanted to be close enough to read every nuance of his expression. 'What is it like, then, *Benedikt*?'

Annalena dropped her voice on his name, allowing him to hear the ponderous weight of her distrust and disapproval.

A muscle flicked in his jaw and he rolled his shoulders, standing taller. 'There's no partner, but I *have* been thinking about marriage.'

Surely the two went together. 'I don't understand.'

'Isn't it obvious? I've been considering potential brides. Someone to share the burden of royalty.'

Considering potential brides. He didn't sound happy about it. Did he have a list of requirements? Did he interview candidates? Or did he delegate that to his staff?

No doubt every woman on his list was gorgeous, talented and would make an admirable royal hostess. She'd have to be sexy too. Annalena couldn't imagine him accepting anything less. Especially as sharing the burdens of royalty no doubt included producing an heir.

Swallowing an acid taste, she asked, 'You have someone particular in mind?'

A brief pause before he nodded. 'But there was no agreement, no proposal.'

Annalena shook her head, folding her arms across her chest. 'Oh, that's all right, then. If there was no *agreement*.' Her lip curled. 'You've led her on to believe—'

'Marriage hasn't been mentioned. I haven't led her on.'

Did he really believe that? He must know the effect he had on women. If he'd been seeing her seriously he must have raised expectations.

Benedikt was well-built and imposingly tall with even—okay, handsome—features. Charismatic. Not to mention rich and royal. She suspected he merely had to smile at a woman to raise her hopes.

Unless that woman was clear-eyed enough to recognise his autocratic tendencies. His unyielding drive to get what he wanted. How else could you describe his idea of them marrying?

Cold-blooded, that was what he was. Even if he made her feel hot and bothered.

His gaze snared hers and held it. And despite her distaste for what he was doing, she felt that frisson of awareness, not just of him, but of herself. The heat under her skin, the weight of her breasts against her lace bra and an achy emptiness in her pelvis.

'It's true. I take my duty seriously and that includes choosing a queen. I was in no rush. The woman in question and I know each other but that's all. No promises were made.'

Just how well did they know each other? It wasn't any of Annalena's business, but she couldn't help wondering.

That worried her. *He* worried her.

Their interactions had been fraught with tension and distrust. Yet there'd been brief moments of something like communion, as when they'd entered this room. And too many other moments when she'd thought of him as a man instead of an opponent.

He messed with her head and she knew it wasn't all intentional. Much of the time she sabotaged herself with her wayward thoughts. Her mind strayed to last night's restless sleep and those disturbing dreams, all featuring Benedikt. And he hadn't always been so formally dressed.

Her gaze skittered away.

'Even so, it wouldn't work. I couldn't marry a man I can't respect.' In her peripheral vision she saw his head rock back. 'Not even for my country.'

'I told you, I'm not my father.'

His voice was colourless, the deliberate absence of emotion making her nerves jangle. Because only someone suppressing every emotion could sound so barren.

She looked back at him. Sure enough, despite his stillness, she saw traces of anger and wounded pride in his strong features.

'Yet, even knowing how disastrous that hydroelectric project will be, you didn't stop it when you came to power. You ignored all the evidence that proves it's a mistake. Do you have a personal financial interest in it too?'

Benedikt didn't step closer but his deep breath lifted his shoulders, expanding his chest, making her more aware than ever that she faced a formidable adversary. She felt a jitter of nerves but stood her ground.

'That project is one of many. Until yesterday I hadn't dug deeply into it. I'd accepted that a full feasibility study had been completed.' As if anticipating her protest, he raised his hand. 'Last night I read all the files. The only material there fully supports the benefits of the project. There's no record of representations against the scheme. No other studies, no petitions, nothing.'

'What?' She moved closer, as if proximity could force the truth. 'They have to be there.'

He shook his head, and this close, his expression looked more like regret than anger. 'I read it all and my personal staff double-checked every file. There's nothing negative except an acknowledgement of losses by a few farmers, and a plan to recompense them generously for losing their land.'

Annalena gaped. 'I *knew* the process was rigged. But this…!' It was inconceivable. 'How could they *do* that?'

'My father didn't like dissent, particularly when he'd already made up his mind.'

Benedikt's expression was so grim it cut through her fury. What had it been like, growing up with a father like that?

Worse than growing up fatherless.

He spoke again. 'I'm rapidly learning how deeply that's affected the administration here. I suspect that to keep their jobs, staff learnt to tell him only what he wanted to hear.'

'To the point of falsifying public records?'

'So it seems.' For a moment he was silent. 'The next ruler will have plenty to deal with.'

There was deliberate provocation in the way he watched her. As if daring her to reassert her claim to the throne. Almost as if he'd like her to take it. But that couldn't be.

More to the point, did she believe that he hadn't been part of this corrupt plan?

Her position would be much easier if she doubted his word. The trouble was that she couldn't typecast him as a villain. He was so angry and resentful about what his father had done. And looked serious about the task ahead to make things right.

'So you're not pro-dam?'

'Not if the evidence proves it's a bad idea.'

'I can get you that evidence today.'

Her fingers itched to reach for her phone but now wasn't the time. He was right, there was more at stake than a single infrastructure project.

'Do that. Nothing will proceed until it's reassessed.'

Relief was a mass of butterflies in her stomach. 'Once you have proof of the true situation you'll stop the project.'

She made it a statement, not a question.

Yet instead of agreeing, he stepped up to her, making her pulse thrum and her breath catch.

'I could say the same to you, Annalena. You know the precarious situation created by your claim to the throne. Unless it's settled definitively the country faces a possible power vacuum and uncertainty in all levels of government. That could take ages to sort out. Just when we need stability and good leadership more than ever.' He leaned close and the air between them fizzed with energy. 'If you're as principled as you imply, you'll do your part to rectify that once and for all.'

She swallowed, almost choking on the knot of dismay clogging her throat.

'By marrying you.'

Her tone was supposed to be scoffing. Instead it was a raw whisper. But he heard it. How could he not when he stood so close that his body heat made her temperature spike?

'Exactly.'

What worried her most wasn't that he looked triumphant or smug. He didn't. This wasn't the expression of a man who *wanted* to marry her. He looked determined and expectant.

Her brain whirled with all the reasons marriage was impossible. But every objection she could raise faded before the need to put her country first.

And he knew it. She saw it in his eyes.

Her upbringing had centred around duty. To family, to her people, to Edelforst, and yes, to Prinzenberg.

From a child she'd learned to put others first. Her grandmother had seen to that and had provided a strong role model, counselling, leading and representing her people for decades.

Annalena had always known at some point in the future she'd carry on that role after her grandmother. That was why she'd come here.

But not to marry a stranger!

'There must be another option.'

The lift of one dark eyebrow told her what Benedikt thought of that. 'If you can come up with a better solution, let me know.'

He didn't look any more impressed by the idea than she was. After all, he'd already chosen a suitable bride. He didn't want Annalena any more than she wanted to tie herself to him.

Maybe she could use that to her advantage.

'Marriage between us wouldn't work.'

'We'd make it work.'

Annalena looked away. 'We're not compatible. That would make for a very uncomfortable marriage. *And* everyone would see through the sham of it once we were in the spotlight together. The days are long gone when royals marry solely for dynastic reasons.'

'Not compatible?'

His voice held a note she couldn't identify, but it made her turn to meet his stare.

Instead of looking argumentative, his expression was even blanker than before. As if he couldn't even be bothered to argue the point. Those brief moments of connection she'd felt earlier must have been in her head.

That bland stare riled her.

Once or twice, early in her career, male colleagues had tried to blank her, pretending her input wasn't as valuable as theirs. They'd attempted to undermine her confidence and others' belief in her. It didn't happen any more because she refused to be put down.

Her hands found her hips as she stared into Benedikt's strong features. And noticed again how disturbingly good-looking he was.

Her pulse quickened in self-castigation.

'Exactly. Not compatible. Not attracted.'

It was only a partial lie. She might be strangely drawn to him but he'd given no indication he felt the same way about her. These inconvenient feelings were one-sided. The gleam she'd seen in his remarkable eyes was impatience, not attraction.

For the longest time he said nothing. Annalena was about to turn on her heel and head into the palace when he said, 'I disagree.'

Just that. As if his opinion were all that counted.

Maybe he was like his father after all.

She shrugged. 'There's no point discussing this any further. I'll—'

'It wasn't discussion I had in mind.' His voice dropped to a low burring note that rolled across her skin, making the fine hairs on her arms lift.

'Sorry?'

Suddenly he seemed much closer, though she hadn't noticed him move. 'No need to be sorry.'

Annalena frowned. It hadn't been meant as an apology.

'Can't you feel it?'

Now he *did* move nearer. Their feet almost touched and his breath warmed her face. To her dismay that made a decadent little shiver unfurl down her spine.

Light sparked in his eyes and she caught once more the glimmer of gold in dark brown irises.

Something whispered through her. A warning? An invitation? Whatever it was, it evoked a strange quiver in her stomach. She swallowed. 'Feel what?'

His head tilted closer, as if he wanted to read every nuance of her expression.

Not, absolutely *not* to kiss her.

Even so her heartbeat became a rapid flurry, as when lazy flakes of snow turned into a sudden blizzard.

Her nostrils flared as she detected an intriguing scent. It reminded her of verdant forests and crisp mountain air with a warm undertone of virile male. She inhaled deeply, drawing it in and feeling something tight in her chest give way.

Her brain blared an alarm but her body didn't notice.

She leaned in, chin rising, as if inviting him to close the space between them.

The realisation shuddered through her and she snapped her head back. She was about to move away when his hand closed on her shoulder.

His grip wasn't hard. She could step free, if she wanted to.

But there was something about the touch of those hard fingers through the cotton of her T-shirt that made her want to stay.

'This. Between us. It's been there from the first.'

An automatic denial formed in her head. She'd seen his initial reaction to her and it wasn't attraction. He was just pretending to make a point. But despite knowing that, her objection didn't make it to her tongue. Because, even understanding this was one-upmanship, she couldn't bring herself to stop it.

Another little tremor down her spine, through her legs and right to the soles of her feet.

That golden gaze dipped to her mouth and the beat of her blood turned to a roar in her ears. Her lips parted so she could suck in more air.

His eyes lifted to hers and the world telescoped so there was just him. Him and her. Every sense clamoured and her toes curled as awareness stirred.

Softly, so gently she thought at first she'd imagined it, something stroked her cheek. She caught a glimpse of his raised hand and his finger skimmed from her cheekbone to her chin, creating warmth deep in her body.

She had to break free. Now.

Resolute, she grabbed his wrist and pulled his hand away just as he leaned closer. Her breath snatched as his heat engulfed her. Wide shoulders filled her vision and gleaming golden-brown eyes fixed on her mouth as he brought his face to hers.

Annalena told herself to step back but was transfixed, waiting for the moment his mouth touched hers.

Surely one moment of curiosity was allowed? One moment before sanity returned.

He was so near her vision blurred, her eyes fluttering closed.

The moment stretched, her every sense on alert.

But when his mouth touched her it wasn't on the lips. She felt his mouth caress her earlobe as he whispered, 'Actually, we're *very* compatible. Attuned, even.' His voice was a rumble that turned her insides to a quivering mess and her knees to jelly. 'You're shaking in anticipation, did you know? If you'd just relax…'

'What? You'd seduce me in your summerhouse?'

Her nails dug into his wrist as she flung his hand away and stepped back. Eyes snapping open, she saw him blink, his expression for a second almost confused as he straightened to his full height. Her one consolation was that he looked almost as dazed as she felt.

But Annalena couldn't let that show. Desperately she reined in her anger, knowing if he saw it he'd realise it had its roots in disappointment.

He'd be right. She'd felt the drag of attraction from the first, while he'd felt *nothing*. He was playing on her weakness.

She thrust her shoulders back, hoping he wouldn't notice the way her nipples had hardened.

A lifetime concealing feelings behind a smile came to her rescue. Yet she didn't trust herself to meet his eyes. Instead she focused on the tiny scar above his left cheek.

'I'd rather you didn't practise your wiles on me, Benedikt.' She dragged air into too-tight lungs. 'This situation is hard enough without pretending attraction that's not there.'

'Annalena—'

'Let's talk later. I've had enough for now.' She turned and strode out the door.

CHAPTER SEVEN

'It's completely outrageous,' Annalena repeated into the phone as she stared at the dusk-darkened gardens.

She wished she could be anywhere else but she couldn't leave until she and Benedikt came to some agreement. So she'd turned to her grandmother and they'd discussed the situation at length. It had been a relief talking to Oma. She'd been sympathetic and supportive. Unfortunately she hadn't been able to suggest a way out of this mess.

'Actually,' Oma said, after a long silence, 'in some ways it's an elegant solution, to have you share the throne.'

'Oma! How can you say that? It's horrible and—'

'I know, I know. I was obviously wrong about him, my information was flawed. He's an appalling man and you hate him. But then he's Karl's son. The apple doesn't fall far from the tree and if the tree's rotten…'

Annalena bit her lip then forced the words out. 'He's not like that. I don't like him but he's not like his father. He seems genuinely concerned about the country, for one thing.'

'Ah.' There was a wealth of meaning in that single syllable. 'You don't hate him after all.'

'Just because I don't think he'd kill for the throne, doesn't mean I *like* him. He's the most arrogant, infuriating man. He even tried to convince me—'

'Convince you of what?'

'Nothing important. It doesn't matter.'

Annalena was *not* going to admit how he'd undone her with the touch of his lips to her ear and the caress of his breath. That said more about her dormant love life than about him.

She shifted as that ache started up again deep inside. It had been there all day and every time she remembered those moments in the summerhouse she felt edgy all over again.

It was shaming. He'd merely been playing games while she'd reacted to him as if…

She cut off the thought, unwilling to go there.

'If you say so, darling. He's despicable but at least he knows his duty to the country.'

Annalena frowned. 'Despicable might be a bit too strong. But he thinks his way is the only way. He's too used to getting what he wants, particularly with women.'

'Ah, like that, is he? A puffed-up peacock. That's interesting. I'd heard he was actually quite sensible.'

Annalena didn't say anything. She supposed he *was* sensible, when it suited him. The way he'd outlined their situation had been compelling. But that didn't mean his conclusion was right.

'But he's wrong. There must be another way out of this.'

The silence lengthened and her tension grew.

When she was little her grandmother had always been there to comfort her, assuring her everything would be okay. But she wasn't a little girl now. She and her grandmother shared a relationship based on love but also honesty. Nowadays the Grand Duchess didn't soften the truth to make it more palatable. It was something Annalena admired, the old lady's determination to face problems.

Her silence now was a bad sign. Annalena had been so sure she'd have another option to offer.

'I'm afraid I agree with his analysis.' The old lady's tone made Annalena's stomach drop. 'He might be conceited but he's acutely aware of the pitfalls. This secret is growing too big. There's no guarantee we can keep it quiet. If it becomes public knowledge the fallout could be disastrous.' She sighed. 'I've lived through uncertain times. I don't want to see that again.'

Deflated, Annalena leaned against the window sill. 'But there must be an answer that doesn't involve marriage and me becoming Queen.'

Another silence, longer this time.

Sharp claws dug into Annalena's chest, dragging down, lower and lower. She drew in a shuddering breath.

'I'm not cut out to be Queen. I don't want to be.'

'We don't always get what we want, my darling.'

'You *want* this?'

She heard a drawn-out sigh. 'I'd hoped you'd find happiness. At the same time, this *is* your destiny. Your right and your duty. It's what your parents would have wanted, for you to rule the country.'

Annalena didn't know what to say. It was all well and good to talk about duty but this... Marrying a stranger! Taking a role for which she hadn't prepared.

'You know,' her grandmother said eventually, 'sometimes things aren't as they seem. Did I tell you how I met your grandfather?'

Annalena frowned at the ugly gilded clock on the other side of the room, her mind still on Benedikt and his proposition. 'I don't think you have.'

'Ah. I didn't like him you know, not at all.'

Annalena stiffened, shocked. 'That can't be. The way you've always talked about him!' And it wasn't just what Oma had said but her tone and the soft light in her eyes when she spoke of her dead husband. Everyone knew the pair had been devoted.

'Oh, I *came* to love him. He was a wonderful man. But at first... Pfft. I thought him a pompous waste of space.'

An unwilling smile curved Annalena's mouth. 'Really? I can't imagine you giving such a man a chance to make a better impression.'

'That's just it. He was a visitor and I had to entertain him, though it was obvious my mother was matchmaking. It's a wonder he survived. I was sorely tempted to push him into the lake or over a cliff.'

'He can't have been that bad.'

'Well, no. As I eventually found out. But to begin with we rubbed each other the wrong way. Sparks flew whenever we were together. I found him completely infuriating. But first impressions aren't always right, my darling.' She paused. 'Maybe you should take a step back. Maybe your Benedikt isn't as bad as you think.'

He wasn't *her* Benedikt but Annalena saved her breath. There was no point protesting. Her grandmother's take on the situation was completely different to hers.

Soon after, Annalena said goodnight and ended the call.

Far from calming her, talking with Oma had unsettled her more. To the old lady, duty was a given. While she sympathised, she didn't view a royal marriage and coronation as a disaster. She'd probably be delighted to see her granddaughter as Queen.

Annalena frowned, rubbing her arms.

A wayward thought tickled her brain, stirred by the reference to matchmaking.

Had Oma suspected Annalena's trip to the capital might lead to this debacle? Surely not. Even her canny grandmother couldn't have foreseen that.

Annalena stared into the night, wishing she could swap the floodlit gardens and city lights for her familiar view of mountain peaks.

Tomorrow she'd see Benedikt and he'd demand her answer. She *wanted* to say no. But this had gone far beyond what she wanted personally.

We rubbed each other the wrong way. Sparks flew whenever we were together. I found him completely infuriating.

Oma's words circled in her head. They were so apt, perfectly describing Annalena's situation.

Except for two things. First, her Oma had had the freedom to make up her own mind. Annalena's situation felt like a noose around her neck, tightening with each passing hour.

Second, what she and Benedikt felt for each other wasn't the beginnings of love. He was calculating and coldly pragmatic and she had no need for any man to tell her what to do. That moment of searing connection in the summerhouse, when she'd read something like hunger in his eyes, when the very air had felt charged with awareness—it had occurred *after* he decided he needed to marry her.

He wasn't interested in *her*, just what she represented. She wanted to save Edelforst and he, what did he want? It sounded as if he worried about the stability of the kingdom, yet, at the same time, was he like his father, driven by the need for personal gain?

They were mismatched. Even if their marriage benefited the kingdom, it would be a personal disaster.

'The Princess Annalena, sir.'

Frowning, Benedikt looked up from his desk. The fact the morning sky was still pink didn't bode well.

Annalena wouldn't visit at dawn to bring good news. Yesterday she'd looked at him as if he were something that slithered under the forest leaf litter.

That had stung, not least because he was used to attracting women, not repelling them.

His proposal might be unconventional but it was a perfect solution. How many generations had sealed a dynastic agreement with marriage? Though he'd rather avoid marriage, he told himself needs must, ignoring the cold shiver down his spine. His parents' marriage and the dysfunctional family in which he'd been raised had given him an aversion to marriage.

But a king needed an heir. He'd even started taking steps in that direction before this disaster blew up. Annalena's news just made the need to marry urgent.

Yet he recalled her horror when he'd suggested it and felt

the spectre of his father stalking his conscience. Was he cornering her into marriage because beneath his lofty ideals he simply wanted the crown for himself?

He shoved his chair back, repelled by the idea. He was on his feet as she walked in and Matthias exited, closing the door.

She looked as if she hadn't had much more sleep than Benedikt. Yet the sight of her made his pulse quicken and his belly clench.

Because she held the security of the nation in her hands.

But it was more. This woman drew him in ways that had nothing to do with her claim to the throne. That, above all else, raised his hackles in wariness. He didn't have time for further complications. The situation was already convoluted enough.

'Won't you sit?' He rounded the desk and gestured towards a sofa.

Bright green eyes met his and his chest tightened.

Yet she wasn't trying to dazzle him. Again she wore casual clothes. Making a point that she wasn't impressed enough to dress up for him? Or because she hadn't planned to stay in the palace?

Jeans and a pale blue shirt that complemented her clear skin. In this place where everyone dressed formally, even behind the scenes, she was like a breath of fresh air.

'Thank you.'

She turned and took a seat and Benedikt had to wrench his gaze from the loving fit of denim against female curves and the supple sway of her hips.

'I wasn't sure you'd be in the office yet.'

Benedikt shrugged as he sat opposite her. 'I'm an early riser.' And sleep had been impossible. 'How did you sleep?'

Her eyes widened as if surprised. Annoyance stirred. Just how much of his father's reputation was she attributing to him? He felt like saying his mother had insisted on impeccable manners. That he wasn't an ogre who ate pretty little girls for breakfast.

Annalena shrugged. 'Not well. I had a lot on my mind. You?'

'The same.'

'What's so amusing?'

He hadn't realised he was smiling. 'In the short time we've known each other we've never beaten around the bush, have we? I appreciate that. I prefer unvarnished fact to polite untruths.'

'So do I.'

He believed it. Her reaction to his proposal had been forthright. His bruised ego was testament to that.

'I assume you're here to give me your answer.'

She inclined her head, her mouth pinching. 'Not that you actually asked.'

Benedikt frowned. 'I did you the courtesy of sharing the truth, Annalena. What is it you want? For me to get down on bended knee—?'

'No!' Her eyes rounded in horror. He couldn't decide whether it was because she wanted nothing to do with him, or because she didn't want to enact a farce. 'There's no need to insult us both with such a performance.'

Relief stirred, but so did annoyance. She had a unique ability to discomfort him.

'So you've made a decision.'

Her hands twisted in her lap before she saw him watching. Instantly she lifted her hands to the arms of her chair, adopting a pose that looked graceful and nonchalant. Except for the quickened pulse at her throat.

He liked it, he realised. The combination of outward serenity on a woman who, he'd learned, was volatile. Passionate.

Something stirred at the prospect of knowing her better.

Because, he realised, he *would* be knowing her better. If she planned to reject his proposal she wouldn't be jittery. Not that an ordinary observer would see her nerves. She pulled her collar close then sat straighter, the image of royal composure.

Inside him a tiny demon danced with glee. She was going to say yes.

'I *have* made a decision.' Her needle-sharp gaze skewered him. 'I'll accept the throne and marriage. With provisos.'

'Naturally.' He should have known she wouldn't make this straightforward. 'Go on.'

'I want your signature on a document stating that the dam won't go ahead and I want your decision announced publicly, before the engagement is made public.'

'My decision?' he scoffed. 'Don't you mean *yours*?'

He'd yet to see the detailed argument against the project. Yet he couldn't fault her logic or her bargaining skills. He admired her for both.

'I'm happy to wait until you've read the papers. I sent them again to your office last night. In fact, take your time. I'm in no rush.'

'No. We'll finalise this quickly. And while we're talking about conditions, I have one. I want you to stay here until we announce the engagement.'

She blinked, pupils darkening the green of her eyes. Her skin paled. But instead of making her look fragile, the changes emphasised her allure and that elusive touch-me-not air.

Excitement stirred. She might have perfected the look but he'd learned her body sent a different message. Yesterday when they'd got close he'd felt her change from aloof to breathless anticipation.

Before Annalena's arrival he'd forced himself to consider marriage despite his own antipathy. Now though, he saw definite compensations.

'But I have work. Meetings. I can't just cancel everything.'

'It won't be for long. There's a grand ball at the end of the week, an official welcome to me as the incoming King. It will be a perfect opportunity to introduce you and announce our engagement.'

She shook her head. 'That's too soon.'

'The sooner the better. Your people in Edelforst will welcome an early resolution to the dam issue and there's no reason for us to delay, not with our coronation approaching so quickly. It's much better if people get used to the news in advance of the coronation.'

Annalena might have been carved from stone. She sat so still, as if she'd forgotten how to breathe. Yet when she spoke her tone was even.

'Do you have any idea how long it takes to create a ball gown, made to measure? Not only made-to-measure but spectacular? Because, believe me, only spectacular will do if you intend to announce our sudden engagement.'

He didn't, but that wasn't going to stop him. 'I'm sure there are any number of suppliers who'd move heaven and earth to fit you with a suitable dress in time. Designing for a queen would make their name.'

Her jaw worked. Was she grinding her teeth? Still her composure didn't crack. 'I can't persuade you to put off the coronation a little?'

'You assume correctly. The date is set. The only thing that will change is that it will be a double coronation and a wedding on the same day. It will make things much easier for us, for you, in the long term.'

He waited for the outburst but it didn't come. Instead she surveyed some point on the far side of the room. He could almost hear her brain working.

'Very well. I'll attend the ball but I can't stay here. At the very least I need to be visiting couturiers and—'

'No need. They'll come here. My staff will organise it this morning.'

Her head snapped around, her gaze fixing on his. He felt the sizzle of energy under his skin as if he'd been zapped by a live wire.

'An excellent idea.' Even white teeth bit off the word. 'But they can come to my home in Edelforst.'

Benedikt shook his head. He had no intention of allowing her off the premises until this deal was sealed. Not just with a marriage contract but with a public announcement so she couldn't back out. He needed to control the information around her right to the crown and their agreement until everything was settled.

He'd have security bar the palace exits if need be. But that would only cause fuss and bother. Annalena would be outraged and storm at him. He'd rather channel her energies into more productive directions.

'Time is of the essence, Annalena, remember? If you're here for fittings we'll make the deadline. If everyone has to traipse into the provinces...' He shrugged and spread his hands. 'Besides, a couple of days in the palace means you'll be available to sign relevant documents. You can get up to speed on any unfamiliar royal protocol. Better to be prepared, don't you agree?'

'I could still be available if I stayed in a hotel.' She paused, one eyebrow arching. 'Or don't you trust me out of your sight?'

Benedikt silently cursed. He'd promised honesty. 'Would you, if our situations were reversed? Would you trust *me*?'

Her gaze flickered. Her mouth tucked in at the corners as if suppressing disapproval or disappointment.

She rose in one graceful movement. 'Very well. I'll stay until the ball. But the morning after, I go home.'

She waited long enough to see him nod then swept from the room.

Benedikt was torn between relief and admiration.

Already she looked and acted every inch the Queen. He suspected she had the makings of an excellent ruler. For all her unpredictability and lack of training, she was focused on the public good, not herself. She listened, even when she didn't want to hear unpalatable truths.

Marrying her had been an impulsive idea, triggered by bizarre circumstances. But it was one of his best.

The question was whether he could break through her wall

of disdain so they could forge a workable marriage. A mutually...acceptable marriage.

Another challenge to add to the long list, Benno.

Along with turning around a failing administration, rooting out corruption, announcing a betrothal that would stun the world and taking on the burden of ruling a country that had begun to lose faith in its leadership.

He had to win over the most determined, proud, distrustful, *distracting* woman he'd ever met and persuade her he wasn't some sort of Bluebeard. Easy!

He raked his hand through his hair and closed his eyes, ignoring the ache pounding at the back of his skull. He'd always liked a challenge but this...

CHAPTER EIGHT

'Madam, may we come in? His Majesty sent us.'

There was a sharp rap on the door to Annalena's suite but before she could reach it, the door opened.

She met a familiar, assessing gaze. It was less dismissive today yet she couldn't see anything akin to respect there. It was the woman who, a bare couple of days before, had tried to evict her from the palace. The woman who hadn't passed on the news that Annalena was waiting to see the King.

Unless Benedikt was lying and he'd known she was there all along.

It was profitless to ponder that now. In time she'd uncover the truth, when she had more than instinct to guide her. The man's actions would speak for his character.

'Madam?' From the threshold, impatience coloured the woman's tone. As if she had every right to intrude without invitation.

Annalena spoke into her phone. 'I'm sorry. The people I was expecting have arrived early. I'll call back later.'

She ended the call and walked to the door, rather than call across the vast room.

Her visitor looked sleek and self-important, again in a tightly tailored skirt and jacket, another silk shirt and high heels. Making Annalena aware of her jeans and casual shirt.

'You have the advantage of me. Clearly you know who I am but I don't know who you are.'

It was time someone taught the woman manners.

Annalena saw her eyes widen then narrow speculatively, and wondered at her attitude. Was she such a favourite she thought she could get by without common courtesy?

She *was* beautiful with her dark eyes and striking bone structure.

Was she a favourite of Benedikt's? Could that explain her arrogance?

Annalena tasted bitterness on her tongue.

No, he might be manipulative but surely he wasn't crass enough to make her deal with his mistress.

'Ida Becker, madam. I work for His Majesty.'

Did Annalena imagine the woman's taut expression softened as she mentioned him? She swung her gaze beyond her visitor's shoulder. 'Please come in.'

Annalena positioned herself beside the door, greeting the dress designer and her staff who followed, wheeling in rack after tall rack of gowns.

The sight of them filled her with dread. In only a few days she'd attend her first royal ball. At which time her engagement would be proclaimed.

After that there'd be no escape.

She could hear her Oma's voice in her head, talking about duty.

Her stomach churned, nausea stirring, until she sensed all eyes on her and turned, a serene mask firmly in place.

For the next fifteen minutes the discussion was all about the ball, Annalena's colouring and dress styles. She found herself saying less and less, which didn't seem to matter as everyone else had opinions.

The fact was she didn't know anything about formal ball gowns. Technically she might be a princess and, yes, Oma had insisted she learn to dance gracefully, but she'd never been to a ball. The glamorous events her grandparents hosted had ended with the death of their only child. As for attending regal events in the capital, the family had avoided them from that date.

Annalena knew how to dress well for conferences and civic events in what she thought of as business formal. Or wear traditional clothes for festivals. But a full-length ball gown? She'd never needed one.

For the first time she wished she'd spent less time researching botany and a little time pondering fashion. Could she pull this off and not look like the country bumpkin she suddenly felt? How many would be waiting, after Benedikt made his announcement, to see her fail?

'How about something like this?'

Ida Becker held out a long dress's voluminous skirt that seemed to consist of puffy tulle flowers. Annalena thought instantly of an oversized meringue. Worse, while some yellows worked for her, others, like this, would make her look jaundiced.

Annalena surveyed the woman's blank expression. Did Ida have no eye for colour, or was she trying to sabotage her?

If so, why? Once more, Benedikt's name came to mind.

Before Annalena could object to the dress, the designer did. She shook her head emphatically and requested that Ms Becker stop fingering the delicate fabric, so crisply that Annalena had to stifle a smile.

Then the woman turned to her. 'Now, madam, if you'll permit, we need to take your measurements. If you wouldn't mind stripping to your underwear.'

Four sets of eyes scrutinised her and she felt a flicker of nerves. The last time she'd undressed before a stranger was when her grandmother had insisted she be fitted for her first bra, an experience she'd never wanted to repeat.

Annalena rose and reached for her shirt's top button. 'Thank you, Ms Becker, that will be all.'

'But—'

'I'll call if you're needed.'

By the time she'd finished unbuttoning, Ida had left, the door closing hard behind her.

'Sensible decision,' the designer said. 'She obviously has no idea what suits you. Why she thought she could add anything useful I don't know.' She clicked her fingers and one of the assistants scurried forward with a tape measure. 'Now, let's begin.'

'Hello?'

Her voice wasn't as Benedikt had ever heard it. He was used to clipped words and a shadow of suspicion. But her voice was mellow, with a warm, husky edge that made the flesh at his nape tighten and his groin stir.

He frowned. 'Annalena? Where are you?'

His staff had assured him she hadn't left her rooms, but he'd tried the landline several times already, finally resorting to her mobile phone.

'Where do you think, since you sent a stream of visitors to keep me out of mischief?'

She didn't sound quite so languid now, but there was still something about her tone...

'So you admit you're a mischief-maker?'

To his surprise that elicited a gurgle of laughter, rich and velvety. He shifted in his office chair on the far side of the palace, horrified at how her casual laugh went straight to his gonads.

'If only you knew. I was always the good girl. Serious, studious.'

Benedikt's imagination took the idea and ran with it.

Instead of a dirndl or jeans and T-shirt, his mind supplied a fitted pencil skirt, high-collared shirt and heels. Her green eyes surveyed him over clear glasses with an invitation at odds with her buttoned-up clothes. And she was pouting, her plush mouth pure invitation.

She looked like an incredibly alluring librarian. He could imagine her descending a tall library ladder, book in hand, the tight fit of her skirt lovingly outlining her backside and slender legs. His fingers twitched as if to reach for her.

Benedikt cleared his throat. Since when did he have librarian fantasies?

Not librarian fantasies. Fantasies about Annalena. Remember last night's dreams?

He adjusted his trousers where they'd grown tight.

She spoke again, saving him from the need to reply. 'My grandmother demanded good behaviour. I had to be a role model.'

Benedikt rubbed his jaw and sank back in his chair. 'I know how that feels.'

Even if he baulked at sharing real power, his father had been adamant Benedikt be the perfect crown prince because that reflected on him.

'You too? Did you ever rebel?'

'All the time. But not in public.'

From the moment he could choose for himself he'd spent most of his time outside Prinzenberg, returning only when necessary. It had made his father furious but he'd put up with it when he'd realised Benedikt's growing business acumen led to sizeable profits. Profits he'd hoped to redirect to his own coffers.

'And you? Were you serious and studious all the time?'

Her next breath held a hint of another chuckle and Benedikt felt his skin heat. 'I might, *occasionally*, have let my hair down.'

For a man who considered himself pragmatic and achievement-orientated his imagination was suddenly working overtime. Now it supplied a tantalising image of Annalena with her gleaming hair loose across her breasts. She leant back against heaped pillows, her only garment a lace negligée that revealed more than it concealed of her body. He was kneeling above her, lowering himself...

'How?' he croaked. 'How did you let your hair down?'

'The usual. Sneaking down to the local festival late at night, hanging out with other teenagers, tasting the local beer.'

'Just as well your grandmother didn't find out.'

She had the reputation of being a tartar.

'Oh, she knew. She told me later she was pleased to see I had the spirit and ingenuity to sneak out to be with my friends. She might be a stickler for duty and protocol but she's no snob. She believes in the value of individuals, no matter what their supposed social status.'

He digested that. There was more to the old lady than he'd thought. Just like her granddaughter.

'That's where our families differ. My father wanted me to spend my time only with *important* people. Ones who could be of value to him in future. He wasn't what you call a man of the people.'

Benedikt spun his office chair to face the window, taking in the nightscape of the capital's lights.

'That doesn't sound like much fun.'

He frowned. Was that a trace of pity he heard?

'Don't worry, you weren't the only one to sneak out and enjoy themselves.'

Though in his case he hadn't just sat around, drinking beer. He'd developed a taste for fast cars and hot women early. At one stage he'd also sought to deaden the emptiness of his personal life at the roulette wheel, before he realised how pointless that was. After that, and with his grandfather's encouragement, he'd sought his thrills in the business sphere and occasional rock climbing. As for women, he'd become much more discriminating, while avoiding serious relationships.

'Why did you call, Benedikt?'

'I thought we'd eat together. Discuss how you got on today. But I'm told you requested a meal on a tray. Are you all right?'

'Perfectly fine, thanks. But I want a quiet night. I assumed we'd talk tomorrow.'

He should be pleased. That gave him the evening free to work.

Strangely though, he felt…let down. Had he been looking forward to sharing a meal with her?

No, it was merely that he'd planned to discuss some of the many things they needed to cover before the coronation.

'You're exhausted from trying on dresses?'

He heard what sounded strangely like a splash then she spoke, not quite so relaxed now. 'You should try it some time. It takes *hours*. It's easier for men. Once they have your measurements, making formal clothes is pretty standard. But for women there are so many variables, not only colour and style but how you stand and carry yourself. And that's just one dress. Your Ms Becker said you'd given orders for a whole new wardrobe.'

Annalena's voice was suddenly razor-sharp.

Because he wanted her to look like a queen? What was wrong with that?

'It's necessary. From the night of the ball you'll be in the public eye. You'll need to look the part, not only when our engagement photos are taken and at the coronation.'

'I understand that and I've agreed on a dress for the ball and a couple of others. But I prefer not to use just one designer. I'll organise the rest myself, including the wedding dress.'

It was better to patronise a variety of makers yet Benedikt hesitated. Annalena had admitted she wasn't used to the royal court and what he'd seen of her wardrobe…

'My team can provide a list of designers. Your dress for the wedding and our coronation needs to be spectacular.'

He heard an impatient huff. 'Don't worry, I'm not going to sabotage the day by wearing something that lets us both down. I've already contacted a designer in Edelforst.'

Edelforst! The province was best known for agriculture and traditional handcrafts. It *was* beginning to make a name in medical research and robotics, but not, as far as he knew, women's fashion.

He had a momentary picture of her arriving at the grand cathedral in a dirndl and apron.

'I—'

'This isn't negotiable, Benedikt. If I have to go through with this marriage, I'll at least wear something designed and made in my home province.'

He pinched the bridge of his nose, trying to relinquish the need to keep control of every important detail.

Just because she chooses tradition and comfort over glamour it doesn't mean she doesn't know how to dress for the occasion.

This was a test. If they were going to marry, a level of trust was needed.

Unfortunate that the real legacy he'd got from his father was to trust sparingly. There'd been his mother and grandfather and now Matthias. He could count those he'd ever trusted completely on the fingers of one hand.

His father had mercilessly used any weakness to coerce others into doing his bidding, or to hurt them just because he could. No one had been spared, especially not his wife and son. Karl had only been interested in people for what he could take from them.

Annalena wasn't like that. Given the chance, she'd run from him and this marriage. Her honesty about that was strangely reassuring.

'As long as they can guarantee finishing in time.'

'Don't worry, the design's already sorted and she's calling in favours to get the hand-stitching done in time.'

Hand stitching. That sounded disturbingly amateur. But what did he know about dressmaking? All that mattered was that they married.

'Right.' He swivelled to face the desk and the work waiting for him. 'I'm glad you're okay. But we've got a lot to discuss. I'll meet you at eight tomorrow in my office.'

'I'll be there. I—' There was a clatter as if she'd dropped the phone.

'Annalena?'

'Sorry, I was reaching for my glass of wine and almost dropped the phone in the bath.'

She was drinking wine in the bath while he was sitting here facing a load of paperwork? Negotiating over her official wardrobe while lolling, naked...?

'Benedikt? Are you there?'

He scrubbed a hand around his neck. 'Yes, still here. But I have to go. I'll see you at eight.'

He ended the call before she could say more. What she'd already said was enough.

A ragged laugh escaped.

The woman had surely been sent to test his limits, as a king and an all too fallible man.

Forget librarian fantasies. In the far wing of the palace, Annalena reclined in a bath, naked, drinking wine. He could be there in minutes. He *wanted* to be there.

Except when they became intimate it would be on *his* terms, after they'd signed a marriage contract. After he'd got what he wanted: both the throne and therefore the country safe.

He gritted his teeth, opening the detailed reports on the dam. The print blurred because his unruly imagination kept relaying images of a naked, glistening Annalena.

It was going to be a long, hard evening.

CHAPTER NINE

THREE DAYS LATER Annalena stood in Benedikt's study. The room with its full bookshelves and comfortable leather chesterfields felt familiar, almost cosy, since she'd spent so much time here.

There'd been so many details to discuss and agree on. But today was different. It wasn't just the pair of them.

Apart from Benedikt's assistant, Matthias, there were half a dozen witnesses to today's formalities. All male, all holding important government positions, and all serious, their expressions ranging from sombre to aghast, making her feel more than ever like an unwelcome outsider.

Annalena kept her expression serene despite the crash of her heart against her ribs.

Benedikt sat at the desk, signing document after document with a confident flourish.

With their dark suits and long faces, the men gave a funereal air to the proceedings.

Annalena's green and silver dirndl seemed festive, almost frivolous by comparison. But her new wardrobe wasn't ready and these were the only formal clothes she'd brought.

How would these disapproving men have looked if she'd appeared in jeans and a T-shirt, the ones she wore for exploring the vast palace grounds? Her lips twitched and she looked up to see Matthias nod genially in her direction.

That tiny show of solidarity warmed her. She'd tried not to dwell on negative thoughts but felt very much alone.

Half an hour ago Benedikt had told her she was doing the right thing. But it was hard to believe, now their agreement was about to become real.

He put his pen down and stood, his gaze catching hers.

More warmth, a sizzle that flooded her body and made her pulse beat hard and low, but Annalena didn't trust it. He made her feel things she shouldn't. How could she believe his reassurances?

You have no other option.

She was in a corner with no escape.

Squaring her shoulders, she walked to the desk and sat. The royal desk, a huge antique used by generations of kings. Now here she was, an interloper.

She might have a right to sit here because of the blood that flowed in her veins, but it felt wrong. Obviously those around her felt the same. Her life was supposed to be elsewhere. She had a career, friends—

Benedikt's strong hand appeared before her, holding a gold fountain pen. 'When you're ready, Annalena.'

He stood close but didn't crowd her. She had a momentary flash of surprise, registering that she'd grown accustomed to him being near. Her body still reacted with regrettable predictability when he got close, but he didn't intimidate her. It was the disapproving old men glowering from the far side of the desk who did that.

She took the pen, straightened her shoulders and smiled coolly at her audience, refusing to let them see she was rattled. A couple of nervous smiles met hers.

Perhaps they weren't all disapproving, just concerned.

Who could blame them? She wasn't cut out for this, knew nothing about ruling the country.

Focus on the positive. You're a quick learner. You have some skills and people you can consult when in doubt.

Suppressing a sigh, she looked at the papers before her. In a gesture of good faith, Benedikt had signed first, ending the dam project, then signing the marriage contract and the documents giving her the right to rule jointly with him.

Even so, she read every word, ignoring the restless shuffle of feet. Finally, when she managed to steady her hand, she began to sign.

The final document was the marriage agreement.

Annalena flexed her fingers. They were stiff as if she'd been writing all morning. The words blurred, formal clauses turning into gobbledygook.

She blinked, trying to clear her vision.

She wasn't a romantic, but she'd assumed one day she'd marry for love. Or at least marry someone she liked.

Did she like Benedikt?

Sometimes she liked him too much. There were times when it felt as if they hovered on the brink of something more than reluctant acceptance.

Don't you want more than acceptance? Don't you want to be valued for yourself? Not for your claim to the throne?

Annalena swallowed over the constriction in her throat. She didn't have that luxury. Yet this felt wrong, promising to share her life, *herself* with a man she barely knew.

Someone on the other side of the desk coughed but beside her Benedikt stood steady, unmoving. As usual, she felt his presence without even turning her head.

Repressing a sigh, she grabbed the pen and signed.

There was no going back. She only hoped she hadn't just made the biggest mistake of her life.

'Don't leave, Annalena.'

She cast a longing look at the door closing behind the departing men. Now it was done, she needed time to gather her thoughts and her shaky equilibrium.

Because no matter what duty decreed, it was tough knowing her life would never be the same.

An hour in the woodland beyond the formal gardens would

restore her calm. Being outside in the natural world had always been her go to when things got tough.

Was it any wonder she'd become a botanist?

'I have phone calls to make.'

She'd promised to phone her grandmother after the contract was signed. She turned to find Benedikt watching her, head tilted as if the better to scrutinise her.

The man who was going to be her husband.

Adrenaline shot through her bloodstream.

'I won't keep you long.'

'Of course.' She stifled an unfamiliar sensation that felt too much like panic and made herself walk back to the desk where he stood.

'It will be okay, Annalena, as long as we work together.'

His words and the expression in his eyes surprised her. She'd spent the days resenting the situation she found herself in. Yet he wasn't an ogre, just, she hoped, a man trying to do right by his country.

Had he read her fear? The idea was insupportable. She didn't want his pity. She'd spent her life standing up for herself and her people. Now she needed to be his equal if she were to have any chance of making this relationship work. A lifetime's lessons from her redoubtable Oma came to her aid as she wiped the frown from her face, offering him an expression of calm certainty.

'Yes, that's the only way. What did you want to discuss?'

For a second longer his gaze held hers then he looked down to something in his hand. 'We'll announce our betrothal at the ball in a couple of days. Plus there's a session booked for official photos. You'll need this.'

He held his hand out to reveal a green velvet box. A ring box.

'Oh.'

Her heart pounded so high it felt as if it tried to escape via her throat. Her cheeks flushed on a rush of heat before the ice forming in the pit of her stomach counteracted it.

He pressed a button and the lid popped to reveal a dazzling ring. It was plain but for the large, emerald-cut stone of clear, deep green that shone with inner fire.

Her grandmother owned a substantial jewellery collection but Annalena had never seen any piece so beautiful.

'It's from the treasury. You're welcome to choose something else if you prefer, but I thought this suited you.'

She raised her eyes. 'Oh?'

'The colour matches your eyes. And—' he lifted his shoulders '—because of its simplicity.'

Everything inside stilled. 'Because I'm simple?'

The last few days, with endless sessions about royal responsibilities and protocol, had left her fully aware of her ignorance in such matters, feeling more than ever out of her depth. But she'd thought she'd learned well.

She and Benedikt had been at loggerheads from the first but he'd never offered insults.

'Of course not!' Lines carved across his forehead. 'If anything, you're complex and not to be underestimated.' He paused. 'I was referring to your beauty. It's unfussy and natural. The ring reminded me of that.'

Annalena had no words. He thought her complex and not to be underestimated? That made her sound like a worthy opponent.

But beautiful? She had even features and her eyes were an unusually pure green. Did he think she needed flattery? Did unfussy and natural mean unsophisticated? But her self-esteem didn't hinge on what he thought.

He probably felt it necessary to say *something* complimentary when presenting an engagement ring. Words of affection, much less love, would be insulting.

Yet she couldn't banish the tiny curl of delight deep inside at the compliment. Remarkably he'd made her feel special. Not what she envisaged from the man forcing her hand.

'Thank you, Benedikt. It's good you thought of a ring. I'd

completely forgotten. It would have looked odd if I'd appeared without the appropriate prop.'

She took it out and slipped it on. It was a little snug, making her hyperconscious of its weight around her finger. Or perhaps that was because she didn't usually wear rings.

She moved her hand, transfixed by the gorgeous ring. An emerald? Probably, since it came from the treasury.

Annalena forced a smile to her lips. 'It looks regal, doesn't it? Perfect for the part I'm playing.'

Benedikt strode the long corridor to the guest wing. They were due to open the ball soon, but first he needed to see Annalena in her suite.

In case she's a no-show?

No, she'd given her word.

Because you want to vet what she's wearing? You don't trust her fashion sense?

That was the least of his worries. The designer knew what was needed. Annalena's outfit for the engagement photos couldn't have been better. The tailored skirt and jacket in a deep rose colour had been a perfect foil for her colouring. She'd looked elegant and attractive.

Yet her smiles hadn't reached her eyes and she'd been as wooden as a marionette when the photographer asked them to stand together. It had been hard finding convincing photos to project the image of an eager bride and groom.

She hadn't deliberately tried to sabotage the shoot, but her discomfort had been clear.

His jaw clenched. Photos could be airbrushed but tonight they'd be on show before hundreds of curious spectators. When he announced their engagement everyone needed to be convinced it was real. That it was what they both wanted.

What he *didn't* need was a bride-to-be who looked as if she were stepping onto a hangman's scaffold. Or one who regarded the flawless emerald on her ring finger as a *prop*.

How mistaken he'd been, thinking she'd like the ring. As soon as he'd seen it he'd wanted to see it on her finger. Almost as if he wanted to mark her as his own. It was a primitive, possessive instinct that didn't match their situation at all and made him uncomfortable whenever he thought of it.

Her response had drained his satisfaction at finding the perfect piece.

Stupid to feel rebuffed over a piece of jewellery. There were more important things at stake. Like making tonight look convincing.

Women had always been easy for him. He was used to their interest, their attention, their desire. He'd never imagined he'd have to coach a woman into acting as if she wanted to be with him.

He reached her suite, knocked and entered at the sound of her voice.

Midstride over the threshold, he halted. His hand clenched on the doorknob, his bow tie seemed to tighten around his throat. There was a thrumming in his ears as she moved towards him. He tried to swallow but it felt ridiculously difficult, as if he'd forgotten how.

All that in just a second. Then he stepped forward, closing the door behind him.

'Annalena, you look spectacular.' So spectacular, his voice sounded as if he spoke over ground glass.

He'd come intending to compliment her, to put her at ease before tonight's function. But this was no compliment, just a statement of fact.

She wore her hair up, not in an old-fashioned plaited coronet, but a sleek twist. Her face was different, her eyes smokier, her cheekbones accentuated and her mouth...

Her mouth.

He made himself drag his gaze away.

Her dress was simple yet stunning. Strapless, it was shaped to skim her body, glorying in her curves before falling in a straight column to the floor. There were no puffy skirts or outlandish ornamentation. Just Annalena, classically sophisticated and heartbreakingly beautiful.

The dress was emerald green like her eyes. The neckline dipped a little between her breasts, edged with what looked like diamonds.

She wore no jewellery except her ring, but from her shoulders, attached to the dress, hung a transparent, full-length cape of green studded with a galaxy of diamonds.

Benedikt hauled in air to constricted lungs.

'Thank you.' Her voice had a husky edge he liked. 'So do you. Formal evening clothes suit you.'

He shook his head. There was no comparison. He moved closer, something inside him dipping as she stiffened.

That wouldn't do, not tonight.

His concern wasn't just for the image they'd project. He hated her instinctive withdrawal.

Deliberately he conjured a light tone as he stopped before her. 'They look like tiny stars. Did you raid the treasury for diamonds?'

Her eyes widened and she looked down at the filmy material cascading from her shoulders. Her hand lifted as if to touch, then fell. 'Just diamantés, not the real thing. Don't worry. The royal coffers are safe.'

A tiny smile curved her lips and lit her face.

If only he could entice that smile more often. Get her to smile that way at *him*. At this rate no one would be convinced by their betrothal announcement.

He dragged in much-needed oxygen and with it came an elusive scent. The light but seductive perfume of mountain meadows and spring flowers.

Warmth enveloped him like Alpine sunshine and he leaned in. Instantly she took a half-step back, making him clamp his jaw.

'You're early. We're not due to open the ball for a while.'

'Yet you're ready.'

She lifted her shoulders in a shrug that should have been casual but seemed jerky. 'I didn't want to run late. I wanted to look…right.'

It was the first time she'd come close to admitting to nerves or uncertainty. As if to make up for it, she held her head high, her expression calm.

Benedikt wasn't fooled. He felt her tension. 'You look amazing. You'd be the belle of the ball even without our announcement.'

Her expression was quizzical. 'Thank you. Let's hope it goes smoothly.'

'That's why I'm here. There's something we need to fix before we appear in public.'

She frowned. 'Fix? All the arrangements are made. Your staff have been force-feeding me information on the guests for days, not to mention details of how the evening will proceed and every possible etiquette issue.'

'You'll deal with all that easily. And I'll be with you if you're unsure about anything.'

'So what's the problem?'

'This.'

He reached out and touched her hand. Immediately she flinched before standing stiffly, as unresponsive as a piece of wood.

'Are you scared of me?'

'Of course I'm not scared.'

Predictably her chin lifted. But her poise was undercut by the way she clamped her teeth into her bottom lip. He wanted to soothe the soft flesh with his own.

'Do you find me abhorrent?' He didn't believe it but had to ask. 'Every time we come close you stiffen up. At the photo shoot you looked like you wanted to be anywhere else but with me.'

'What do you want me to say, Benedikt? I didn't ask for

this.' She waved her hand in a gesture that encompassed both him and the palace. 'You know I don't want it.'

He'd had a long, difficult week too, as difficult as hers. His patience snapped.

'You think I wanted things to work out this way?' He'd never wanted to marry. He'd seen close up how poisonous and destructive marriage could be. Only his sense of duty forced his hand, and the hope he'd do better than his parents. 'This is bigger than you or me. Bigger than our personal wants. We agreed that.'

Her head tipped back, making him realise he'd stepped in close. But she didn't look intimidated. Her hands were on her hips, her eyebrows arching superciliously. She'd never looked more desirable.

Light flashed off her emerald ring as she gesticulated. 'Which is why I'm dressed like this, ready to go through with tonight's farce. I'm delivering on my side of the deal.'

Her eyes glittered, diffidence replaced by pride and a challenge he felt deep in his gut.

Now this wasn't about a show for the world to see. It was about him and her.

He wanted to curl his arm around her back, tug her close and feel those soft curves against his hardness. He wanted her eyes to turn brilliant with sensual invitation and later, with sated delight.

He wanted Annalena. And despite her anger now, he'd seen the looks she'd sent him this last week when she thought he wasn't paying attention. Looks that made him suspect her tension wasn't about repugnance but something quite different.

Benedikt forced his hands to stay at his sides rather than reach for her.

'It's not enough. You need to do more.'

'More? I'm *marrying* you. There *is* no more.'

He was already shaking his head. 'It's not enough to go through the motions. You have to make it look convincing.

If you flinch every time I get near, no one will believe in our marriage or our partnership as rulers.'

Her eyes darkened and for a second he wondered if he read fear in her eyes. Then the illusion disintegrated. He saw only impatience.

'You want me to nestle close and simper?'

A bark of laughter escaped. 'I can't imagine you simpering but I'd love to see you try.'

He'd enjoy her nestling close, reaching for him.

Slowly her mouth curled into a rueful smile. 'You're right, I wouldn't have a clue how.'

Benedikt waited. Now her flash of anger had disintegrated, she seemed to mull over his words.

'I'm not a good actor.'

'Of course you are. Remember the day you strode into my office and threatened to take the crown from me? You were so self-assured, as if you had no doubts that you'd succeed. But you can't have known for sure it would work.'

'Anger can make anyone brave.'

'Maybe. But what about when we signed the marriage agreement? The witnesses commented later on your poise. You took it all in your stride with complete confidence.' Benedikt lowered his voice. 'But I saw how your hand shook and how you needed time to bring yourself to sign.'

She chewed her lip. 'You weren't supposed to notice.'

But he had and his admiration for her had soared.

'Think of all those times when you've had to project the image people expect, as Princess of Edelforst, or presenting at some academic conference. You're good at hiding trepidation, good at being the person people need you to be.'

Her eyes were wide and her lips parted as if he'd shocked her to the core.

'Did you really think I was so oblivious I wouldn't notice? You play a good game, Annalena, but don't forget I grew up learning those same skills. I can hide my feelings and put on a public face too.'

She breathed deeply, her sigh fluttering across his chin. 'This isn't quite the same.'

He didn't have a name for the emotion that rippled across her features, but it made him regret that he'd had to force her hand.

'No. Not for either of us.'

Though he had no qualms about touching her. Increasingly it seemed the most natural thing in the world.

Warmth closed around his hand and he looked down to see slim fingers curling around his. His heart lurched. It felt like a breakthrough. Instantly he was reminded of those breathless moments in the summerhouse when he'd caressed her and been so sure she wanted him.

'Is that better?'

He looked up to find his gaze snared by gorgeous green eyes. 'It's a start.'

A hint of a frown skated over her forehead. 'What more do you want? We're standing close and I'm touching you.'

'But what if I reach for you? Will you startle and pull away before you have a chance to school your features?'

Her mouth crimped at the corners. 'I'll work on it, okay? Maybe you could warn me if you're going to touch me.'

'And how would that play out in public?' He shook his head. 'That won't always be possible.'

'Okay, okay.' She blew out a gusty breath. 'I take your point. I promise not to tense up if you touch me.'

'Easily said, Annalena.'

Her eyes narrowed. 'You don't trust me?'

He shrugged, enjoying the spark in her eyes. Seeing her feisty and fearless did something to him, his libido especially.

'It's not a matter of trust, but getting acclimatised to my touch. But we don't have time to take things slowly. How about we take a short cut?'

She tilted her head, scrutinising him like some scientific specimen. Did she even notice that he'd turned his hand to thread his fingers through hers?

'What sort of short cut?'

Benedikt failed to repress his smile. 'A kiss. Then you'll see you've nothing to fear from me. After that having me touch your back or your arm will be a walk in the park. What do you say? Shall we?'

CHAPTER TEN

WHAT SHE SHOULD say was a resounding *'No'*. Especially when he looked at her with that gleam in his eyes. He didn't look like a man worried about public opinion. He *looked* like a man who wanted…her.

That stopped her throat and quickened her pulse. He was dangerous. But in that heady moment she welcomed his attention.

Was she projecting her own desire? He had few scruples about doing whatever it took to secure the throne and the country. Appearing interested in her was part of the deal. She'd be crazy to believe it was more than a calculated act.

But he had a point. What if she jumped at his touch in public? This marriage would elicit enough consternation without that.

Maybe a kiss would work as exposure therapy.

Maybe she'd grow blasé about his touch.

Maybe you want to find out what kissing Benedikt is like.

'One kiss.'

Where had that come from? She hadn't planned the words.

Annalena watched a smile unfurl across his face. She read approval but more too. Something that made her wonder if this was a good idea. But she couldn't back out. Showing fear was always a mistake.

Determined to get it over before she could think too much, she stepped so close their bodies almost touched.

She felt his body heat down her whole length. Except it was more than heat. It felt like thousands of sparks igniting across her skin.

All the more reason not to linger. Planting one hand on his chest, she tilted her head.

But her intention to press a brief kiss to his lips died as she registered the thud of his heart beneath his jacket. Watched his eyes zero in on her lips.

Her breath escaped in a sigh because she *felt* that look like a caress. Her pulse hammered and her chest shuddered as she sucked in air.

Just get it done. A few seconds and it will be over.

She rose to brush her mouth against his.

Annalena blinked, stunned to discover his lips were soft. Even that cursory touch brought with it a taste of... She couldn't name the flavour except she liked it.

Benedikt didn't respond, didn't move, his gaze focused on her mouth in a way that made her imagine her lips throbbed. They parted and she licked them, trying to draw in more of that taste. *His* taste.

A fiery arc of heat shot down her body, past her nipples and stomach to the hollow between her thighs.

Golden-brown eyes met hers and one slashing dark eyebrow lifted as if to say *Is that the best you can do?*

He was right. That wasn't a kiss. Yet she was torn between competing instincts. To be cautious and step away. Or be bold and fit her mouth to his.

In the end it was a mix of determination not to be seen as weak and the lure of irresistible temptation.

She put her other hand on his shoulder, holding herself steady as she rose and covered his mouth with hers.

He didn't move but that didn't matter because she knew exactly what she wanted. Tilting her head, she closed her eyes and moved her lips, brushing, nibbling, tasting. The rich, unique taste of him was addictive and she wanted more.

Her fingers drifted up to cup the hot flesh of his neck, thumb on his jaw and fingertips buried in his short hair.

Finally he moved, angling his head to give better access.

Her breath stalled as delight punched hard. She wanted…

Too much. Far more than this tentative caress, yet still Benedikt didn't reciprocate. Did he feel nothing? Not the tiniest spark of pleasure? Was this truly just about her acclimatising to his presence?

Hurt pride seared.

Maybe, like some of his staff, he found her unsophisticated. She'd heard a stifled giggle in the royal offices the other day. From the corner of her eye she'd seen Ida Becker whispering to another woman and caught the words '…wearing a dirndl like a milkmaid.'

As if their national dress were embarrassing!

As if *Annalena* had anything to be ashamed of because she tried to deal with people honestly, not playing at one-upmanship.

Annalena didn't stop to ponder why that provoked her. Why Benedikt's unresponsiveness became unbearable. She simply followed her instinct, stroking her tongue between his lips, demanding entry, then following that delicious taste and exploring the lush mystery of his mouth.

She clasped his head with both hands, tentative no longer as she delved deep and discovered…

Oh.

A shudder raced from her head to her soles as his tongue slid against hers, curling and drawing her deep into plush, velvety warmth that was more inviting than any place she'd ever been.

Something jolted through her like an electric shock. Every sense deepened. Colours appeared in the darkness behind her eyes like a kaleidoscope reflecting sunlight. The scent and taste of him deepened. The satin of his skin beneath her palms and the thick silk of his hair against her fingertips made her hands curl possessively. She *heard* the twin thrum of their pulses, beating in sync.

She'd kissed before. But the last time had been a long time ago. How could she have forgotten?

Unless it hadn't been like this.

Disquiet filtered into her brain. Did he sense it? A second later it vanished as he roped his arms around her, tugging her flush against his body.

Annalena gasped at the myriad sensations. All that hard, masculine heat. The heavy cushion of muscled thighs and broad chest. The slow track of one large hand settling low on her back and drawing her in. Benedikt's mouth moving with hers, his tongue coaxing and enticing.

Goosebumps broke out across her skin as he came alive against her, turning her foray into a mutual caress, deep and slow.

It felt as easy as if they'd done this a million times before. As inevitable as the sun rising over the Alps.

But more exciting than anything she knew.

Annalena stretched high, revelling in his solidity against her yearning body, the strength of long arms encircling her, pulling her close.

There was a muffled sound, a low hum, almost a growl, that she tasted in the back of her throat, and easy familiarity turned urgent. He led her deeper, into places she hadn't gone and she followed eagerly, utterly entranced.

She clung, grasping for purchase as her knees loosened and only his embrace kept her upright. Her blood effervesced like champagne and her toes curled as ribbons of delight danced through her.

Benedikt supported the back of her head in one hand as he bent low, taking her mouth with devastating thoroughness. Making her nipples pucker and her brain atrophy.

Deep within she felt a hungry twist of need. A hollow throb that began in her pelvis but resonated everywhere. Moisture dampened her new silk undies as arousal stirred.

The truth slammed into her brain. This kiss had nothing to do with hurt pride or proving a point, but everything to do with her response to Benedikt.

Annalena's hands tightened on his skull as she tried to climb his body, curving her spine to align her pelvis with his.

She tasted another low, masculine growl that sent her libido into overdrive.

Then, abruptly, nothing.

She heard breathing, harsh and uneven, gulped lungfuls of cold air and felt strong hands at her elbows. They held her as she wobbled on high heels, legs like overcooked spaghetti. Her hands clenched and opened, empty.

Stunned, she lifted impossibly heavy eyelids.

Benedikt loomed over her, dishevelled, lipstick-smeared and distant. His jaw was set, the mouth that had kissed her so voraciously a flat line.

Annalena blinked, barely taking in his rumpled hair and bow tie hanging loose, trying to read his searing gaze. She saw heat but was it from arousal or something else?

His gaze roved her face and her lips throbbed and parted. A second later he withdrew totally, stepping back and putting a world of space between them.

Well, that went well. You came undone while he...

She didn't want to think about how he felt. She had a horrible feeling that passionate kiss had been an experiment on his part, the passion all hers.

Annalena watched him roll his shoulders and straighten to his full height. He wasn't even out of breath whereas her heart hammered as she struggled to draw in oxygen, making her breasts rise and fall quickly.

That's the least of your worries. Never show weakness to an enemy, remember?

Except he hadn't felt like an enemy.

'Was that enthusiastic enough?' she murmured, hiding a wince at her husky, broken voice. 'Not that we'll have to go that far to convince our guests.'

His eyes narrowed and she'd swear she saw annoyance flicker across his set features.

'You're saying that was an act?'

Benedikt's tone was clipped. She hated the contrast, hated herself for what she'd done. How could she let him affect her that way?

She shrugged and walked past him, grateful for the sheer determination that kept her steady on high heels despite feeling as if her bones had melted. 'It wasn't...unpleasant and I wanted to be thorough. Isn't that how exposure therapy works?'

She didn't want to see his reaction to her lie. But she'd tramp over hot coals rather than admit she'd lost her senses as soon as he'd kissed her back.

A shiver ran through her. Their upcoming marriage was more daunting now than ever. She'd just proved she wanted her husband-to-be. But he'd pulled back from her. He might simulate passion but that was all it was, a sham.

Hurt welled. An echo of the ancient self-pity she'd thought she'd conquered years ago. At never wholly fitting in. At always being different. The orphan brought up by an old lady regarded locally with mixed awe, reverence and trepidation. The girl from the castle, privileged but hemmed in by duty and expectation.

Annalena stopped at a mirror over the fireplace to gather her tattered control. She was a mess. Lipstick gone, hair coming down and a flush of sexual arousal emblazoned her throat and cheeks. Even her eyes looked different, heavy-lidded as if she'd just woken. Or left a lover's bed.

'It wasn't *unpleasant*?'

His voice was edged like a sharpened blade. She should have known he'd take her words as a challenge. She *had* known, and struck out rather than admit he'd affected her. But she didn't have the energy to deal with his ego. Not when her world was crumbling.

It had just been a kiss yet it felt like far more. Shockwaves reverberated through her and she wanted to curl up, alone in her room. Better yet, leave this place and never face him again.

A huff of laughter escaped as she tidied her hair. No chance of that!

'You find this funny, Annalena?'

In the mirror she saw he'd moved to stand behind her, tall, broad-shouldered and compelling. Something turned over in her belly and her pelvic muscles pulled tight.

You really are in trouble.

He could use her susceptibility against her. She had to defend against that.

'Not at all.' Defiantly she met his stare in the glass. 'I was thinking how much I'd give to be anywhere else.'

His expression shifted and she almost fancied she saw understanding in his eyes. 'It will get easier, Annalena. I'm not your enemy.'

She wished she could believe it.

You have to believe it or this marriage will destroy you.

Was it possible their relationship might be like Oma's marriage? Not that there'd be love, she wasn't naive. But was friendship possible, or at least respect and cooperation?

Benedikt held her gaze. 'Whatever you're thinking, Annalena, this isn't the end of the world. It will be tough but we'll find a way.'

She pivoted and he was closer than she'd anticipated. So close her unrepentant heart thrummed in excitement. So much for gathering her tattered self-possession! Yet there was no glint of smugness in his eyes. Nothing but calm certainty.

Despite the gnawing hurt that he hadn't shared her desperate yearning, his expression settled a little of her tension. 'We'll be partners, Annalena. Is that so bad?'

Strange how the idea drew her. For so long she'd strived alone, fighting her battles with only her beloved Oma in the background, urging her on. Day to day Annalena had only herself. The thought of a partner, even if just for her formal responsibilities, was strangely attractive.

If she could set aside her doubts and trust him.

'Help me?' He took a handkerchief from his pocket and held it out.

After a moment Annalena took it, avoiding his fingers. She held the fabric that bore the warmth of his body. Then stepped close and raised the fine cotton to the lipstick smudge beside his mouth.

Again his scent engulfed her, making her insides squirm in excitement. But she concentrated on the stain, trying not to think of how it got there. Refusing to notice how his lips looked fuller from their kiss, or the quick pulse throbbing at his jaw.

When she stepped back it was to discover he'd retied his bow tie. Of course he could do it perfectly without a mirror! She held out his handkerchief.

Benedikt retrieved it without brushing her fingers.

She was grateful, not disturbed that he understood her need for distance. But her movements were abrupt as she stepped away.

'I'll just be a moment.'

Annalena could have finished tidying her hair where she was. Her purse with her lipstick was nearby. But she needed more, needed something to shore up her courage.

Thirty seconds later she was in the bathroom, reaching for the other lipstick the make-up expert had suggested for tonight. A deep scarlet rather than the pink she'd initially worn, it smoothed across her swollen lips, creamy and soothing. The colour was darker and defiant.

No, she amended, not defiant. Assured. She looked like a confident woman unfazed by the stunning couture gown, the imposing man who'd be her companion or the pomp and glitter of a royal celebration. A woman at home among hordes of people who'd wonder if she had what it took to be Queen.

Fake it till you make it.

She grimaced at her reflection, then thought of the Grand Duchess of Edelforst who for thirty years had protected Annalena's true identity and safety, while single-handedly ensuring their homeland wasn't eviscerated by King Karl and his greedy cohort.

It's your turn to step up, Annalena. No going back.

The grand ballroom had never looked more stupendous.

Rows of antique chandeliers glittered brilliantly after staff had spent a week polishing every crystal facet. Enormous mirrors lined the walls, reflecting an infinity of light and the shifting colours of the formally dressed crowd. On one side, French doors stood open to a terrace with views over the gardens where fountains played and spotlights turned night into day.

Everybody who was anybody in Prinzenberg, and for that matter Europe, was here.

And none, Benedikt realised as he escorted Annalena down the length of the room, outshone the woman beside him.

She took his breath away. Still.

The way she'd looked when he'd entered her room, soignée and alluring. But that was only part of it. The way she *tasted*. He'd kissed many women but none tasted like her. Delicious. Intriguing. *Addictive.*

When she'd clutched him, leaning up to take what she wanted, he'd rejoiced. Not because of how they'd look together at the ball, but because finally he had the real Annalena without artifice or caution.

It had been like holding a goddess in his arms, seductive and awe-inspiring, her passion so powerful it called to him at an elemental level.

What had begun as an exercise to make their partnership look convincing had escalated into a lust-fuelled adventure.

His one saving grace was that he hadn't backed her onto a sofa and ravished her so thoroughly that neither of them would have been fit to attend the ball. She had no idea how close he'd come to lifting those silky skirts and having her there and then.

He could have because, despite her horrified reaction later, she'd been as swept away as he.

When he'd forced himself away and seen her, eyes slumbrous with invitation, hair tumbling about her shoulders from his urgent grasping, lips dark and swollen... She'd tempt a saint, something Benedikt had never aspired to be.

His stride now was shorter than usual. Not only because of the need to acknowledge greetings and make introductions, but because walking in his semi-aroused state was uncomfortable.

He glanced at the woman beside him, so composed, wearing the hint of a smile. Any concerns she mightn't cope tonight disintegrated. She looked every inch the Queen she was about to become.

Except for that mouth. He swallowed, trying to ignore the increasing pressure in his groin. Those scarlet lips belonged to a seductress, not a monarch.

His gaze raked their audience and sure enough most of the men were gaping as if they'd never seen a woman before.

And she's all mine...or will be soon.

'Your Majesty.'

He paused, recognising Colonel Ditmar bowing before him.

'Colonel, I'm pleased you could be here.'

'Thank you.' The old man shifted his attention to Annalena. 'Princess, may I say you look ravishing?'

'You may, Colonel. I'll accept such flattery since you're an old friend.'

Ditmar protested there was no flattery and Annalena's smile grew wide. Benedikt was glad she had at least one friend here.

'Your Majesty.'

He turned and there was Countess Heldenbruck. Her black hair shone like a raven's wing, the deep blue of her dress highlighting her creamy complexion and dark eyes.

Regret slammed into Benedikt. Not because he couldn't marry her as he'd once considered, but because he'd have preferred to tell her of his impending wedding in private. That hadn't been an option. He couldn't have risked a leak of the news he'd announce tonight before everything was in place.

'Elise, it's good to see you. You're looking very fine.'

'So are you, Your Majesty.'

They exchanged light pleasantries, but he was acutely aware of her questioning stare, almost hidden by her smile. And how, after one quick glance at Annalena's ring finger, she hadn't looked that way again.

Suddenly his collar felt too snug. Was Annalena right? He and Elise had never discussed marriage or a relationship. But had he inadvertently raised expectations?

He'd been so determined to identify a suitable spouse who wouldn't demand too much, he hadn't considered her perspective.

His gut tightened. He'd told himself he never used people the way his father had. But the lines between them were more blurred than he'd thought. He'd been as ruthless as Karl, fixated only on getting what he wanted without considering others.

Too late to worry about your conscience. You're making Annalena marry you, even knowing she hates the idea.

'Elise, let me introduce you.' He turned to Annalena. 'Princess, I'd like to introduce Countess Heldenbruck. Countess, I don't believe you know Princess Annalena of Edelforst.'

After greetings were exchanged, Annalena surprised him by saying, 'I believe I know your cousin Paul, Countess.'

'Really?' Elise's smile looked less brittle than a moment ago. 'He hasn't lived in Prinzenberg for years.'

'I met him on a field trip in Scandinavia.' She continued with an amusing anecdote about a research trip that involved dog sledding into the wilderness. She painted Elise's cousin as a saviour when the team ran into difficulties. Benedikt watched with gratitude as the Countess's expression eased.

A few minutes later they moved through the press of guests towards a dais. The buzz of conversation grew loud with speculation. Some of those closest had noticed the emerald on Annalena's finger and hurried to spread the word.

But no one broached the subject with him. Protocol demanded a royal announcement.

Between nods and smiles Annalena murmured, 'That was her? The woman you mentioned?'

Benedikt's pace faltered, his head snapping round. But Annalena's expression revealed only the same mild pleasure she'd shown since entering the room.

She was even more perspicacious than he'd thought. Neither he nor Elise had uttered anything but social niceties.

He should feel embarrassed, introducing his fiancée to the woman he'd considered marrying. But he'd planned a convenient marriage, not a love match. Annalena could hardly be jealous.

'It was.'

'She's extremely beautiful, and, I think, intelligent.'

She was right. Benedikt wouldn't accept any less in a wife, but he couldn't say that to the woman he was forcing into marriage.

'Yes, she is.'

But no more than you.

Something else he couldn't say.

'Thanks for putting her at ease. I hadn't realised…' He shook his head. 'I put her in a difficult position. It was cruel of me not to warn her about tonight.'

To his surprise Annalena's expression softened. 'I don't see how you could. There was too much at stake. But I'm glad you realise it.'

At the end of the room he slowed his step, holding her gaze. 'Ready?'

She nodded, making the crystals on her translucent cape shiver like winking stars. Her eyes were just as bright. He wished he knew what she was thinking.

Taking her hand, he guided her up the steps. The room hushed as they turned to face their audience.

He could have heard a pin drop when he made the announcements. First he introduced Annalena then explained they planned to marry and rule jointly.

Stunned silence spun out until someone nearby broke into

cheers that were rapidly taken up until the ballroom swelled with the din.

There was no way of knowing how genuine the applause was. He saw stunned expressions, one or two heads shaking. But there were plenty of smiles too.

Meeting Annalena's eyes, he saw a flash of something he couldn't name. His conscience wavered and he realised with devastating clarity how much he asked of this woman. But he couldn't pull back.

'Shall we?'

He led her onto the dance floor. The crowd parted and the musicians struck up 'The Emperor Waltz'.

Annalena's fingers spasmed in his and he paused mid-step but she seemed to gather herself. 'Let's do this,' she whispered.

They paced to the centre of the enormous room and as the music swelled, he slipped his arm around her waist and drew her into a slow-turning circle.

She was posture perfect, breathtaking under the blaze of lights, and their steps matched as if they'd danced together for years.

Benedikt pulled her closer for their sedate duty waltz under curious eyes. But when the pace of the music accelerated the dance turned into something more. The swirling music beat in his blood. The feel of Annalena, supple yet strong in his embrace, ignited an excitement, a mix of satisfaction and hunger that had nothing to do with the crowd or the crown.

Mysterious green eyes held his. Her breasts rose quickly and her lips parted as they sped down the room. The audience was a glittering blur.

His vision telescoped to the woman he held, the sensuality of her body against his and the heady, possessive beat of his blood.

Soon, soon, soon.

Suddenly he couldn't wait for their wedding.

CHAPTER ELEVEN

THEY MARRIED A scant two weeks later.

Never had time rushed so quickly. Annalena had returned to Edelforst, seeking solace in familiar work and faces but didn't find it. As she delivered on research goals and finalised contract negotiations, her inbox filled with messages from the palace. Questions to be answered, decisions to be made, reams of material to digest.

Then there were the calls. To be fair, Benedikt rarely called during business hours, like her, busy with his work. But early in the morning and in the evening she'd hear his deep voice, sometimes scratchy with tiredness, and her senses did an unwanted little shimmy of anticipation.

Those calls catapulted her back to the ball. The whirl of them dancing in harmony as if they *were* the perfect couple they tried to appear.

To the kiss. The wretched kiss that had upended all her certainty about what she *didn't* want from Benedikt.

'Annalena?'

Colonel Ditmar stood beside her, imposing in dress uniform. His kindly eyes met hers.

'Sorry. I was...' What? Wishing herself anywhere but here? 'Gathering myself.'

A brisk wind caught them on the cathedral's porch, making her glad she had no veil and wore her hair up. She refused to appear veiled like some virgin, passed from one male protector to another.

Even if the virgin part was true. How was she meant to navigate this marriage when Benedikt undid her so easily? His impact on her *had* to be down to her inexperience. The alternative was untenable.

'It's a big thing you're doing, my dear, but you're up to it. You'll make a wonderful queen. Your grandmother is proud of you and your parents would have been too.'

The colonel's sincerity as much as his words cut through her jangling nerves. She felt a warm glow, even as her mouth wobbled and she blinked suddenly scratchy eyes.

The thought of her parents approving was surprisingly strengthening. As for Oma, how Annalena wished she could be here. But the old lady's agoraphobia made that impossible. Annalena knew how frustrated she was by it, and how she hid it behind a brisk manner. Even now she'd be watching the live broadcast.

The realisation made Annalena straighten and grip her bouquet tighter.

'Thank you, Colonel, that means a lot.'

She turned to her attendants, a colleague's twelve-year-old twins. Wearing coronets of wildflowers and pretty dresses of pale spring green, they twitched the hem of her dress. 'Ready, girls?'

They hurried into position, their eagerness a stark contrast to her feelings.

The colonel nodded to an attendant. A trumpet fanfare sounded then the resonant notes of the massive pipe organ. Music rolled through the doorway, grand and ebullient. Celebratory. Annalena refused to acknowledge her stomach's nauseating churn. Instead she lifted her chin and let the colonel lead her forward.

Shafts of sunlight, coloured by ancient stained-glass windows, lit the massive heraldic flags hanging high above the congregation. The cathedral was packed. She saw suits and traditional festive clothes, beaming smiles and stares. All those people and she probably only knew a dozen.

It was easier to look at the guests than the tall figure at the end of the aisle. Yet how could she *not* look?

It felt as though a taut, invisible cord stretched between her and the man waiting at the end of the long red carpet.

Despite her best efforts, her gaze lifted. His eyes were on her, even from this distance she felt the snap and sizzle of his stare. His face looked chiselled, proud and imposing. Her insides did that appalling dance of awareness and her mouth tightened.

Then she remembered the millions watching the televised ceremony and forced a smile.

He was so close now she saw the amber-gold glow of his eyes. But she couldn't read his expression, just that his focus was totally on her. Was that triumph she read? Satisfaction? It couldn't be eagerness except for what this marriage brought him—the crown.

There was no more time for thinking. Her attendants took the bouquet. The colonel squeezed her hand and placed it in Benedikt's.

A tumble of feelings rocked her. Emotions she didn't want to acknowledge. How could one man's touch be so different to another's?

The priest spoke her name and she snapped her head around. But all through the ceremony Annalena felt distanced from it, as if separated by a wall of glass. She was aware only of Benedikt's hand holding hers and the thrum of her heartbeat. And her stilted voice as she spoke her vows.

Until the moment when a pleased voice said, 'You may now kiss the bride.'

Inevitably her thoughts flew to the kiss that had left her limp with need. Heat flooded her cheeks as she turned to her husband.

Her husband!

She swallowed and tilted her chin, lifting her face.

An expression cut across his sculpted face, so quickly she almost missed it. Annoyance. A fleeting frown of annoyance!

What the hell did he have to be annoyed about?

Then warm lips covered hers. She inhaled sharply, drawing in the stunningly familiar scent-taste of him. His hand covered her cheek as he tilted his head, a gesture that to the onlookers would appear tender, even possessive. His mouth moved on hers and suddenly she felt—

'That's enough,' she whispered through stiff lips.

Benedikt paused, mouth still brushing hers, then slowly lifted his head as a roar of delight rose from the crowd.

He smiled down at her and she knew the world would see a fairy-tale prince besotted with his bride. Only she knew his smile didn't reach eyes that stayed serious and watchful.

'One ceremony down,' he murmured. 'Only the coronation to go.'

Hours later Annalena stood in the sitting room of the new suite she'd been allocated, adjoining Benedikt's. Her face ached from smiling and her feet felt hot from so many hours in heels.

She'd discarded her shoes by the door. She'd thought of running herself a bath since she'd sent away the maid who'd been eager to assist. She wasn't up to dealing with other people, however helpful. But instead of relaxing in warm water, she found herself at the window, still in her heavy, satin wedding dress, watching the fireworks explode over the city as Prinzenberg celebrated.

'I thought you might like some refreshment. You didn't eat at the reception.'

Annalena swung around in a swish of long skirts, one hand going to her throat. Across the room, in the doorway to his rooms, stood Benedikt.

He'd discarded his jacket and cufflinks and rolled his

sleeves to the elbow, baring strong, tanned forearms. His bow tie hung loose and his formal shirt was undone at the throat.

His air of undiluted sexiness stopped her breath. He had a vitality that proclaimed him far more than an office-bound administrator. Annalena wondered what he did in his spare time.

It took a second to register the tray he carried.

'I didn't hear you knock.' Was her voice too high?

'No. You were oblivious. You're a fan of fireworks?'

He moved into the room and put the tray on a low table. She saw canapés and fruit, pastries and a wine bottle nestled in the silver cooler.

A tickle of something that might have been excitement stroked her backbone. That wouldn't do. She couldn't allow herself to be wined, dined and charmed. Not if she wanted to be his equal. Benedikt threatened her equilibrium in ways she'd never experienced. She couldn't trust the yearning he made her feel because she feared that would make her vulnerable. Emotions had made her mother vulnerable and destroyed her.

'It's been a long day. I'm sorry, I'm not in the mood for company.'

'And I'm in no mood to be ignored.' His tone was even but his words made her head rock back in shock. 'Listen, Annalena.' He moved closer. 'We've embarked on something together. Something big. We need to share, not shut each other out.'

In other circumstances his words might have softened her. But she remembered, vividly, his expression in the cathedral. He'd barely hidden his distaste.

'I agree. We need to work as a team. But not now. I'm tired.'

For a long moment Benedikt said nothing, merely surveyed her, then slowly shook his head. 'No, you're not. You're wired. I can see it from here, *feel* it. You're tense with excess energy.'

He was right. The adrenaline that had ridden her all day

was still in her bloodstream. How did he know? It couldn't be that obvious.

'Okay, then. I'm not tired but I'd rather be alone.'

His gaze narrowed on hers and she felt like a specimen under a microscope. What did he see? The trouble was, the longer he stood there, so effortlessly charismatic, so annoyingly virile, the more her nerves jittered and her composure cracked.

Because for two weeks, underlying everything else she did had run the desire for *more* from Benedikt. More than that ravishing kiss. Though she knew it would leave her wide open in a way she couldn't afford. Though she now had confirmation that he really wasn't into her.

'If you feel that way I'll leave. But first tell me what's wrong. There's something, isn't there?'

A ragged laugh escaped. 'Apart from being blackmailed into marriage?'

Benedikt said nothing, merely waited, leaving her with the disturbing feeling that she was overly emotional. She folded her arms across her waist, palms flat against heavy satin.

'You come to my room as if we're friends or lovers.' She licked dry lips. 'You talk about sharing, but I know what I saw in the cathedral. I'd rather you were honest about your feelings.'

His eyebrows scrunched down, furrows lining his brow. 'What did you see?'

Annalena gestured to his face. 'That. Your frown when you had to kiss me. Your feelings were obvious, to me at least.' She turned her palm towards him when he would have spoken. 'I don't mind that you don't *want* me in that way. But I'd rather you didn't lie and pretend we're anything more than partners in a cold-blooded, convenient match.'

She hurried on, gesturing to the tray he'd brought. 'I don't want champagne and midnight seduction, especially from a man who's not attracted to me. But give me time and I'm sure we can develop a good working relationship.'

'You read all that into a single frown?'

She shrugged. 'A frown you were quick to hide. I understand that. I know the kiss was just for show. But that expression was *real*.'

Benedikt moved closer, his face sombre. 'You're right. It was.'

Crazy how the confirmation felt like a punch to the chest. She felt winded, bracing her hands between the deep V of her neckline and her stomach. The sumptuous embroidery covering her bodice scratched her palms.

'I *wasn't* happy,' he went on with a bluntness that made her want to cringe. 'Because when you turned to me *your* expression gave you away. You held yourself like some stoic martyr, like a virgin about to be ravished. As if you couldn't bear my touch.'

Her breath hissed. Did he somehow know she was a virgin? Impossible.

'I thought we'd moved past that, Annalena. Our kiss the night of the ball proved that however much our actions are driven by duty, there's something personal here too.'

'All that kiss proved was that you're willing to use your… wiles to get what you want.'

One dark eyebrow shot high. 'Wiles?'

'You know what I mean. You're a good-looking man and know your way around women. That doesn't mean you were invested in the kiss, any more than I was.'

He studied her intently and a tide of heat rose over her breasts and throat.

'You're lying again. Just like you lied when you said you were tired.'

His words scratched her pride. Since when had she resorted to untruths? She'd been brought up to value honesty and honour.

Fury and frustration at herself bubbled so high it felt as though her skin was too tight to contain her feelings. She'd gone into this with her eyes open but tonight everything felt twisted and wrong. As if she were in danger of being overwhelmed.

'You want honesty? I honestly want you to leave this minute.'

'Because you think I don't want you.' Did the gold flecks in his eyes flare brighter? 'Because if I kiss you, you'll think I'm using *wiles*.'

Behind that serious expression he was laughing at her, she knew it. Annalena stalked across the space between them, getting in his face, releasing the pure blaze of anger that had burned for weeks.

'Don't mock me, Benedikt.'

She glared up at him, hating the sharp pang of appreciation at his sheer magnetism. Even now it tugged at something deep-seated and needy inside her.

His eyes danced and his mouth curved into a hard, tight smile that looked edgy and, if she didn't know better…ravenous. Instead of being cowed, she felt excitement stir. As if she welcomed the fact he wasn't so sanguine now.

'I wouldn't dare mock, Annalena. But you've accused me of lying and I can't let that stand.' He spread his hands, shoulders lifting. 'I can't convince you with words and I can't convince you with a kiss.'

His gaze zeroed in on her mouth and she had to resist the urgent need to moisten her lips.

'How can I show you that I want you, Annalena? Not just as a queen but a woman? Perhaps with this?'

Before she had time to register his intent, long fingers curled around her hand, pulling it down between them. Down to his groin.

He pressed her palm to the front of his dark trousers, against the long, rigid heat of an erection.

Annalena dragged in a stunned breath as her hand instinctively curled around him. Her grip firmed and she felt an answering throb.

Fascinated, she raised rounded eyes to his. 'Satisfied? That's one thing I can't feign. My *wiles* don't stretch that far.' That smile looked more like a grimace now. 'Just so we're absolutely clear, I want you. In my bed.'

Rocked to her core, she planted her other hand on his chest for balance, only to discover his heartbeat, pounding fast like hers. Fire pinpricked her skin as she surveyed that proud, angry face and felt his body's reaction. To *her*.

It felt glorious, *right* that they were in this together. This had nothing to do with duty. Seeing him grapple with the same desire evoked a pang of tenderness that only amplified her response to him.

Her legs were wobbly and there was a melting sensation low in her body. She shifted, realising the strip of silk and lace between her legs was wet with arousal.

'Nothing to say, Annalena?'

He spoke through clenched teeth, like a man struggling for control, which made her realise she should release her hold. But she didn't want to. For the first time in her life she wanted to take a step she'd avoided since she was old enough to understand desire could be dangerous. Instead of nerves she felt only anticipation, as if she'd waited for this moment. This man.

Rather than releasing him, she slid her hand lower, squeezing gently.

Colour streaked his high-cut cheekbones and his eyes glittered more gold than brown. His hips rocked forward in an explicit thrust.

'You want me.' The words tasted wonderful. 'I like that.'

A laugh cracked the taut air between them. His eyes blazed with approval but at the same time she saw his jaw clench, a muscle spasming.

Reluctantly she let him go, fingers twitching as she took a

half-step back. Needing a second to absorb the enormity of the moment.

'And you want me.'

It was a statement not a question, and she nodded. They'd gone past prevarication and point scoring. Only honesty would do. 'Yes. I'm…curious.'

And awestruck. Excited and nervous. But above all she wanted more of Benedikt. Avoiding him wasn't possible. Abstinence made her a wreck. The need in her was too strong.

'We can work with curious.' He paused. 'If you agree.'

No sign now of that fierce amusement. His expression was grave.

'We're partners, Annalena. Husband and wife. We've committed our lives to our nation. Love isn't on the table. But there's respect and attraction. We're entitled to find what pleasure we can in a marriage neither of us sought.'

As he spoke he lifted his hand to trail his knuckles down her cheek. Annalena exhaled, turning into his touch, relieved as the barriers tumbled. This truth she could deal with. 'Yes. We're entitled to that.'

Because it was mutual passion, not one-sided yearning, which she couldn't have borne. She ignored the blip of her heartbeat when he'd acknowledged love was an impossibility.

'Respect and passion sound good to me.' She pressed her mouth to his knuckles, delighting in this connection between them.

'In that case…'

He drew her hard against him with one arm wrapped around her waist.

'I suppose you have no idea how you've tantalised me in this dress.' His gaze dropped to the narrow V of her neckline that plunged between her breasts. His stare shot fire into her blood and made her push her shoulders back. 'I thought brides were supposed to be demure.'

'I didn't want to look dowdy.' Especially when she'd feared

some would expect that. 'My designer friend had this amazing design she said would be perfect, formal but feminine.'

Heavy ivory satin dropped in folds to the floor. Long sleeves fell in pleats that became soft, belling folds. A high collar plunged to a deep opening between her breasts and the whole bodice, which arrowed down to her abdomen in an almost mediaeval style, was heavily embroidered.

It was unlike anything she'd ever worn and she loved it. Wearing it made her feel feminine and powerful.

Especially when Benedikt looked at her like that, his gaze eating her up.

'She was right. It's perfect.'

His voice was gravel and had the same effect as flint striking stone. Sparks ignited across her skin. His hand dropped from her face to her collarbone and her breath stopped as skin met skin. Slowly his palm slid lower, the weight of it delicious. When he reached the place between her breasts he splayed his fingers.

'There's tape there,' she explained as he met resistance. But she needn't have worried. He found the double-sided tape that kept her breasts fully covered and deftly stripped it free.

Hadn't she said he knew his way around women?

Annalena sighed as her unfettered breasts eased towards the opening while Benedikt explored. Teased, more like. He stroked the inner curve of each breast, stretching his fingers under the fabric but not quite far enough to reach her pebbled nipples.

She grabbed his shoulders as arousal quaked through her.

'You like that, Annalena? What about this?'

He bent to kiss from her collarbone to her breasts. His tongue caressed the tender, sensitive skin bared to his caress, trailing ribbons of fire wherever he touched and making her hands clench into his shoulders.

She wanted him to touch her like that everywhere.

All too soon he stopped. Yet instead of rising to possess her mouth, Benedikt dropped to his knees. Pure gold gleamed in eyes that regarded her steadily while he grabbed the voluminous skirt, bunching it up her shins, to her knees, then higher.

Her breasts rose on a snatched breath as his smile became a devilish grin. Breathless, she watched him skim his mouth over her inner thighs.

It was the most decadent thing she'd ever experienced. Even through sheer pantyhose, the touch of his mouth to her trembling thigh created a jolt of lightning, driving down through her body.

Her fingers curled into his shoulders as he pushed the heavy skirt up to her abdomen. Now his gaze wasn't on her face. From this angle his honed features looked taut, the pulse at his neck jumping as he surveyed what he'd bared.

'Push down your pantyhose, Annalena.'

It sounded like an order in that roughened voice and for once she didn't think to object. Excitement burred through her.

Wordlessly she hooked her thumbs through the waistband and slid the tights down.

'And the rest. I want you bare.' Though she wanted that too, hearing him spell it out made her pause for a millisecond. Instantly he looked up and what she saw in his face told her his brusque tone had more to do with his own excitement than the need to give orders. 'Please.'

She swallowed the knot clogging her throat and hooked her fingers into lace and silk, dragging pantyhose and underwear together down her thighs. But when she would have lifted one knee to free herself he stopped her. Not with words but the simple act of leaning in to brush his mouth across her thatch of blonde hair.

Annalena jumped and clung to his shoulders, her knees wobbling.

'You smell so good.'

The words vibrated against her skin, making her twitch and widen her stance, only to be stopped by the restriction of the tights above her knees. She should feel foolish standing, half undressed. Or embarrassed with Benedikt nuzzling her *there*.

She felt nothing of the kind. She liked it.

Cogent thought frayed when he adjusted his grip on her skirt so he could explore her folds with one hand while he kissed her.

Lips pressed as fingers stroked and her hips bucked. Annalena felt his smile but before she could react, his tongue followed the same route, pausing to swirl and press.

She gasped, a raw, keening sound that made the hairs on her nape stand up. Or perhaps that was because of where his fingers delved while his tongue worked that incredibly sensitive nub.

Her hands found his scalp, fingers in thick hair as if to stop him moving away. This was so amazing she didn't want it to end, even as her pelvis rolled against his touch, meeting his stroking.

She shuddered as delight bombarded her. Instinct, formed by a life governed by duty and work, told her anything that felt so impossibly wonderful had to be dangerous. Eyes she hadn't remembered closing fluttered open to discover Benedikt looking up at her.

She gasped, undone by the blast of emotion that hit her as she met that molten stare.

'Come for me, Annalena. Let go.'

How she wanted to. Yet some stubborn part of her resisted. It was only as he caressed her again and her hips rolled in response that she saw a flicker of movement in the corner of her eye.

Lifting her head, she caught a reflection in the antique mirror. A woman, mouth open and red-cheeked, hands clamped on the man kneeling before her, his head dark against bare skin and ivory satin.

Shock exploded as she saw him bend closer, his hand moving between her legs. She'd never seen anything, experienced anything so...

'Benedikt!'

Her cry went on and on, primal and triumphant as her body exploded in a climax unlike anything she'd known. Colours burst against closed eyelids. Showers of gold and silver rained down, molten. She felt the climax deep in her body as she rode his hand through the final, desperate throes of delight.

Ages later she was aware of her fingers tight in his hair and the hot, moist touch of his breath against her thigh. There were words too, murmured words she couldn't make out but which sounded like praise and gentling noises designed to soothe.

She didn't need soothing. Despite the rackety beat of her heart she felt lax as if every bone and muscle melted. Her legs gave way. 'Benedikt.' Her voice was unrecognisable. 'I need…'

He read her body quickly. An instant later he was on his feet, scooping her against his chest. His eyes glowed and his smiling mouth was wet with the taste of her. The sight of him made something roll over in her chest.

'I know. It's time to find a bed.'

CHAPTER TWELVE

DIVESTING HIS WIFE of her glorious wedding gown was an experience Benedikt would remember for years to come.

He felt alternately eager excitement and something else, strong yet tender, as he took in her hazy, slightly unfocused stare, her body blush and her fumbling efforts to assist. He felt a need to cherish and protect.

It was as if the orgasm he'd given her had truly undone her.

Sure! You don't think the long, long day and the stress of the past weeks have anything to do with it?

The proud, argumentative woman who didn't hesitate to question when she thought he was wrong, or step up to daunting royal responsibilities, lay limp and delectably biddable as he carefully wrangled her out of the dress that had driven him crazy since she'd walked down the aisle.

She'd looked...perfect, a word he rarely used.

He told himself it was because of the clever dress design. It harked back to ancient tradition with its embroidery, full sleeves and shape that drew attention to her small waist. Yet it was thoroughly modern with that tantalising slice of bare flesh that defied anyone to label it old-fashioned.

It's not the dress and you know it. It's Annalena. You couldn't have chosen a better bride. She may be a novice at court but she understands duty and dedication to her people.

He wasn't thinking about duty or dedication as he dropped the heavy satin over the side of the bed.

His heart hammered as he surveyed her, bare flesh pink with the flush of satiation. She had a slender frame, gentle curves and long legs. Pale breasts tipped with rose pink. Pubic hair a dark, burnished gold. Her lazy green gaze made his blood rush and sizzle.

Slowly he stripped her fine pantyhose and the wet scrap of lace and silk from her legs, tossing them over his shoulder, watching her eyes widen then narrow, sending a bolt of fire through his belly.

Benedikt slowed his breathing, battling the urge to wrench open his trousers and plunge into her.

'Take down your hair,' he instructed, wincing at his telltale huskiness.

'Don't get too used to giving orders. And shouldn't you be undressing? Or would you like me to do that for you?' She propped herself up against the bank of plump pillows.

So much for his wife being undone by bliss. His wife! That would take some getting used to.

But he could definitely get used to having her in his bed. Especially when she surveyed him with a glittering challenge that held neither anger nor doubt but pure sexual anticipation.

Benedikt lifted his hand to his shirt, undoing the studs as Annalena shuffled higher in the bed, her breasts jiggling invitingly. He fumbled, fingers seemingly too big and clumsy, so he grabbed both sides of the shirt and tugged. That was better. Cool air caressed overheated flesh as he shrugged free.

The look on Annalena's face as she watched made him still for a second before reaching for his belt buckle. Her stare branded as surely as fire. That look—as if she'd never seen anything so good as his naked torso—ramped up the arousal he struggled to control.

She lifted her hands behind her head and her hair uncoiled, rolling down over one shoulder, past her breast, towards her waist. He swallowed over a scratchy lump in his throat.

Once more he was reminded of someone mediaeval. A maiden letting down her hair for a lover.

The eroticism of shining tresses against flushed feminine skin was new to him, a man experienced in the art of sex. Benedikt felt a beat of something harsh and unfamiliar, something dark and untamed. Sex had always been fun, a need, a release. Now he fought the idea it could be more.

Not because of her long hair. But because of the way each moment since he'd walked into her suite felt invested with deeper significance, a meaning he couldn't quite grasp.

Now who's letting weeks of stress affect them?

A frown wrinkled Annalena's brow, her attention going to his groin and his half-undone belt buckle. 'Why have you stopped?'

He smiled, taut facial muscles pulling. 'I'm taking a moment to admire you.'

To his surprise, the colour in her throat and cheeks intensified. She looked delighted, as if she weren't used to a lover's compliments.

No time to ponder that. Benedikt stepped off the bed, stripping away shoes, socks and the last of his clothes, retrieving the condoms he'd shoved in a pocket.

'You came prepared.'

He couldn't decipher her tone and forbore to admit he'd been carrying condoms for weeks. He knew she'd viewed him as an opponent but he hadn't been able to deny his rising hunger for her. Or the hope she'd admit to the attraction she'd been so determined to repudiate.

'I assumed you weren't ready to conceive a child.'

She sat higher, crossing her arms and inadvertently plumping up her breasts, making his shaft twitch as he rolled on protection. 'You assumed right.'

He nodded, trying to focus on the conversation, not the bewitching sight of tight nipples cresting her arms like treats displayed for him to taste. He failed. How could he not notice?

'Good. Nor am I.'

Though at some stage a child had to be on the agenda.

His mouth tightened. He was already doing what he could to secure the throne. So was Annalena. The thought of them coming together, solely to create an heir, felt wrong. Like the way his father had manipulated his mother, convincing her he cared for her to get the heir he needed. Not to mention access to her fortune and international connections.

'What is it, Benedikt? Having second thoughts?'

'Does it look like I am having second thoughts?' he asked as he turned to the bed, his erection heavy and his flesh too tight from the effort of holding back.

She shook her head but he saw the way her crossed arms tightened and the upward tilt of her jaw. He recalled how she'd believed him uninterested in her.

Did she still think, even a little, that he didn't desire her? He knelt on the end of the bed, knees wide, gripped her ankles and, in one quick movement, tugged till she lay flat before him.

'I want you, Annalena, and it has nothing to do with making an heir or satisfying duty.' Their eyes locked and he felt that familiar electric pulse between them. 'Frankly, I've had it up to my neck with duty. I refuse to take it to bed with me. This is personal. I want *you*. Just like you want *me*.'

He waited and eventually she relented, her eyes like emerald fire. 'I do. So much.'

Her words stroked fire through his already eager body but he made himself go slowly, kissing his leisurely way up from her ankles. The musky, enticing scent of female satisfaction teased as he reached silky inner thighs. But before he could settle between her legs and bring her back to the verge of climax, she wriggled and tugged at his shoulders.

'Not that. I want *you*.'

She'd get no argument from him. Making his movements slow, forcing himself not to rush, he moved higher, nudged her legs wide and settled between them. His eyes closed as a powerful throb of pleasure rocked him. Their bodies, naked together, evoked powerful magic. When he lowered his head to her breast and she wound her arms around him, pressing him close, need rose sharply.

His hand was between them, guiding himself to her slick passage when she spoke. 'I should tell you I haven't done this before. It mightn't be easy.'

Disbelief blasted Benedikt. And the desperate urge to ignore the words and bury himself deep.

He closed his eyes, lowering his forehead to her neck and exhaling slowly. It took a moment or ten, but finally he trusted himself to move. He lifted his head to discover her chewing the corner of her mouth. She looked earnest and adorable.

Adorable? The feisty woman who never conceded a point?

'I thought you should know,' she said quickly. 'In case it's difficult. It could be...not what you're used to.'

She was right. He'd never been with a virgin. Having seen the debacle of his parents' marriage, he'd shied from potentially emotional relationships. He'd only been with experienced women who understood he wasn't looking for for ever.

'It could be disappointing for you,' she murmured.

'I won't be disappointed, Annalena. But this may be difficult for *you*.'

The idea made his gut churn and a heavy ache settle in his chest. He'd do everything to ensure that wasn't the case but even so...

'That's okay. I know the first time mightn't be good. But hopefully the time after will be better.'

He rose to his knees, disturbed by her low expectations, even if he applauded her common sense.

Benedikt didn't want this to be anything less than wondrous for her. He should be pleased she was pragmatic but he wanted, he realised with startling clarity, to see stars in her eyes. He wanted her to come around him, muscles clenching and heart pounding, her cries of ecstasy filling the room.

He wanted Annalena to shatter with delight. Then turn to him again and again and again.

Nothing less would do.

Annalena surveyed Benedikt's serious expression and wondered if frankness had been a mistake.

She bit her lip and almost...almost wished herself elsewhere. But how could she wish to be anywhere but here, about to have sex with the one man who'd ever roused her to such passion?

'Why?' He frowned. 'Is there someone else? Someone you've been waiting for?'

The question flustered her. The head of his erection was notched at her core, the heat impossible to describe, yet he found time to interrogate her!

She shifted and was rewarded by the sight of muscles and tendons in his neck and chest drawing tight. Relief pulsed through her at the visible proof he was strung out too.

'I was tempted but somehow it never seemed right.' She'd been raised to think of sex in terms of a committed, lifelong relationship. That and her intrinsic distrust of passionate love, courtesy of her parents' tragedy, had made her too ready to see flaws in the men who'd tried to persuade her into bed. 'Maybe my standards are too high.'

'Or you didn't meet the right man.'

Benedikt sounded smug, as well he might, looking like some immortal god full of devastating masculine power.

'You think you're the right man? You have to prove— Oh!'

He'd flexed his hips and she felt the strangest sensation as her body opened for him. There was weight and heat and a mix of trepidation and thrilling anticipation that tensed her whole body.

To her surprise, Benedikt didn't thrust further. He lowered his head to her breast, fondling and kissing, squeezing until she squirmed beneath him, inching her legs wider so his solid thighs sank between them.

There, that was better. With one hand he nudged her clitoris, stoking the fire, then pressed in, a little further this time. He was so big, so solid, she didn't know how this could possibly work, though of course it must.

She was bracing to take him when he withdrew, the heaviness of his shaft shockingly virile against her thigh as he lavished attention on her other breast. Meanwhile his fingers teased and stroked until everything gathered in a rush towards orgasm.

He stopped before she fell over the edge.

Blinking up, Annalena met his serious stare as he slid forward, prodding gently till her breath caught on the edge of being overwhelmed.

So it continued, Benedikt kissing and caressing, building up the need in her, letting her acclimatise to his possession, one slow centimetre at a time.

It was either the most thoughtful, considerate introduction to sex or a refined form of torture, designed to drive her out of her mind.

Her need was so intense, the suspense so great, that finally she lifted her knees and anchored them around his hips so he couldn't pull away. To make doubly sure she grabbed his buttocks, digging in her fingers.

'More,' she whispered. 'Give me everything.'

Above her his face was a mask of pared lines and brutal restraint. His nostrils flared. 'Everything?'

Heart thrumming, she nodded. He gathered himself and plunged deep, so deep there were no words to describe such intimacy.

Annalena blinked, trying to catch her breath.

Instantly Benedikt frowned. 'I hurt you?'

'No!' How could she explain? It felt too extraordinary. 'Not hurt.'

She hefted in air, feeling the friction of her breasts against his hairy chest. That distracted her, sending delight corkscrewing through her. Everything about him felt so good.

There'd been no pain. Trepidation, yes, and she realised her tension would have worked against her if not for Benedikt's patient attentions.

She felt his strain, saw it in his almost-grimace, and felt a wave of tenderness for this man who put her needs beyond his own. If she weren't careful, she might read too much into that.

'Show me more.'

The grimace became a surprisingly endearing lopsided smile. 'Demanding woman.'

She raised her eyebrows, delighted. 'I *am* a queen.'

'Ah. Well, then, if it's a royal command…'

Benedikt moved back then bucked his hips. Annalena clung tight through his rhythm of surge and retreat, slowly testing her own response. She thrilled at the sensations he evoked, gasping at each new level of heightened arousal, mutually shared.

His breaths shortened, his movements grew quicker and less fluid. He lowered his dark head, grazing his teeth at a tender spot on her neck she hadn't known existed. Fire jolted through her and when his fingers caressed her too…

White light exploded, engulfing her, drawing her up and up as she shattered into stardust. But still the ecstasy went on, so acute it had no beginning or end. There was only bliss and Benedikt, golden eyes, convulsing body and then hot, cushioning muscles drawing her close and holding her through the maelstrom.

Benedikt stood before the bathroom mirror, concentrating on the razor's glide through the shaving foam on his jaw. An electric razor wasn't good enough today, not when he'd seen the stubble burn he'd left on Annalena.

Hard to believe they'd only shared a bed for one night. It felt like more. It felt *momentous*.

So momentous, so different, it worried him. He couldn't recall anything like it. He shook his head and flicked excess foam from the blade into the sink.

Who was he kidding? It had been compelling, exciting, but not—as he'd imagined in the early hours—extraordinary. That had been his hormones talking. And lingering shock that his bride had been a virgin.

No wonder he'd felt that sudden surge of protectiveness.

Except, he realised, it couldn't have been protectiveness, just surprise and the need to ensure she enjoyed the experience. Her pleasure added to his own and he wanted a wife who enjoyed intimacy, not who avoided it.

Protectiveness! The only protection she ever needed was from you. You've used her again and again, forcing her into marriage and a crown she doesn't want, just to safeguard your position. Making her give up a career she loves because you alone decided it was necessary. Revelling not only in her passion but her virginity.

He grimaced, avoiding his eyes in the mirror, not wanting to discover what he'd see there.

Today he'd woken to sunlight illuminating Annalena sprawled and exhausted in her rumpled bed. Because even her inexperience hadn't been enough to stop him having her again, and again, egged on by her enthusiastic responses.

Right. Blame her, when what drove you was your own selfish need. You might talk the talk but underneath are you any better than your father?

Benedikt winced as he nicked his throat, dark red blood welling against white foam.

That was what had catapulted him out of her bed. The fear that, despite the altruistic spin he put on his actions to protect the country, he was a chip off the old block. So intent on getting his own way that he saw others as necessary collateral damage.

Would Annalena really have been such a threat to the

crown? He understood her well enough now to know she'd have abided by an agreement never to undermine his rule or that of his heirs.

Heirs.

His pulse quickened. Not because he was eager for kids, but imagining Annalena, rounded and ripe with his child. His visceral response was so profound he almost dropped the razor, finally collecting his wits and reaching for something to staunch the dribble of blood down his throat.

Despite the condoms it was possible he'd made her pregnant. They'd been very…enthusiastic and he'd enjoyed foreplay so much that at least once he'd been tardy putting on protection.

Yet he felt no panic, or sense of walls closing in as he had before when considering a family of his own.

Coming from a nightmare family situation, marriage and children had never appealed. Only the eventual need for a royal heir had made him consider taking a bride, hence his pragmatic interest in the Countess.

It wasn't just that his father had been cruel. Even without that, his mother would have been desperately unhappy, in love initially at least with a man incapable of softer emotion.

As for raising children… He'd always thought bringing a child into an unhappy family was a crime. He knew how a child could be used as both a hostage and a prize. Then there was the question of whether he had what it took to be a good parent. His father had been appalling and anything but a good role model and his mother, though she'd tried, hadn't been able to make up for her husband.

Listen to yourself! It's still all about you, isn't it? What about Annalena and her needs?

He rinsed the razor then washed his face, blotting it with a towel.

He couldn't give Annalena what she wanted. The full-time career to which she'd dedicated herself. A man who'd cherish her. She'd admitted when he'd first mentioned marriage that she'd hoped one day to find someone *right* for her. Benedikt knew that was code for love.

Pragmatic in other ways, she was still a romantic.

He didn't trust love. He'd never seen it work. It had brought his mother only unhappiness. Even his much-admired grandfather had married a woman who'd helped him make his first million.

But Benedikt would do everything to make this new royal life as easy as possible for Annalena. He'd respect and trust her.

They'd be partners. Partners with benefits.

He'd find a way to make that enough for her.

CHAPTER THIRTEEN

ANNALENA WOKE TO find her head turned towards the car window as they drove through darkness. Benedikt was beside her in the driver's seat. The vehicle was climate-controlled but she *felt* the warmth of his body and registered the unique tangy scent of his skin.

After last night's intimacies her physical awareness of him had turned into something more, as if he'd imprinted himself on her psyche and her body.

She knew she'd be able to *sense* his presence anywhere. She felt that awareness now in the pit of her stomach, a coiling consciousness, and in her chest, expanding as she inhaled that tantalising scent.

All the more reason to her keep eyes closed while she gathered her wits. It had been an eventful day and she needed to process it.

She'd woken feeling more alive than she ever had in her life. But disappointment had consumed her on discovering Benedikt's absence. They'd spent the night entwined, even when they weren't having sex. Annalena was careful not to confuse sex with making love. Even if that was what it had felt like—his gentleness, his care and his passion.

Just as well she was a pragmatist. She understood the way she'd felt last night, and her searing disappointment at his desertion this morning, must be products of her inexperience. Losing her virginity was a major event on top of weeks of strain and high emotion.

No wonder she'd felt so much.

When she became acclimatised to physical intimacy she'd be able to separate her emotions. It was just that last night had been so...

She had no words. Wonderful didn't encompass the depth of her emotions as she'd hugged Benedikt to her and felt him spill himself inside her. When he'd taken such care with her that it had seemed not like calculated patience but tenderness, almost reverence.

She stifled a snort. The illusion hadn't lasted. Waking alone and naked, the bed cold around her, had brought her back to reality.

They'd share the crown and their bodies but emotions weren't part of the deal.

Of course he'd had a plausible reason for leaving, as he'd explained over breakfast. He hadn't wanted to wake her, knowing she'd be exhausted and possibly sore. His solicitousness about that had made her blush despite her best efforts.

So, he'd explained, he'd worked in his own suite with the door open so he'd hear when she got up.

She *had* needed the sleep. And she wasn't sore but tender, aware of her body as never before. All day, at the most inconvenient times, she'd felt that tenderness, remembered last night and wished...

There's no point wishing for the impossible.

Despite Benedikt's solicitude over breakfast, there'd been no breath-stealing kisses, just reminders that theirs was a pragmatic marriage. He'd ushered her to a seat, his hand hovering close but not touching. As for a good morning kiss, he'd pressed his lips to her forehead as she'd sat and when she'd tilted her head up for more he'd already turned away to sit on the other side of the table.

They'd discussed allocating her a security detail and a private secretary. That was when he'd surprised her, asking if she'd like Udo, the guard she'd first met in the palace foyer, on her security team. She'd seen Udo several times in the palace and had always stopped to exchange greetings.

Annalena didn't know whether to be worried that such minor interactions had been noted, or pleased at Benedikt's thoughtfulness, suggesting a friendly face on the team she'd need, despite her protests.

When they'd discussed candidates for her secretary there'd been another surprise. 'As long as it's not Ida Becker,' Annalena had said.

Only to have Benedikt declare, 'Ms Becker has left palace employment.' Seeing her stare, he'd added, 'I discovered she was the one who rudely left you waiting that first day, and her attitude since…' He shook his head, his expression grim. 'I won't have her near you, or the palace.'

Benedikt's words, his protectiveness, had disarmed her. It was impossible to believe now that Ida had had a relationship with him. He had better taste and he wasn't the sort to dally with staff. When Annalena had accused him of toying with the Countess's feelings he'd looked appalled at the suggestion, and that was the woman he'd considered marrying.

Benedikt confused her. His thoughtfulness was real, as was his passion, but he deliberately distanced himself.

Organising a surprise honeymoon is hardly distancing himself.

That had been utterly unexpected. He hadn't mentioned a honeymoon, nor had she anticipated one, for they weren't ordinary newly-weds, eager to be alone together. The news that he'd organised one had stunned her. She knew his workload. How had he carved out time for a bridal trip, and why?

Obvious. Benedikt wanted the world to believe theirs was more than a convenient marriage. He wanted it to appear solid.

Annalena remembered her shock as the motorcade had left the palace and headed, not for the airport, but towards Edelforst.

It seemed she was the only one who hadn't known. When

they'd reached her province people had lined the roads in every town and village, sometimes even in forests and farmland. Her throat had closed as she'd seen beaming faces, flags waving, and wildflowers strewn across the road. And when they'd taken the road to her grandmother's home...

'I know you're awake, Annalena. I can hear you thinking.'

Had his senses become attuned to her the way hers were to him? Then she realised how ludicrous that was. She sat up, blinking as the headlights cut the darkness, following a winding, well-made road.

'It was kind of you to visit my grandmother.' She blamed her scratchy voice on the fact she'd just woken. 'It meant a lot to her, and me.'

'She's a formidable lady. I can see where you get your strength.'

Annalena turned, surveying his profile in the light from the dashboard. Her heart did a funny little somersault and for a second she felt a jab of distress. Would it always be like this now? This weakness for a man who could never be the sort of husband she wanted?

'She's strong-willed, but she's caring too.'

Some people only saw Oma's formality and didn't realise the kindness that made her the special person she was.

A wry smile curved Benedikt's mouth. 'I know. It's there in the respect her people have for her. And the obvious love she has for you. But I wouldn't like to get on her bad side.'

'I don't think you need worry about that. She approves of you.'

That hadn't entirely surprised Annalena, given Oma's comments about him as a potential husband. Yet she'd been surprised at how well the pair had got on. Oma had unbent enough to let him kiss her cheek, a rare privilege.

'I take that as a huge compliment. I admire her enormously.'

'I didn't think you knew her.'

'No, but I knew of her years ago. She was one of the few

people in all Prinzenberg able to hold my father to account. I always admired the way she spoke up for what she believed was right, even when he tried to bully her.'

His words created an inner glow. 'She's been my heroine all my life.' And the closest she'd had to a mother.

'I thought she'd come to the capital for the wedding.' Benedikt glanced her way. 'You said she was unwell and so I didn't expect someone so spry.'

Annalena hesitated, about to prevaricate. But they'd agreed to be truthful with each other and there'd be other times when Oma's incapacity would become obvious.

'Not all disability is visible.' She turned to look at the windscreen, trying to work out where they were, but the forest wasn't familiar.

'Oma is strong in many ways but the trauma of my parents' death took a toll. She refused to enter the rest of Prinzenberg again, but when I was little I travelled with her regularly all through Edelforst. Then, gradually, I realised she wasn't travelling as far as before. Her physical boundaries have narrowed, even though her interests and her mind haven't. Nowadays she barely goes beyond our valley. People come to her instead.'

Warmth closed around her fisted hand. Warmth from Benedikt's long fingers, gently squeezing. 'Agoraphobia?'

Annalena nodded. 'I know she wanted to be at my wedding.' She'd wanted it too.

'I'm sorry she couldn't be. It was tough for you not having family there.' He lifted his hand to the wheel as they took a bend and Annalena was surprised how much she missed his touch. 'We'll just have to visit her often.'

Annalena's head swung around. In the dim light he looked serious, and he'd said *we* not *you*. 'You'd do that?'

'She's important to you and you to her. Why would I get in the way of that? My father was deplorable but other members of my family saved me from the worst of him. And from myself. If you have good people in your life you need to cherish them.'

That surprised her. Talk of cherishing seemed at odds with the tough negotiator who'd put their wishes behind the country's future. He seemed genuinely taken with her grandmother but to decide they should both visit her, as if he wanted to build a relationship with the old lady, was something she'd never considered.

Because you've spent so long thinking of him as your enemy. You know there's more to him than that.

Then there was his candour about his family. How had they saved him and from what? Did he mean his mother? But why not say so? Annalena was ashamed she had no idea what other family he had. None were at the wedding.

She was about to ask when Benedikt said, 'We're here.'

The car swung out of the forest, the road curving up to a wide-eaved chalet overlooking a meadow. Lights shone at the windows and along a deep balcony with a carved wooden balustrade where scarlet flowers spilled. High beyond the chalet sat the dark bulk of a mountain.

Annalena blinked. If Benedikt had said they were flying to New York or a private Caribbean island she wouldn't have been surprised. A private mountain chalet, for this was no bustling resort hotel, was the last place she'd have imagined him taking her.

That was reinforced when they neared the building and she saw part of the floodlit white stucco decorated with a large painting. Such paintings were a local tradition. This one represented the Almabtrieb, the autumn procession down the mountains as dairy herds, wearing bells and flowers, left their Alpine pastures for the valley. It was charming but a far cry from the glitz and elegant sophistication she'd thought he'd favour.

But how well do you know him?

Last night she'd begun to believe she knew Benedikt in

ways no one else did. Nonsense, of course. He must have had lots of lovers. Hadn't she warned herself not to bring emotion into a purely physical connection?

'We can be private here. The security team will be in accommodation on the edge of the clearing.' He switched off the engine and she felt his eyes on her. 'You like it?'

Annalena turned. The chalet lights illuminated his strong, familiar features. But his expression wasn't familiar. He looked expectant and concerned, as if unsure of her reaction.

No. As if it *mattered* what she thought.

The thought snatched the air from her lungs. Was this an olive branch? Like visiting Oma straight after their wedding?

He looked like a man who wanted to please her.

'Annalena?'

She moistened her dry mouth and was unprepared for the shaft of searing fire that shot through her as his frowning eyes narrowed on the movement, lingering on her lips before lifting to meet hers.

'It's wonderful. In fact…'

'In fact?'

Did he lean closer? She swallowed, finding it hard to speak because she wanted to move closer and kiss him. Abruptly she sat back.

'It's the sort of place I'd have chosen.' Belatedly she tugged her gaze free and looked over the dark meadow, fringing forest and outline of craggy mountains. 'It's so peaceful.'

'I'm glad.' His hand captured hers and she felt that deep unfurling sensation, as if vital parts of her body softened and melted. 'I thought you'd had enough of cities and schedules for a while.'

Annalena's vocal cords tightened. Because, despite the jampacked diary of appointments she'd seen him and Matthias pore over, Benedikt had conjured time away from the stress and busyness of royal life for her.

Because he knew she needed it. Even if he'd been partly

motivated by public perception, she *knew* this trip wasn't part of his original plan.

'When did you organise this?'

Benedikt tilted his head as if surprised by the question. 'The beginning of the week. Why?'

She shrugged. 'I'm amazed Matthias managed to reschedule your diary so quickly.'

'It was a miracle. Anyone else would have quit on the spot when I raised it. I owe him a terrific bonus.'

She'd seen how hard Matthias worked. 'Good idea. Maybe a long holiday?'

'That's the plan, as soon as we train a couple of secretaries to stand in for him. Right now I'd be lost without him.'

'He didn't work for your father?'

It was a guess, but Annalena liked the man too much to believe he'd been part of the previous King's court.

Benedikt's deep chuckle was inviting and it struck her that here in the dim confines of the car it was far easier to talk than at the palace. 'Absolutely not. Matthias has been with me for years.'

Annalena had suspected as much. The pair had a camaraderie that spoke of mutual respect and friendship. Matthias was competent, friendly and honest. Interesting that such a man was so loyal to Benedikt over a long time. That told her a lot about her new husband.

'What are you frowning over, Annalena?'

'Just thinking what a formidable pair you are, turning things around for the better, taking on your father's administration and rooting out problems.'

Like removing Ida Becker, whose negativity and rudeness had no place in the palace. But there was far more. Annalena had heard enough in the past few weeks to realise wholesale changes were under way to how royal business was conducted and contracts let.

'You know, I think that's the nicest thing you've said to me. Thank you, Annalena.'

Benedikt's grin caught something in her chest, drawing it tight. To her astonishment, he lifted her hand and kissed it, lips lingering to brush slowly across her knuckles.

Suddenly it felt like last night all over again. The spark of desire and connection, the rippling sensation across her flesh and the softening low in her body.

Annalena's fingers tightened on his. 'You don't seem to mind touching me now.'

'Mind?' He frowned. 'I like touching you.' His voice dropped to a low note that made her tremble. 'You know that.'

'Do I? You haven't touched me all day.' Her chin lifted. 'Or kissed me properly.'

She'd instinctively avoided the subject but now the constraint between them had dropped.

'Ah.' He looked at their joined hands then to her. 'There were reasons.'

When he didn't continue she prompted, 'We agreed to be honest.'

Benedikt released her hand and leaned back against the door. Finally he spoke. 'I was…on unfamiliar ground.'

'*You* were on unfamiliar ground? I'd never had a morning after but you had.'

Slowly he nodded. 'That was part of it. I felt *concerned*. You'd been saving yourself for someone who clearly wasn't me. It brought home what I'd taken from you, the future you wanted and couldn't have… I regretted that.' He crossed his arms, all humour vanished. 'You *were* waiting, weren't you?'

Annalena tried to interpret his tone, stunned at the idea her inexperience had impacted anything other than his physical pleasure.

'No. Maybe.' She clasped her hands. 'I don't know. Oma would tell you I've always been career focused. I've been attracted to men but never enough to…' She shrugged, reminding herself she'd promised honesty too. 'I suppose I held back. For as long as I can remember romance and tragedy have been tangled together in my mind. I suppose that was a barrier.'

'Because of your parents.'

She nodded. 'I was never going to be swept off my feet. I'm too cautious for that. But I always imagined I'd find a partner and have children one day.' Benedikt looked as if he were about to say something but she'd had enough of this subject. 'You said there were reasons, plural, why you didn't touch me today. What was the other?'

Light danced in his eyes and the flat line of his mouth curved into a smile that made her pulse quicken. 'I was afraid if I touched you I wouldn't want to stop. And we had places to be, your grandmother to see.'

Her heart was doing a polka, or maybe following the rhythm of a sensual dance like a samba or tango. Because Benedikt wanted her, had wanted her all along. Her lips curved into an answering smile. 'Keeping your distance seems a bit extreme.'

'You think so?' His nostrils flared and his expression grew hungry. 'Do you have any idea how tough it's been, holding back? Making polite conversation with your grandmother and local dignitaries, meeting people in towns along the way. And all the time you've been beside me, close enough that I can smell your perfume and feel the warmth of your skin. But I haven't been able to take you in my arms.'

Annalena had told herself she wouldn't fall into those arms again, not easily. Because she'd yearned for his warmth from the moment she'd woken and he'd denied her that. As if what they'd shared last night was easily put aside.

Discovering his reasons broke down the wall she'd spent all day rebuilding.

Because you want him. You want the passion you discovered last night.

It was true, but she wanted more too. His tenderness and

the sense of belonging she'd never expected but which had blown her away.

For a moment she felt that old caution rise. The fear of committing to something over which she had no control. But it was too late. She'd gone too far. She knew what she wanted and she wasn't going to deny herself because of some nebulous fear.

Anyway, what was the worst that could happen? They were committed to this marriage. It made sense to find what pleasure she could in it.

Annalena held his gaze as she unclipped her seat belt and reached for the door. 'Well, we've done our duty for the day. There's no reason to hold back any longer.'

Benedikt drew the cork from the bottle. The wine was pale gold like Annalena's hair as he poured it into an etched goblet.

With her bare feet curled beneath her on the sofa and a faint smile on her lips, she was entrancing. Every minute the housekeeper had spent giving them a tour of the place, Benedikt had chafed at the need for restraint.

He wanted Annalena. His need was tangible, a torsion in his body heavier and harder than anything he'd known.

Now the housekeeper was gone they were alone in the chalet. Yet he needed to maintain the veneer of a civilised man. He was mindful of Annalena's inexperience. She could be tender after last night. He turned away to pour the second glass.

'Benedikt.' Her voice came from just behind him. 'Put the wine down.'

He swung around, meeting sparkling green eyes less than an arm's length away. In the time it had taken to pour the glass she'd let her hair down. It rippled like a sunlit river over her shoulders and around her breasts.

He heard the chink of glass on silver as he put the bottle down, then he was drawing her close, an impossible mixture of relief and urgency sighing through his body as he pulled her flush against him.

Last night he'd told himself his celibacy over the last six months had made intimacy with Annalena seem unique. Or her virginity. Or his guilt. Even the fact it had been such a stressful time. Maybe they were all factors but here it was again, the sense that he'd found something both fragile and powerful. Something precious and new. Sexual desire on steroids but more too.

Dipping his head, he pulled her up and fused his mouth with hers.

Annalena wrapped her arms around his neck, grabbing his hair as she surged against him. He kissed her hard, delving between soft lips, one hand on her buttocks, pulling her to his pelvis. Fire streaked through him as she ground herself against his erection, making him buck hard.

Go slow. Go slow.

Reluctantly he lifted his head, dragging in air, lungs on fire.

Slumbrous eyes met his and something broke free inside. 'Benedikt, what is it?'

'I'm trying to pace myself. Not ravish you where you stand.' His facial muscles ached as he attempted a smile. 'I'm trying to be considerate.'

She lifted herself on tiptoe, in the process sliding up his aroused length and making him shudder. 'Can't you ravish me then pace yourself next time? I've waited so long.'

Annalena hadn't finished talking when he put both hands to her backside and hoisted her high. So good, so incredibly good. Especially when she wrapped her legs around his waist.

Benedikt stilled, poised on the brink of losing himself though they were fully clothed. No woman had ever affected him like this.

A minute later they were on the sofa, she sitting astride him, arms around his neck, and they were kissing with a desperation that made him feel bizarrely as if he'd never done this before.

'Annalena,' he mumbled against her lips, stunned by how desperate he was. How much he needed her.

Her hands went to his belt buckle. 'Yes. Please.'

Benedikt must have found his wallet because soon he was sheathing himself, rolling the rubber on while Annalena watched. For a second he shut his eyes, needing to assert some self-control. Instead he felt soft fingers slide down his length.

Vice-like, he wrapped his hand around her wrist and pulled it away, shaking his head.

She pouted as if disappointed. Did she have any idea what that did to him? How often he'd fantasised about those plump lips on him?

Still holding her wrist, he burrowed his other hand under her skirt, grateful she'd worn it instead of jeans. Questing fingers met warm flesh then damp lace. One tug and it tore away. Over the thrum in his ears he heard Annalena's gasp but it was excitement, not outrage he saw in her shining eyes.

Releasing her hand, he pulled her skirt up. 'Come to me, sweetheart.'

He watched her shuffle closer, rising as she knelt above him.

'That's it,' he crooned, hands sliding around her hips. 'Now down.'

She paused as they came in contact, heat meeting heat, need against need. Then, with an ease that emptied his lungs of oxygen, she sank until they were completely joined.

Benedikt saw her wonder and knew she'd see the same in his eyes. It was utterly new to her but inexplicably it felt new to him too. He barely had time to register that when his primitive self took over.

His hands were tight on her hips as he thrust, pulling her to him. His mouth crushed hers. But as she rose then fell again, learning the rhythm, she slanted her mouth fiercely against his. Her fingers dug into his shoulders as the urgency he'd tried to rein in took them both.

It was a desperate, wild ride. Acute sensation, driving hunger and a crescendo of pleasure.

Benedikt felt pressure build at the base of his spine then in his groin. He couldn't last. He captured her face and poured all his jumbled yearning and unresolved emotions into their kiss, stunned to receive the same from her.

His hand slid to claim her breast and she jolted against him. He swallowed her cry, convinced he heard his name on her lips as they toppled over the edge together. His life force spilled into velvety heat as bliss took him.

CHAPTER FOURTEEN

ANNALENA SHADED HER EYES, squinting into sunshine. Her heart was in her mouth yet she felt a mix of awe and pride as she watched Benedikt climb the rockface.

The sheer rockface.

When she'd said as much he'd laughed and assured her there were plenty of hand and footholds on the cliff.

Nevertheless nerves nibbled her stomach. If anything happened to him…

A few short weeks ago she'd have thought it a solution to her problems to hear the new King had died. Now the thought made her shudder. Ten days after their wedding and so much had changed.

She'd changed and her feelings about Benedikt too.

With a final surge of flexing, impressive strength, he pulled himself over the cliff top. Then he stood, waving at her. He didn't even seem to be breathing heavily. Whereas her heart hammered and her breathing was shallow.

She waved back, smiling as he grinned. The breeze riffled his hair and he looked carefree and young, not the severe man she'd met in Prinzenberg.

She dropped her hand as he stepped out of sight to explore before walking down the steep but navigable slope beyond the rockface.

Annalena turned and sank onto the blanket where they'd lunched.

Each day they made love, hiked, and talked about everything and nothing. She told him about her fieldwork and her fascination with lichens and mosses. He talked of his time in the US and some of his climbing adventures.

She found herself ever more drawn to Benedikt. Even the word *husband* didn't faze her now.

It wasn't his looks. It was his essence, that charisma she'd always felt. His character. Far from being callous and unsympathetic, he was a man of compassion and deep humanity. A man who attracted her in ways that had nothing to do with sex.

Though the sex was phenomenal. Just thinking about their sex life made her toes curl.

Even his occasional retreat into thoughtful silence didn't seem negative now. Before, she'd imagined his every reaction a response to her, imagining him judging and finding her wanting. Now she saw a man who'd faced his own problems. Yes, he brooded occasionally but didn't she too sometimes? Usually she kept her own counsel, working through problems alone rather than turning to others. Once in a while she'd share concerns with Oma.

Who did Benedikt share with? Matthias?

To her delight he'd begun sharing with her.

He'd been open when they'd discussed his plans for the state, his reforms and snags blocking his way. Yesterday, picnicking by a mountain tarn, he'd mentioned problems in a local tender process and asked her opinion.

It had felt the most natural thing to thrash out the issues with him.

That was when she'd realised he already knew about her work, not only as a botanist. She'd done her share of contract negotiations. The centre where she'd worked, initially funded by an endowment from her grandparents, was at the forefront of research into Alpine plants. That research was leading to potential new medications.

Would she be able to continue her scientific work part-time? It seemed unlikely. She couldn't imagine life without it. She sighed. Was that the lot of all royals, putting their personal lives aside?

Annalena lay back on the rug and closed her eyes, wondering what dreams Benedikt might have set aside.

She was drowsing when a deep voice murmured, 'Sleeping beauty, I presume?'

Lips brushed hers, brushed and clung. She raised a hand to stroke Benedikt's lean cheek and thick hair. He smelt of mountain sunshine and tasted tantalisingly masculine. She sighed against his mouth as her body softened.

Would she ever get enough of him? Their sexual connection was amazing but it wasn't the whole of what she felt. Her link to him grew stronger with each hour yet she still had so much to learn about him.

Benedikt pulled back, expression unreadable with the sunlight behind his head. 'That was a big sigh. What were you thinking about?'

About how big my feelings are for you. About how I've begun to yearn for more.

Yearning was dangerous. He'd been clear in what he could offer—partnership based on duty with lovemaking to soften the edges. Because it *was* lovemaking, she realised, at least on her part. She mightn't actually be in love but she wasn't as heart whole as she'd once been. The realisation made her tremble.

'I was wondering about you, actually.'

'What exactly?'

She wished she could see his face clearly. 'What you'd do if you weren't King. What were your dreams? And,' she hurried on, 'you said your family saved you from your father and yourself—'

'And you want to understand.' His voice held an edge she couldn't decipher. Not anger but something hard. So she was surprised when he said, 'I know I owe you more. You've shared so much with me.'

Abruptly he moved away and Annalena was about to protest when she realised he was just leaning across to the picnic basket. 'Would you like to share an apple?'

She nodded, watching as he took a paring knife, neatly coring and segmenting the fruit.

He frowned as if in concentration, but his expression transformed into a teasing smile as he held a segment to her lips until she opened and took a bite, tasting crisp sweetness.

Satisfaction flared in those golden-brown eyes and, she'd swear, sensual interest. But for once Benedikt didn't pursue that. He put the knife away then leaned back, propped on one elbow, munching.

'What would I do if I weren't King? Easy. Focus on my business. I thought I had years left to pursue my own commercial interests.'

'Tell me about them.'

He offered her another bite of apple. 'I began in media and advertising. That's where my grandfather made his fortune. I still have some investments there in North America, but my main interest became IT. Software development, cyber security, a range of areas. I finance start-up companies. I suppose I'm drawn to the industry's creativeness. But I dabble in other things too.'

'You have a nose for business.'

He shrugged as if unwilling to accept praise. Most men she knew loved accolades but Benedikt wasn't most men.

'So, you'd devote yourself to business.'

That boyish grin returned and her heart pattered faster. 'I'd make time for mountaineering. And skiing.'

'I love skiing.'

'This winter, we'll go together.'

He leaned across and he offered her another piece of apple. She took a bite, watching him watch her, and felt a febrile thread of arousal run through her body. But she wouldn't let herself be distracted... Yet.

'I'd like that.' She imagined them speeding down the slopes, blood pumping from the exertion and exhilaration. Afterwards, alone in their chalet... 'But was business your dream when you were young?'

The shadow crossed his features. 'The only dream I had then was getting away from my father. You know what sort of man he was. He treated his family no better. He didn't care about anyone but himself.'

Benedikt paused, looking into the distance. What did he see? She was sure it wasn't the beauty of the Alpine scene.

'He destroyed my mother.'

The words were shocking for their matter-of-factness. Annalena had hoped he'd let her in, sharing details of his life, yet his frankness surprised.

'For reasons I never understood she cared about him. Their marriage was a convenient one but she loved him at least in the beginning. He took that love and twisted it into a weapon.'

Annalena sat up, covering Benedikt's hand with hers.

He gave her a tight smile. 'As for me, I was a necessary evil. He wanted an heir and insisted I do him proud yet he took every opportunity to alienate me. I think he resented the fact I'd eventually inherit. He didn't want to share power with anyone. Usually he'd ignore or belittle me, but other times he'd micromanage my life and he was never satisfied.'

'Oh, Benedikt! That's awful.' She'd been an orphan yet she'd known love and support.

'It's okay. *I'm* okay. I had my mother, when she was well enough, and I had her father, my grandfather. He was the role model who saved me.'

Benedikt squeezed her hand, darkened eyes snaring hers.

'You said your family saved you from yourself.'

After a moment he nodded. 'He and my mother. They showed me another way to live. Taught me to think of people other than myself.'

He huffed a laugh that didn't sound like amusement. 'My

father insisted I spend my early years in the palace. Much as I learned to fear and loathe him, I also learned his ways. By the time he grew bored with being a father and let me travel to the States each summer, his poison had infected me. I was a sullen, selfish kid focused on myself, on getting what I wanted and, of course, keeping out of my father's way.'

His self-hatred astonished her and she leaned closer. 'You were only a child.'

Benedikt hitched those broad shoulders. 'A child raised by a cruel, narcissistic man. Being away from him, learning about kindness and decency, was like discovering a whole new world. I began to believe maybe I could find a place for myself in that world.

'My family had a lot of patience. They persevered through the bad behaviour, the acting out, the time in my late teens when I decided that despite everything I'd learned, selfish hedonism was the way to go.'

He looked down at her hand clutching his. 'With their help I fought *not* to be like my father, even if sometimes I feel his darkness inside.'

Benedikt's words pierced her. 'You're not like him. How can you think it?' He raised a quizzical eyebrow but said nothing. 'You're dismantling everything bad he created in this country. You and Matthias.'

And now she was too. She felt an uprush of pride at the thought of helping that endeavour.

Finally he inclined his head, his mouth twisting as he lifted his hand to stroke her jaw. 'You're so earnest on my behalf. Thank you, sweetheart. After the way I corralled you into marriage that's kind of you.'

Annalena jerked her head back. 'Don't patronise me, Benedikt. It's not kind. I'm speaking the truth.'

That cynical twist of his lips disappeared and the bleakness left his eyes.

'That's something you always deliver.' This time his smile

was genuine. 'After dealing with my father's Byzantine arrangements and secret back-room deals, it's refreshing to have someone who says what they mean and doesn't shy from the truth.'

'What else could you expect from a plain, unsophisticated scientist who spends more time with plants than people?'

'Plain? Unsophisticated? You're neither of those things.'

She hadn't been fishing for compliments. 'I meant—'

He leaned in, crowding her back towards the picnic blanket. 'You're anything but plain and you have one of the most sophisticated minds I know.' His eyes glinted with intent as her shoulder blades hit the ground. 'As for your looks, your body...' He settled over her, hard muscle against yielding flesh. 'You know I approve wholeheartedly.'

He nuzzled her neck, nibbling against that sensitive spot, making her gasp as need rose.

Annalena knew he was deliberately diverting her. She was amazed he'd shared such intimate details. Amazed and horrified that it wasn't just his father he viewed negatively, but himself.

Her heart felt raw. Remembering his stark expression as he spoke about darkness inside, she felt sympathy rise for the troubled boy he'd been and the man who devoted his life to others yet believed himself so flawed.

'Benedikt, you—'

His mouth covered hers in a caress so potent it thickened the blood in her veins and the thoughts in her brain. She cupped his face in her hands, holding him to her as she opened for him, curling her tongue against his lips and inviting him in.

He accepted the invitation. His mouth was hard and needy, his hands too, though she felt the restraint he tried to impose on himself.

The air turned smoky with searing need, the sharp tang of arousal in her nostrils, the taste of desire and Benedikt in her mouth.

He was iron hard against her belly as he lifted his head enough to meet her eyes, his blazing like molten metal. She felt him tremble, this powerful man who was so much stronger and better than he believed. 'I need you—'

Her fingers on his lips stopped his words, her heart curvetting against her ribs as she read his desperation. Her need quickened. 'Then take me. I want this. I want *you*.'

She shuffled her legs wider, glad that she'd worn a skirt in today's heat. Anticipation spiked as he settled lower. Minutes later she was naked from the waist down and his trousers were around his thighs, his erection sheathed.

She saw the tendons in his throat jerk as he swallowed. He nudged her entrance. 'I can't do finesse. I—'

'Shh...'

She wrapped her arms around his neck, drawing his mouth to hers as she lifted her knees to cradle him. Benedikt drove home, slow and deep, impossibly deep. Nothing had ever felt so good.

A sigh wafted on the still air, followed by a deep groan as all the energy he'd leashed erupted. He bucked, his movements jerky and her attempts to match his rhythm more clumsy still. But within seconds she felt that telltale quiver, the spasm of muscles, the unstoppable force.

Annalena clutched him close, her hand on his skull holding his face to her neck. Hot breaths on her throat, his possessive hand at her breast squeezing with just the right pressure. And between her legs and deep inside, Benedikt, stealing her soul and flinging her into rapture.

He shouted, her name thrown up to the sky, his throat arching as he pounded into her and she met him with mindless abandon. Finally they collapsed, spent, and a wave of tenderness swept through her as she held him tight.

Much later, when she opened her eyes and looked into the blue sky above, the world looked different.

* * *

Benedikt pulled Annalena into a deserted anteroom, pushing the door shut and drawing her close. She came eagerly, eyes shining, smile alluring. She wore red lipstick to match the dress she'd worn to the lunch they'd hosted for charity volunteers. All through the proceedings he'd wanted to haul her to him and kiss the scarlet lipstick away.

His wife was tempting, gorgeous, sexy and clever. She was overcoming her hesitancy about taking on a royal role and he couldn't imagine doing his job without her. She had a way of connecting with people that he wished he'd learnt. He was improving but he doubted he'd ever have the knack for it that she did.

The day she'd stormed into his office and made her ultimatum was one of the best of his life.

She made him feel... She made him *feel*.

In the past he'd avoided emotion and what he had felt had often been negative, a trait inherited from his father.

Warm fingers stroked his cheek. 'Why the serious face, Benno?'

Even after four months of marriage, his heart thudded when she used the diminutive so tenderly.

His mother had loved him but was often unwell, retreating to her rooms. His grandfather had shown his affection, but never through soft words. His wife, with her directness tempered with warmth, was a revelation.

His Lena. Did she have any idea how she'd changed his world?

'I'm calculating if there's time to ravish my wife before my meeting.'

Her gurgle of laughter flowed like warm honey through his veins. 'You know there's not. And I promised the research team I'd review the draft report this afternoon.'

He nodded, pleased they'd found a way to give her a couple

of days each week to pursue the vocation she loved. His arms tightened, pulling her flush against him, torture for both of them, but impossible to resist.

Mischief sparked in her eyes as she pressed her hand to his burgeoning erection. Sheet lightning blasted his vision as she tugged his belt.

'But we do have a little time.' Her smile turned sultry as she sank to her knees. 'I could—'

'No!' He pulled her high against him and the impact of soft femininity against urgent arousal almost undid him. He clenched his teeth. 'What I need is *you*. *All* of you.' He watched her turn rose pink, lips parting. 'Besides, I'd never be able to concentrate on the meeting. I'd be in a stupor of sexual satisfaction.'

She slid her hand over his lapel, pouting. 'So what do you suggest?'

'I'm sure I can finish early. In the meantime we'll have to be satisfied with a kiss.'

'Not what I want to hear, Your Majesty, but I suppose it will have to do.'

'Believe me, Your Majesty,' he murmured against her throat, feeling her shiver, 'it will be worth waiting for.'

Inevitably he was late for his meeting, but Lena had insisted on combing his tousled hair and removing the lipstick smudges. Fortunately Matthias and his new team had used the time to brief the attendees, so in the end the meeting finished in good time.

Benedikt should dally with his wife during business hours more often. Now he'd put the time to good use, getting through some of his mail.

But his thoughts were of her as he settled at his desk.

They worked well together. She lightened his darkness and called him on his autocratic tendencies. Matthias tried but had to concede if Benedikt pushed the point. Lena conceded nothing.

He opened his emails, a flagged message catching his attention.

Urgent. Confidential. Legitimacy of Sovereignty.

Benedikt's heart missed a beat then quickened as he opened it. He read the missive quickly then again, testing every word, ensuring he didn't miss any detail.

Finally he sat back, heart pounding and adrenaline thundering. This changed everything.

CHAPTER FIFTEEN

ANNALENA HURRIED DOWN the corridor. Her old laptop had died and though IT had promised to fix it quickly, she'd belatedly realised there was an urgent item she'd promised to read.

She *could* have made do with her phone but instead made for her husband's office.

Any excuse to see him!

Once that would have disturbed her, now it made her smile. Where once there'd been distrust, now there was intimacy, emotional intimacy. Trust and, with it, hope.

Hope that their convenient, dynastic marriage had become something more meaningful.

She hugged that hope to herself as she turned a corner. Benno respected and cherished her. He might not realise it but he'd changed, as she had.

How much she'd changed! She remembered opening her eyes and seeing the world altered. Because she'd finally made sense of her feelings. Benno was complex, with faults and strengths. He wasn't always right and he still tended to think his way was the best way, but he listened and he genuinely cared.

He understood how she thought and, so often, how she felt. They'd both been trained to keep emotions hidden and sublimate their own wishes for the greater good. With Benedikt she felt truly *seen* for the first time.

He could be so tender, so generous. So lovable.

She was in love with her husband!

Instead of her thinking that a disaster, it gave her hope for the future.

Look at the trouble he was going to, converting a more modern part of the palace into their private accommodation. Far from the state rooms, it would be comfortable and streamlined, with no overblown ornamentation, and it would have an unrivalled view of the pretty walled garden. He knew how much she loved that.

With a rap on the door and a smile on her lips, she entered, only to discover the offices empty. Matthias and Benno were absent.

Huffing a sigh of disappointment she made for Benno's desk. He wouldn't mind her logging on to access her mail.

He mustn't have gone far for the screen was still on. She settled in the chair, about to minimise that screen when something caught her eye.

Urgent. Confidential. Legitimacy of Sovereignty.

She didn't consciously decide to open it but a second later she was reading the extraordinary message sent by a legal expert who'd unearthed a long-forgotten document.

To rule in their own right, future sovereigns must be the child of a member of the House of Prinzenberg and born into a marriage that was celebrated publicly in the Royal Cathedral of Prinzenberg.

Annalena stared, unable to believe what she read. There was more, extolling the importance of giving the public certainty about claimants to the throne.

The lawyer explained there was no doubt the document was real and valid. He'd confidentially checked with the most senior constitutional lawmakers. So, he concluded, he felt it necessary to bring this to His Majesty's attention, given the current unique situation.

He means you sharing the crown with Benno.

Benno must have consulted the man about his options when she first came to the palace.

She swallowed. Benedikt's parents had married in the cathedral but hers hadn't.

This document destroyed her claim to the throne.

Oma had always said her parents had planned to renew their marriage vows in public, at the cathedral. Was this why? Had they known about this decree? Whatever they'd intended, it hadn't happened because her father had died.

So you never had a claim to the throne.

Oma couldn't have known that.

Benno's power-sharing deal, his marriage offer, was based on a lie. Her threat to take the crown from him had been no threat at all.

She pressed a hand to her throat where it felt as if her heart were trying to escape. The whole basis of their marriage was invalid.

Aghast, she looked at the date of the email. Two weeks ago. She slumped back in his chair, disbelieving.

He'd known for a fortnight and hadn't said a word to her! Why? Annalena's nape prickled, skin tightening as a chill enveloped her.

So much for trust, for sharing.

She pressed her other hand to her churning stomach. While she'd been reading so much into their improved relationship, Benedikt had kept this from her.

She'd believed their relationship was open and honest. *Special*. Yet he'd lied by omission.

Lied about something fundamental. For two weeks!

Did Benno, the man who'd inveigled his way into her trust and her heart, truly exist? Or had she imagined him, reading too much into physical intimacy and her husband's efforts to make their relationship easier? Had he simply been making the best of it? He'd said more than once that sex was their compensation for a dynastic union.

Said too that love was off the table, and after his revelations she understood that love wouldn't come easily to him. His dysfunctional family had damaged his view of himself and his ability to trust.

Had she let great sex and a little consideration turn her head? Had she confused physical intimacy with real affection? It didn't seem possible, yet...

She shot to her feet and crossed the room, as far from the email as she could get. Backed up against a bookcase, she wrapped her arms around her middle, fighting shudders as she thought back over the past two weeks.

He'd been more distracted though he'd denied it. Meanwhile he'd encouraged her to devote more time to her scientific work. Her heart had melted when he'd called that work valuable, saying it would be criminal for her to give up her career completely. When he'd suggested a plan to give her more time for that, devoting only a few days a week to royal obligations, she'd rejoiced.

You thought he cared. But maybe it wasn't that at all. Maybe it's the first step in...

Separation? Divorce? Unseating her from the throne?

Once she'd have jumped at anything that took her away from royal responsibilities. Now she'd begun to feel pride and satisfaction in some of them, feeling she was contributing to her country. The work stretched her and she welcomed that.

But her husband didn't need her any more. He encouraged her to spend more time at the research and development centre in Edelforst. It had been *she* who'd hesitated. Because she didn't want to be away from him, restricting herself to working from the palace except when they visited Edelforst and she'd catch up with her colleagues and Oma.

While you were dreaming of happy-ever-afters and a family with him, he was pushing you away.

Could it be true? Everything rebelled at the idea.

You're the wife he had to have. Never the wife he wanted. Now he's learned he doesn't need you and he's already looking for distance.

Had she been living a fool's dream, building castles in the air? She *knew* he didn't love her. Just because she'd fallen in love with him, she'd told herself he might eventually feel the same way about her.

The fact is, he's happier without you around. You were always the outsider. You never fitted here. You weren't even his first choice of bride!

Her emotions hit rock bottom. Did he feel *anything* for her apart from lust? As for manipulating her towards a separation via the career she loved, did he think that the easiest way, or was he trying to be kind?

The thought he might *pity* her, on top of his deviousness, was the final straw.

She dragged in a shallow breath then another and another but couldn't suck in enough oxygen. She needed to think and she couldn't do that here.

Swallowing choking emotion, furious with herself for her naivety, Annalena stumbled from the room.

Benedikt's worry grew when he found their new rooms deserted, bar the team refurbishing the floorboards. He'd pinned his hopes on finding her there. He'd already tried their current suite and questioned every staff member he saw, but none had seen Lena.

Returning to the office twenty minutes ago, he'd only got as far as Matthias's desk when his assistant said he'd seen the Queen hurrying down the corridor, visibly upset.

Matthias never exaggerated and Lena never broadcast her

emotions in public. If she looked upset something was badly wrong. Benedikt had spun on his heel and gone to find her.

Unease gripped him. What had happened? Why hadn't she waited to talk with him? He'd thought they could discuss anything now that she trusted him.

Lena spoke with him openly and they'd found commonality in their odd childhoods, separate from their peers, always different, coping with others' expectations while finding their own way in the world.

He'd told her things he'd hugged to himself all his life. Lena insisted that his tendency to strategise and command weren't proof that he'd inherited even worse traits from his father. She saw positives in his character and her habit of asking for clarification on decisions made him pause more often now before taking action.

She'd changed his life, given him so much.

The thought of her hurting created a physical ache.

His gaze lighted on the walled garden beyond the window where his mother had so often sought refuge. Had Lena gone there too? He strode towards an exit.

Pausing outside the summerhouse, he breathed deep. Whatever was wrong, Lena needed him strong and supportive.

'Lena! Sweetheart?'

For a moment he didn't see her against the light streaming in the windows, then a shadow shifted, a figure moving to sit up straight on the sofa.

Relief caught his breath as he strode across and sank down beside her. 'What's wrong?'

Her mouth was drawn with pain and her eyes were pink and puffy. His alarm intensified. Lena didn't cry. Even when he'd cornered her into an unwanted marriage she'd been upset and defiant, not teary.

'Your grandmother?'

Had something happened to the old lady? The two were close. He reached for Lena's hand but she pulled away.

The gesture, small but definite, made everything inside him go cold and still. 'Lena, what is it?'

Instead of turning to him as he'd got used to, she fixed her gaze on the far side of the room. Something surged inside him, a stark emotion so powerful he'd swear his heart stopped.

'I needed time alone to think.'

Her voice was dull, her shoulders slumped. This wasn't the woman he knew. And why time alone? Often as not they shared the challenges facing them, bouncing ideas off each other. Just yesterday Lena had used him as a sounding board for a complication that had arisen in her research team.

'Talk to me, Lena. What's on your mind?'

Slowly she turned, chin lifting in that familiar way. But there was something different this time.

'It's been good getting back into more research work. I missed it and you're right, it's really where I belong.'

He frowned, not liking the finality of her words or the implication he thought that was the only place she belonged.

'You don't need me here and I'm much happier in Edelforst.' She moistened her bottom lip. 'I want to live there full-time.'

'What?' It was so unexpected Benedikt had trouble believing his ears. 'You mean until you finish this current project?'

Her gaze slipped away. 'I mean permanently, at least in time.' Deep green eyes met his and the force of her tightly leashed emotion rocked him back in his seat. 'After the first few years, your mother lived most of the time in the US. The country will survive if I move back to Edelforst.'

Benedikt felt his jaw sag, his mouth drop open. It wasn't only what she said, it was the way she said it, the way she refused to let him in. He *felt* her roiling emotions but she blocked him like a stranger.

He wanted to remind her they were married. That their relationship grew stronger and better every day. They were joint rulers of a country that needed them. Her words were a hammer blow to the chest. He could barely catch his breath.

'Why, Lena? Tell me the truth. We've been happy together.'

Something shimmered in her eyes and hope stirred. But then she shook her head. 'I thought I could do this, but I was wrong. I don't want a dynastic marriage for the country's sake. I want a *real* marriage, not a power-sharing agreement. I want to be with a man I can *trust*, someone I can believe in.'

Benedikt felt his blood freeze. 'You don't trust me?'

Her long pause carved a chasm through his soul. The fact she hurt him so easily should have surprised him, for he didn't *do* emotional relationships. But deep down he'd known Lena was different. *They* were different.

Their marriage wasn't like any previous relationship, and that had nothing to do with duty or public expectations. It had everything to do with Lena and how she made him feel.

Yet now she swept all that aside, everything he'd felt and hoped, as if they meant nothing.

'You don't believe in me? In us?'

The words almost choked him. For the first time in his life he'd let down his guard. Being with Lena had made him want to believe in a better life, in *them*.

'How can I when you lie to me?'

His head jerked back as if she'd hit him. Didn't she know him better than that? It was one more lacerating hurt. Each felt deeper and more devastating. Had nothing about their relationship been as it seemed?

How could he have been so wrong about her feelings? He knew he had little aptitude for deep relationships but he'd been so sure...

'We promised each other honesty and I've never lied to you.' His voice ground low as he forced out the words. 'I'm not my father, Lena. How many times do I have to prove it?'

Finally hurt gave way to anger. Bruised pride surfaced, but it was no consolation for the anguish that twisted him inside out.

For the first time he'd opened himself fully to another person. He'd ignored the tough lessons that had taught self-reliance and a mistrust of emotion. He'd trusted and felt and believed in things he never had before.

'You're lying now, Benedikt.' Her voice a curious mix of ice and heat as she spat out his name. 'For two weeks you've known I had no claim to the throne and what did you do? Instead of telling me, you pushed me away, saying I should spend more time away from the palace. What was the plan? To gradually edge me out? Isolate me then divorce me? Well, don't bother. I'll divorce you and renounce my claim to the throne.'

Lena surged to her feet only to halt, swaying as if unsteady. Benedikt was at her side in a moment, grasping her arm and turning her to face him.

Despite her fiery words her face told another story and it broke his heart. Her chin crumpled, her mouth quivered as she blinked. 'Let me go. I want to be alone.'

'I don't believe you.'

He loosened his grip so she could step away if she wanted. She didn't move and hope leapt.

'You're right. I should have told you about that email immediately. I tried to bury it, hoping it would go away.'

'Go away?' Her glittering green gaze, sharp as a faceted emerald, snared his. 'Don't you mean hide it until the time was right to push me away fully?' Her face pinched. 'It doesn't matter. I know the truth and that you want—'

'You don't know what I want!'

He tugged her to him, bodies colliding, and felt some of his impossible tension ease. This was where he needed her. He wrapped his arms around her, feeling a hit of satisfaction when she didn't pull free.

'I was never going to push you away, Lena. I don't want you going anywhere.'

His heart curled over on itself as she angled her chin up in a gesture of defiance, belied by the misery on her face. Her gallantry, her fighting spirit as she tried to hide hurt, made everything he felt for her well up.

'You expect me to believe that, when you hid something *so* vital from me? I was idiot enough to believe we trusted each other but I was wrong.'

He stroked his hands up her arms. 'I didn't tell you about the email because I wanted to protect you. I double-checked and that clause doesn't delegitimise your position as joint ruler.'

'But it means I could never have ruled alone. I was never a danger to your authority. The whole basis of this farcical marriage no longer exists.'

Benedikt winced. She couldn't really think their marriage farcical. His heart thudded faster. 'I don't care about that, Lena.'

'You say that, yet you've done everything you could to encourage me back to scientific work.'

'Because I thought that made you happy!' He paused when he heard his voice grow strident. He leaned closer. 'I want you happy in this marriage. I want you to feel fulfilled. I know how much botany means to you. I was afraid you'd grow to resent a life spent focused only on regal obligations.'

Her eyes widened, doubt glimmering.

'It doesn't matter now what some fusty old document says. We're married and I want us to stay that way.' He dragged in a deep breath, chest rising against hers as he struggled to find words for what he felt. 'What we've shared has changed everything. It's changed *me*.'

'You don't want to rule alone?'

Her hands had crept to his upper arms. Was that a good sign or did she just need support?

'No, I don't, but this isn't about the crown—'

'It's all about the crown. It always has been.'

'Not any more.' Benedikt gathered her closer, fitting her snug against him. 'This is about *us*. I said I'd changed and I meant it. What I feel for you, Lena, it's taken over everything.

It's bigger than duty or Prinzenberg. Nothing is more important to me than your happiness.' To his amazement his voice wobbled. 'You make me feel things I've never felt before. You give me perspective and happiness. For the first time I feel like my life, *our* life, could be about joy and fulfilment, not just obligation and work. I want to make you happy.'

Gentle hands cupped his face, wondering eyes holding his. 'Why didn't you say anything if you felt that way?'

'You doubt me?' His shoulders lifted. 'I shouldn't be surprised. I doubted myself. I told you about my upbringing. I've always had trouble trusting, much less forming meaningful relationships. I told you love wasn't on the agenda.'

'Love!'

'Yes, love.' He drew a sustaining breath but found he didn't need it. The truth wasn't such a challenge after all. 'I love you, Lena. I want to spend my life with you and that's got nothing to do with the crown. I should have told you about the email but I was afraid you'd fret about being here under false pretences or...'

'Or what?' He couldn't read her expression.

'Use it as an excuse to leave me.'

He hadn't admitted that even to himself before this moment. It made him realise that once again he'd manipulated things to get what he wanted, hiding what Lena deserved to know. He'd talked about trusting her but he'd still tried to take control for his own selfish ends. Horrified, he dropped his arms and stepped back.

But Lena followed, closing the gap so they were toe to toe. '*That's* what you thought?'

He swallowed. 'I didn't know.' Had he blown his chance of happiness, proving himself unable to relinquish control and trust her? The thought sickened him. 'I thought you were happy, I hoped so. That means everything to me.' He shook his head. 'But you're right. I owed you the truth. I convinced myself that document didn't matter because it didn't affect what we have now. It was a convenient lie because I wasn't sure you felt the same way about me.'

'Hiding an explosive secret like that,' she murmured. 'That's extreme. I would have found out some time.'

'I wasn't thinking clearly.'

'I know the feeling.' To his amazement she placed her palm on his chest. He felt it like a brand, the way she'd branded his heart as hers. 'I know the feeling exactly.' Her voice dropped. 'That's why I was so upset, because I'm in love with you, Benno, and I thought you wanted to get rid of me. I decided to pre-empt you and go straight away.'

His heart gave a mighty jolt as she called him Benno. As if he really was forgiven. He covered her hand with both of his. 'You love me?' The sick feeling in the pit of his belly disappeared, replaced by warmth. 'How can you after what I did? I should have been honest with you.'

'You're not the only one. We should have talked more about our feelings, but I was too scared.' A soft smile trembled on her lips. 'Do you really—?'

'I really love you.' Just saying the words made him feel ten feet tall. 'I never believed I could feel anything as glorious as this. I was an idiot and I was scared. I could say I thought it was too soon to tell you how I felt but it was fear that held me back.'

She nodded and lifted his hands to her mouth, pressing kisses across his knuckles, making his heart melt as his fingers curled around hers. 'I was the same. I never expected to feel this way.'

Benedikt drew in a shaky breath. He felt as if he'd swallowed the sun, as if she'd given him the moon and the stars. But all he wanted was her, his precious Lena.

His voice was as serious as when he'd made his vows in the cathedral. 'I promise to be completely honest with you, my love, including about my feelings.'

'And I promise to be completely honest with you, my darling husband, *especially* about my feelings.'

For a moment they stood solemn and still, eyes locked on each other. Then Benedikt drew her towards the sofa.

'In the interests of complete honesty,' he murmured, 'I need to be upfront about my intentions.'

'Intentions?' The glimmer in her eyes made his breath hitch. 'Tell me more.'

Benedikt sat down and pulled her onto his lap. As she settled, warm and soft in his embrace, eyes turned to his, he knew this was going to be all right. More than all right, it was going to be perfect.

'We did this the wrong way around. We married but had no courtship. I intend to rectify that, starting now.'

'You're going to court me? I like the sound of that.'

He nuzzled the base of her neck, drawing in the scent of flowers and Lena. 'Good. I need to do this thoroughly. It could take months.'

Her chuckle was liquid sunshine as she put his hand to her breast. 'Definitely, my darling. Maybe even years.'

Her darling.

His heart had never felt so full. And this was only the first day of the rest of their lives together.

EPILOGUE

THE CASTLE OF EDELFORST had never looked so good. Chandeliers glittered, mirrors shone and flowers scented the air as guests mingled in the ballroom.

From the minstrels' gallery above, music began and the guests retreated to the sides of the room. Annalena watched a couple approach and her breath caught. Even now her husband had that effect, especially when he wore formal evening dress.

They'd been married a year today. A year that had been blissful and challenging. They were both strong-willed and didn't always see eye to eye, but the promise of honesty had seen them through both testing and wonderful times.

In his stark clothes Benno looked incredibly sexy but serious, as befitted a king. But then, uncaring of the crowd, he lifted his hand and blew her a kiss, stealing her heart all over again. There was a ripple among the throng as women sighed in delight.

The man Annalena had met a year ago was still there, conscientious and determined. But now Benno embraced happiness with an enthusiasm that transformed him.

She smiled as he escorted her Oma, resplendent in navy and silver, onto the dance floor. Annalena turned to the man beside her. Young and handsome, Harald Ditmar said, 'Ready, Your Majesty?'

She nodded first at Harald then at his beaming grandfather, the colonel, who sat with his ankle strapped up. 'Absolutely.'

The crowd applauded as the musicians struck up a waltz. Annalena circled the room with Harald, while Benno and Oma danced in the opposite direction.

Incredible to think it was only a year ago that she'd attended her first royal ball. Now, confident in her abilities and in Benno's affections, she no longer felt like a fish out of water. She actually enjoyed dressing up once in a while, though she'd remove the emerald and diamond tiara after the dancing.

When the waltz ended the couples met. Oma's cheeks were flushed and her eyes glittered as she thanked Benno for the dance. 'But one waltz is enough for me.' She turned to Harald. 'Let's go and check on your grandfather, young man.'

'She really is a wonderful lady,' Benno murmured as the pair left and he gathered Annalena close.

'She's absolutely delighted we're celebrating our anniversary here.' His smile warmed her as the music began and other couples spilled onto the floor. 'Thank you for suggesting it.'

He shrugged as they began dancing. 'It's good to celebrate with family. Besides, we can head up to the chalet tomorrow for a break.'

He'd bought the chalet where they'd honeymooned as a belated wedding gift. Weekends there were some of their happiest times.

As they moved down the room Annalena frowned. 'They're playing the same music again, that's unusual.'

'I asked them to. Do you like it?'

It was light and lovely. 'I do. I've never heard it before.'

Golden brown eyes met hers. 'You wouldn't have. It's "Lena's Waltz". I commissioned it for you. Happy anniversary, my love.'

Annalena's eyes widened and she would have stumbled but for Benno's encircling arm. 'You commissioned a waltz?' What an amazing gift, especially from a man who'd once been totally absorbed in business and strategy, with no time for anything that wasn't 'useful'. But her husband was caring and thoughtful and knew how she enjoyed music. 'Oh, Benno. That's…' She swallowed.

He tsked in mock admonishment but smiled tenderly as he swung them into a turn. 'No need to get emotional.' He pressed a kiss to her forehead. 'But I love that you like it so much.'

'Like it? It's so special.'

'*You're* special.'

There she was blinking again but how could she help it when he looked at her like that? On the other hand she did have another reason for feeling a little emotional. 'You'll have to wait until we're at the chalet for your gift.'

How would he react to the news she'd had confirmed this morning, that they were going to be parents?

She didn't have to wonder. She knew he'd be thrilled, and he'd make the best father.

His breath tickled as he murmured, 'You're plotting something, Lena. Perhaps I'll have to persuade you to tell me about it when we're alone tonight.'

She grinned in anticipation, thinking of Benno's persuasiveness. Besides, they'd promised not to keep secrets and this was one she couldn't wait to share.

'That sounds like a wonderful idea, Your Majesty.'

* * * * *

MILLS & BOON®

Coming next month

TWINS FOR HIS MAJESTY
Clare Connelly

'The baby is fine?'

'Oh, the baby is fine. In fact, both babies are fine,' she snapped, almost maniacally now. 'It's twins,' she added, and then she sobbed, lifting a hand to her mouth to stop the torrent of emotion from pouring out in a large wail.

Silence cracked around them but she barely noticed. She was shaking now, processing the truth of the scan, the reality that lay before her.

'Well, then.' His voice was low and silky, as though she hadn't just told him they were going to have *two babies* in a matter of months. 'That makes our decision even easier.'

'What decision?' she asked, whirling around to face him.

'There is no way on earth you are leaving the country whilst pregnant with my children, so forget about returning to New Zealand.'

She flinched. She hadn't expected that.

'Nor will my children be born under a cloud of illegitimacy.'

Her heart almost stopped beating; his words made no sense. 'I—don't—what are you saying?'

'That you must marry me—and quickly.'

Continue reading

TWINS FOR HIS MAJESTY
Clare Connelly

Available next month
millsandboon.co.uk

Copyright ©2025 by Clare Connelly

COMING SOON!

We really hope you enjoyed reading this book. If you're looking for more romance be sure to head to the shops when new books are available on

Thursday 17th July

To see which titles are coming soon, please visit
millsandboon.co.uk/nextmonth

MILLS & BOON

FOUR BRAND NEW BOOKS FROM
MILLS & BOON MODERN

The same great stories you love, a stylish new look!

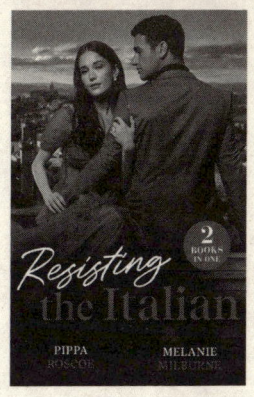

OUT NOW

Eight Modern stories published every month, find them all at:

millsandboon.co.uk

afterglow BOOKS

Afterglow Books is a trend-led, trope-filled list of books with diverse, authentic and relatable characters, a wide array of voices and representations, plus real world trials and tribulations. Featuring all the tropes you could possibly want (think small-town settings, fake relationships, grumpy vs sunshine, enemies to lovers) and all with a generous dose of spice in every story.

@millsandboonuk
@millsandboonuk
afterglowbooks.co.uk

#AfterglowBooks

For all the latest book news, exclusive content and giveaways scan the QR code below to sign up to the Afterglow newsletter:

afterglow BOOKS

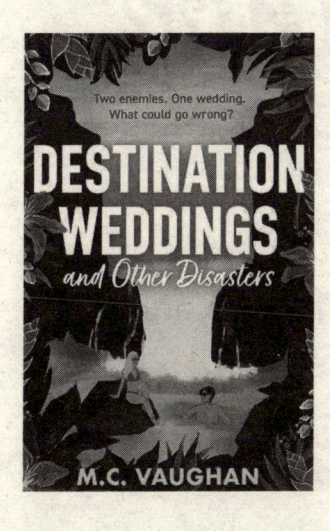

Destination Weddings and Other Disasters
M.C. VAUGHAN

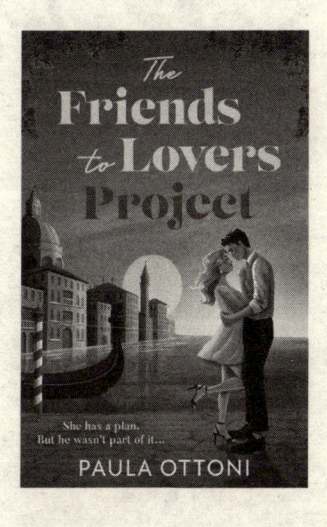

- ✈ International
- 🔥 Enemies to lovers
- 💓 Forced proximity

The Friends to Lovers Project
PAULA OTTONI

- 👪 Friends to lovers
- ✈ International
- 🔺 Love triangle

OUT NOW

Two stories published every month. Discover more at:
Afterglowbooks.co.uk

LET'S TALK
Romance

For exclusive extracts, competitions and special offers, find us online:

- **f** MillsandBoon
- **X** @MillsandBoon
- **◉** @MillsandBoonUK
- **♪** @MillsandBoonUK

Get in touch on 01413 063 232

For all the latest titles coming soon, visit
millsandboon.co.uk/nextmonth

OUT NOW!

Opposites Attract: Workplace Temptation

3 BOOKS IN ONE

CHRISTY McKELLEN
BARBARA WALLACE
STEFANIE LONDON

Available at
millsandboon.co.uk

MILLS & BOON

OUT NOW!

A DARK ROMANCE SERIES

Veil of Deception

CLARE CONNELLY FAYE AVALON JENNIE LUCAS

Available at
millsandboon.co.uk

MILLS & BOON